Ken Kesey's previous work includes *One Flew Over the Cuckoo's Nest*, *Sometimes a Great Notion*, *Kesey's Garage Sale*, *Demon Box*, *Caverns* (with O.U. Levon), *The Further Inquiry*, and *Sailor Song*. His children's books include *Little Tricker the Squirrel Meets Big Double the Bear* and *The Sea Lion*. He lives in Oregon.

Ken Babbs (on the right of the photograph) and his wife, Eileen, and daughter, Elizabeth, live in Lost Creek, Oregon, where he writes and does his constructions.

Also by Ken Kesey

SAILOR SONG

and published by Black Swan

Last Go Round

Ken Kesey

with Ken Babbs

BLACK SWAN

LAST GO ROUND
A BLACK SWAN BOOK : 0 552 99621 1

First publication in Great Britain

PRINTING HISTORY
Black Swan edition published 1995

PHOTOGRAPH CREDITS
In first photo section, pages 1, 2 (top), and 2–3 (bottom): from *Let 'Er Buck*
by Charles Wellington Furlong (G.P. Putnam's Sons, 1921); pages 3 (top), 6
(top), and 8: The Department of Special Collections, The Knight Library,
University of Oregon; pages 4, 5 (top), and 7 (top): Wayne Low Historical
Photographs, Pilot Rock, Oregon; page 5 (bottom – left and right): from
Gotch to Gable by Mike Chapman (University of Iowa, 1981); pages 6
(bottom) and 7 (bottom): Howdyshell Collection/Matt Johnson.
In second photo section, pages 1, 2 (top – right figure in background), 4
(top), and 5 (top; bottom – left and middle figures in background): Wayne
Low Historical Photographs, Pilot Rock, Oregon; pages 2 (top – figure in
foreground, left and middle figures in background; bottom), 3 (top and
bottom) and 6 (bottom): The Department of Special Collections, The Knight
Library, University of Oregon; page 4 (bottom): Reproduced from the
Pioneer Cowgirl series, Volume 2, No. 6, published by Pendleton Cowgirl
Company, all rights reserved: pages 5 (bottom – figure in foreground, right
figure in background), 6 (top), and 8: Howdyshell Collection/Matt Johnson;
page 7: Reproduced from the Pioneer Cowgirl series, Volume 1, No. 3,
published by Pendleton Cowgirl Company, all rights reserved.

Set in 11pt Linotype Melior by County Typesetters, Margate, Kent.

Black Swan Books are published by Transworld Publishers Ltd,
61–63 Uxbridge Road, Ealing, London W5 5SA,
in Australia by Transworld Publishers (Australia) Pty Ltd,
15–25 Helles Avenue, Moorebank, NSW 2170,
and in New Zealand by Transworld Publishers (NZ) Ltd,
3 William Pickering Drive, Albany, Auckland.

Reproduced, printed and bound in Great Britain by
Cox & Wyman Ltd, Reading, Berks.

Disclaimers and Dedications

Three immortal riders stand out on our northwestern horizon – distant, hazy, lit from behind by so many tall tales the shadows seem more solid than the silhouettes.

Nearly a century of dusty summers and smoky autumns sprawl out between us. Newspaper accounts of that first weekend (September 16, 17, 18, 1911) read like a slanted crossbreed of Jimmy the Greek and Howard Cosell – more interested in complexions than achievements. In one rare 8 × 10 print of the trio together, the complexions are even hand-tinted, to make sure posterity gets the point: one rider's face is tinted Indian copper, one Caucasian pink, one a deep molasses brown.

At length we conclude that the best way to summon up these spirits is not by combing through the musty archives, but by studying the shadows they still cast across the years. What high-bucking brilliance must have occurred on that long gone weekend to stretch these shades out so long! What cowboy glories! This is why we elect to conjure our three spectral riders out of the old tall tales, told over hot coffee around a warm campfire, instead of the cold facts and half-baked truths served up by library stacks.

I first heard the story from my father when I was fourteen. I was in the backseat with my younger brother in our big Red Ram Dodge. An old hard-of-hearing farmer friend named Riley was riding shotgun. All four of our applications for antelope tags had been drawn in the Special Hunts lottery, and we were on our way to the Ochoco mountains. We didn't even know it was rodeo week until we suddenly found ourselves in a bumper-to-bumper traffic jam right out in the middle of rolling nowhere.

'Oh no!' Daddy shouted. 'The Pendleton Round Up! Look for us a turn-out, Riley — else we'll end up camping with longhorns 'stead of pronghorns!'

'Never liked longhorns,' Riley shouted back.

By the time we got out of the traffic the sun was sinking and so was Riley. Daddy found a promising pair of ruts and we pitched camp beneath a rimrock above the town. Mom's cold chicken was available in the cooler but Dad was in a cooking mood. My brother and I built a fire of sage and cedar while he opened and poured into a big iron pot cans of Vienna sausages, pork and beans, and sardines — his camp-cook specialty.

'Beans, 'deens, and 'weens,' he announced. 'Sticks to the ribs, right, Riley?'

'I like ribs,' Riley allowed. He was looking past the unappetizing stew toward the lights far below us. Ferris wheels stirred the night. Street dances. Barbecue pits belching greasy flames. 'Ribs would do just fine.'

My brother and I nodded agreement. Hoping to disperse the wistful pall hanging over our camp, Daddy started reminiscing about previous Round Ups he had attended.

'Gets wild and wooly and full of fleas, Pendleton

6

does at Round Up time. Tell you what: next fall we'll bring the ladies and take in the whole show, from the Friday morn parade to the Sunday eve awards ceremony. How about that?'

We stared toward the festive lights below and were not mollified.

'Say, Riley! You heard about that first one, didn't you? First Round Up?'

'Many the time,' Riley answered.

'Well these boys haven't. Tell 'em.'

'You tell it. Now that we aint having ribth I got my teef out.'

So my father told it, with the fire crackling and the beans bubbling and old Riley making sounds of toothless affirmation. A great yarn. He told it again a couple of Septembers later when he made good on his promise to take us to the Round Up, ladies and all. A marvelous yarn. It never occurred to me to believe it until I drove over by myself years later and heard the same story from a teepee full of Indians.

I was a junior at the U of Oregon, majoring in radio and television. Our midterm assignment in screenwriting was to write an outline for a documentary about some town we considered particularly unique. Due Monday. I skipped my Friday classes and headed for Pendleton, driving my Nash Ambassador with seats that folded down into a lumpy bed. I wore a black beret and carried a big wine bota so people would know I was there as an artist, not a tourist.

I was at a wooden table in the park after the Saturday show, jotting down impressions and squirting Chianti at my mouth, when I noticed that a thin Indian had stopped to scowl. He was dressed in customary rodeo costume: boots, Levi's, U-roll hat, and pearl-button shirt. Everything Round Up regulation except for his gloves. He wore a tattered cowhide work glove on his left hand, an unscuffed black kid on his right. I held out the bota.

'It's a wine bag. Want to try?'

The man nodded. He took the bag in the shabby work glove, pulled the stopper with his teeth and let it dangle. He squirted wine at his face until his collar was soaked and the bag was squirting air.

'It's empty.' He took the stopper back between his teeth, stoppered the bag, and handed it back. The black-gloved hand hung at his side the whole time.

'Time for a refill,' I decided.

He followed me across the park to the Nash and held the bag while I poured from my gallon of Gallo. He noticed my sleeping bag spread over the reclining seats.

'Bring your bags, you can bed down in our tent. I'll carry the bottle. My name is David Sleeping Good. Call me Dave.'

It was my first time in a teepee. My first taste of hot frybread and honey, and my first glimpse into the dry, ironic world of Indian wit.

When my host peeled out of his wine-soaked shirt I saw that he was missing his right arm. A tree limb was harnessed to the shoulder, the rough pinebark still on it. Only the hand and wrist had been peeled and carved. He saw me staring at his crude prosthesis.

'I pass out on the train tracks in Walla Walla. I wake up – no right arm. I was lucky, though. I'm a left-hander.'

I could think of other ways to be lucky, but I didn't venture them. I asked why he hadn't peeled the rest of the bark. Dave raised the wooden replacement with his other hand and looked on it with affection.

'It keeps the limb from drying out and splitting.'

Later that night, when the camp grew still and the Gallo was gone, Dave treated me to his grandfather's version of that famous first Round Up, and those three legendary finalists. His granddad's tale was very much like my father's. Grander, even, inside a flickering teepee. More wonderful. More . . . powerful!

So we begin our thank-yous and dedications with David Sleeping Good. He took me into his enchanted circle and he shared his wonders. All I had to do was share my wine.

I would next like to thank old Les Hagen, rest his ornery bones, and his family both ways. Les proved that a good poker player is never too far gone to win.

And the Roy family, who nourished the lily of culture in the land of the cocklebur.

And the McCormmachs, with their down-to-earth wisdom: 'Shoot, so you stepped in some. It aint nothin' but grass what's been run through a cow.'

And Bill Severe and Marty Wood and Kendall Early.

And MiSchelle McMindes and Dave Webb and Doug Minthorn.

And the Rainbow Bar and Cimmiyotti's.

And, of course, my old saddle pal and trail boss, Ken Babbs.

And, finally, the town of Pendleton. If we offend the facts with our tall tale, pray accept our contrition and our excuse:

A short little stub of a tale just would not serve.

—Ken Kesey

I first got to know Mike Hagen and Ken Kesey in 1958 at Palo Alto and Stanford. They were continuously blowing smoke about the glories of the Pendleton Round Up. It wasn't until 1972 that I got to savor these glories for myself. A bunch of us got decked out in jeans and boots and pearl-button shirts and Stetsons and drove up the Columbia Gorge to join the hordes filling the roped-off streets of Pendleton.

We fought through the mob to the outskirts of town where the Hagen family was located: We deposited our pokes and bedrolls in the bunkhouse and headed for the kitchen, where Mike's dad, Les Hagen, presided over an ongoing poker game while his wife, Janet, presided over a massive six-burner, two-oven, gas-burning stove.

Les took all our money and used it to keep the liquor cabinet full. Janet stuffed us with dumplings and gravy and mugs of hot coffee to keep our energy up. We needed all the energy we could get. At noon every day we headed for the arena. It was a proud melee of cowboys and Indians and ball-busting bulls and spine-rattling broncs. An official finally asked if we had any business in the chutes. We admitted we didn't. 'Then get out of the way. Go to the Let 'Er Buck Room if you're lookin' for local color.'

Below the stands the Let 'Er Buck Room was packed shoulder to shoulder, belly to butt. This was more local color than I could bear. I found relief exploring the walls of the adjoining rooms. They were covered with framed photos of Round Ups from the first year in 1911 to the present. A wonderful history was etched into those bygone faces, like wagon ruts across the sage-brush.

While we were working on this book more visual histories turned up. We received a package of postcards from Polly Helm, a Pendleton native. These pictures depicted the role women played in the old Round Ups. Polly calls her collection She Is My Hero, and she graciously offered us whatever photos we needed. Photo researcher Genie Murphy contacted Wayne Low and Matt Johnson in Pendleton, who each had a large collection of old Round Up photographs. Our final batch came from the University of Oregon Library's Moorhouse collection, again thanks to Genie Murphy's efforts.

With deep gratitude to all these fine contributors, and with the invaluable assistance of Chief Word Wrangler David Stanford, I set to work organizing and selecting from hundreds of pictures the ones we finally used in the book. I'm also indebted to Charles W. Furlong for much of the information I used in the captions, borrowing freely from his 1917 book, *Let 'Er Buck*.

—Ken Babbs

Last Go Round

Chapter One

Giddy with Outrage and Whiskey

It was a picture of you, matter of fact, on the front page of an *Oregonian* sports section. I came across it last Sunday in the Portland Free Library reading room. It was the way they had dressed you up to look like him, and the way that reporter kept finding all those comparisons between the pair of you ... it set me studying about the old times. But I found my once-gleaming memories had gone alarmingly dim. I could barely make them out. I got to thinking Do I have to break down and buy me a bus ticket, make my own comparisons? Wal, Old-Timer, I finally says to myself – the Pendleton Round Up; the first time in a couple decades. Let 'er buck!

It was the reason I happened to be in that damn Let 'Er Buck Room, too. The Let 'Er Buck was never my style, even back in my high-riding heel-kicking days. I have never cared for a crowd, especially a loud crowd, but it was one place I knew for sure I could find a particular photo to compare with the *Oregonian* picture. This is that rare pose of him bareheaded, taken as he was accepting that famous First World Championship saddle that he supposedly won. They keep that original daguerreotype in the display case, so folks can see his likeness along with the very bronc he rode

– supposedly rode – in that famous last go round. The citizens had hauled the carcass to a taxidermist when it died, and had it stuffed.

That's where I got tangled up with all these Indians, too.

I had intended to put off my visit to the Let 'Er Buck till later – catch some of the day's events first – but the show was plumb sold out. The ticket lady informed me with obvious pride: 'We're filled full to the brim. *Wide World of Sports* is broadcasting us live this year.' Then closed her window in my face. This was after standing in line in the brutal sun for two hours with nothing in my belly but yesterday's braised ribs and mashed potatoes and nothing for my parched throat but a pink Sno-Cone. The Let 'Er Buck Room right there beneath the stands was the next logical stop.

The room was packed tighter than a three-wire bale of green alfalfa, shoulder-to-shoulder, belly-to-belly, wall-to-wall. Everybody sloshing drinks and hollering at the top of their lungs. Full glasses flowed across the bar and empty glasses and dollars flowed back. No ice, either, though the place was boiling hot. The only thing keeping the whole business from blowing up like an over-stoked steamboat was a bespectacled deputy sheriff on a raised platform at one end of the bar. His eyes looked like a pair of brass-rimmed pressure gauges. I was glad my scarecrow stature stretched me somewhat above it all, too. I could make out the saddle and stuffed horse across a bobbing expanse of cowboy hats. I set sail in that direction.

The sea of hatbrims was entirely unbroken except for one little island near the bar. As I worked my way near it I saw this circle was a half-dozen or so Indians that didn't have hats. They were wearing matching red

16

T-shirts and similar scowls. The T-shirts had the word SURVIVAL printed across the shoulders. They didn't have drinks, either, and I conjectured that was what accounted for the scowls. I know the feeling. I called down into their forlorn circle that I'd be gratified if they would let an old-timer buy them a round, for old times' sake. They looked up at me, their scowls turning to curiosity at the sight of such a teetering relic. Before they could respond a bell began to clang.

'Fancy that,' I marveled. 'They still have that old brassiere bell. Hooray for tradition.'

Two cowboy-clad buckle-bunnies have climbed onto the bar. The taller of the pair, a palomino blonde, is yanking the bell's rope with drunken determination. Her back is to us, but you can tell her shirt is already unbuttoned by the way it hangs out of her jeans. At last the bartender manages to tug the rope out of her hand: 'All right, honey. You got our attention get on with it.'

There's a lull in the din as the crowd turns to watch her shuck out of the shirt. She reaches behind her back and unsnaps her undergarment and hands it to the bartender. He tosses it over a clothesline alongside hundreds of others. 'What size?' he asks, stepping to four stacks of folded T-shirts. She arches her back. 'Extra large,' she boasts. 'I say medium and barely that,' he opines – in a manner most unchivalrous, I thought – and hands her one of the printed T-shirts. She pirouettes in a circle, her silk-screened prize held high: – I LET IT ALL HANG OUT AT THE LET 'ER BUCK ROOM!

The crowd sizes her up and agrees with the bartender – 'Mee-dee-um!' – then turns back to business of hollering and drinking. I'm wondering Whatever in the world happened to the famous cowboy chivalry?

17

when somebody gooses me in the ribs. It's one of the Indians, handing me a brimful bourbon and water. In fact, the entire red-shirted circle, while still hatless, now *all* hold drinks. Two apiece, some of the scamps. I raise my bourbon in a genteel acknowledgment, thinking On the other hand isn't it odd how often survival and chivalry seem to turn up together? Hand-in-glove, cheek-to-cheek, potbelly-to-belly?

I leave the Indians and by the time I've struggled through the crowd to the display case the bell is clanging for the palomino's plump little pal. I lean close to the glass, panting hard from the struggle. The dilapidated horse is a testament to why taxidermy has fallen out of fashion. The saddle is dry-cracked and warped. I am peering around for the picture when I see a ghostly face reflected in the glass, as dry-cracked and time-warped as the ancient saddle or the stuffed horse.

The bell stops clanging, and I hear a fuss commence back toward the bar, something about underage buckle-bunnies and unpaid-for drinks, but I pay no mind. I pant in the heat and gape at the reflection, scarcely able to believe this gaunt stranger was what I had become. These new electric razors. A man doesn't need to subject himself to a mirror. He can mow his whiskers while reading the morning papers and sipping his coffee; never have to notice the old mug getting cracked and chipped. I was still gaping when a gloved hand jostles me from my trance:

'You too, Grandpa. I'm easing you out of here, right along with the immature and the indigent.'

It was the deputy sheriff and a pair of deputy deputies. They were herding the two buckle-bunnies and the half-dozen Indians toward the side door. He intended to move me along with the herd.

'Just a darn minute!' I protested. 'I've got money. And I'm certainly *old* enough.'

'Old enough to get trampled. And if you got money how come you never paid for that whiskey? Look at you, panting like a lizard. Why aren't you up in the nice shady seats with the rest of the tourists?'

'Tourists?' I was outraged. 'You call me a *tourist?*' I made no attempt to explain that the drink had been given me, or that the stands were sold out. 'I'm part of this damn place's *history!* Some folks in Pendleton are still familiar with the name of Johnathan Spain.'

'Could be, Gramps, but I'm not one of them. Now finish your freebee and mosey along. If I catch any of you back in here you *will* be history.'

The next thing I know I'm outside staggering around in the afternoon glare, downright giddy with outrage and whiskey. I must have looked pretty dangerous because my banished compatriots were wanting to get me someplace safe. The buckle-bunnies wanted to drive me to the hospital. The Indians wanted to take me to their spread in the teepee camp. I chose the Indians. I told the girls I appreciated their concern but I had seen enough of the Pendleton Hospital the year a tangled lariat pulled my hand off, thank you, and had no intention of ever visiting it again. *Now* look at our predicament. It goes to show you.

My Indian escort turns out to be from different tribes all over the nation. They got acquainted in some Dakota jail after a big protest powwow. They've been rendezvousing every fall ever since. Across the red belly of their SURVIVAL shirts they've written their various nicknames. The one that gave me the filched bourbon is Mended Knee. The lightest-complected is Uncle Tomahawk. The darkest is Number Nine, after

19

the Roger Miller song. Number Nine is local, like the underage bunnies.

They escort me across the park toward the teepee grounds. The girls fuss along, full of boozy worry about my welfare. The palomino blonde even offers me her ticket if I'll let her drive me first to a doctor. 'My father reserves the best seats in the place.' Number Nine says he bets the SURVIVALS have better. He says they got a private viewing booth with multiple TV's. The girls say this they got to see and we all troop in the gate and through the zigzag of teepees to their campsite, clear over where the Cyclone fence fences the Indians off from the access road to the chutes. They couldn't have picked a dustier hotter spot.

They do have multiple screens, however – though not exactly a booth. *Wide World of Sports* has their big TV trailer backed right up to the fence with its rear door rolled all the way open for the river breeze. The SURVIVAL boys have scrounged up a sizable pyramid of hay, then stretched black plastic up to the pyramid peak. This gives us a nice shady cave and we can see the whole TV operation through the crisscross wire. The girls concede that it is a very comfortable arrangement. The plump one digs a pint of tequila out of her shoulder bag and Mended Knee digs some peanuts and lemons out of the hay and we make ourselves at home. The people in the trailer pay us no more mind than if we were a pen full of roosting chickens.

On the bank of monitors we can see a bunch of different angles of the action inside the arena, plus hear the announcer's voice. It reaches us over the TV a good second and a half before we hear it boom from the loudspeakers. 'The Squaw Race, folks . . . and it looks like cute little—' then, echoing from the arena:

'THE SQUAW RACE, FOLKS ... AND IT LOOKS LIKE CUTE LITTLE BIRD-IN-BLUE-HAT IS FLYING AWAY WITH THE BLUE RIBBON.'

'Yeah, but not very high, ratings-wise,' one of the trailer people says. 'I call it dull and juiceless.' She's a sharp-chinned lady in a swivel chair.

'It's tradition,' her assistant says, hovering behind her. He is a baggy-eyed man in a baggy velour sweater. 'They've been holding this Squaw Race since the first Round Up.'

'Tradition isn't television,' she lets him know. 'We got anything with more juice?'

He looks at his notes. 'Bull Riding's next, Ange. Juice to the max. And lookee. The next one up is that Mister Hots from Watts.'

'The arrogant little bastard from the press conference?'

'The very one. In his proud purple hat. How about setting up on him with the Steadycam?'

'Arrogant is better than dull. Let's do it.' She swings around to her mike. 'Felix? Get me up tight on the black bullrider.'

This rouses me to closer attention. Maybe I'm going to get to compare faces after all.

'Use the Steady, Felix. I want up close and personal on our hotshot from Watts. He'll be coming out of chute number—?'

The announcer supplies it for her. 'Next up, in chute number two on the Christensen Brothers' bull, Lullaby, is a hoss of a totally different – ah – well, *breed*. But heck, folks, *any* fan of professional rodeo savvies who I'm talking about: Drew Washington. One of the most popular young cowboys on the circuit and a blue-chip natural if I ever saw one. Drew was last

21

year's runner-up and he's *way* in the lead this year after two days of competition. All Drew needs now, folks, is a completed ride. Nothing fancy. If he can just hang on till the bell he'll not only *be* first, he will also be *the* first of his race to win the prize saddle since that immortal black buckaroo at the *first* Pendleton Round Up.'

This brought me reeling to my feet. 'Hold yer horses,' I said. 'George Fletcher never *won* it.'

The cameraman has made it to his position at chute two but all we see through the slats of the chute is the rider's foot. It's a ragged tennis shoe with a spur taped on the rubber heel. The picture heaves and surges against the slats.

'Looks like Drew's having trouble getting a grip on old Lullaby, even with his Nike's. What's that you say, Typhoon?' He's answering the clown, down in the arena. 'You ask if I know why so many of our cowboys are starting to wear running shoes instead of boots? I don't have a clue, Ty. Why don't you tell me? I see; so people won't mistake them for truckdrivers.'

The audience moans.

'OK, Typhoon, here's one for you: Can you tell me who it was Fletcher beat out for that prize saddle? Right. Jackson Sundown, the Nez Percé nation's immortal "Red Rider." Sundown eventually – Look out! *Here* he comes! Bad bull, short fuse. Ride, you buckaroo!'

The rider's hat fills the screen, bobbing wildly as the bull booms out of the chute. Pressed right up to the Cyclone fence, blurred glimpses are all I get, mostly of that purple hat tilted over a cocky grin. Supple of joint, though, I do see that. For a while you was supple as smoke.

22

'Go to three!' the boss lady hisses into her mike. 'Camera three, focus! More face! I want focus and more face!'

The TV switches to a telescope shot from across the arena. The announcer's voice follows the ride: 'Bad bull, good rider. *Eee*-haww! Drew Washington from Watts, ladies and gentlemen, a natural blue-chip world-beater! And *there's* the buzzer. He's done it, folks! He's won it! For the first time in more than half a century it looks like we've got us a – and I trust you folks all know I mean absolutely no slur by it; it's the name history gave him . . .' And we hear it twice, once in the trailer, then a second and a half later, booming out of the arena loudspeakers: '—another NIGGER GEORGE FLETCHER!'

That's when I saw the suppleness leave you; even on those tiny TV screens I saw it.

'This year's *All Round!* top-dollar *grand—!*'

A gasp from the stands changes the announcer's acclaim to horror.

'Oh no he's hung. He's hung up! Come on, Drew. Ah God, he's pinned backwards.'

The screens show it in full detail, from every angle: how the reinforced glove wedged under the rope is across the body . . . how the elbow is bent the wrong way . . . how the head keeps snapping back against the bull's vast flank, hard, over and over. The proud hat snaps away, revealing a childlike face, contorted with pain and terror. Our worldbeater is just a boy, just a skinny kid being slung about like a rag doll. The bullfighter clowns rush in to help, then the mounted hazers. It takes four ropes before they can hold the bull still enough to pry the gloved hand free of the surcingle rope. Then the siren and the lights. The TV's show slow-motion reruns while the medics examine the injuries. The announcer provides the details.

'There's where it happens, folks. He's a left-handed rider and dismounts left for some reason . . . and gets pinned on the bull's left side, backwards. There! Oh! Oh my! Now the bull loads him up . . . and again . . . ! Lullaby: one of the rankest bulls in all rodeo . . . Oh my Lord . . .'

The rankest in all rodeo oh my oh my Lord. I was glad I had that fence to hang on to. All that slow motion and siren wail was throwing me for a loop. Silly thing for a rattleboned old swayback, drinking hard whiskey in the hot sun on an empty stomach. I knew better. I knew I oughta sit down and calm myself, but I wanted to see. I wanted more face, just like that TV woman. And when the ambulance came blaring through the dust I took off along the fence after it like a blamed idiot. I don't know if I expected to head it off or flag it down or what. I do know I never expected to find myself following along behind it in an ambulance of my own a few minutes later, siren whistling. Back to this damn old Pendleton Hospital after all, for observation, just like you . . . back to another time as well, another train of thought: steam . . . whistling down the rusty rails of my memory.

Chapter Two

A Surprise

Well that train whistle was a ways back, blame near into another century. Before any World War Two or World War One, let alone *Wide World of Sports*. It was the first time any of our family had ever crossed the Mason-Dixon Line, let alone come this far north, and I was proud to be the one who had accomplished it: the youngest son – scarcely seventeen, bright-eyed as a babe, and nearly as naive.

I was watching this new world through the slats of an open-topped stock car. My rail accommodations weren't fancy, I admit, but I had made myself quite comfortable. Fresh straw cushioned my skinny rear and my head rested against my saddle. My feet were bare so I could enjoy the wiggle of my filthy toes in the cinder-filled air. During the long miles west everything about me had got filthy with those cinders, except for my boots. My boots got special consideration, protected by a windbreak of crates and canvas. I'd kept them polished, for all the blowing cinders. The Confederate flag was tooled into their leather fronts and they gleamed from days of rubbing. I still continued to give them an occasional swipe. It was a whole night's ride yet to Pendleton, and when I got there I wanted to be sure I rode in shining.

The whistle tooted again and through the slats I spotted the sight it was tooting at.

'Antelopes, Stoney! Pronghorn antelopes! Look at 'em go!'

Standing next to me was my horse, Stonewall. His long legs were spread against the train's sway as he watched over the top rail with his ears laid back. Stonewall was a big gray gelding, sixteen hands, tall enough to accommodate my beanpole build. He was a fretful and suspicious animal, but reliable in the long run even if it happened to be by rail. We'd growed up and strung out together since Tennessee.

'Say there you other passengers!' I yelled toward the front of the car. 'You see them yonder? Real prong-horns . . .'

A blue shoat and a kick-crazy pony stood at the other end of the car, unimpressed. They were a pretty spectacular pair theirselves. The pig was spangled all over with silver stars and the pony's rump and shoulders were printed with bright-green shamrocks. They were fellow travelers on their way to the big show. Veteran troupers.

A clatter rose ahead and the antelopes veered away. The train rattled across a trestle bridge spanning a deep gorge. I had to pull myself up on the slats to see the river below. It was steep and far away, just a tiny blue ribbon at the bottom of an enormous crack. Once across I let myself down out of the wind and, for the hundredth time, I drew the printed handbill out of my shirt pocket and unfolded it.

**ROUND*UP*SPECIAL * MODERN TRAIN RIDE
AUTHENTIC FRONTIER FOOD +
SPORTING CARS * DANCING + GAMBLING.**

The central body of the broadside boasted a map of the Round Up Special's run: DENVER to PENDLETON. I traced the route with my finger until I reached the river line.

'Gentlemen,' I smiled about at my traveling companions, 'that was the Snake River we just crossed. We are now in Oh-ree-gone. How does that suit you?'

The star-spangled pig grunted, still unimpressed, and the shamrock pony responded by kicking a packing crate.

'Well,' I shrugged, 'I reckon you can't suit everybody.'

I watched the passing panorama until the sun went down and I had to move back away from the chilly wind coming through the slats. I gathered wood from the kicked crate and started a small fire in my big skillet. I rooted a huge yam up from the bottom of my tucker bag. Along with a mason jar of her yellow moon, my Great-Aunt Ruth had pressed a bundle of tubers on me when I stopped by her farm in Arkansas, weeks before. 'You *take* them,' she commanded. 'Yams'll outlast all that other fiddle-faddle you're totin'.' She was right. The coffee and corn muffins and cheese and tinned fish were gone right away, and the apples finished hundreds of miles ago. I was not short of cash and I still had the unopened jar of yellow moon, but my route had not taken me and Stonewall near any mercantile stores nor given me cause to drink. Yams had been our staple for days now, and this one was the last and the largest. I sliced a point on a piece of slat with my knife and spitted the yam on the end. Stonewall leaned forward and sniffed.

'I say, sir -- patience,' I told the sniffer. I knew he could eat his portion raw but it was another of my

Southern conceits to make him wait until supper was served for all.

I propped the slat over the fire, leaned back against my saddle, and looked at the stars. A long ways from Tennessee. I was the youngest of the six Spain boys, as I mentioned, and the youngest of the whole family except for my little sister. She was the only one close. By the time I was ten and she was eight, our older brothers had hit the outbound trail, a-roving. But only as far as New Orleans, Galveston, and the like, and always south. I used to tell my sister that when I left home I was by golly gonna do better than that. I was gonna rove *north*, I vowed, and keep on a-roving till I reached whatever real frontier was still left in our swiftly settling nation.

'A long ways, Little Sis,' I said, grinning up at those northern stars, proud as a frog eating fire.

The train began laboring up a steep grade. My eyelids grew heavy as the engine chugged and the stars twinkled down. I was just about to doze off when, from absolutely out of nowhere, I was assailed by a noise that sounded like suddenly approaching thunder. Yet there wasn't a cloud between me and the stars! This thundering got rapidly louder and louder until it turned into a screaming whinny coming from behind. My eyes rolled back just in time to see a wild black shape soar across the starry sky directly over my head. The shape clattered to a scrambling stop in the dim front end of my stock car, stampeding pig and pony before it. Dumbstruck, I rose to my elbows, just in time to hear the oncoming gallop of a second set of hoofbeats, and see a second black shape sail over. This shadowy shape skidded to a stop alongside the first one. Both shapes reined about and came looming toward me in the firelight. I grabbed the yam stick and aimed it like a bayonet at the towering pair.

My ridiculous weapon seemed to impress the riders. As they swung down from their mounts and stepped into the firelight, they kept their attention fixed on the tuberous tip of it. The first man was an Indian, thin and straight, wearing a flat-brim hat and a thin-lipped scowl. His boots were soft-top, Indian style, and worn nearly to death. His face was blank, eyes just pinpoints beneath his hat-brim. He was rubbing a queer coin against his cheek with an air of contemplation. The second was a black man with a grin as merry as his partner's was somber. The hat on his head was so old and floppy it was hard to say what its style had originally been. I waited for them to make the first move. The Indian pushed back the hat and I saw that his eyes were wildly bright and entirely innocent of fear. They were ravenous.

'Nice yam,' he said.

'Certainly *is*,' the black rider nodded. 'Suppose our highbred young humdinger here might consider cuttin' high card for it?'

Chapter Three

Real Dime Western

It didn't take me long to appreciate what a rare pair had sailed into my life. Even the most naive of eyes could see that these were a couple of real old-time dime-western ripsnorters. The black cowboy was the smaller of the pair but he made up for it with his mouth: it was bright as the moon dancing in the stars over his shoulder. He introduced himself as Mister Fletcher but just call him George, and his taciturn partner as Mister Jackson. 'You can call him Sun Gone Jack Down or Dog Gone Sun Jack or anything thereabouts – Injun names're always changing.'

I judged Mister Fletcher to be an easy half-foot shorter than me and maybe three times older. It's hard to say what revealed him so much my senior. The skin on his face was smooth as a baby's, and his eyes danced like ageless imps. Everything about him seemed to dance, in fact, from the features of his face right down to his booted feet. As he bustled about it looked for all the world like he was dancing a reel, with his mouth the fiddle he danced to.

'Sure,' he was saying, 'we knowed this train was going to the Round Up. What aint, this side of the Rockies? But the thing is, this aint no ordinary train. You been back here with a imitation Irish pony and a star-spangled sow, son. You got no notion of the *diversions* they got up ahead. Hold this mirror, would you, please? I aim to brush me in some pomade.'

He had bustled out of his dusty work clothes and into dress-up duds from his saddlebag. Now that he was plumed like a peacock he was ready to attend to his grizzled topknot. I held the mirror.

The Indian had his own dress-ups — a severe three-piece suit and starched white shirt. I guessed from his furrowed face that he was even older than Fletcher. He had that same lean-hipped build, only ramrod stiff. His eyes were as bright as his black friend's, but they didn't dance. They didn't even blink. They bored, like a pair of carbon-tip drills. His glossy hair was braided down each side of his face, then braided into one under his chin, like a necktie. He was poking the end of this doubled braid at a large gold nugget pitted with holes. Apparently one of the holes went all the way through.

'Give me some of that grease,' he said.

'Why certainly, Sundog.' George slapped a dollop of pomade into the Indian's hand and gave me a wink. 'I'm always happy to assist in anything that might sweeten Mister Jackson's sour puss.'

The Indian worked the pomade into the frayed end of his braid while George resumed his chatter.

'I mean this ol' rattler contains a *world* of opportunities, all ripe and waiting for them that's game enough to climb after 'em. You think you're game enough?' he asked me.

'I'm game enough,' I said. I was feeling a little reckless. After helping me finish off Great-Aunt Ruth's last yam they had moved right along to her jar of yellow moon. 'Just show me which way we climb.'

'First you better get shod.' He gave a nod at my dirty bare feet. 'We're going to be mingling with some high society.'

I sat down and put on my socks, then took my boots out from behind their windbreak. Both men's eyes popped. For the first time since they had galloped aboard miles back, George Fletcher seemed to be at a loss for words. It was the Indian who finally spoke.

'How much they cost, them boots?'

'I can't rightly say, Mister Jackson. My father purchased them in Nashville, for my sixteenth birthday. I do know I wouldn't take a fortune for them.'

This declaration broke George's trance. 'Nashville? Nashville, Tennessee? I once knew a vet come from Nashville. Terrible at horsedoctoring but the fanciest dresser you ever *see!* He'd show up to pull a colt primped out like a plantation owner. But I swear he never had nothing fancy as that footwear. Mm! Well Ol' George'll do his best not to look too shabby 'longside you dandies. If you would be so kind as to hand me that box yonder?'

I reached behind the man's dilapidated saddle for a round box. He untied the lid and took out a high crowned Stetson, the color of fresh-churned butter. Now my eyes popped. He spun it on his finger, grinning at me.

'You ever walk the high spine, Mister Nashville? I didn't think so. There's never going to be a better train to learn on, or a nicer moon to light the way. Just watch your footing and do like I do and you'll be fine.' He put the Stetson on and drew the string tight under his chin.

I put my own hat on and drew the string under my chin. The Indian lifted his braid atop his head and screwed his flat-brim tight over it. He was still looking at my boots.

'Mind the ladders,' he advised solemnly. 'The rust can be rough on good leather.'

It was nice to know my new friends were looking out for my footing and my footware, both. It turned out that rusty ladders were the least of my worries. I was across the coupling and up on the roof of the boxcar ahead of us before I quite appreciated how high up that high spine was. The moon gave me ample illumination but not much confidence. I tried to ignore the jagged landscape ripping past, and concentrate on putting one foot in front of the other. When I reached the yawning roar between the two cars it seemed as deep as the Snake River gorge. George and Sundown leapt without hesitation, landing in a splash of gold. When the splash cleared I saw they were standing waist-deep in an open-topped wheat gondola. They beckoned me to come ahead. I signaled them I would, just as soon as I worked up enough gumption. I was still working it up when that train blew its whistle.

'Do it now, Nashville!' the black man hollered. 'You got to!' His partner's thin face was craned around into the flying cinders. '*Right* now!'

The whistle shrieked again and both men laid back down in the wheat. Up ahead the engine had roared onto another trestle, smaller than the one over the Snake – and much lower! Only inches between the smokestack and the girder beam! I pulled a deep breath and dived, an instant before the girder boomed past. Wheat filled my mouth and jammed my nostrils. I came up coughing but they snatched me back down. We lay on our backs in the fresh wheat and watched the girders slashing past. When the trestle was behind us George sat up and grinned down at me.

'He look a little peevish to you, Jack?' he kidded. 'Like he got wheat up his nose, maybe?'

The Indian sat up on the other side. 'He come from yam country. Maybe not much acquainted with wheat.'

He might have been kidding, too; except he never smiled. He seemed to be without any sense of humor whatsoever.

We crawled the distance of the wheat gondola and jumped to the boxcar ahead. It was easy after the fright I had just survived. Next was a flatcar with a solitary shrouded chunk chained in the center, about the size of one of the new gasoline-powered farm machines. We climbed down and leaned against the mysterious chunk and scrabbled the grain out of our cuffs and crannies. George Fletcher's curiosity got the better of him. He untied a corner of tarp and peeked underneath. He gave a low whistle and tied the canvas carefully back in place.

'What is it?' I asked. 'A combine?'

He shook his head. 'Not less'n Mister Rolls and Mister Royce has took to making farm equipment. I *tole* you this train was plump with prizes, didn't I? Giddyup, Jack! Time's a-wasting.'

The next car was decorated with grimy red-white-and-blue bunting. We hopped across into a little foyer. The laughter and loud talk from beyond the door was a little intimidating. I fidgeted after the wheat under my belt. 'I feel like a hayseed,' I whispered.

'I feel like a Mississippi gambler, myself,' the black man boasted. 'Fortune's own chile.' His boasting was done in a whisper, though. I wasn't the only one intimidated. 'You bring your joo-joo, Jack?'

The Indian was bent looking through the small window of the foyer's door. Without turning, he dipped a finger into the watch pocket of his vest and pulled out that queer coin. It was heavy copper and about the size of a milk-bottle cap. He rubbed it against the side of his chin.

'What's that?' I asked. I was whispering, too.

'That's Mister Jackson's big medicine,' George said. 'A Injun-head penny from the Nineteen-O-Four World's Fair in St Louis. The Bureau of Injun Fairs sent him back to St Louis, *gratis!* On account he is so picturesque.'

'I am Chief Joseph's last living relative,' the Indian said. 'Son of his brother.'

'Oh yes, Mister Jackson's the right full hair to the Nez Percé throne, to hear him tell it. Iffen they *had* any throne, hee hee hee. Tell the boy about the magic coin, Your Majesty.'

The Indian turned from the window and looked me up and down, to make sure I was worthy. He began to pretend he was poking the copper piece at an imagined slot.

'There was a machine. It had a crack in the top, like in a piggy bank. Twenty-five little pennies go in, and then—'

The poking halted and the copper coin sunk out of sight into the copper fingers, disappeared, not in a showy way like a coin in the fingers of a stage magician, but naturally, like a crawdad sinking backward into wet mud. The Indian pantomimed pulling down a lever and the coin popped into his other palm.

'—out comes one big one. Twenty-five times as lucky.'

'Injun arithmetic,' George explained. 'We civilized

people, we know it can't work. On the other hand we know that it sometimes *do*. I personally have coin-flipped against that dang penny one whole Christmas without winning *oncet*.'

I looked skeptical. 'Without averaging out ahead, you must mean.'

'I mean without winning ary a flip! Heads, tails, or odd man out! The dang thing never loses.'

'Never? That's not possible.'

The Indian gave me what might have been just the slightest smile. 'Want to bet?'

'Bet? Bet against what?'

'My gold nugget . . . that you can't call one flip right out of twenty-five tries.' His thumb sent the big coin spinning toward me. 'With you flippin'.'

I one-handed the coin out of the air and slapped it down on the back of my hand. If I was ever going to get any respect from these old sports I couldn't let them bluff me down. 'You're on,' I said. 'I call tails.'

I lifted my palm. The copper profile of an Indian chief shined in the light from the little window. I flipped again. 'One correct call out of twenty-five gets me your gold nugget, right?'

'Out of twenty-four, now.'

'Twenty-four, then – I call heads – and what am I putting up, in the unlikely event that I lose?'

Fletcher giggled. The Indian's face was blank. 'Something equally fine,' he said. He looked under my palm. It was tails. 'Twenty-three flips left.'

I gave up somewhere around fifteen. I was tired of hearing that hee hee hee of George Fletcher. So when my cowboy boots finally stepped grandly through the door and into the car they were on another cowboy. I was wearing Indian soft-tops.

We stood blinking in unexpected grandeur – carpets and polished trim and stuffed trophies, like a gentleman's den in a mansion.

'Shoot,' Fletcher realized with dismay. 'This aint a public car, this is Oliver Nordstrum's private coach.'

The car was hazy with smoke and filled with a bewildering assortment of gamblers, tourists, cowboys, barbers, and ordinary citizens. Most of the men were crowded around a big tote board at the other end of the room, placing bets with a fat man on a riser. The man was chalking them up and drinking champagne and sweating like a tea kettle. A waitress with a tray and bottle was replacing his empty glass with a full one. She was what they called in New Orleans a French High Yellow. She was costumed Southern Belle style – off-the-shoulder blue silk and high-heeled blue boots that laced up the front. The outfit would have fit right in at any high-society ball, except for her sash. It was a gaudy mischief of a thing of parrot orange and peacock green knotted around her waist. She was laughing and filling glasses and swishing that sash like a feisty Gypsy until she saw us. She excused herself and came striding our direction with such a glare of outrage I wasn't sure whether she intended to brain us with the bottle or smash us with the tray full of glasses.

'George Fletcher! What are you *doing* here? I heard you went to a branding contest on the Culdesac and got infection from a mule bite. I was hoping it was fatal.'

'Evening, Miss Jubal,' George said, touching his hat brim. 'It was the mule what expired, not Ol' George. Nice to know you was thinking about me, though.' He was sparkling his smile at her but his eyes were on the champagne. 'I did some thinking about you, too. Every time I put the iron to a pretty little heifer's rump, I thought about you.'

'I don't care to know what you did or didn't think about. What I want to know is what are you doing on my train?'

'Aint you read? I'm going to Pendleton to win the big World Champeenship rodeo. It's front page all over Idaho.' The car lurched her a step nearer and he managed to catch a corner of her silk sash. 'The Boise newspaper calls me the Black King of the Broncbusters, just waitin' to be crowned.'

'Don't expect no coon-ass crown from *me*.' She was twisting this way and that to keep the bottle and trayful of glasses out of his reach. 'It was insult enough that you never showed up to take me to the Harney County Fair like you promised. I waited in that depot the better part of my Sunday in case there was a telegraph you'd been knife-cut or something. Then I find out you was off at some pissant little cowboy foolishness!'

George was weaving the silk in and out of his fingers. 'You oughtn't talk trashy that way, Louise. It don't become you.' He gave her a look both sincere and lascivious. 'I'm sorry about that mix-up. I musta got my days confused. But I promise you this, honor bright: just as soon as they crown me king I'm gonna make you my *queen*. What do you say about that?'

'I say horse malarky.' She spun free, leaving the sash hanging in George's hand. 'You're due to get crowned, George Fletcher, but not as no *king*.'

George sighed and turned to his partner. 'How come this woman doubts me, Jack? I should have brought that Idaho newspaper—'

'She doubts you because she's got good sense,' was Sundown's reply.

'Good *sense?*' George's eyes went wide. 'Why everybody with any real sense knows George Fletcher is gonna win.'

'Not everybody with any real dollars, King Buster.' The woman pointed to the tote board. A column of names were chalked up on one side. 'Injun Jack Sundown' was at the top, 8 to 5 over the second-place favorite, 'Niggar George.' George snorted.

'Nordstrum and them other tenderfoots? What do they know? About half of nothing, that's what! For all they know Nashville here might beat the both of us. Louise, I want you to meet our young gentleman, if you stop being trashy long enough—'

Our introduction was cut short by a call from the crowd: 'George Fletcher? Wah-*hoo*, George, is that you?'

'Look out,' George groaned. 'It's the main nabob hisself.'

The fat man had climbed down from the riser and was gimping toward us. I noticed he wore an orthopedic cowboy boot on one short leg.

'And Sundown Jack, *too!*' His voice positively oozed with goodfellowship. 'You gentlemen on this train? This is absolutely splendid. I had no idea. And by God don't you both look the cat's pajamas! Your gold chapeau has never looked spiffier, George. And aren't those new boots you're sporting, Jack? Magnificent, finest I've ever seen. Here, both of you. Do me the honor?' He called Louise back and took two glasses from her tinkling tray. This drew an ironic smile from the woman in spite of herself. She plucked her sash from George's hand.

'Where have you two been quartered?' Nordstrum continued. 'One of the public cars, up forward, I expect?'

'Not exactly,' George hedged.

'We been backward,' the Indian answered in his humorless monotone. 'In our own private car.'

Other people were drifting over, attracted by the sweaty to-do Mister Nordstrum was making over the black man and the Indian.

'Boys—?' Nordstrum put his arms around their shoulders and gave them a big squeeze. '—how about giving it to us straight from the horse's mouth, as they say. Which one of you aces is going to walk out of that arena Saturday with that World Champion saddle?'

Neither answered straightaway. Even George's breezy chatter seemed stifled by all this sweaty goodfellowship. There was a long moment of silence. Then, as though they had rehearsed, George and Sundown simultaneously raised their right hands Indian fashion and said, 'This one.' That got a big guffaw from everybody, and another squeeze from Nordstrum.

'Spoken like true aces,' the fat man laughed. 'Which reminds me: I want to introduce you to some of the other kings and queens and jacks visiting our little Pendleton card game this week. Bill?' He waved a fat hand. 'Here's one of the very gents you said you wanted to look over. Come join us, sir. All of you, all of you . . .'

The crowd parted and an impressive wedge of people emerged from the upholstered shadows. In the lead was the obvious 'sir' Nordstrum had called to: a striking figure with pearl-white hair down to his shoulders and a mustache and goatee to match. He was wearing a suit and trousers made out of tan buckskin, cut and tailored in the latest gentleman's fashion except for the scabbard and knife built into one pant leg and a canteen pouch hanging from a beaded strap.

Tight on his heels was a well-worn cowgirl with hair the color of a tangerine, and a terrier-faced fellow in maroon sleeve-garters. In back of this couple was a trio as nondescript as the other three were singular – charcoal suits, charcoal toppers, faces like cold ashes. Behind this rank the last member followed, an unbelievably huge man, or at least something that walked enough upright like a man to have been squeezed into a man's suit. He was hatless and he was hairless – not even any eyelashes. You could see the machinery of his muscles right through his skin and he was muscled all the way to his scalp. His ears were so muscled the earhole was about squeezed shut. He stood as tall as or taller than me, and weighed maybe twice my stringy one-sixty. But he wasn't fat. Big as he was, there was something starved about him; cramped, as though his body was still growing and hungered for room. His chest swelled against the shirt buttons and suspenders. His arms were too long for the straining sleeves. His wrists were too thick for the fancy linen cuffs. He looked like an ape that had been unnaturally dressed up and shaved for an act in the circus ring. But it was something you couldn't see that was far more unnatural: it drifted around the giant like an invisible cloud of virulent air. Even the dead-faced charcoal-dressed men tried to keep clear.

Oliver Nordstrum puffed up and beamed at the peculiar group, his eyes like buttered yolks. He made you think of some soft-pouched little rich kid who had been inexplicably accepted into a gang of some pretty hard-boiled eggs. He took the leader of the group by his buckskin cuff and pulled him forward.

'Bill, I'd like you to shake hands with the two best bronc riders in the whole world: Jack Sundown and George Fletcher. Boys, meet Mister William Cody.'

I knew Nordstrum had been puffing up to something big, but I hadn't expected anything of this proportion. 'Buffalo *Bill*?' I gasped. I imagined he'd passed away years before. But here he was, in the flesh, and still an impressive-looking sight. 'Buffalo Bill *Cody*?'

George and Sundown nodded politely. Buffalo Bill didn't offer to shake. He barely gave the black man a glance. The red man, on the other hand, he sized up for quite a long moment, like he was inspecting livestock. Nordstrum broke the silence.

'So, Bill, now that you've looked our pair of aces over, what's your best gambler guess? Where would you put *your* wad?'

'I'm not a gambler, Oliver. That's Mister Handles corner of the ring.'

'Not me, not me,' the little man yapped. 'Not up on this boon-dock chuck-a-luck as yet. Don't know who's got the horseflesh, yet. Don't know who's got the horseradish.'

Buffalo Bill turned to the giant. 'How about you, Frank? You are a judge of horseflesh and mustard. Which one would you bank on?'

The three charcoal-dressed men gave way so the giant could have an unobstructed look. His eyes fixed on George first, blue and cold as icicles. He forced a little sound out of his swollen nose that might have been intended as a sarcastic snort and continued to stare.

'Frank Gotch,' Nordstrum stage-whispered behind

his hand. 'Took the belt from Farmer Burns in 'aught one and's held it ever since.'

George stood the pressure of Gotch's heavy blue stare without changing expression – his eyes friendly, his grin good-natured. But I had seen that kind of stare before, through eyeholes in white sheets.

'Frank Gotch?' I said to divert the pressure. 'Now where have I heard that name before . . . ?' I knew exactly where. My father had taken me to the Memphis Fair for my tenth birthday. We had watched a wavy-haired young Adonis named Frank Gotch pin Strangler Lewis twice in forty-five minutes. It was difficult for me to believe this swollen brute was that same Adonis. 'Do you wrestle, Mister Gotch?'

The surrounding crowd held back their amusement while those little eyes swung to me. His answer was both pent up and soft, like the rumble of something sleeping in a cage.

'Does a fat puppy fart when you kick it?'

Now the crowd whooped. Nordstrum slapped his gimpy leg and Buffalo Bill cackled through his whiskers like a billy goat bleating. It was Mister Handles who answered.

'Why yes, he does wrassle, Slim. Wrassles real good. But that aint why you heard the name of Frank Gotch afore. *Lots* of gents wrassle real good. Frank here does more than that. He crushes, d'ye see? *Crushes*, with *un*human strength. *That's* what the name Gotch is known for.' Mister Handles had turned to the whole crowd now. 'He *crushes*. He *punishes*. He *mashes*. Shall we show 'em, Frank? What we can do with just *two fingers*? Someone got a coin? Be sure it's a big *thick* one. A cartwheel? A peso?'

Before thinking better of it, George and I both

glanced at Sundown. Sundown quickly closed his fingers into a fist but it was too late – *again*. Everybody in the little circle we had attracted saw it. They edged closer, leaning to look. Sundown was caught. He had to open up or seem uncivil. He uncurled his fingers, displaying the big penny in his copper palm. Mister Handles snagged it up quick as a snake snagging a mouse.

'This do, Frank?'

Gotch took the coin and turned it over to eye its thickness. Satisfied, he rolled his shoulders and stepped back. The circle spread to accommodate the wrestler.

'Here he is, gentlemen and sports,' the barker yapped out of the side of his mouth, 'your World Champeen wrassler and international famous strongman, Frank "The Crusher" Gotch! . . . in a demonstration of that very unhuman strength of which we spoke. And, for your edification, this evening's demonstration is absolutely *free!* Do it, champ . . .'

Gotch squared his stance and stuck up the first two fingers of his right hand in a V. They were big and pink as frankfurters. He situated the coin between the fingers, sucked a breath through his teeth, and began to squeeze. His face got red. For a long moment nothing happened, then the coin started to bend. It kept bending, slowly but surely, until it was folded at a perfect right angle. The crowd hollered and clapped. Gotch grinned at the result of his effort, then casually flipped the coin wobbling into the air. Sundown snatched it out of the smoke and held it in his closed fist.

'Never seen a man do that before, I'd wager.' Buffalo Bill grinned to the crowd, looking more goatlike than ever.

'How about it, folks?' the barker challenged. 'Ever seen anything like that? And with just *two fingers?*'

All the circle could do was shake their heads and murmur, 'Never seen nothing like it,' and, 'Takes superhuman strength,' and so on . . . until a flat voice shocked the murmurings into silence.

'One other time; one other man.' It was Sundown. He had stuck the coin in the pocket of his serge trousers. 'Only he didn't need *no* fingers.'

Gotch's scowl returned. He swiveled toward Sundown but Buffalo Bill waved him off with a laugh.

'Just crazy Injun talk, Frank,' he said. 'You don't know 'em like I do. They got their own way of joking.'

'That's right!' Mister Handles interjected. He hopped back in the center of the circle and clapped the wrestler on the shoulder. 'Crazy Injun talk. You'll get used to it, too, champ, given a little time.'

'I wouldn't wager on it,' Gotch said darkly, but his scowl, I noticed, had become more appraising. In fact the whole Buffalo Bill contingent was looking the Indian up and down. I realized Sundown was undergoing some kind of job interview, and that it was by no means concluded.

'Wagering!' George said, terminating the interview with a loud snap of his fingers. '*Dat's* what I come here about – to put down a wager. An' yawl better watch, cuz anybody got the brains of a bullfrog be putting his the same place I put mine.'

Digging in his pocket he stepped between Sundown and Gotch and strode through the car to the betting table. He looked at the tote board where they'd scrawled his name in chalk: NIGGAR GEORGE. He shook his head at the epithet, then slapped down a dusty roll of cash.

'Put this on *Mister* George Fletcher—' he declared with a clownish toss of his head and tipped his butter-gold Stetson sidways over one merry eye. '—representin' *Pendleton*, state of *O*-regon!'

The circle broke apart, laughing. Sundown walked up to the table, unwrinkling some cash of his own. He put it beside George's roll and looked at the board. They'd chalked his name down as Indian Jack.

'Jackson Sundown,' he said. 'Nation of the Nez Percé.'

Behind him the others surged forward, clamoring to get more bets down. George took advantage of the commotion to swoop a fresh drink off the tray. When Louise didn't pull the tray back, George swooped another and handed it to me. She favored me with a bright smile and pranced away in a swish of crinoline. George went prancing after her. Sundown and I were headed off by a sweet-faced woman holding a little black notebook in front of a bosom big as a buggy bumper. She bumpered square into Sundown.

'Oh, I am sorry,' she sang out. 'These trains are so un*steady*—'

It was hard to believe such a sweet shy violet of a face could harbor such a blaring bugle of a voice. Sundown held her elbow like a gentleman while she smoothed her gabardine and straightened her glasses. When Sundown decided she was sufficiently steadied he let go of her arm and started to leave. She headed him off again.

'Mister *Sun*down – I mean Mister Jackson . . . Please; I'm Nadine Rose, with the *Salt Lake Intelligencer.* You are a rider of some renown, even in Utah, and I'd be most grateful if you could give me a quote for our readers. Pretty please? Just a word?'

She plucked a matchstick-thin pen out of the little notebook and waited, breathing up and down. The only response she got from the Indian was his soft all-purpose grunt. It could have meant uh-huh or huh-uh or perhaps just his opinion of lady reporters, but it was clear that was all the word she was going to get from this renowned rider. When she tired of waiting for more she turned to George, who had reappeared with more drinks.

'Mister *Fletch*er,' she brayed. 'I have *heard* that Mister Jackson taught you *everything* he knew about rodeoing. Is this true?'

'Yes ma'am,' George politely responded. 'And it didn't take him hardly more'n a minute.'

The onlookers laughed and Sundown repeated his grunt. I saw some of our circle was drifting back our way from the board, leaving an opening. I downed the drink and, while my new pards were sporting with the reporter, decided to attend to another of the reckless impulses that came on me after every drink. I would show them that Southern boys also possessed a fair share of sporting dash, if not much good betting sense. I bowed – 'If you all will excuse me?' – and stepped to the table. I felt every eye burning the back of my scrawny neck, but I kept my poise. I reached into my shirt and extracted a bill out of my money belt, cool and collected as any high-card sport. I was so cool and collected, in fact, that I didn't even glance at the greenback's denomination.

'I'd be obliged,' I announced, 'if you would put this on Johnathan Spain.'

'Johnathan wha-*what*?' the clerk stammered, blinking at the bill I'd laid down.

'S-P-A-I-N,' I spelled out. 'Just like the country.'

He took the money and wrote the name and then chalked up the bet. One hundred dollars. I never let on. I walked back the length of the car with the tiny wager chit I'd been given in place of my big hundred-dollar bill. George and Sundown were staring at me like all the rest of the high-flying stuffed shirts – eyes big as moons. I shrugged and put the chit in my pocket.

George affirmed my brash move with a slap on the back.

'By gosh, Nashville, I like the way you root right in. My daddy used to say, "If you're gonna eat watermelon, eat watermelon."'

Still, I knew it had been a foolish thing I'd done, betting all that money on myself. Yet it did seem to go with the rest of the foolishness in that private car. The gold-fringed window curtains where there wasn't any windows, wasn't that foolish? The big desk pushed up against the wall and the stuffed leather chair alongside, weren't they foolish, too? The long-stemmed champagne glasses teetering and tipping in a swaying railcar, on a backwater track in raw America? Wasn't that grandly foolish? Everything, from the fancy trappings to the exuberant goodfellowship, was pure Yankee Yokel. Who was I to go against that grain?

In the next half-hour I learned that this crowd of stuffed shirts wasn't merely high from tippling; they were uplifted, elevated, soaring like aeroplanes, and fueled by a concoction of spirits stronger than any champagne, stronger even than Great-Aunt Ruth's yellow moon. Something extraordinary was happening, and it made them feel special. Weren't they in the most special car in the Round Up Special?

I learned that these citizens were part of a delegation of investors that had journeyed east to Boise over these same rails four days earlier. They had gone to the big city partly to purchase supplies for the growing throng of visitors they anticipated were coming to their event – hams, sausages, lumber, potatoes, and all the barrels of beer that could be hunted out of that part of Idaho in those few days. Their main purpose, though, was to convince the First National Bank of Boise to loan them enough cold cash to pay for it. The Boise bankers had adamantly refused to grant the loan, for all the supplications of the merchants and ranchers and dairymen, until – and it was the mustachioed barker who kept mentioning this every chance he had – Buffalo Bill signed on. The aging showman just *happened* to be booked on the Pendleton Special himself, bound for Portland to do advance publicity for his famous Wild West Extravaganza, and just happened to be an acquaintance of Oliver Nordstrum. A deal was struck. The benevolent old buffalo-hunter agreed to a few days' layover in Pendleton, gratis, for the sake of the desperate citizens and their little punkin-roller rodeo in the prairie. More*over*, as the pinch-backed little barker went on to volunteer, as an extra *added* attraction, the World Champion wrestler, Frank Gotch, would do some public demonstrations of his *unhuman* strength and maybe even a little catch-as-catch-can, if a challenger could be found. This had been enough to tip the Idaho bankers' scales and loosen their purse strings.

More power to them, I thought, bankers and barkers, barbers and farmers and fools and all. I felt special right along with them. And I was eager to sample whatever other treats this special train held in store.

Chapter Four

Bet Your Boots

The atmosphere of the next car forward was just as heady and rarefied as Mister Nordstrum's private coach, and a whole lot rawer. This was the *cow*pokes' car. There was no fancy furniture or lamps or rugs; just a packed wad of waddies with sweet-smelling hay for furniture and cedar shavings for a carpet. One lone lantern hung swaying from the ceiling. Beneath it the men were jammed in a yelling circle, stretching their necks to watch what was happening. A high voice rose out of the hubbub, counting backward: '. . . fifteen . . . fourteen . . . thirteen . . .'

Through the yelling and underneath the numbers, I hear another sound: this strange, low humming.

George and Sundown stepped up on a bale at the back of the pack so they could see. I was tall enough I didn't have to stand on anything. When my eyes penetrated the smoke and the shadows I saw that the counting was coming from a skinny fellow with a pocket watch standing in the ring's center. Two other men were hunkered down at opposing sides of the circle facing each other.

The strange smothered humming was coming from the smaller of the hunkered pair. He was holding the entire head of a black rooster in his mouth, humming

50

air into the fowl like it was a feathered bagpipe. On the other side of the ring his pockfaced opponent held a fat fire-red rooster clamped tight between his knees. The big red was a straining coil of feathered fury. It was all Pockface could do to keep it from attacking the little black rooster before the count was up.

'I seen them reds fight before,' Sundown said over the noise. 'They're plenty tough.'

'That fat old fake?' George countered. 'Why, anybody can see he's pure yeller under that ruckus and red feathers.'

'You don't know birds,' Sundown said without much interest.

'Oh? Wanta bet?'

The Indian looked more interested. 'Bet what?'

The din of the crowd was rising as fast as the numbers went down. George leaned over and yelled something in Sundown's ear. The Indian nodded. '. . . three . . . two . . . one . . .' the timekeeper counted. *'Pit 'em!'*

The black rooster's head plopped out of the hummer's mouth. He was turned to face his adversary, barely conscious, blinking and staggering stupidly. He was bowled over backward by the furious charge of Big Red. Red's backers hooted and waved fists full of money. Big Red spun around and charged again, right over the smaller bird. The worried-looker's humming turned to groans as he watched his fowl lie blinking on his back in the shavings. Once more the red rooster spun and charged, steel flashing. For the next few furious seconds he was raging all over the poor, dazed darker bird, like a windy flame dancing on the tip of a wick. Then, as though a sudden black gust had blown out his flames, Big Red flopped on *his* back, split from

51

gizzard to gut. The bedraggled black rooster rolled standing. He staggered over and pecked once at the dimming eye of his gutted opponent – the winning peck – then keeled over dead himself. I hadn't even seen the kick that did Big Red in.

'Slashers,' Sundown spat, glaring at the dead rooster's spurs. 'I thought this was gaffs, not slashers. I would never have bet.'

George grinned. 'Looks like that big bald ape bent some of the luck out of your medicine penny, Sundog, with his unhuman strength. Maybe it's a unlucky penny now . . .'

'No,' Sundown said. He stepped down off the bale and sat on it, looking forlornly at his feet. 'It was just an unlucky kick.' Then his dark gaze turned on me, like a teacher turning from a blackboard to a student. 'Never bet a fight where the birds are spurred with Spanish slash knives. No margin for consistency with slashers. With gaff spurs you can suffer a unlucky kick and keep on fighting.'

'That's the trouble with you redskins,' George declared. 'You never want to admit you're whipped. Shuck 'em.'

Sundown shucked 'em. A few minutes later my boots were stepping grandly through the cedar shavings and chicken feathers, this time on George's feet. I followed along, eager to see what was next. Sundown stayed behind, seated on the hay bale, gazing at the bent penny in his palm. He claimed some gaff fights were coming up and he wanted to win some bets.

I took advantage of the next car's foyer to ask George about that other strongman wonder. 'The one Sundown said could bend a coin with no fingers?'

'That would be Jackson's Yakima cousin, Montanic,'

George told me. '*Parson* Montanic. But nevermind him, we got more immediate wonders to investigate' – and swung the door open on the unlikely spectacle of a Viennese waltz.

This car was decked out like a decorous little ballroom, all velvet and walnut. Shaded gas lamps lined the walls and richly attired couples waltzed to and fro to the strained strains of Strauss. This wheezy racket was being pumped out of a gold-leafed pump organ. George hesitated a moment on the brink of this unaccustomed elegance, then gave me a brave grin and went on in.

His grin faded quickly once we were inside. One after another the dancers stopped and stared. The golden pump organ gave a little sob and stopped. George doffed his big yellow Stetson and begged forgiveness for our interruption, mumbling and shuffling like a field hand. A worn-faced, white-shocked rancher stepped forward with a friendly smile, his wife alongside. 'Good evening, Mister Fletcher,' the rancher said, and held out a callused palm. As the two men shook hands the mood of the car changed like magic. Frowns fled from troubled brows. Thin lips lifted into smiles. The organ recovered from its shock and wheezed back to life.

'Good evenin', Mister Kell. Nice to see you and that's the truth.'

'You also, George,' the rancher said. 'New boots?'

George's familiar grin flooded across his face. He reached down and tugged up his pant legs, exposing the stars and bars of the beautiful boots.

'New for me,' George said, throwing a sidelong grin my way. 'Kind of you to notice, though, Mister Cecil.' He turned to the woman and bowed low. 'Evening,

Miz Kell. Just waltzing through, me'n my young fren'. Please pardon our innertrusion.'

Missus Kell reached out a long, graceful hand. 'Good evening, George. And good luck. The whole town is pulling for you.'

George pressed his hat over his chest. 'Thank you, Miz Kell,' he said, respectfully. 'I just hopes I don't disappoint 'em.'

He pulled me forward for introductions. Her long hand was warm and soft, the very opposite of her husband's rawhide grip. It was like the hand of one of my aunts, and it squeezed a sharp pain from my bosom.

After a short palaver we said goodbye and continued through the crowd, begging pardons in every direction. I wasn't sure if George knew everyone or not, nor did I really care. My mind was still taken up with the Kells. These were people of worth, equal to any Southern gentility I ever encountered. Kell was a Westerner of a special cut – exceptional, but not a bit like Buffalo Bill or Gotch were exceptional. The famous Indian fighter's worth was washed out and faded, like a fake banknote. There was nothing fakey about Gotch but he was what you might say somewhat removed from the regular order of *Homo sapiens.* Cecil Kell struck me as both exceptional and regular at the same time, high-minded, but with both boots planted firmly in the dirt.

When we had worked our way to the end of the car, I mentioned Sundown was still back there with the roosters.

'Might take him all night to get them boots of mine on,' George said. He was whispering again. 'You got any more of that Big Green, by the by?'

'A little bit,' I admitted.

He took me by the arm. 'Good. Your Uncle George is going to show you how to turn that little bit into a whole lot.' He led the way into the next car.

It was a sleeper car and not a soul in sight. Everyone was either already in bed, or else visiting one of the other cars. The aisle along the windows was so narrow we had to go single file. As George tiptoed past one of the compartment doors it swung open behind him and an outlandishly enormous bundle of linen stepped out, supported by two tiny legs. I decided to help out.

'Let me give you a hand, sonny.'

When I lifted the bundle I found myself staring into the face of a beautiful Oriental girl. She was blushing from color to color beneath my stare, like Chinese fireworks. The train rocked and she had to wrap both arms around my waist to keep from going down. I felt those pyrotechnics light my face up, too.

'Thank you prease thank you,' she stammered. She started working her way around me, stammering all the while. 'Good evening velly much.' She spotted George and turned toward him with relief. 'Oh! Good *evening*, Misteh Fretcher.'

'Good evening indeed, Miss Sue Lin,' he said. 'This here is my new pard, Johnny Reb Nashville, the *Third*.'

I was still struggling with the bundle, but I was darned if I was going to let him fun me like that. 'That's Johnathan Spain, ma'am,' I corrected. 'Johnathan E. Lee Spain. And I'm *most* gratified to meet you. En*chant*ed.'

I used what I considered my suavest genteel manner, for I yearned to become better acquainted with this color-changing will-o'-the-wisp. George ignored my gentility and my yearning both.

'Where's the rest of the hired help, Sue honey?' he asked in a low voice. 'Maybe hid out?'

She answered his low whisper with her own high one. 'Keep going way you go, maybe. Maybe next car. Maybe last door. I must go other away.'

She reached up to take the bundle and the train swayed her against me again – the merest brush – but I was set burning anew. George shook my sleeve.

'All right, Misteh Enchanted,' he said. 'You come with me *this*-away, maybe. Less'n you plan to stand there gaping like a hooked bullhead!'

The next car was also a sleeper, but older, and partially made over into kind of a utility compartment. The doors had been recently marked STORAGE, or TELEGRAPH, or EMERGENCY EQUIP, with a butcher's crayon. The last door was labeled RR PERSONNEL ONLY. George eased it open a crack so we could peek in. The room was full of hanging dust and men kneeling prayerfully in a half-circle. A zigzag Indian blanket was spread on the floor and a brakeman's lantern glowed like an altar. I made out the black faces and stark uniforms of waiters, porters, cooks, dishwashers. Menials. They weren't praying; they were gambling. Dice galloped across the blanket and greenbacks passed back and forth. The crapshooters were all betting intensely, cursing or celebrating, calling on the assistance of Dame Fortune – but only in whispers. George banged the door full wide and burst in, yelling, 'All right, the jig is up!'

There was instant pandemonium. Hands snatching for money; people scrambling to their feet. Then they saw who it was hoo-hawing at them.

'Goddamn your ass, George Fletcher,' one of the men yelled. 'Don't *never* fool like that!'

'Truly, George,' an older, somber-faced man said, the only one still on his knees. 'Very poor taste.'

'My apologies, Reverend Linkhorn.' George removed his hat and made a humble bow. 'The devil made me do it, as my daddy said. It was too good a foolin' to pass up.'

'A man must forbear from being the devil's fool, George,' the kneeler said in a voice like a muffled funeral bell. He was a thin sad-mouthed man with gold-rimmed glasses and a suit as stiff and black and somber as his face. 'Especially a man done been just about everybody *else's* fool one time or another.'

'Yes sir, Reverend,' George answered, contrite. Then he brightened and waved his hand at the stirred dust. 'Can y'awl use any fresh air in this dusty ol' game?'

The Reverend brightened at the query. 'Fresh blood us can always use.'

'Good. 'Cause I got a peckerwood here so fresh he might make us *all* rich.'

George tugged me forward into the musty room. I was still flustered from my encounter with Sue Lin, to say nothing of the innermingling of those two glasses of bubbly and Aunt Ruth's yellow moon, so I fear I was more tongue-tied than ever. Reverend Linkhorn leaned forward for a better look, but it wasn't at me. He was squinting through his specs at George's feet.

'New boots, Brother Fletcher? Or have you sunk to grave-robbing?'

'Dame Fortune has been seeing to my needs all evening, Reverend. These boots was won fair and square, just ask Nashville.'

Reverend Linkhorn looked somberly at me and I somberly nodded back. He picked up the dice and patted a spot on the blanket. 'Please join us, then,

57

cousins. *Dear* friends and cousins all—' He looked around at the others. 'Let us kneel and *see* if Miss Fortune persists in her tasteless consort with Cousin Fletcher.'

I knelt beside the Reverend and unbuttoned my shirt to have my money belt handy. George squatted down, took a bill from me and the dice from Linkhorn. He blew on the cubes. 'Shady ladies, get hot. Seven come eleven and no boxcars. Let's hear you bones *talk*.' His hand came down in a sweeping circle and the dice went spinning across the blanket. Snake eyes. George groaned and the circle jeered. I yawned. All these sports in all these different cars were beginning to shuffle together. The train whistle blew a long mournful wail and the wheels clackety-clacked under our knees. I recall rolling a time or two, but I had trouble counting the spots, let alone following the bet. I kept yawning. The drink, the low murmur of the voices, the close quarters, the dark shapes in the tight-packed warmth – all had lulled me into a dreamy torpor. The faces were cured hams hanging in our smokehouse, where I wasn't supposed to play – not with the children of our crop hands, anyway. The dice were my two best shooter marbles. The zigzag Indian blanket was the circle scratched in the smokehouse dirt floor and I plunked whirlies and rubies and puries out of the ring, into the swelling marble pouch between my knees.

I wasn't aware that the dicing had ended until a chill rush of fresh air snapped me full out of my trance. I was outside on the roof of the train again! In the shell of gray dawn I saw George crabbing across the roof ahead of me, sideways. He was leading the woman, Louise, holding her arm with one hand and Sundown's

58

elkskin boots with the other. Louise was clutching that zigzag blanket around her shoulders. She giggled and shrilled as the wind flapped at the cloth.

'Lord Jee-sus I don't believe I'm doing this! I swear George Fletcher you must have a snake for a tongue to talk me into – oh Lord *Jee*-sus—!'

The train answered and the pair splashed into the moony wheat.

Sundown was already in our stock car, rolled up in his blanket. George and the squealing Louise tumbled down next to him on the zigzag blanket. I sat on my own blanket and began tugging off my boots – my *own* boots. I was a better marble shooter than I remembered.

Sundown opened one eye. 'Damn fine boots.'

I set them in their box under the tarp. The train whistle blew and I leaned back on my saddle. A pearly ribbon of steam fluttered across the face of the moon and the engine chugged. The next thing I knew, that chugging had slowed and we were coming to a stop. The sky was killing bright and I got my first glimpse of Pendleton through a pair of eyeballs red as the sun itself.

Chapter Five

Boomtown Excitement

I wasn't ready to wake up just yet; I'd have preferred to sleep until my head and body settled back to normal. But there was too much going on around me. The train was coasting to a stop in the station yard. The engine lurched one final time and let out a loud yawn of steam. I shook my head to clear the cobwebs and scooted to the slats. The sign across the way said PENDLETON DEPOT in fresh letters. The yard was totally deserted except for one old horse asleep in the traces of one old baggage cart. The streets beyond were empty and quiet, except – as I listened closer – I could make out the tooting of a distant march, and it seemed to be tooting our direction.

I rose on my elbow to get a better look. A disorderly line of citizens was marching around a far corner, heading straight for the train. They were followed by a meager brass band and two Indians riding side by side on painted horses. The Indians' lances had a banner tied between them. When they got it to hang straight I was able to make out the words: WELCOME TO THE ROUND UP – LET 'ER BUCK!

Behind me I heard the fumbling of a bedroll. George Fletcher crawled out from his blankets, wearing a pair of long johns. They were patched so many times it looked like a clown's costume.

'Wouldn't you know,' he fretted, pawing for his clothes. 'Just when a saddlebronc champ got nothing to ride but a ratty U.S. Army saddle they want him for Grand Marshal of the parade. Sundog! Better wake up and get curried, partner. Here come our red carpet.'

'Already curried,' Sundown said. He was sitting atop a wooden crate, dressed in his blue serge suit. 'All I need's a little more of that grease.'

George mumbled something about his brother's keeper and dug out the pomade. I rolled around and poked my head through the slats. Tousled gamblers and weary-eyed passengers were gawking out windows at the unexpected parade. The door of the private coach opened and Nordstrum stepped out, beaming like a politician. Buffalo Bill and Frank Gotch followed, and after them, Mister Handles.

'The hungry eye, right, fellas?' Handles said to his colleagues. 'The price of fame. "The world is ever famished after famous wonders," Salome says with one veil left. Or was it Bubble Bath Sheba?'

Buffalo Bill nodded wearily. Gotch unbuttoned his coat, the better to show off his World Wrestling belt and buckle. The three charcoal-dressed men appeared, eyeing the parade suspiciously. The ragged ranks of the welcoming committee finally reached the station and the groggy band tooted to a stop: ta *duh!* Gotch commenced to swell, and Buffalo Bill swept off his white hat with a practiced flourish. Nobody cheered. Nordstrum cleared his throat to address the delegation but an earsplitting clang of metal turned all our heads. It was the gate of our stock car tipped forward to create a steep ramp. The painted pig rushed down the ramp, squealing. Right behind, about to trample on the pig's star-spangled hamhocks, galloped George and Sundown. Now the welcoming committee cheered. George had been right with his bragging jest: he *was* the one the citizens had crawled out of a warm bed and marched to the depot to welcome – the hometown hero and his Nez Percé nemesis! The band came to attention with a version of 'Buffalo Gal,' played like a march. The two bronc riders passed in review like conquering generals.

Sundown had put sheepskin chaps on over his blue serge trousers. Gauntlet gloves covered his coat cuffs, a beadwork red rose on the back of each glove. The saddle on his paint horse was painstakingly decorated and tooled. George's old army saddle was pitiful by comparison – drab and tattered. To spruce things up he'd spread the zigzag Indian blanket over the back of his bay gelding, and he'd tied Louise's orange-and-green silk sash around his throat for a bandana. Crowned with his butter-gold Stetson, it's doubtful many even noticed the shabby saddle.

'Yep, Stonewall,' I said to my ear-pricked horse. 'Real pronghorns.'

When the parade had passed, Buffalo Bill slammed his hat back on and Gotch removed his thumbs from his championship belt and let his long arms hang. Nordstrum and the barker chewed their cigars, exasperated.

Out in the street the crowd folded around George and Sundown and escorted them back around the corner, toward town. The rest of the passengers straggled after, taking their time. I washed myself up as best I could with my canteen. By the time I was packed and saddled the station master had offloaded the Rolls-Royce automobile. It cranked over the first spin and went fuming away. The wrestler and the Indian scout were in the back seat, Mister Handles in the rumble behind. Oliver Nordstrum was riding shotgun, twisting around and pointing out local landmarks like a tour guide. The three Pinkertons rode the running boards. Behind the wheel was the orange-haired woman: She was driving one-handed and looking bored. When the car was swallowed in its dust and fumes I led Stonewall down the ramp and mounted up.

We eased into the heart of the little town. It soon became apparent that Pendleton had put considerable effort into getting itself all decked out for a real whoopte-do. People were everywhere, clamoring like cattle buyers at a spring auction. Cowboys had on their brightest shirts and cleanest jeans. Broad-brimmed hats were fresh-blocked and decorated with horsehair bands and wild-bird feathers. Boots were buffed to a high shine and spurs made a constant jingling. Cowgirls in fringed buckskin dresses laughed and bantered with barbers and barkeeps. Merchants dickered with drummers. Loggers and bankers exchanged loud pleasantries with miners and ministers. And, milling in and out among all these clamorous pillars of Pendleton society, were the Indians. Squads and scores and tribes of Indians, of every condition and complexion: from burnt brick red to buckskin brown; from eagle-eyed proud in full feathered grandeur to rummy-eyed wrecks shuffling along in rags. The thing that set them apart, though, wasn't their skin color or their clothes; it was their silence. They didn't even talk to each other.

The storefronts were festooned with patriotic bunting. Streamers and flags bulged and flapped on ropes strung across the street. Every hotel window showed a

NO VACANCY sign. The vacant lots were completely filled with tarpaulin tents.

To a considerable degree downtown Pendleton looked a lot like it does today. Not as much electric light after dark, of course, nor as much afternoon shade as the full-grown elms and poplars afford the folks now. Fresh plank sidewalks and nice wide streets. Like a lot of little prairie towns that were settled and developed in the West, everything was laid out neatly north and south, east and west. Everything except the Umatilla County Courthouse. Even through the crowd and clamor I couldn't help but notice that the two-story brick courthouse had been built askew on its lot. *Real* askew. A bucktoothed baritone in a high collar and straw hat was apologizing to a crowd of tourists how the whole town would have been all straight and true but for this one misaligned mistake. His deep voice was heavy with authority. Penned to his lapel was one of those I'M A ROUND UP VOLUNTEER: ASK ME buttons.

'And you want to hear whose fault it was?' he was saying. 'That bantylegged Moses Godwin and his featherbrained wife, is whose! If it hadn't been fer him being so henpecked and her being so cockeyed our little town woulda been un*packable*!'

He meant 'impeccable.' Six months ago he would never have attempted such a word, let alone made such a claim. But a boomtown fever was on him. He was proud and critical both at once. I understand better now how he felt. I've lived here long enough and often enough to feel proud of the straight and true of it, myself, and critical of the crooked and the false.

I read the whole story of that famous wrong-angled courthouse the winter I was healing my wrist, in this very hospital. They have a good little library of local histories down in the chapel. Moses Godwin had built a toll bridge across the river and a hotel on this side, but the land around it never amounted to much until Umatilla County began looking for a new county seat. Moses immediately offered two and a half acres for county buildings. Thanks to the help of his neighbor, Judge Bailey, and a jug of Keye's whiskey, his land got the nod.

It was the passion of these early Pendletonians to lay the land out in perfect lines, running true to the compass. This wasn't from an overwhelming sense of orderliness or a consuming desire to tame the wilderness. Profit fueled their passion. The straight and true makes money, whereas things a little off kilter tend to remind us that it was once *all* off kilter, and might get that way again, wild and untamed, if we don't watch out. I think that's why the citizens have always been so vexed by that off-kilter courthouse. Moses Godwin's cockeyed bride bears the most blame.

In a fit of connubial generosity, he allowed her to pick the spot where the new courthouse would sit. She chose a prime site and promptly scratched out the outline in the dirt with a stick. She said she'd lived here all her life and was downright positive which way north and south were. There was no reason for dilly-dallying around with surveying. There's the outline. Build the building. Not that it's any big deal that the courthouse turned out cockeyed. I mention it to give you the benefit of a little trick I have discovered to tell the difference between true history and false; the True is generally uncertain, wishy-washy, vague, while the False is often downright positive.

I kicked Stonewall through the crowd of listeners and

headed down the street. Everywhere I looked, people were betting on something. Mumbly-peg; horseshoes; anything. Down in the dirt next to the boardwalk farm boys in overalls were wagering marbles on two dogs that were hung rear-to-rear after copulation. I didn't stick around to find out what criteria determined the winner. I needed lodging and a bath. And food! That yam was long gone. At the end of the main street I finally spotted a large white house with a ROOM AND BOARD sign on the door.

I tied my horse to the gate and continued up a cobbled path to a broad white porch. I nodded at the boarders sipping iced tea and eating deviled eggs. We exchanged pleasantries. When the proprietress answered my knock she told me there was no vacancy, shaking her head for emphasis. The porch crowd all agreed: no vacancies no place. I stared at the mustard-scented eggs. This time the crowd shook their heads: *no* free lunch, either. Provisions and liquids were fast becoming scarce.

I untied my mount and walked on. I spotted a sidewalk vendor selling sliced watermelon. Here was lunch and liquid all in one. I bought two big slices and led Stonewall toward a dusty cloud of activity. This had to be the rodeo grounds. We penetrated the cloud and I found myself in the middle of a frantic last-minute turmoil of preparation: lumber carrying and hammering and sawing everywhere. The same Round Up volunteer from the courthouse was illuminating the onlookers.

'The crowd was three thousand strong last year. I bet we got three, four times that many this year, already. We got to expand and quick. As you see, we're adding on fast as we can.' He gave me a wink. 'We can't wait for surveyors, no more than Moses Godwin's wife could.'

Two men walked past carrying a meager load of lumber on their shoulders. Both men were breathing hard and the man on the tail end of the load was looking a bit faint. The volunteer gave me another wink. 'Barbers,' he said behind his hand. They dumped their load in front of a bunch of men similarly sunburned and equally winded. The bleachers they were building extended slapdash along a rail fence that surrounded a quarter-mile dirt track.

Every way I looked it was a mix of boomtown excitement and carnival hustle. One man was running a three-card-monte game on an upsidedown wheelbarrow. Another was demonstrating a knife sharpener on an Indian tomahawk. A disorderly mob heaved and pushed in front of two ticket windows. Horses and buggies and buckboards and jalopies were tethered and parked everywhere.

I led Stonewall toward a throng of cowboys. They were gathered in front of an unfinished room beneath the stadium's main bleachers. There was no front wall, but a pair of swinging saloon doors had been installed, and a painted shingle hung above: ROUND UP HDQTRS REGISTER HERE. The swinging doors were a precursor of things to come: they're still there in front of the Let 'Er Buck, still swinging. To the left of the unwalled headquarters an army tent had been set up. Chalk on the khaki tarpaulin informed one and all this was the PRESS ROOM. On a table in front of the tent a man in a green eyeshade was rattling out Morse code. Nadine Rose, the big-bumpered reporter from the train, was striding back and forth, loudly dictating her latest dispatch. Her claxon voice carried over the hammering of the workers and the yammering of the crowd. The telegraph operator winced at every enunciated syllable.

'—incredibly *heart*-stirring . . . is the pano*rama* before us . . . as these stalwart front*iersmen* rise to the tempestuous occasion – What? Tempestuous? Oh, for heaven's sake! T-E-M-P . . .' Now the telegraph operator was given the opportunity to wince at every enunciated letter.

Alongside the press-room tent was parked an enormous circus wagon with a matched pair of mules in the traces. It was strung with the same bunting I'd seen on Nordstrum's private coach. Sideshow banners advertising Buffalo Bill's Wild West Extravaganza were hung up as a back wall. The show's star stood in front of the banner of his likeness, gazing out toward the horizon, trying to look picturesque. The orange-haired woman stood on a plank between two barrels, twirling two bright-orange lariats. The banner behind her proclaimed: MAGGIE O'GRADY – COLLEEN OF THE COWGIRLS.

A third banner advertised FRANK GOTCH – WORLD HEAVYWEIGHT CHAMPION. In garish colors and ghastly detail this painting depicted the wrestler tearing a horseshoe apart with his bare hands while crushing a coconut in a scissorlock. The actual Gotch stood in front wearing nothing but blood-red tights, looking even more garish and ghastly than his painted likeness. He was pumping his hairless chest to its fullest while a photographer charged his flash bar with powder. Mister Handles was barking and pointing at the wrestler with a wooden-stock cane. I looked around. Sure enough, I saw the three ash-faced men in the shadow of the banners, keeping an eye on things.

Handles saw I had noticed the lurking trio and turned his spiel my direction.

'Why if it isn't Dixie Slim! Still wondering about our three boys, aintcha, Slim. Rightly so, rightly so. A sharp-eyed lad like you ought to be encouraged. So, for your benefit as well as all these other fine citizens, allow me to explain their ominous presence.' He aimed his cane at the wrestler. 'As I was saying, folks, that behemoth right there is pow! the great Frank Gotch, undisputed catch-as-catch-can Champeen of the *World!* Accept no substitutes! And this right *here!'* He held up a canvas money bag by its drawstring. '—is one! thousand! dollars! Not paper. *Hard* currency! *And!* lurking yonder in the background—' He aimed the cane at the three ashen faces, pow! pow! pow! The faces didn't change. '—is the trio of Pinks Buffalo Bill has hired especially to pertect this precious pouch. Pinkerton's finest! And *why*, you ask, are we traveling this wild country with this tempting sack of cartwheels? To give it away! That's right! Give it away!' He held the bag higher. 'Buffalo Bill's Wild West Extravaganza has put up this one thousand silver simoleons as a *prize!* to any man, beast, or *savage!* that can last a mere ten minutes in the ring with Fearsome Frank! Not *win*, folks. Just *last*! Any takers out there, gents? No? Wal, don't be ashamed. There's no shame in a man not wanting to tangle with a unhuman giant.'

The men shuffled in the dust. Maybe there was no shame, but the tone of the barker's voice let every man know what the barker thought of them.

'So! If there ain't no local challengers, and should you want to see this physical phenomenon in action, you folks can still catch the champ in action at the Great Buffalo Bill Wild West Extravaganza in the

Portland Armory this coming Sunday! Mister Gotch will defend his belt *officially* against the champion of the European nations: Carl! The Cruel! *Hammer-shlagger!* Two falls out of three. Portland Armory, Sunday next! Flex some flesh at 'em, Frank. Show 'em what you got.'

Gotch flexed. The flash powder popped. The mules snorted and the circus wagon lurched ahead. The barker jumped for the reins. The cow ponies, already skittish, reared and snorted.

'Easy,' I said to Stonewall, 'it's just show business, don't take it serious.'

When the barker managed to rein the wagon to a stop it was very conveniently right in front of the rodeo headquarters. The barker halfheartedly tried to get the mules to move on but they had planted their feet. A group wearing official Round Up buttons came through the swinging doors. Cecil Kell was in the lead. His shock of white hair hung over his forehead. He was carrying a big stone jug, glazed with frost.

'We kind of need to keep this lane cleared, Mister Cody,' he called up to the wagon. 'If you fine people would move your rig on a ways we'd all appreciate it . . .'

'Aint us fine people *trying* to move,' the barker cried, tugging and grunting. The mules didn't move an inch and neither did the picturesque Indian scout's profile. The barker tugged a while more, then wiped his brow in mock exhaustion. 'How 'bout some of you local pony boys lending a hand? Or do I have to get Frank to come down here to *prompt* the brutes . . . ?'

It was clear by then the whole thing was an act to show off the wrestler. Some volunteers stepped up to help the barker tug, but those mules were dug in.

They knew the routine. The barker finally threw up his hands. 'Looks like it's gonna be up to you, Frank—' But somebody said Wait, here come the Beesons, they'll try anything. Two young redheads came through the crowd. They were twins, identical reflections of each other, from the rust-colored cowlicks across their sunburnt foreheads to the stogies smoking in their freckled hands. This definitely wasn't part of the act. The barker glared from one twin to the other as they ambled back to the mules' rumps. They removed their cigars and grinned at each other across the wagon traces. Suddenly both mules lurched again. It was such a lurch this time that Buffalo Bill fell into the wrestler's sweaty arms. The barker was pulled clear off his feet, hollering unspeakable epithets. The orange-haired woman didn't flutter an eyelash, though, balanced on her plank.

Everybody but the Bill Cody troupe laughed. The twins relit the mashed end of their cigars. 'Just in case your team needs more prompting, Mister Cody,' one of them said. The old Indian scout did not think it at all amusing. The wrestler came looming to the edge of the wagon bed and the Pinkertons eased out of the shadows. The twins melted back into the crowd but Gotch's heavy blue stare stuck with them. Mister Kell tried to smooth things over by handing up the crockery jug.

'Hookners bonded reserve, buried six months in last winter's ice. I bet it'd take the edge off this hot sun, Mister Gotch.'

The wrestler switched his eyes back and forth. He finally decided the frosty jug looked more inviting than the cigar-smoking redheads, and accepted the offering. His huge neck pumped down three huge swallows, then he handed the jug on to his boss. Cody had a silver canteen, ready for just such an offer. He held it out and the wrestler poured it full. He sipped critically.

'I wouldn't any of you boys pull that cigar caper again,' he advised everybody. 'Frank don't like to see dumb animals mistreated.'

'Neither do I, Mister Cody, neither do any of us,' Mister Kell said. 'I apologize. The Beeson boys usually got better sense. I guess the unexpected success of our harvest-time punkin roller has made all us folks a little loco. Used to be just a baseball game. Last year we added a trial balloon rodeo. Now look—' He gestured at the milling multitudes. '—we got our *own* extravaganza.'

'Not bad for a punkin roller,' the old showman conceded. 'It could turn into a real sweet investment, but you'd have to get some professionals to run the event. For, mark my words, sir; I've seen shows come and shows go. Forgive me if I speak frankly, but if you brush poppers hope to keep this punkin rolling you positively *must* have outside investors and experienced promoters. Abso*lutely*.'

This pronouncement was delivered like a gauntlet. Everybody could hear the slap. Mister Kell's white hair ruffled even more.

'You're dead wrong about *this* punkin roller. Mister Cody. This aint show business. What us brush poppers have here isn't an investment, it's a tradition! The Indians have been coming to this valley every fall since before Jesus was a pup! For powwows and Indian wrestling and pony races! Don't get me wrong, sir. I aint saying there's anything wrong with treating a traveling show like a business, the way you folks do,

72

but our little whoop-te-do is strictly for the purpose of tradition and good, clean sport.'

Everybody could see the scout's old eyes narrow. 'Is that a fact?' Buffalo Bill said in a measured voice. 'Sport. Did I not hear you refer to Injun Rassling? Then what have you got against Whiteman Rassling? And if one of these lads were to try his luck in the ring with Frank Gotch for ten minutes at ten-to-one odds, would you not call it sport?'

'Back east a feller might.' Mister Kell's face was getting redder; he could tell he was being herded into a corner. 'But none of these lads is professional athletes. They're cowboys, plain old sunup-to-sundown small-town cowboys, not prizefighters.'

The old Indian Fighter looked us over to verify this. 'You mean to tell me there's not a manjack in this town willing to go up against Frank for a thousand-dollar prize, yet they're willing to ride an untamed mankiller for the sake of *tradition?* If that's what you folks call sport, I'll stick to show business.'

The old rancher elected to clamp his teeth down on the cigar and keep quiet. He wasn't used to this much iced spirits and hot sparring in the early afternoon. A young waddie from the crowd filled in. 'I thought that thousand-dollar offer referred only to big cities like Portland and Seattle.'

'That thousand-dollar offer's good anywhere, son,' Bill said. 'We mainly publicize the challenge in cities. We've learned there's not likely anybody in these little one-horse towns – as Mister Kell pointed out and you lads have just reaffirmed – that's man enough to take us up on it.'

'Mister Cody,' the rancher said through his clamped teeth, 'I'd love to discuss this further but I aint got the

73

time or the expertise. I've got some show-business business of my own champing at the bit.' He turned on his heel and stalked through the swinging doors, the back of his neck flaming.

Business was the right word, to tell the truth. For all Mister Kell's talk about tradition there was a succulent smell of a big, rich pot in the Pendleton air this weekend, and a lot of these amateur mouths were drooling for a taste. Well, judge not, I reminded myself; aint your mouth watering, too, just a bit? It looked like it was time for me to make sure my name was in that pot.

I found a homey spot for my horse at the edge of the park. It was in the shade of a big hay wagon ricked high with manure and stable straw. It was not only cool, it was exclusive. The only other horse taking advantage of the place was George's tall gelding. I asked him where his master was. He paid me no heed but whickered a friendly greeting to Stonewall. I put the remainder of my watermelon for them to nuzzle and headed for the swinging doors.

Chapter Six

Fool's Throne

They hadn't named it the Let 'Er Buck in those days, nor instituted anything as titillating as the brassiere bell. Half the ceiling was nothing but rafters and sky. But as it has been every Round Up since, the room was jampacked. Cowboys and townspeople and tourists crammed together, drinking, laughing, and betting. After standing a long time in a long serpentine line I reached the entry table. Cecil Kell had put aside his stogie and jug and was soberly signing up the cowboys. He'd cooled off a bit. 'Johnny Nashville, as I recall?' he said up to me.

'It's actually Johnathan Spain, Mister Kell,' I told him. 'Just like the country. What's the entry fee?'

'Ten dollars a day per event, twenty-five an event for all three days. Or fifty big bucks for All Round, if that prize saddle's your considered hope. You might just stand a chance, too. Only about a dozen big bucks have signed on. Everybody else figures George or Sundown have the All Round tied up.'

I unbuttoned my shirt; and this time I made sure I got a tenspot instead of a hundred. 'Put me down in the calf-roping, sir,' I said. 'One day only.' I leaned forward to sign, but a hand drifted out of the crowd and enfolded my wrist, dark as smoke.

'You can put this cowboy down for the whole shebang. Mistah Kell – Best All Round.' George had appeared out of nowhere again, to help me with my decisions. 'I mean *look* at him – young, limber, handsome . . . I bet he got the nachul ability, and I *know* he got the wherewithal.'

The rancher raised his eyebrows at me and waited.

'I'm a roper, Mister Kell. Our grandiose friend is exaggerating as usual.'

George didn't lift the hand. 'Listen to me, Nashville . . .' He leaned close to my ear. 'The Best All Round entry gives you the same chance at winning the roping money *plus* gives you a shot at the saddle. You hearin' your Uncle George? You done already bet a hundred dollars on yourself back on the train, if you recollect. Now's no time to get cold feet. You got to ride *all* these events *all* three days to pertect your investment, see what I'm saying? You see what I'm saying don't you, Mister Kell? Aint I right?'

Before either Mister Kell or I could think up an answer, another voice hummed at my other ear. 'Nice saddle.'

Sundown had slipped up from my other side. He pointed toward the end of the table, where a grand saddle was displayed on a sawhorse. It did look nice, gleaming in the sunbeams slanting through the rafters. With all its polished turquoise-and-silver inlay it glowed like a huge jewel.

'Hamley's tooled it special,' Sundown went on. 'First ever.'

'First World Champeen saddle *ever*,' George emphasized. 'Come *on*, pardner. Even if you aint rider enough to win it, aint you gambler enough to take a longshot at it? Invest a couple of measly bills more for a chance at something worth a fortune?'

'They're right, son,' Mister Kell had to admit. 'Raw silver alone for all that inlay cost more than three hundred dollars. Meyerhoff showed me the silversmith's bill. What do you say?'

It occurred to me the room had gone very still. I heard someone in the crowd elaborate on Sundown's evaluation – '*Real* nice damn saddle, Johnny Reb,' and someone else added, 'Go good with your boots.' I knew I was surrounded. The room cheered while I counted out four more tens from my moneybelt.

'You got a local address, Spain, Johnathan?' Mister Kell asked. 'Where you're bunking?'

'For tonight I plan to bunk down with my horse, sir,' I said. 'Soon's I find my horse accommodations.'

The cheers turned to horselaughs. 'Slim,' a slope-nose cowboy hooted, 'you're gonna have a tougher time finding accommodations for your *horse* than for your ass.'

'They're right, too, son,' Mister Kell said. 'Every stall and stable is booked this weekend.'

'Excuse me, Mister Kell,' George said. 'I reckon Nashville's horse can bunk with mine, for tonight.'

Kell was still waiting with his pencil. 'We need a nearest of kin or something, son. Just in case.'

I let out a sigh. 'Might's well put down my home address. Four hundred Founder Lane, Mister Kell.'

'Johnathan Spain,' Kell wrote. 'Four hundred Founder Lane. And with a nickname like "Nashville" I guess I put down that you hail from Tennessee?'

'Yessir. T-E-N-N—'

'I know how to spell it, son. Just like the state. Next.'

Ears burning, I stepped away from the table, thankful to have George and Sundown to follow behind. The crowd slapped the two men on the shoulders as we passed, wishing them luck. 'Took that silver saddle to bring the two of you head to head, didn't it, hombres?' Slope-Nose called.

'Does kinda look like it,' George admitted. Sundown responded with his customary direct stare. We made it through the surging sea of drinkers and out the swinging doors. I was grateful for the fresh air.

'Now listen, Nashville,' George said, striding along purposefully. 'I *can* stable your horse at my roost easy enough, but as for accommodations *other*wise I might be booked up full – if I'm lucky.' He gave me a wink and pointed across the park by way of explanation. His horse was still tied in the shade of the hay wagon, but no longer riderless. Up behind George's old saddle on top of the zigzag blanket was Louise Jubal. She was sitting sideways in her Southern Belle costume, fanning the flies away with a Chinese fan. 'You *sabe, amigo?*'

'*Sí*, I savvy,' I winked back. I was becoming a man of the world.

'My Idaho family got a teepee in camp,' Sundown said. I took this as an invitation and thanked him. George held a finger to his lips, tiptoeing.

Louise had climbed up the wagon wheel to her perch on the blanket, the better to see. The Wild West wagon had pulled around to the main road. The troupe had spread their web in the shade of a big maple and netted a nice catch of foot traffic. Louise was stretching her neck, fascinated. I couldn't imagine a lady of her quality climbing up a manure wagon just to watch that hairless gorilla flex his flesh. Then I saw it wasn't his flesh being flexed; it was that orange-haired O'Grady woman's. She had peeled off her cowgirl cover and was down to beads and cheesecloth, doing the Little Egypt belly dance while the barker played snake music on a flute. Louise was totally oblivious to our approach. When George whispered, 'Naughty, child,' I thought she was going to jump out of those blue boots.

'Don't *ever* do that! None of you. Not when a girl's watching hairless *mon*sters.'

'Hairless monsters, my foot,' George laughed. 'You was watching that hootchy-kootch, hopin' to pick up some new steps. Ol' George got here just in time to keep you from seeing sights a good girl oughtn't to see.'

'I climbed up here so I *could* see, you backdoor hypocrite. I like the view and I'll see what I wants to see and that's the end of it.'

'So you likes the view and that's the end of it?' He untied his reins from the wagon spoke. 'Well, you better grab hold of the tail on that end, Little Miss Big Eyes, because I'm leading you away from this trashy-ness.'

'You ain't leading me nowhere, nigger! I been led down your road before.'

'I wouldn't try to squirm off, sinner girl. This animal is seventeen hands high at the saddle and higher than that back where you're perched.'

Louise hissed and spit for a while about Who was *he* to say what was trashy! a no-count over-the-hill cowboy with a saddle look like was salvaged from a trash heap. Then she saw what he meant about the horse's height – seventeen hands was a long ways down with nothing to break your fall but those blue boots – and she crossed her arms in resignation. She rode in rigid silence until she saw where we were headed. Then she grabbed that tail.

'The Indian Camp! You fret about my sensibilities watching a white lady do the jellyroll yet all the while intending to drag me off to a stinky old Indian camp? Huh-*uh*, and that's final. I'll twist this horse handle plumb *off*, you try to take me in that circle of howling savages!'

'Louise!' George cried in disbelief. 'What a insensitive thing to say—'

The horse stopped dead in his tracks, rolling his eyes. Louise sat there, adamant, the horse tail in one hand, the Chinese fan in the other. Fanning her face, she turned to Sundown.

'I apologize, Mr Jackson. I didn't really mean savages. Nor stinky and howling, neither. But you got to admit these teepee camps tend to be hard on the ears and nose.'

'Loo-*eez!*' George was scandalized. 'You got to stop behaving in ways not becoming a lady. We're in the twentieth century.'

Louise fanned herself harder. 'Still smells like the eighteenth to me.'

'You remember that far back?' George teased, monkeying his eyebrows up and down. Louise sat glowering. Her expression didn't soften even when Sundown interceded.

'We can take the river path.'

'Sure,' George said. 'It goes around the teepees.'

'I *know* where that path goes, if you'll recall . . .'

They kept after her. She finally threw up her hands in surrender, releasing the tail. George led the horse through the gate, then took a cutoff, away from the teepees. He was whistling a little tune to the rhythm of his steps. He seemed greatly relieved. He hadn't liked the idea of leaving such an exotic flower unwatched.

I was secretly relieved, myself. That ring of tents looked wild and threatening, like arrowheads aimed at the sky. There weren't as many teepees as nowadays, of course, but the styles were more various. All sizes and shapes, some still covered with animal hides and some of those hides still rank with fat and flies. The hodge-podge of tribes and clans hadn't agreed on one central fire for the camp, so the air between the dwellings was choked with the smoke of hundreds of cooking pits. Squaws and maidens, tourists and kids, dogs and horses drifted in and out of a hanging haze. Indian men hunkered in whatever shade they could find, drumming and singing and drinking. The sun was hammering down.

George led the gelding into a scrub-oak thicket. Sundown dismounted and followed him on foot. It was brushy going but Louise refused to quit her seat on George's horse. I got off Stoney and walked, too. My head was ringing, both from today's heat and last night's carousing. I concentrated on the back of Sundown's blue serge suit. The stiff shoulders looked like rolled tin, the cloth was so worn. The old-fashioned cut of the collar reminded me of the suit I saw Great-Grandfather Spain buried in.

We broke into the clear and found ourselves following the bank of the Umatilla. The river rushed past, down a narrow channel and over a little falls. There was a moil of bare-bottomed Indian boys in the pool below the falls, yelling and tussling. They were playing a kind of King of the Mountain. Their mountain was a single spectacular boulder in the middle of the falls. Unlike the rest of the granite dam, this boulder was glistening yellow and amber and was as big as a Brahma bull. Eons of water had polished the rock naturally, but the summit looked handmade, carved into a smoother basin. This saddle-sized declivity was green with slime and glistening with spray.

'That big rock looks like some kind of throne,' I observed.

'It is a throne,' George said. 'A Ko Shar throne, carved out of obsidian. Nobody knows where it came from.'

'Mahogany obsidian,' Sundown emphasized. 'It comes from Glass Butte, south of here.'

'Alright, alright. It comes from Glass Butte. But nobody knows how it got here. In case you hadn't noticed, Nashville, Sundog is of the opinion that the seat gives the sitter some kind of power.'

One of the boys broke free from the pack and scrambled his way up the rushing current and plopped his brown rump into the green hollow. Then, to my amazement, he commenced whooping and jabbering like a madman.

'What kind of power?' I asked. 'The power to jabber?'

'The Power of Tongues,' the Indian said.

'Ko Shar is the Spirit of Truth,' George said.

'Truth Running,' Sundown corrected

'Injuns believe you can hear him in the jabber of river water if you listen long enough.'

'Hear him speak the truth.' Sundown seemed practically verbose on this subject.

George was his usual gabby self: 'They claim that the man that keeps his seat and jabbers along with the water will eventually speak the truth, too – if he's able to sit and jabber *long* enough. That ain't exactly easy on the Ko Shar throne.'

I saw what he meant. All that jabbering in the slick saddle was already unbalancing the lad. He couldn't keep his seat in this bucking current. With a yelp of despair he slid back into the moil of lesser beings churning the water below. Louise shook her head at the sight.

'Don't you two get started about that crazy rock. A *fool's* throne is what you mean, and I for one am not amused. I want you both to swear you'll let them *other* little boys play the fool with that rock this year. It's their turn, don't you think?'

George snickered. Sundown stood looking at the rock.

'Promise me, this instant, both of you! Swear you'll leave that damn rock alone or I'll fry up some bayou joo-joo that'll burn your insides like fire ants.'

They both raised their palms in their all-purpose gesture. Louise seemed satisfied.

'Good. Now, you big boys go on with your business; I'll wait right here in the cool. I'm comfortable up on this fat old horse. And this is not an unpleasant place – in the daylight, with naked children playing in the pool instead of ugly old men.'

Laughing, George dropped the reins so his horse could crop the shoreside grass. Louise remained reclined across the gelding's blanket-covered rump like a lady on a divan. I unlashed my bedroll and tied it up behind Sundown's saddle, then tethered Stoney to a willow where he could get at the miner's lettuce. Sundown chose to lead his horse at a leisurely pace. He seemed as reluctant as Louise to enter the clamorous teepee camp. George ribbed him about it all the long, slow walk, but the Indian didn't say a word.

Sundown's wife's family had pitched camp clear on the far side of the teepee ring, along the back fence. Their teepee had a buffalo-skin covering painted with scenes of battles and hunts, some very old, some brightly recent. The scenes were all mixed together. Ancient stick figures fired rifles at blue-coated cavalrymen; a ferocious warrior held a bloody hatchet in his right fist, a Bible in his left; breechclothed braves in the back of a Stanley Steamer were shooting arrows at long-gone buffalo herds. My perusal of the teepee's art was interrupted by George's snickering.

'What you waiting for, Dog? hee hee hee. You're the cock of the walk this year. Go in there and give 'em a big cock-a-doodle howdy-do.'

'I have to tend my horse.' Sundown untied his bedroll from behind his saddle and placed it next to the teepee's flap door. I dropped mine alongside. Then he removed the saddle and carefully situated it on a straw bale. He tied a lead rope from the paint horse to the saddle horn and poured a pouch full of grain on the ground. George kept snickering at his partner's procrastinating pace. He cupped his ear toward the teepee.

'Why are you so hesitant, Dog? It sounds right peaceful, compared with the rest of the neighborhood. Maybe nobody's home. Maybe your kinfolks just set it up and left, knowing how you hates socializing.'

Sundown didn't respond to George's ribbing. He raised his hand in that stiff gesture and ducked into the teepee. The flap closed behind him like a page in a book.

But this chapter wasn't over. Within seconds after his entrance a hellacious chorus of complaint arose from the teepee. Dogs and babies and women, all voicing their grievances simultaneously. Sundown hopped back out the flap like a spooked coyote. He had his hand cupped to his ear this time, but it wasn't toward the turbulent teepee.

'Do you hear that?' he inquired, squinting on up the fence line.

'Hear that warm welcome you just got?' George said. 'How could we miss it, less'n we was deaf?'

'No. That way. I hear bells. Christmas bells.'

I looked up the rail-fence line to see what he was talking about. Two small crowds of cowboys and Indians had gathered, each on their respective sides of the fence. I couldn't see what they were so interested in, but above the racket of the camp and the bellering of the stock I could make out the unlikely tinkle of sleighbells. Sundown began striding that direction.

'It's Cousin Montanic. He's run into that fence they built across the trail.'

George hastened to catch up. 'Parson Montanic aint likely to need any help and he *aint* any real cousin. You're just hoping to avoid your *real* family is what I think.'

'No. I'm hoping to get my penny straightened.'

I followed, wondering if this was an Indian euphemism, like us getting our ashes hauled.

As we approached the two crowds of onlookers I saw that one of the fenceposts had been pulled free of the ground and the rails piled aside. The dirt line on the post showed it had been planted nearly three feet deep. I was looking around to see what kind of lever-and-fulcrum had been used to extract the post when the two crowds suddenly stepped aside. I beheld a startling sight.

A draft wagon came jingling through the open fence, traces empty. It was an ordinary wooden four-wheel freight wagon, the kind you still see in some freight yards, but it was by no means ordinary-looking. The entire rig was painted with biblical illuminations. The seatback depicted Jonah being coughed forth by the whale. The sideboard showed angels and winged horses hovering around an aboriginal nativity scene: Baby Jesus was sitting bolt upright on the back of a tender-eyed mule deer; the three feathered wise men rode paint ponies. Except for the broken spare all the wheels were decorated with feathers and colored ribbons woven through the spokes. The whole contraption looked like something Ezekiel might have haywired together after his vision of wheels within wheels.

But the most extraordinary feature of this jingling altar was – as I mentioned – the fact that it was jingling along without benefit of horsepower. Or mule or ox or *any* beast-of-burden power, that I could see. There wasn't even a wagontongue to harness an animal to!

While I was puzzling at this mystery, the proprietor of this colorful conveyance finally came plodding into view at the rear corner of his load, an old gimpy coyote at his heels for a companion. The man was of indeterminate years, the drab shape and color of a potato. Yet he was decked out in the most elaborate Indian getup I had seen so far, from his eagle-feather headdress down to his deerskin moccasins. His headband was beaded, his vest was beaded, his leather pants were beaded. An animal-tail mantle around his shoulders hung all the way to his knees. A four-strand necklace hung clear down over his baked-potato belly – alternating red beads and long white tubes. These tubes, I later found out, were the boiled spines of a rare sea urchin, and highly esteemed. In the midst of all this Indian grandeur, however, one tiny piece of jewelry stood out – a silver crucifix on a delicate chain.

Sundown stepped through the onlookers and raised his hand.

'Haw, Cousin Parson! *Ya kacha katah.*'

The potato-shaped man and the painted vehicle stopped. The cousins talked in Indian across the junk-filled wagon bed until an understanding was reached. Sundown held out the coin. With a look of heavy deliberation, Montanic rotated his head and studied the bent copper. The movement seemed unnaturally slow, like a sloth studying a leaf. George stepped alongside his partner.

'C'mon, Parson. Straighten poor Sundog's penny out. I doubt it'll bring the luck back but all these folks is starvin' to see *some*thing happen.'

Sundown's cousin dragged his gaze across the crowd and nodded. He began to sink slowly down. His corner of his wagon sunk with him until it rested on the axle. I saw then that the lashed-on wheel hadn't been a spare at all. This pious potato in feathers and beads had been the whole replacement, rear wheel and horsepower all in one.

Montanic walked around the rear of the wagon, flexing the fingers of the hand that had held the axle. The crowd watched in silence as he took the coin from Sundown and began turning it over and over. After examining it a long time, he raised his face.

'What kind of Philistine do this?'

Sundown was at a loss for an answer. Montanic rotated his face to George.

'*Big* kind, Parson,' George answered. 'Strong as the very devil. Can you *un*do it?'

'Render undo Caesar,' Montanic answered. He carefully pinched each half of the coin between thumbs and fingers and drew a breath. George spoke again.

'With*out* hands, Parson. I want to give our visitor from the South the full glory.'

Montanic raised his head to me. After a while he gave me a spreading smile, very wide and very white. It kept spreading wider and whiter until a prodigious jawful of perfect teeth was displayed. It was truly glorious.

'Do it, Parson,' someone from the cowboy side yelled. Several Indian voices concurred: 'Haw!'

Montanic placed the coin between his molars and began clamping down. It was like watching a porcelain vise. When he took the coin out of his mouth it was flat. Sundown solemnly accepted the restored coin and gave a nod of thanks. Montanic returned to the wheelless axle. The wagon raised and began to move. It jingled on toward the teepees. The crowds drifted their respective directions.

'I best be getting back to the Ko Shar pool, Dog,' George said. 'I don't like leaving my horse *nor* Louise unhobbled too long; either one is liable to get itchy-footed.'

We returned along the rail fence. I was still wondering about the vise-jawed Indian. 'Where in the world did that fellow come from?' I asked. 'Why do people call him Parson?'

'He came from the same place as me,' George said. 'Parents unknown. White folks brand us orphans; Indians don't have that concept. Indian families will always take a stray kid in and feed him.'

'Until he shows hair under the arms,' Sundown added. 'Then he gets pushed out on his own.'

'Right, forage – hee hee hee. *I* found out about forage. It aint so bad in the summer with all the grasshoppers and blueberries. Come wintertime, foragin' can get a little rough on a skinny youth. Montanic, though, he started foragin' even before he showed fuzz. He's been at it ever since.'

'He lives in a cave by himself now,' Sundown said. 'Except for the coyote.'

'Coyote must have been an orphan, too,' George said. 'Just a pup. He slunk into the cave one night and crawled under the blanket. Montanic let him stay, figuring two orphans in a blanket are warmer than one. It wasn't long after that he claims he heard it.'

'Christmas Eve it was,' Sundown said.

'Heard it?' I said peevishly. 'Heard *what*?'

'A voice,' George said, 'calling him from the forest: "Monnn-tannn-ic." He crawled out from under his robes but the shivering pup refused to move. He followed the voice way up the ridge but he couldn't catch up with it. The moon come out from behind a cloud and . . . he saw something.'

'It flew from the other side of the moon,' Sundown said.

'Well?' This pair could string a parable out longer than a preacher. 'What was it?'

'A white eagle,' Sundown said. 'It landed on a rock and called. The boy climbed up. The eagle flew to a higher rock. The boy climbed up. The eagle flew to a higher rock. The boy climbed up. He was in a dreamworld. He kept climbing until the voice told him what it wanted to tell him.'

'Which *was*?'

'That he was going to be a warrior for Jesus.'

''Course, when he came *out* of that dreamworld,' George said, 'he wasn't a warrior for nobody. He was lost and cold and scared.'

'He heard another voice then. The coyote was

89

howling. He followed the howl back to his cave.'

'And, laying there under the warm covers with his wild pet, Montanic understood what his life was for. He was sup*posed* to become a travelin' preacher.'

'He had found his *weweykin*,' Sundown said.

'Is that like your guardian angel?' I asked. 'Your special spirit?'

'Your *weweykin* can be many spirits,' Sundown said. 'Young Montanic's was the eagle that called him away and the coyote that called him back. For a long time he denied what he was told.'

'Who wouldn't?' George snorted. 'He was young and strong and full of vinegar! He wanted to be a *hell*raiser, not no pious preacher! He had oats to sow.'

'He was trouble to tribes all over the territory. Drinking, gambling, hurting people. He was strong. We would tie him up and he would chew off the ropes. Then another cold night he heard the voice again. Another Christmastime. In a saloon in Yakima. He followed the voice outside but he was too drunk to make it up the mountain. He keeled over in the gutter and fouled himself. Nobody would touch him. Not even the Yakimas.'

'They say even his coyote wouldn't get close to him,' George added. 'Then, this whopper goes, just as this stinkin' scapegrace was sliding down into his final sleep, a *babe* appeared in the heavens, naked as a jaybird and glowing like a red-hot ember. It came down and curled up next to him and kept him from freezing to death. *N*aturally, Montanic says it was the baby Jesus.'

'Many people saw it,' Sundown said. 'They saw Mary and Joseph, too, and the Holy Ghost beat a drum all night for the babe and Montanic. Since then he's been Parson Montanic. He baptizes and does weddings all over the Northwest.'

'Maybe that part about the eagle and the coyote got some truth to it,' George said, 'but the Holy Ghost don't visit drunk Indians in the gutter in Yakima, Washington. He don't play no drum, either.'

'Have it your way,' Sundown said. 'Montanic is still Parson.'

George huffed and gave up. The noise in the camp forbade more talk, anyway. It sounded like there were Holy Ghost drummers by the hundreds, and they were just getting warmed up. Sundown's teepee was still emitting an uproar of babies and women. Not one male voice that I could hear. Sundown gave a groan of resignation and picked up my bedroll under one arm and his under the other. As a last resort he invited George and me inside to look around.

'I seen that parlor before, and our Southern guest can look it over later after we have some grub and check the sights,' George said. 'Come along, Nashville. All that lady buzz I'm hearing got me worried. Nighty-night, Sundog. Sleep tight, don't let the ladybugs bite.'

Sundown stooped through the slanted opening. A full fanfare of domestic demands welcomed him.

'Don't worry after your gear,' George reassured me. 'Injuns are *famous* for not stealing.'

The drums were beating louder. The longer I was here, it occurred to me, the more I was getting shed of everything I called my own: my bankroll, my bedroll, even my given name. What would they think back home? That I had been relieved of my senses and my sensibilities and my booty to boot.

When we got back to the river the pool was empty

and the Ko Shar stone unassailed. Stonewall was peacefully cropping the miner's lettuce along the bank. George's bay gelding was nowhere to be seen, and neither was Louise.

Chapter Seven

Jenny Lynne

George guessed exactly where Louise had flitted off to. 'That trashy flashy show-cart – like a moth to a candle flame! Your horse is gonna have to tote us double, Nashville.'

The crowd around the wagon had grown so dense we weren't able to penetrate by way of the park. We had to circle north and come at the spectacle from the Dalles road. We spotted her across the throng at once.

Buffalo Bill was seated in the shade of the banners. The orange-haired woman was gathering up her six veils.

Gotch was striding back and forth on the fold-out wagon bed while the barker began barking the same old challenges. The look in the wrestler's eyes had gone from bullying to bored, while the tone in the pitchman's voice was more insulting than ever, like a slap in the face.

'A hundred bucks a minute, you craven clod-hoppers! For just ten! short! little minutes! Those that can do sums know that tallies up to one thousand dollars! One thousand *doll* ears! In silver cartwheels! To any hoss, filly, or *colt!* what's got gizzard enough to climb into this square ring with this magnificent physical specimen for ten measly minutes!'

He turned to Gotch and confided in a loud aside, 'I include fillies and colts, Frank, because I so far aint seen any sign of studs. You seen any?'

Without breaking his routine, the giant turned his baleful gaze on the faces. One man after the other he began to stare deliberately down.

'Not yet,' he told the barker. 'I'll keep looking.'

George and I were on the rear-stage side of the wagon, getting Gotch's back more than his face, but it was clear he was enjoying the sport. Gotch continued to methodically browbeat one man after another. After a few moments beneath his bored, blue stare, every face would cringe groundward, like a whipped dog. It made you sad to see it.

Every face, until he came to Louise's. She just wouldn't browbeat. For one thing, she was up in the saddle of George's tall horse so she wasn't looking up like the rest of the rubberneckers; she was eye-level to him, and just as unblinking. For another, she knew she was quite the physical specimen herself, sitting up there in her blue boots and her off-the-shoulder gown. She matched Mr Gotch glare for glare and would not relent! Nor would he. His eyes narrowed and the look of boredom left his face. You could almost hear the actual hum of their staredown, like the hum of juice through telegraph wires.

Gotch broke off first, making like it was time for him to go to a new and more difficult flex position and he had to close his eyes to concentrate. It was an opportunity for both parties to back off with grace. But when Gotch's lids reopened the brassy little beauty was still eyeballing him, casually fanning her generous front with the fan – and she was the one looking bored.

'O me, O my,' George fretted anxiously from his seat

behind my saddle. 'That girl would kick a porkypine barefooted.'

Just then Gotch recognized the fan. He snapped his big fingers.

'I *knew* I seen that look-out look before. You're that little yeller hammer from the train. You hunting for a tree trunk to hammer, Yeller-honey?'

'It is a very challening look, Frank,' the barker put in. 'Maybe she's the one goin' to take us up on our offer.'

'Is that so, Yeller?' Gotch asked. 'Want to rassle? Going ten minutes catch-as-catch-can with you might be worth a thousand. Whatcha say?'

The crowd of men guffawed. They were glad somebody else had drawn Gotch's fire, even if it was a woman. Everybody turned toward her, waiting, but Louise didn't reply. The fan never faltered; her eyes never wavered. I could see why George was anxious. She'd got herself in a thorny situation, being the only woman around for Gotch and the boys to sport with.

'Whatcher think, Bill?' Gotch went on. 'Think we can afford to drop a grand for the opportunity of me going ten minutes with Cindy Lou here?'

Buffalo Bill raised a beaded gauntlet against the late-afternoon sun and studied the woman on the horse.

'Tell you what, Frank. How about you go nine and a half minutes, *then* pin her? That way you'd have your fun, the fans would get their money's worth, and I'd save a thousand dollars.'

Everybody thought this was a great tease. They hooted and slapped their knees and carried on like lodge brothers at a stag show. This was more than Louise could hold up under. Her eyes dropped and a startling blush rose up her proud neck like the temperature up a weather thermometer. The hoots and horselaughs rose with it. She squirmed on the saddle, glancing desperately every direction for a hero to help her out of her predicament. Naturally, this desperate glance fell on George. The giant swiveled his face around to see who it was she had found.

'Bless my buttons, if it isn't Uncle George, spooning a ride with the Dixie dandy. You hear the sporting news, Uncle? Me and Yeller Hammer are negotiating a catch-as-catch-can contest – right here and right now, 'less she crawfishes. She ain't the crawfishin' kind, is she?'

George didn't answer. Gotch shifted into a new flex, the better to talk our direction. His words were soft as a cat's paw with the claws out of sight.

'She'll be needing a second, of course. You'd kneel in her corner with a towel and a bucket, wouldn't you, Uncle George? Be her bucket boy?'

George still diplomatically declined to answer. I couldn't see his face but I heard his breath sizzle through his teeth. It sent a shameful shudder of panic through me. Who knew how long this cowboy diplomat would be able to keep a tight rein on his tongue? Any minute he might sass some foolish crack back at Gotch and bring the brute's wrath down on *all* our shoulders. I found myself wondering if I shouldn't have stayed with Sundown. At least Indians had their tribesmen for reinforcements should some hotheaded fool make a dangerous retort. George Fletcher wasn't that kind of a fool, thank God. He merely shrugged and lifted his open palms.

'Dat's up to de lady, Mars Gotch,' George said. 'Ol' George'll kneel anywhere he needed. She want to fuss with you, that's none of my affair.'

Gotch looked disappointed. Mister Handles stepped forward with his stock cane.

'That's the spirit! Spoken like a true Republican. But these folks deserve *some* kind of action, don'tcha think – standing all this time in the heat? Tell you what, George: how about *you* come up here and defend your little lady's honor? That thousand-dollar prize still holds good. Whatcha say?'

'Yeah,' Gotch said. 'I'll even give you one free swing at the ol' tomato can.'

He grinned and knotted his hands behind his back to tighten his abdominal muscles. They looked like corrugated-iron siding. George grinned back, and when he didn't say anything, Gotch moved his heavy gaze on to me.

'How 'bout you there, Dixie? One free swing at my unguarded guts. Let's see some of that famous Southern spunk. It shore don't appear any of these Northern bucks got any.'

'Oh, I don't know about that, Mister Gotch,' I blurted out. 'You remember that coin you bent one-handed? I just saw a fellow straighten it out.'

'Das right, das right!' George cried, goosing me in the back to shut me up. 'Straighten it out! Only he didn't use *no* hands. *Der's* you opponent, Mars Gotch. Parson Montanic! You let dat girl bring me my horse an' we'll go *get* him for you, on my word of honor.'

When they heard this, dozens of onlookers shouted their concurrence: 'Parson Montanic, of *course*! Strongest Injun in the world, and a preacher in the bargain!' Gotch's interest was piqued. So was the interest of Mister Handles and Buffalo Bill. The old promoter perceived there might be an event worth promoting in these boondocks yet. If enough of the crowd thought this Indian preacher was a match for Gotch, the Wild West troupe knew that's all it took. They promptly dispatched the three of us to locate this local strong boy and sign him up – preferably before evening, tomorrow noon at the latest. Nodding and scraping, George slid down off Stoney and up behind his own saddle.

'Be back in a wink soon's I find the Parson and talk him into a wrassle-match. I'll tell him it's for the glory of God.'

To seal the deal, Gotch flipped George a silver dollar. They looked at each other a moment more before we rode off. When we were safely clear George dropped the coin in his shirt pocket.

'If I *can't* talk cousin Montanic into it, well, I'll just hafta bring Mars Gotch his silver cartwheel back . . . bent. Ee Yah!' He spurred the horse to a lope.

Louise knew nothing of posting and the horse's gait was spanking her good against George's hard old saddle. She knew she deserved it.

George headed upriver, exactly opposite from the direction of Montanic's wagon. At a roaring ford he traded seats with Louise and picked out an underwater path across the current. Stoney and I both had doubts but we followed. We passed a suspension bridge of plank and heavy hawser, wide enough for horse and rider. The bridge looked to me like it would have been a better choice than that churn of rapids and riverweed where we'd forded, but I made no comment. It likely wouldn't have been heard anyway. The river was guzzling loudly at its ferny banks along the path. Behind me the town was wah-hooing its rehearsal for tomorrow's opening-day festivities, and up ahead the double-riding couple were arguing. Louise had recovered her poise and George his quick-tongued equanimity; the pair was fussing at each other like two kingfishers fussing over limb space. I couldn't tell if they were finishing an old dispute or stirring up a new one. They finally reached some mutual disagreement and rode on in a brooding truce.

The wah-hooing behind us grew dimmer as we climbed, and the trail narrower. The occasional riverside shacks got smaller and emptier. After crossing a second ford, George reined left, up an overgrown wagon road. The weedy ruts crested a knoll and opened into a cleared pasture. A doe and two spotted fawns bounded through the tall clover and over a tumbledown stone fence. At the far end of the meadow unpruned fruit trees hung heavy before unpainted buildings. It was the remains of a failed dairy ranch. It must have been an ambitious attempt, and probably a costly failure. The barn was immense. The silos and milking sheds were large enough to have once accommodated nine or ten dozen head, twice a day. The house was three-fourths burned, but you could see it had been quite a fetching domicile in its day. It had been built between two tall maples for the shade. The twin gables on the roof had been made long and low, so their windows could peek from under the leafy green lashes of the maples. Now the maples were leafless, killed by the fire, and sooty stains fanned out around the empty windows like mascara on a witch.

George rode right on past the burned house to the massive barn and reined up outside a sliding door. This split-plank portal was enormous, a good twenty foot from its slotted wooden base to the iron track and rollers at its top, and almost as wide as it was tall. Two doors, actually, built the way barn doors used to be built before the hay baler, to open in the center and slide each direction so a high-pitched hay wagon could enter. Whoever had built this double monstrosity had a godawful big hay wagon or hellaciously big intentions.

The two halves were chained shut in the middle with a rusty log-chain that went through one augered hole, around the uprights, and back out through the hole in the other half. A padlock the size of a mule's hoof kept the two ends of the chain secured. A herd of hay-starved African elephants could not have stampeded their way in.

George hopped down and dug a key from somewhere deep in his longjohns. It was the size of a hunting knife. He probed at the rusty keyhole. Louise and I waited on our impatient horses.

'You'd think the old rip had the treasures of a royal castle in there,' Louise remarked to me in a taunting aside. 'Something valuable as jewels, maybe.'

Finally the key turned and the big lock creaked open. George hung it on a spike and began rattling the chain links through the holes.

'Sorry, no. Ol' George aint got no jewel crown in his c'lection *yet*. But don't they say a man's home is his castle? Well my home and castle's got royal treasures, *too* . . . and they needs protected just like anybody's.'

'*Your* home?' Louise said. 'I bet that aint what you say when Millicent McConkey sashays out on one of her surprise inspections.'

'Alright, my *temporary* home and castle.' He turned to me. 'This used to be the McConkey dairy. I helped Dad McConkey and his two brothers work it while I was still a pup – watched the herd grow till we was milking more than a hundred head of prize Guernseys. They was milkers, them McConkeys, but terrible stiff-necked and stingy. The milk of human kindness was not one of their products. They druv their help like niggers. Finally nobody would work for them no more, 'cept family members. And me, of course: I was used to being druv like that. They eventually kind of druv one another off – all but Dad McConkey and his poor little motherless daughter, Millicent.'

'Motherless aint how I heard it,' Louise said. 'I heard Dad McConkey was intimate with several of those pretty heifers. Millicent likely had a whole *herd* of mamas and aunts and grandmamas.'

'Louise! Listen at you. No wonder you're attracted to that wagonload of lowlifes.'

'Something wasn't proper! Else why did she turn out to be such a egg-addled mooncalf.'

'She aint addled!' George retorted. 'She runs a successful beauty parlor all day, then teaches at the Umatilla College of Beauticians of an evening! You think a person could do that if they was egg-addled?'

'It probably even helps,' Louise answered. 'Are you going to open that door or not?'

George resumed his task. 'Dad McConkey just up and set the house on fire one day, and hiked off into the hills. His dog didn't even go with him. When seven years passed they declared him legally dead and passed the deed on to his daughter. Miss Millicent appointed me watchman over what's left. In case old Dad comes down out of the hills with a box of matches to finish the job. Like I say, Nashville: it's home. Hop down and give me a hand, would you?'

With both of us pulling, the door popped free and

rolled open with a deep rumble. George cupped a hand stirrup for Louise to dismount, then led his horse into the cavernous gloom. It was a vast enclosure, echoing and dim and cluttered with black, ribby forms that smelled of axle grease and old wood. George clambered up one of these dark forms and opened a high shutter. A golden beam of sunlight streamed in through the roused dust, spotlighting a carpeted circle across the immense space. In this golden ring sat a chair and a neatly made brass bed. As my eyes adjusted I saw that rodeo pictures and prizes adorned the wall above the bed. A guitar hung from a carved peg. A cedar chest gleamed at the foot of the bed with a matching pitcher and basin arranged on its polished lid. In the midst of the barn's vast clutter and dirt this little carpeted island was lovingly maintained. George spun his yellow Stetson in a perfect ringer atop a bedpost and stood grinning, awaiting my reaction.

'It's first rate, George,' I said. 'A castle.'

'Just a drafty ol' barn,' he answered, flattered. 'Serves well enough for a raggedy ol' batchlor, I reckon.'

'I'm always amazed, George Fletcher,' Louise said, 'that a raggedy batchlor like you can be so *neat*. You sure this is without benefit of any female influence?'

'Well of *course* I got female influence,' George declared. 'I got Miss Jenny Lynne, aint I?'

He reached up through the sunbeam and twanged a line. Something dark moved in the shadows, like a giant black widow in her web. George shimmied up a ladder to reach an even higher shutter. The beam through this window revealed the dark thing to be a common wooden barrel hung in the center of a wall-to-wall network of plowlines. George hopped down and strummed another lather line. The barrel shuddered.

'Meet my chilehood sweetheart, Nashville – Jumpin' Jenny Lynne. She can pace, she can gait, she can pitch you on yo' pate.'

I stepped closer. The barrel was rigged with brass eyebolts and lashed horizontally, about six feet above the barn floor. A saddle horn was mounted at one end. In the bunghole at the other was a horsetail flywhisk. Stirrups hung from each side, U.S. Cavalry stirrups, shined to a soft sheen. I reached up and stroked the barrel's underbelly; it was smooth as a baby's. The whole apparatus was polished to the same deep sheen as the stirrups. The staves looked like the waxed wood of expensive furniture. The iron hoops and brass fittings gleamed like Great-Aunt Ruth's Sunday silver. I gave a low whistle.

'Uh-huh,' George beamed, 'aint she ever. A sly old buffalo-soldier veteran named T. Spoon constructed her for me. Them stirrups? They off that saddle I use. Spoon modified it for ranch work. He was the original McConkey handyman and I was his apprentice – which means I learned to be just about as knock-around sly as T. Spoon was. But his army life had trained him to keep neat – shaved and shined and shirttail tucked in – and he learned me that. He kept my nose clean and my trousers washed and my boots shined – nevermind if they all had holes in them. I try to do the same for Jenny here.'

He ran a hand over the wooden flank for a moment, then turned with a slight smile.

'What do you say, cowboy? Care to see how she rides? I'll just lead her easy, honest I will.'

'Don't trust him,' Louise warned. 'He's a tricker and a scamp.'

'Honor bright,' George promised. 'Light and easy and no tricks. I merely want you to throw a leg over and *feel* her – tell me how she rides, horseman to horseman.'

George tugged down on one of the lines so I could reach the horn. I got a foot in the stirrup and swung aboard. The barrel shuddered in its web of plowlines. I got my other foot in its stirrup and steadied myself. I rocked carefully a time or two, then smiled down at George. He was still holding the plowline.

'Rides real nice,' I said.

'Don't she just,' George said.

'Kind of antsy-feeling, though,' I observed. 'I'd worry she might have an ornery streak in her.' It was the taut line in George's hand that was really worrying me. 'Could be if you were to turn her loose she'd be less jittery.'

George said, 'Could be you're right—' and let the line go. The whole barn thrummed, like a big bull-fiddle being plucked. As the ripple passed along the stretched leather the wooden barrel gave a quick left-shoulder buck, just the way certain devious ponies will try to unseat a greenhorn before he's settled. But John Spain, even at that tender age, wasn't any greenhorn. I rode the wave easy by adjusting my weight to the left. Then I realized, too late, that quick side buck hadn't been a real buck at all – only a feint. The ripple bounced off the wall and came back from the right, its power amplified. The damn thing had faked me one way then used the energy of my own reaction to double the force of the wave. The next thing I knew I was sitting on the floor, blinking through the dusty sunbeams at George and Louise bent over me. I tried to grin.

'That's one on me. I imagine I must have looked like some kind of fool.'

George gave me a helping hand up and brushed me off. 'It weren't on purpose, Nashville,' he told me. 'You said Turn loose. Anything broke?'

I assured him I was all right. He stopped brushing and stepped back, rubbing his chin. 'You was sittin' too *stiff* if you want to know what it really was. You was stiffed up like a Baptist banker in a private pew. If you hope to do worth beans in this here rodeo business you better take some expert advice. First off, always try and sit *supple*, never mind what sort of foolish you imagine you look. See that horsetail? A horse's tail maybe looks foolish, too, switching and swaying up there like a joke, but you never see a horse buck its tail off, did you? The tail's too *supple*. So limber up and try her once more.'

I did, and I was once more thumped to the floor. Nobody had even touched the lines. I sat coughing in the fresh dustcloud. This time George didn't offer to help me up.

'Too much stiff,' he reiterated sternly. 'And not enough supple. Let's see. Maybe if we try lengthening the stirrups a little bit—'

Louise came to my rescue. 'No you don't!' she said, fanning away George and the dust both with her Chinese fan. 'Leave this boy be. Naturally he's stiff, what with comin' all that way in a stock car and carousing all night on top of a train. Now you vexing him up on your goshdamn old barrel. Shame on you.'

'Now, Sweetenin',' George protested, giving her his brightest, openest grin, 'I'm just offering a little advice to the young pup, one horseman to another.'

'Just leave him be! I don't recall seeing *you* up there in the last few years, Mister Supple. Could it be you aint pup enough no more?'

This made George's eyes flash bright as his grin. Without another word he walked across the room and sat down on his bed. He took off his boots, humming a little tune through his nose. When the boots were neatly stowed side by side he stood up and took his Stetson from the bedpost and put it on. He strolled leisurely back to the barrel, careful not to alarm it, and stood humming at it, the way riders will hum to calm a skittish mount. Suddenly he grabbed the horn and swung himself high in the air, all in one effortless motion. He didn't even try for the stirrups. He landed square atop the barrel on both bare feet. He crouched low, knees rocking, like a tightrope walker waiting for the wire to steady. Gradually, he straightened up and spread his arms.

'Friends?' He looked down at us. 'Is *you all* prepared to witness something – how was it that sideshow snake put it? – downright exter-ordinary? Then pluck some lines and let 'er *buck!*'

Louise gave a delighted yip and plucked the first line she could jump up to. The barrel barely quivered. She gave it a harder strum. George just crossed his arms and let the tremor roll past, like he was bored with such puny action. He started singing his little ditty out loud, in fact, as if to pass the time:

> 'Oh, I'm the constable of Pumpkinville,
> Jist traded horses at the mill,
> My name's Joshua Ebenezer Fry—'

106

'Grab a line, Johnny!' Louise hollered. She plucked harder. George sang louder:

'I know a thing or two, you bet your life I do,
And you can't get me, I'm too derned sly.'

'Grab *two* lines,' she shrieked. 'Let's bring the swole-headed sunofabitch smack down on his uppity rear end!'

We strummed and jerked and sawed the lines for all we were worth, until the barrel was just a blur. George's singing never so much as wavered. His face remained a mocking mask of boredom. Uppity was right! But try as we might we couldn't bring him down. It struck me that we were indeed witnessing something quite extraordinary, rocking with rhythm up there on top of that bucking barrel, singing away like some kind of cork-face angel. Not that there was anything angelic about his singing. He could hit the notes true enough but his voice was as rough and earthy as it gets. Neither was it the way he kept up with the rhythm up on the barrel. If anything, it was the way he kept *off* the rhythm. When one of the waves came at him from the plucked plowlines he didn't jump over it only to get it double coming back – the way I had – he jumped *different* from the wave, in front of it, behind it, or off on a comical sideslant from it the way a clown might jump. *There's* probably the dodge what George would have been best at: a rodeo clown. It takes a contrary kind of skill to be a good clown. I tried some seasons as a bullfighter clown after my mishap with the twisted rope. I found out what the job really requires. The fans think you're there to to save the bullrider's precious hide once he hits the sod. They think you're between the bull and bullrider to confound the one into coming for you instead of the other. They know this demands courage, insight, and a lot of agility – all qualities that George had a double helping of. But they don't know that the *essential* requirement of the profession – of the promoter and his bookkeeper, of the fans, of the *bullrider himself* – is that you got to make it entertaining. The crowd likes to be led to the yawning brink of danger, then, after gazing down into it long enough to feel a good shiver, to be led safely back away from it. This is the rodeo clown's real job. After he drags some peachy-cheeked boy out from under a thundering ton of orneriness the clown has to turn around and dance in that thunderstorm's face. Kick dirt, spit, fart at the beast – *any*thing offbeat enough to turn fear into fun, to mock the monster. Cassius Clay had it against Sonny Liston. Joe Namath had it against the Colts. The first time I saw this offbeat dance in action was when I saw George Fletcher clowning around up on that barrel singing 'Joshua Ebenezer Fry':

> 'Wal, I swan, I must be gettin' on,
> Giddyup Napoleon, it looks like rain—'

Louise and I were finally laughing so hard we couldn't hold the plowlines. She sank to the floor, weak with mirth. I had to sit down on a haybale. The barrel's bucking slowed back to a shudder. George stood with his hand over his heart and his head thrown back, like a singer at the opening game of the World Series finishing strong on 'The Star-Spangled Banner.'

> 'I'll be switched if the hay aint pitched.
> Drop in when you're over to the farm again.'

He dismounted in a lightfooted leap. The barrel barely jiggled. The only dust raised from the old floorboards was stirred up by the sweep of his hat when he made his bow.

Louise curtsied in return, then told us she had to get spruced up for work, if we would wait outside, please. George put his boots on and we headed outside to tend the horses. At least Stonewall was set for the night. We stripped to the waist and splashed our faces at the watering trough. When Louise came out we both gaped at the sight. Her hair had been brushed into a high black bun and fastened with a rhinestone tiara. Her blouse had been turned front to back and pulled low off her shoulders so a frothy fringe of that Southern Belle lace showed, and one of her crinoline petticoats had been promoted from beneath and was now a purple skirt. With the rhinestone crown she looked like a Gypsy queen. The orange sash over one shoulder was her queenly mantle and the folded fan was her scepter.

'Behold the magic of woman,' George said. 'The royal dishwasher's transformed herself into a royal dish. Mm-*mm!*' He started toward her, smacking his lips. 'Flank steak and brown gravy, baked yam and butter. And for dessert – I see carmel custards, *bub*blin' over.'

'Hush that.' Louise halted his advance with a pop of her fan. 'Talking such flim-flam. You wasn't so old and mangy, Mr Fletcher, talk like that could turn a young woman's head.'

'Let's hope so,' he said, offering his arm. 'What say we three stroll downriver and show the town how quality does.'

The afternoon sun was still hammering down and

heat waves were shimmering across the meadow where the deer had grazed. It was hot even along the riverbank. The willows were drooping and the red-wing blackbirds were panting in their branches. The heat didn't seem to bother George, though. When I mentioned to Louise that it was amazing to me that such a mangy old stud could frisk around like a colt in such stifling temperature, she allowed it was on account of the frisky young company he was keeping. George was quick to agree.

'Young blood'll get an old stud to friskin' every time! 'Specially high-steppin', long-legged, coffee-colored *filly* blood.' George quickened his pace and began walking backward so he could look her in the eye. 'Makes the mouth fairly water.'

'I noticed you was lickin' your chops,' Louise said.

'I worked up an appetite introducing Nashville here to Miss Jenny Lynne. I'm hungry enough to eat the whalebone outen certain unmentionables I could mention.'

To keep from laughing, Louise stepped out at a brisker pace. George scurried ahead of her backward, like a crawdad. He begged her to honor us with the pleasure of her company for dinner. She said she already had dinner plans, and they involved work, tending table at the dining car, not pleasure.

'Then meet us down to Hookners after work,' George said. 'We'll dance the do-see-do.'

'*Hook*ners!' She shook her head. 'George, you are a fool and that's a fact. Those peckerwoods at Hookners will dance the do-see-do on your fool black face!'

'Oh no,' George said, 'not this night, they won't. Not *this* weekend.' Then he went to singing again in that raspy voice, skipping along backwards to the tune:

'Coffee gro-o-ows . . . on white-oak trees,
The river flo-o-ows . . . with brandy-*o!*
I'll find someone . . . to go with me,
Sweet as 'lasses candy-*o!*'

I recognized the song, an old Southern schoolyard ditty that George had jazzed up to suit his style. I stretched a blade of grass between my thumbs and started blowing along with the tune. 'You two sound like a stuck pig and a snared rabbit,' Louise laughed. But she joined in on the next verse, her voice high and sweet and her feet keeping step with George's:

'Two in the middle an' I can't dance, Josie,
Three in the middle an' I might fall down.
Four in the middle an' I can't catch Rosie.
Well, hello, Suzi Brown.'

They did it again double-speed, adding a little patty-cake routine they both seemed to know by heart, then again at double-double time. The rhythm got faster and faster until we all three broke down, laughing like kids.

'No more,' Louise said, wheezing for air. 'Here's the footbridge to the depot, and I can't be late. *Some* of us got to work for a livin'.'

'Come on to town, girl,' George coaxed. 'It's gonna be a humdinger. Tell her, Nashville.'

'If tonight's anything like this afternoon,' I said, 'it's going to be a double humdinger. And your company, Miss Louise, would *double* double it.' I was beginning to sound a little like George, I realized. So did Louise. She raised her eyebrows and smiled at me.

'Why, thank you, Johnny,' she said. 'But I got to get

back to that old train. You boys ease by the back side of the dining car and maybe I can slip you out some treats. We're serving "Southern" this evening – backstrap, peas, and spoonbread.'

'That's considerate, Miss Jubal,' George said. 'And tempting. But I want to show our visitor from the South some Northern hospitality. Perchancet later on?'

'Perchance,' she said, and with a swish of her petticoats she went sailing across the rope-and-plank footbridge with all colors flying. I'd never seen anything like her. Down south, back then, there was no place for a woman like Louise Jubal, black or white. Out here in the raw young West they hadn't quite settled into such civilized ruts. A woman like Louise could sail along as toplofty as she saw fit – just as long as she wasn't late for work.

Chapter Eight

*The Cleverest Snare
of the Lot*

As soon as I'm out of bed walking around it isn't any trouble to locate your room. Good thing it's one of the big expensive ones. You had a power of visitors. And here comes the SURVIVAL gang from a supermarket run, Number Nine in the lead.

'Found you by the cigar smell.'

Let me crank open your window. If you were able to look out you could see where that footbridge used to cross. The blizzard of 'twenty-two ripped it away, ice chunks big as Buicks. Or was it 'thirty-two? I've seen lots of changes over the years, but that river stays pretty much the same. It's responsible for this town being here, more than the cattle or the wheat. This little river-carved arena has been a showplace since before we lost our tails. See the way those sheltering hills ring it like bleachers? Cavemen probably came here every fall to ride mastodons and bulldog saber-tooths. As Mister Kell said, it's always provided a good gathering place for the Indian tribes. We know that from the rock carvings. And after the Indians, for the explorers, then the trappers and the settlers. A fellow name Joe Crabbe put up a saloon. A couple of other enterprising fellows expanded the saloon into a trading post and built a ferryboat. Judge J. J. Johnson constructed his house nearby and held court. That meant they had to build a jail. Now, when you got a saloon, a ferryboat, a judge, and a jail, you got a town. You can still see the wagon ruts that led up to the ferry landing.

The footpath George and I were walking on was one of those original ruts. The path enlarged into a road and the road into a street lined with houses. We walked in thoughtful silence. I don't know what George was thinking about but my mind was on supper. The sun had sunk behind the ridge and mouth-watering smells wafted from kitchen windows. This roused George from his reverie. He raised his head and sniffed. His nose swung like a compass needle toward the most magnificent dwelling on the street. It was a three-story mansion, painted sparkling white. A plump man in a white shirt and vest sat smoking in the porch swing. He saw us passing and walked to the rail carrying the cigar box.

'George! George Fletcher! Step over here and have one of these panatellas. They're top quality.'

George turned obediently in the gate. 'Why, thank you kindly, Mister Meyerhoff.' He took a cigar and drew a long sniff. 'Mmmm, yes. That's the smell. You always knows how to get the top quality.' He motioned me over. 'Nashville, this here is one of the Round Up judges. Mind yourself. Mister Meyerhoff, here's a young fren' I meet on the Round Up Special. Shake hands with Johnathan E. Lee Spain. He travel all the way fum Tennessee.'

Mister Meyerhoff's lips were wet and his palm was smooth and soft. 'Ah, Tennessee,' he extolled. 'Tobacco land itself. These panatellas are part of a Southern shipment that came in on that very train.' He held forth the box. 'You too, son. Take one, they're first rate. Take *two*, in honor of General Robert E. Lee.'

'Sir, you're very generous.' I'd breathed enough cigar smoke the night before to honor Lee and the whole rebel army. I was about to decline when George nudged me. 'I'll save it for later.' Another nudge. 'I'll save them *both*.' I slid the cigars into my shirt pocket.

'I walked down to the station myself,' Meyerhoff continued, 'just to unload these smokes fresh off the boxcar. But we are unloading smokables and drinkables *only*, this weekend, right, George? Necessities like beans and barbwire will have to wait until next week.'

'Dat's right,' George agreed. 'Nex' week.' He was sniffing again.

'Let me get you a light for that panatella,' Meyerhoff said. 'They have an even more enjoyable aroma when lit.'

'It's other aromas I was studyin', Mister Meyerhoff. That's kraut an' corn beef, aint it? I recognize it fum de time I hep Miz Meyerhoff wif de cannin'.'

Meyerhoff took a whiff. 'Why I believe it is. Missus Meyerhoff did her best to follow my mother's German recipe. The girls do as well as they can, but one needs the old-country memories to make sauerkraut the way my mother, God rest her, could make. Oy, corned beef and sauerkraut . . .'

A strange expression had come into the man's face. Sad, and a bit crazed, I thought. It looked like he might cloud up and weep. Then something struck him funny. He turned to George with an amused expression.

'I don't suppose you and your young associate could be cajoled into sharing a plate with us? In honor of Missus Meyerhoff, may the Master of the Universe keep her?'

'Nawsah, we couldn't do that, unexpected and all,' George said. 'It wouln' be fittin'. Would it, Nashville? Nawsah, not fittin'.'

George's entire appearance had changed. He looked shorter, bent over. Shambling and subservient. Even his breathing seemed to have an obsequious wheeze to it. I slouched my shoulders, beginning to get the idea. 'Not fitting at all,' I agreed.

'Much obliged jes' de same,' George said. 'Me'n the boy we headed to Hookners Tavrun. Mister Hookner he serve scorched turkey tails out the back door, three fo' a nickel. We appreciate the thought, though.'

George started shambling away and I shuffled after him. Meyerhoff's voice brought us up short.

'George Fletcher! I shall take it as a great insult if you and your young friend don't stay.' His voice was stern but his expression was still amused. 'Missus Meyerhoff would have, also. Remember how she always insisted on giving you a plate? Were she still with us, she would be deeply hurt.'

George turned slowly, his expression hangdog. 'You right, Mister Meyerhoff, you plumb right. Seems I forgot Missus Meyerhoff and my manners both.'

'It's settled, then.' Meyerhoff swept his hand grandly toward the screen door. 'Just follow your noses.' The spicy smells and the plump posterior led us through the front door.

The inside of the house was even more grand than the outside, with dark, deep furniture and shiny hardwood floors. Through the dining-room doors we could see a long linen-covered table laid out for supper. Meyerhoff called toward the kitchen in a language I'd never heard before. A plump young woman swished out and curtsied. Dark locks clung to her face and her long lashes were fluttering. Her hands were clasped beneath the abundant bosom of a tight, white blouse, and she was breathing hard.

'We've already added two more place settings, Papa,' she panted. 'We saw through the kitchen window we might have guests.'

'My eldest daughter, Ruth,' Mister Meyerhoff said. 'Now the lady of the house. Ruth, this is Mister Johnathan Spain, from Tennessee.'

Her lashes fluttered my way and she gave me a look like powdered sugar over strudel; then she swished away around the table. Mister Meyerhoff tucked his cigar ash-up in his vest pocket and took his place at the head. He motioned George and me into the chairs on his right and left.

The kitchen door pushed open and another chubby brunette appeared, rump first and steaming. When she turned I saw the steam was rising from a huge platter of sauerkraut and corned beef. The platter was carried beneath a bosom even more abundant than her sister's.

'My second daughter, Naomi,' Mister Meyerhoff said. 'Naomi – Mister Johnathan Spain.'

The look this daughter poured over me was even stickier than her sister's, like warm caramel. The door burst open again. I feared this next course, if she followed the pattern, would be so sweet that a fellow could get the sugar diabetes just by looking. But this third daughter was as rawboned and salty as her sisters were sweet and voluptuous. She was as willowy as a lad. Nor was she a brunette. Her hair was the color of new hemp-rope and had been pulled tight behind her ears in a hard knot. She was wearing a white blouse like her sisters; an obvious hand-me-down, several sizes too big. The same with her dark skirt.

Sticking from beneath the hem I noticed a pair of silver-toed Spanish boots; she clomped in them like a kid making believe he was a cowboy. In one hand she carried a pitcher of dark beer and in the other a plateful of fresh-baked dinner rolls. She gave me a sharp snap of the eyes, then banged the plate and pitcher on the table, hard. Mister Meyerhoff rolled his eyes to the heavens.

'My *third* daughter. Sarah, say hello to Johnathan E. Lee Spain. Mister Spain hails from the land of the great Southern generals.'

'Hello, Colonel,' the girl said in a voice both polite and barbed. She took the chair next to mine. Though she made a point of keeping her eyes averted I could feel her attention checking me up and down like a horsetrader. I felt surrounded by a trio of traps, and I feared this last one might be the cleverest snare of the lot. I was considerably relieved when Mister Meyerhoff closed his eyes and began the blessing in that foreign tongue. When he stopped they all said Amen but Father Meyerhoff wasn't finished. He raised a pink finger.

'Wait, my daughters. For the benefit of our guests, now in English. *Bless* this food to make *Your* servants strong and willing to do *Your* work, God of our fathers, Master of the Universe. And bless these unwed daughters, that they remain cheerful in their labors. And *bless* this house, for it is the *house* of the Lord . . .'

And so on. There was a lot more. You could recognize it was the same blessing up to a point – the way he put the same emphasis on words in the same places – but as he reached the conclusion he raised his head toward George and let his words loose into new territory. His face had that crazy-sad expression again.

'Also, *God* of our fathers, bless George Fletcher, that he may triumph and be *exalted* . . . for the sake of *all* of God's downtrodden people, for the benefit of the rebuked and scorned, for the healing of the *much-maligned*, and for the chastising of the *maligners*, that they be cast into the *Pit!* For the retribution of those untimely departed and helpless in their graves, unable to rebut the cruel tongues of the slanderers, unable to – to—'

He paused, his wet mouth gulping for air and inspiration. It had turned into a bitter blessing, uncomfortable for us and embarrassing for the girls. Before the poor man could catch his breath George cried, 'Amen!' The skinny daughter next to me seconded him.

'Ah-*men!*' she said in a sardonic voice. 'Can't live with 'em, can't even die with 'em. They keep digging you up to gnaw on.'

'Sarah, be nice,' Meyerhoff said. 'Be like your sisters, sweet.' He reached for the carving knife. As he carved the meat his moist smile returned. 'Forgive my fervor, Mister Spain,' he apologized. 'But you must understand George Fletcher has become for some of us out here our hero. Our *champion.* Quite a rise in status, yes, George? Since the days when they wouldn't let you race riding forwards?'

'Yessir, been a few miles pass under my saddle,' George answered. 'But I'm still jes' the same wu'thless cowhand what used to ride backwards . . . jes' the same wild fool.'

'Don't let him deceive you,' Meyerhoff said to me. 'Though he might have been the fool sometimes, and occasionally wild, he was never worthless. George and men like him are the hand the Master is using to

119

tame this wicked country. That hand sometimes *has* to be wild, you see? To tame a wild land. You see, don't you, George?'

'I reckon.' The tone of George's answer made it clear that further discussions of religion and philosophy would have to wait. He bent to his plate of food without another word. Meyerhoff and I chatted about my home and travels, and the meal progressed smoothly for a piece. Then the girls got into a little sisterly spat over whose turn it was to start coffee. Mister Meyerhoff adjudicated the situation the way most parents do: when in doubt give the chore to the youngest. The youngest said Ah-*men* again in that voice, and went boot-heeling loudly to the kitchen, leaving the door ajar so we could hear her grinding. The middle sister remarked loudly that little Sarah was a spoiled snip. George attempted to pour oil on troubled waters by remarking that little Sarah was looking more and more like her mama looked at that age, back before Mister Meyerhoff brought his business to town. This slight mention of his wife got Meyerhoff sniffling anew. He finally made an excuse to leave the table so we wouldn't have to suffer his grief.

'We have a new roll for the pianola. A Debussy. I think it might go splendidly with dessert.'

Soon a lugubrious piano tune came pumping out of the drawing room, accompanied by wheezy sobs and sighs and moans. Nobody said anything until Sarah returned from the kitchen with the coffee service. She wrinkled her impish nose:

'Sounds like Debussy's got the lungworm strangles.'

The sisters scolded the impertinence, but I was impressed. That this pampered daughter of a small-town merchant had heard of Debussy was not so

120

remarkable, but her offhand allusion to the rare equestrian pulmonary disease came as quite a surprise. This wasn't the sort of thing one expected a spoiled snip to know. Perhaps those silver-toed cowboy boots peeking from beneath the lacy pink hem was more than little-kid make-believe.

'Tell me, Miss Meyerhoff; I couldn't help but notice your fancy footwear. Do you ride?'

'Do I ride, Mister Spain?' Again that laugh and the sharp snap of eyes. 'Does a fat puppy fart when you—'

'*Sarah!*' the sisters cut in, mortified. Sarah finished the wisecrack and the father stepped in from the drawing room to answer my question.

'Sarah not only rides, Johnathan, she is one of our Round Up princesses. The *crown* princess. The only lady that got more votes is the great cowgirl Prairie Rose Henderson.'

'Who is more cow than girl or lady either one,' Sarah elaborated. 'All she needs is two more spigots and a bell around her neck. Yes, I can ride, Colonel Spain. Haven't you noticed who does most of the trotting back and forth around here? Coffee you want? Sarah trots off and brings it. Sugar you want? Trot trot trot. Cream you — whups! Naomi used all the cream in the apple strudel. Maybe I'll trot out and see if Prairie Rose will let me—'

'*Say-rah!*'

'You're right; it's past milking. Maybe the Petersens have some in their porch cooler.'

'Black is fine, Miss Meyerhoff,' I quickly lied. 'I always drink it black.'

'Don't fib, Colonel Spain,' she said, snapping her eyes. 'S'uthern gentlemen *needs* their cream — everybody knows that. No one but saddlebums drink it black. And I won't abide a saddlebum. They all have a cloudy past and a murky future. I'll trot next door and ask if I might borrow a cup.'

'Sarah—?' Meyerhoff said.

'I shall try to be sweet, my father. Though I fear dear Ruth and Naomi used up all the sugar, too.'

When she had clomped down out the hall and out of sight Meyerhoff broke into laughter. 'She is this way because she *likes* you, Johnny. That's good, that's good. Little Sarah does not like so many people since Mother died. But you I detect she likes.'

I found no solace in this detection. If this tongue-lashing was how she treated those she liked I wasn't sure I wanted more of it. She was gone a long, peaceful quarter of an hour while Meyerhoff and George discussed jobs that would require extra help once this weekend of festivities was over. The two older sisters scooted close and plied me with pastries and questions. By the time Sarah returned with the cream pitcher I was feeling a little over-plied. Ruth was trying to get me to try another slice of something called halvah, and Naomi was leaning across the table with her platter full of goodies brazenly displayed.

'Have some more apple blintz, Mister Spain. Very juicy, very sweet.'

'Thanks just the same, ladies, but I'm about blintzed.' This got the first laugh I had heard from Sardonic Sarah.

'Don't they have a tooth for sweet things where you come from, Mister Spain?' I saw now that her eyes were steely grey and sharp with dare and mystery. I'd been right; the wickedest trap of the lot.

'Only in moderation, ma'am,' I managed. 'Too much cake and stuff makes me kinda . . . groggy.'

'Ah,' she said. 'Then Sarah pours you more coffee. This time you can have it with cream.'

She refilled my cup and set it before me. As she bent to pour the cream her loose hand-me-down blouse revealed as tart a pair of little pippins as ever hung from a bough. She was mocking her sister's display, and matching it as well. Pippins could be as interesting to the palate as any Rome Beauties, however juicy and sweet.

Meyerhoff arose, balancing his cup on the saucer.

'What do you say to that smoke now, George? Seeing we've attended to those *other* aromas.' The big wet smile revealed he hadn't been a bit hustled by George's poor-mouthing on the porch. It was an old game between them.

'It would be a pleasure, Mister Meyerhoff,' George said. We excused ourselves from the table and we three men repaired, as they say, to the den.

The worn furniture had enjoyed many long years of after-dinner discussion, somewhere in another time, another country. It sagged with tradition. Meyerhoff rambled on about the condition of the world. 'Europe all bound up . . . new frontiers . . . West meets East . . . trade expansion in China . . .' George listened politely, nodding and puffing like an idling locomotive. I followed George's lead, pretending concentration and trying not to inhale. The more Meyerhoff rambled, the more George fidgeted. When his cigar was politely half-smoked George cleared his throat and stood.

'I'd love to stay an' palaver, Mister Meyerhoff. Truly I would. But I promised the lad here a stroll downtown for a little look at our Pendleton night life. Take the air, as they say.'

Meyerhoff's face filled with concern. 'I'm not so sure

that's wise, George. There's a wildness in that air that could take a sinister and wicked turn. *I* certainly wouldn't stroll down into it, if I were George Fletcher. Why not stay here and chat instead? We could play the pianola.'

'I already give my word,' George insisted. 'An' I promise we'll steer clear of any wicked winds.'

'Then I would most certainly steer clear of Missus Hookner's establishment. Go not thee to the front door *or* the back. Turkey tails aren't the only things those people at Hookners scorch.'

'Good advice, Mistah Meyerhoff. Yassuh, wise advice. And I appreciate yo' concern. Me'n the boy'll keep a tight cinch.'

Outside, in the darkening yard, George's voice returned to its customary ribald rasp. 'I hated to be sudden with Mister Meyerhoff; he usually serves up brandy with his pie-an-ola. But that usually sets him to prayin' and that usually sets him to grieving over his wife. Then he get to cryin'. Besides, too much of that Old World palaver and pastry'll give a man the bloat. It was a A-1 meal, though, weren't it?'

I said it was. A-number-1.

'I hopes that sassypants Sarah didn't vex you too much. She's got a lot of her mama's Irish devilment in her. A man just got to endure it . . .'

I told him she didn't vex me. Not a whit. I was hoping I'd get to endure some more of that devilment sometime soon. A flash of light in an upstairs window caught my eye. She was at the casement in her nightshirt. She held a candle in one hand and a little Irish harp in the other. She saw me looking and raised the candle close to her cheek. A moment before she blew out the flame she gave me a wink, clear as a bell.

'Sarah always been a saucy little filly,' George said, stepping through the picket gate.

I followed him without comment. Out in the street he started singing again.

> 'Coffee gr-o-ows . . . on white-oak trees,
> The river flo-o-ows . . . with brandy-o . . .'

I fell in beside him and matched his stride. It had been quite a day for me as far as firsts were concerned. My first cigar, my first wink from a girl, my first meal eaten beneath any blessing other than Baptist. Tomorrow I was going to ride in the opening day of the first World Championship rodeo. Later on tonight I was supposed to bed down with the Indians, in the same ancestral camp-ground that the tribes had been using for their powwows since before recorded history. And it was still a long way to bedtime.

> 'I'll find some girl to go with me
> Sweet as 'lasses candy-o.'

Chapter Nine

A Good Cleaning

George and I strolled down the middle of the bustling, gaslit street, taking in the sights. The plank sidewalks were crowded three and four abreast and there were buggies and wagons and tin lizzies parked two deep along both curbs. The automobile engines revved and white-eyed ponies stamped. Farmers and farm families lounged around the wagons, talking farm talk. Cowboys leaned and smoked, enjoying that privacy cowboys always find beneath their hatbrims. Kids were playing marbles in the dirt under a corner street-lamp.

George grew quieter as we proceeded into the riotous whirl of downtown Pendleton. That warning from Meyerhoff was bothering him more than he let show. When people called out to him he responded with a tip of his hat and a few muttered words and kept walking. We traveled the entire four blocks of Main like this. By the time we turned about-face to do it again I felt a little apprehensive myself. Violence seemed to lurk beneath the festivities. Every drunken warwhoop and horselaugh could mean trouble. I had experienced this sense of pent-up violence before, on Beale Street the eve of the Dixie Sweepstakes – but not from this side of the color line.

126

'Some whoop-te-do,' I ventured, seeking to allay George's anxiety as well as my own. 'This town is really racing its engine.'

'I reckon so.' George gave me a melancholy look. 'Racin' its engine—'

He was about to say more when we were distracted by a rattle of rapid cracks. They sounded like cheap handguns in a shootout. A Chinese boy came squealing out of a crowd of barroom jokers. He ran past us, yipping and exploding, a string of blazing firecrackers tied to his pigtail. He dropped suddenly out of sight on the other side of the street, as though the earth had swallowed him. George finished his interrupted statement.

'—it just that sometimes I ain't sure it's *my* race.'

He walked on, more melancholy than ever. Poor George, I was thinking; this might not be your night to prance after all. We were passing that mob of horse-laughing jokers again when he suddenly halted.

'Hark! That sounds like the Reverend Linkhorn on the keyboard.'

The jangle of a piano was escaping through the tavern door. A band accompanied the jangle in a dreadful version of 'Buffalo Gal.' It sounded altogether like a riot in a boiler factory.

'Reverend Sylvester Linkhorn is a shirttail cousin of mine,' George informed me. 'From the N'Awleens side of the family. That's the *musical* side. He hires out piano playing when he aint portering for the railroad or working for Jesus. Doggone me, Nashville, it sound like poor ol' Cousin Sylvester could use some help with the Lord's work tonight. I know *us* all could use a drink.'

He squared his shoulders and headed for the tavern

door with me in his wake. As he plowed through that throng of jokers the laughter gave way to stunned stares. I got a look at a name gouged in the wood as we passed through the swinging doors: HOOKNERS. It looked like it had been gouged there with a broken bottle.

The din inside was overwhelming. Hard-drinking cowpokes and townspeople and tourists shoved and shouted under a smoky chandelier. Rough-hewn dining tables with a view of the street were ringed with diners in spindly chairs. At the long bar you had to stand for service – four, five, six drinkers deep. When you could no longer stand, I deduced, you were no longer served. At the far wall, up on a platform, I saw the piano player. He wore a top hat and tails and his face was made up white, like a minstrel clown. His gold-rimmed glasses perched on the end of his nose. A slapdash band surrounded him, playing a two-step for all they were worth. Nobody was dancing, because nobody could hear. The drinkers were trying to holler over the top of the music and the music was trying to play over the top of the drunken hollering.

George managed at last to push his way to the bar. He slapped the wet wood for attention. The two bartenders looked at George, then at each other, their eyebrows lifted in simultaneous disbelief. After a moment they bustled away as though we did not exist. George grinned after them, that reckless glint in his eye again. I started to wonder if we mightn't be better off taking a stroll back to Meyerhoff's, enjoy the brandy and pianola in peace. George slapped the bar again.

'Right here it was,' he bellowed, 'that Nat Love the notorious Negro gunslinger made his dare. Mister Love drew his longnose .44 and laid it on the bar, right *here*—' George slapped the bar again, splattering spilled beer in all directions. '—and 'longside it he laid a one-hundred-dollar bill. The black desperado then dared *any whiteman* who considered hisself fast enough on the draw to step forward and try to take that hundred away. This is not only a historical fact, I myself witnessed it! I was Hookners' maintenance boy at the time and had jes' come in from emptyin' the spit bucket. I saw the entire event. One decrepit old Negro gunslinger calling out a houseful of Caw-casians, right *here!*'

Again he pounded the mahogany. The story needed no more emphasis. To my dismay everybody along the bar was now listening.

'Down at the *other* end,' George continued, 'lean an' mean an' green around the gills from the rotgut rye ol' Mister Hookner used to serve, was Booger Red, formerly the bully of Walla Walla. Booger was never a man to turn down a dare. "I'm right fast," Red says and lays *his* .44 on the bar. After three minutes and thirty-three seconds of nobody moving Jonas Hookner grew impatient. "Go on, dammit!" he yells and they grab for their guns. To tell the truth *both* of them was about as fast as hibernating bears. These old boys were so far over the hill they were sliding down the other side. Nat Love musta been sixty and Booger near that. Their .44's were just as old. They shot a bullet big as your thumb with a muzzle velocity so slow you could actually see the lead tumbling. One bullet splattered into Nat Love's big brass belt buckle and another into Booger Red's. Down they went. Whump! Whump! After a while Nat Love rolled over and got to his feet. He staggered down and helped Booger Red up. "Well," Nat says, "I guess we proved I'm not so fast and you're not so fast, either. Let's have a *drink*.""'

George punctuated his ending with a final slap. The anecdote got a laugh from the surrounding patrons but the bartenders went back to other business. We were left dry. The din of the barroom talk had cranked back up and the band commenced mutilating another tune.

'Your cousin's pretty fair on that piano,' I said to assuage George.

'Cousin Sylvester's doing all right,' George said. 'Considerin'.'

'It's hard for me to believe that under all that clown makeup he's Reverend Linkhorn.'

'One and the same,' George said. 'Cousin Sylvester frees the souls on Saturday night and Reverend Linkhorn saves them on Sunday.'

Alongside the piano stood a bald man with a red mustache and thick glasses. He was holding two brown jugs close to his hairy lips. By blowing back and forth he managed to produce a bull-froggy cadence. Next to him a crooknecked man was sawing away on a violin; he had his eyes shut – to stay in touch with his muse, I supposed. The vocalist was a jelly-fleshed matron wearing too much rouge and a store-bought smile. She had stuffed herself into a sequined gown that sparkled with every jiggle.

'I'll bet that singer purchased her outfit brand-new for tonight,' I told George.

'Pity she couldn't have purchased a brand-new voice while she was at it. Poor ol' Cousin Sylvester ain't gettin' much backup.'

On the other side of the piano a hollow-eyed man thumped away on a gut bucket. He sounded like an undertaker playing in a funeral march. The final member of the ensemble appeared deceased enough to

130

need one. He was passed out in a chair, his chin flopped to his chest, dead drunk. A tin-bellied Dobro guitar leaned between his spraddled legs. George squeezed my elbow.

'Nashville? Use that gooseneck of yours to spot us a pass through. I'd like to ooze up closer to the music.'

I was blessed if I could see why, but I picked an opening and led the way. The band didn't get better as we got closer. They looked half asleep. Everybody's eyes were glazed, even the Reverend's. The funereal beat had pounded them into a trance. Any one of the ensemble looked ready to keel over and join the unconscious Dobro player.

It was comical in its lugubrious way. I turned to see if George appreciated the humor, but he was nowhere to be found. He wasn't at the bar nor at the card tables nor among the crowd packing the little dance floor. Either the din or the dry mouth had driven him back out to the street, I speculated, and began pushing my way through the crowd. I stopped halfway, listening. Something was happening to the music: a new tempo — faster, tighter. I saw the fiddle player's eyes pop open, scowling to have his muse interrupted. The bucketthumper and the jugblower were thumping and bullfrogging faster, and they did not look at all happy about it. The old cowgirl was singing through lips thin with anger. The piano player was the only one not frowning about the new tempo. His painted lips were lifted in a smile of gratitude.

George had climbed up on the platform and commandeered the Dobro. He was thumbing an off-tempo rhythm on the bass strings while ragging out the tune with his fingers. Hookners' entire clientele had turned

131

to stare at this ragtime intrusion. The drinking had ceased. The talking had ceased. For a few tense moments I feared they were going to rise up in redhot outrage and scorch this intruder's tail, just like Louise and Mister Meyerhoff had warned. Then somebody in the crowd wa-hooed an affirmation.

'That's the spirit, George. Kick that mule.'

Cecil Kell had climbed up on a table and was hoisting his beer mug high in salute. 'Kick some life into the lazy old hayburner.'

George began to whang the tin-bellied contraption in earnest. Reverend Sylvester Linkhorn bent over his ivories with equal intensity and the crowd started clapping. The fiddler sawed to catch up. The jug-blower and bucketthumper were right behind. The clapping got louder. The singer's appetite was whetted by the applause and she sunk her storeboughts into the song with ravenous gusto:

> 'Buffalo gal, won't you *come* out tonight,
> *Come* out tonight, *come* out tonight.
> Buffalo gal, won't you *come* out tonight,
> Dance by the light of the moo-*oo*-oon . . .'

George grunted along behind her and the crowd cheered. An old grizzle-faced herder jumped up on the table next to Kell's and broke into a high-kicking reel. Soon all the tables had dancers and the whole place was stomping and whooping.

I felt like I was at a magic show, watching a wizard perform. A desultory herd of plowhorses had been transformed into a thunderstorm of winged steeds assailing the sky. A tent revivalist would have claimed it was a miraculous manifestation of the Holy Spirit descending from the heavens. I knew better. I knew this spirit manifested from the ground up.

'Buffalo Gal' stamped on into 'Pretty Redwing' and 'Redwing' rolled right on into 'State of Arkansas,' nonstop. It went on like that until George had to put down the Dobro, claiming his fingers were raw. Everybody was sweated to a frazzle. George thanked the group for letting him play along with them and suggested it might be time for one of the waltzes they did so nice. The crowd gave George a big hand as he climbed down and crossed the floor, calling out, 'Best of luck tomorrow, George!' 'You're our blue-ribbon boy, George!' One of the barkeeps awarded him a bottle of Johnnie Walker Red. George held it high, like a trophy. The crowd acknowledged the award with another round of applause.

'You all flatter me.' His voice was modest yet orotund, like an actor called out to say a few words after an ovation. 'I wouldn't have been worth beans without the assistance of the rest of the band.'

This stirred up more applause, along with a goodly amount of suppressed laughter. George looked encouraged to say more but there wasn't to be any basking in the afterglow that night. The sharp *ting-ting-ting* of a knife blade on a glass pierced the air. Somebody was ringing for attention from one of the round tabletops near the wall. This table hadn't collected any stompdancers. A chair had been set in the table's center and a thin-legged wooden stool on the chair. On top of this precarious pulpit Mister Handles stood. His legs were as thin as the stool's and crooked as a starved dog's. When he had the room's complete attention he launched into his spiel:

'Citizens of Pendleton and fellow Americans!

Honored visitors and gambling men! And those of you who love sport for the unlucred love of it *alone* . . . your attention if you please. As official representative of the Buffalo Bill Extravaganza Company I have been asked to extend to your community our company's sincerest commendation. By all lights, you people have pitched in and organized an extra*ord*inary show in this far outpost of our country's frontier! And we, as showmen, *salute you!'*

The crowd cheered enthusiastically. The barker waved them silent. 'This week,' he continued, 'in the young borough of Pendleton, Oregon, *history* is being made!'

They cheered some more. They were in a cheering mood. But the barker waved them silent. 'In honor of this championship event, the Wild West Extravaganza Company has decided to lay over and *pitch in as well!'*

The enthusiasm slackened somewhat at this. Mister Handles was undaunted.

'Though your facilities are *yet uncomplete!* and your vending business understandably naive! Mister Cody has avowed to add another contest to your program: a*nother* World Championship contest! Knowledgeable parties have *guaranteed* a contestant *strong* enough! *tough* enough! and *manly* enough to meet our champion!'

He glared about, holding everyone's attention with his blinky little eyes and his balancing act.

'Your own Nigra George yonder made the guarantee. But in the event that for some reason he does not make *good* on said guarantee – no offense, Mister Fletcher – we have upped the odds on our customary challenge! *Double*-upped them, matter of fact. Therefore

134

to-*morrow!* In your arena! World Catch-as-Catch-Can Champion Frank Gotch is prepared to put his championship belt on the *line!* to any man jack who can stay with him in our regulation canvas prizefight ring for a *reduced time* of five fleeting minutes, *plus*—' From his vest pocket the barker produced a fan of greenbacks. '—cover any and all sidebets twenty dollars to *one* cash on the barrelhead! Simple arithmetic: your man stays in the five minutes without getting pinned or crying uncle, and your wager multiplies *twentyfold! Twenty to one,* gents, you heard right. The details are all on the printed handbill our lovely Miss O'Grady will be passing among you.'

A bugle blared and the orange-haired cowgirl came blazing through the swinging doors. The handbills were so fresh off the press you could still smell the benzine. I received a bright-orange smile along with mine.

'MEN OF PENDLETON,' the black blockprint headline challenged. 'WHERE ARE THEE?' The lengthy terms of the contest followed, complete with disclaimers and loopholes. It ended in another blockprint: '*Who among you is bold enough to brave . . . THIS?*'

The last word had been printed in red ink, gory as blood, above an equally grisly photograph. The picture showed the hairless wrestler holding a boar hog aloft upsidedown on his shoulder. The wrestler's hands were locked in an Indian grip and the tusker was popeyed with the pressure being applied to his rib cage. Gotch was smiling. Beneath the lithograph the headline was repeated. 'WHO AMONG YOU?' George threw his flier down like it was a leper's scab. It left a gout of red ink smeared across his sweaty palm.

'Look at George!' someone in the crowd called.

135

'Caught red-handed. Maybe the town's "who" is *you*, George, if you don't come up with that challenger.'

George turned his palm back and forth like a dogeared page. 'I does need a good cleaning,' he drawled. 'No two ways 'bout *dat*. A good forty winks w'unt hurt, nuther.'

He clapped the inky hand on my back. 'C'mon, Nashville. It's sleepytime down souf.'

He headed for the swinging door, Red Label Scotch in one hand, red printer's ink on the other. I followed, walking straight as I could but feeling more than a little queasy. Outside, I grabbed the first post I could find and closed my eyes. I saw a swirl of horses and steers, cowboys and girls. George shook me and we got moving again, his hand under my elbow.

'Take this as another lesson, schoolboy. Another valuable lesson in the course of your education.'

'All right, it's another lesson. May I inquire what the subject of this course happens to be?'

'The subject,' he said, 'is experience. The only subject you eager Southern boys is ever interested in. Here, hold this. I don't want to get red ink all over our nice Scotch. See if you can keep up and uncork a bottle at the same time.'

I showed him I could. He nodded his approval.

'Of course nobody ever learns about experience without they experience what they're learning first. Not even eager Southern boys.'

I protested there was lots I learned that I hadn't experienced. About the Civil War, for instance, from my family lore. About London from the books of Charles Dickens. 'I never went to England but I learned about it, didn't I?'

'Might of,' he said, walking. 'But answer me this,

Mister Book-reader. You think your family lore and your library books is gonna learn you about, say for instance, ladies? Without you get experience *first,* hee hee hee? About *ah-mour?*'

'Respectable people in Tennessee take a very dim view of young bucks experiencing *amour* before wedlock hee hee hee. And now I *think* about it—' I was beginning to giggle, too. '—they also take a dim view of young bucks *not* experiencing it before wedlock.'

'Seems you Tennessee bucks is dimmed if you do and dimmed if you don't. Whoa up!' George stopped, his hand on my elbow. 'Here we are.'

We were standing in front of the most elaborate establishment we had thus far come across in our Pendleton sojourn. Greater even than the Meyerhoff place, and far fancier. The building was three stories high and surrounded on three sides by a pillared porch. Curlicued wooden carvings decorated the eaves and casements. Colored lanterns glowed in every window and seductive shadows swayed on the shades. I wasn't sure I was ready for such advanced studies.

'You're not taking me up there—!'

'Up *there?*' He still held my elbow. 'Certainly *not.* You a respectable Southern gentleman and all.' He turned me carefully and pointed. 'I'm taking you down *here.*'

A dark rectangle yawned in the bordello's sparse lawn, bigger than a grave. A flimsy bamboo rail on three sides was all that prevented some love-blinded customer from falling in. On the unfenced side sat a very old Chinese man. This must have been where that exploding boy had ducked out of sight. The old man was sitting cross-legged on a tiny square of linen, smoking a clay pipe. George led me closer. I saw earthen steps leading down into a misty glow. The old man rose to his feet and bowed to George. George bowed back and the man stepped aside, gesturing toward the clay steps. George descended and the old man gestured for me to follow. I steadied myself and started down, only to be forced back up by a tray full of steaming towels. The huge load was borne by a tiny porcelain figurine.

'Sue Lin?'

A face peered up through the steam.

'Misteh Johnny Lee, is that you? I am happy, thank you velly much.' She was wearing an iridescent blue kimono, embroidered all over with little black-and-white flying horses. Her voice came out of the steam like a tiny bell ringing. 'I be light back, thank you. Take you clothes off, please.'

She hurried away and I descended into the mist. The steps led to a low slanting tunnel. I had to stoop almost to all fours. I was gratified when the tunnel opened into a vast earthen chamber, supported by massive wooden beams that faded from sight in all directions. It could have been as big as George's barn for all I knew. Steam rose from huge tubs simmering above charcoal fires. Men, women, and children hurried in and out of the mist, carrying bundles, buckets, trays. I spotted George seated with his bottle on a plank bench, shucking off his clothes. No one appeared to be paying him the slightest mind. He motioned me over and indicated I was to get undressed, too. I reached first for the bottle. I sat down and closed my eyes and took a long relaxing pull.

When I opened my eyes I was up to my neck in a steaming tub. Workers were still scurrying in and out of the mist. George was reclined in the neighboring tub, talking and smoking, and I suspected the cigar clenched in a corner of his mouth was mine.

'—and *so*,' he was saying, 'when the city officials passed the ordinance against them owning or developing street property, they just dug down underneath. They developed *under*street property.'

I tried to see through the mist. 'It still doesn't look safe,' I said. 'All these tunnels and beams. I wouldn't trust it for a place to live . . .'

'Why not, may I ask? It aint as if the Chinese haven't had plenty of mining experience.'

'Even so, living in tunnels? Good Lord, how do people endure living in such abysmal conditions?'

'Endure? How do they *endure*, do you ask?' George eased deeper into his tub. 'Just like a horsetail in the wind, is how. Whichever way that big rear end jumps they keeps supple and stay on, is how they endures. Now hush. Scoot down shut your mouth and close your eyes. You want Sue Lin to come in here and catch you naked and wet with your eyes open?'

'I do not,' I answered. 'Not wet or dry, thank you; not open or shut.'

That was the last I remember of my first day in Pendleton. When I came to I was still disrobed, it's true, but I was dry. All of my clothes were gone, and so was George. I was lying atop a pile of freshly folded laundry, in an entirely different underground chamber. The only illumination was provided by shafts of sunlight slanting down a pine-pole ladder. I bolted upright in a wide-awake panic – my *money*belt! My watch! My *boots!* I spied the belt sitting next to my boots on an overturned bucket. The money was still inside the zippered pouch. My gold watch was in the belt as well.

I wound the watch, feeling enormously relieved, until I got a look at the time.

I was scheduled to rope a running calf in exactly forty-five minutes.

Chapter Ten

*A Certain Amount
of Initiation*

I went up the ladder cautious as a prairie dog sneaking
out the burrow's back door. I had covered my scrawny
nakedness with the only duds I could find: a standard
coolie outfit – loose black blouse and matching
trousers. The top fit well enough but no matter how far
down I tugged the trousers the cuffs still rode a good
two inches above my boot tops. I knew I looked silly
but I had journeyed a long ways plus put out a lot of
money to enter this rodeo, so my obligation went deep.
I'd inherited my Great-Aunt Ruth's sense of thrift.

The sun was coming through gaps and knotholes in
a slanted storm-cellar door. I pushed it open and
climbed out. I found myself in a weedy alley behind
the bordello. At the side street I made a quick guess
which way the river was and took off running. I had
guessed correctly. There was the footbridge to the river
path. I finally loped up to the McConkey barn, puffing
like a steam engine. The big door was locked but
Stonewall was tied up at the water trough, already
saddled. George was gone. I leaped on Stoney's back
and we hightailed it for the rodeo grounds. We were
galloping into the back chutes just as they announced
the Calf Roping.

The sweating official was bent over his table with

his hat off, busy counting the entry slips. I dismounted and slapped my registration alongside his hatbrim. It wasn't until then that I realized how hungover I was. The lariat wriggled in my fingers like a contrary snake. The official was too busy to notice.

'You better shake it, cowboy, you're coming right up.' He handed back my registration and got a gander at my attire. 'Hold on there, Spain, Johnathan E. You ain't participating in this by Gawd show like by Gawd *that!*'

'My clothing was taken when I slept,' I explained. 'Shirt, vest, pants, *every*thing. This is all I could find to put on.'

'I don't care a doodle in the woods whether you got pants, shirt, vest, or *any*thing on from the neck down. But from the neck *up*—' He pointed to a sign nailed to a post and read it aloud: 'ALL PARTICIPANTS MUST WEAR HATS.'

I was in despair until I saw George lounging with some other cowboys under the judges' stand. 'I'll have a hat by the time I ride,' I promised the official. 'A fine hat.'

George and the other riders got a big kick out of my outfit. 'Good afternoon, Nashville. Looks like you got turned wrong way around when you dressed. This is the Wild West, not the Far East.'

'Where did you disappear to last night?' I demanded. 'What happened to my clothes?'

'Well, it's a long story,' he said. 'After my bath and shave I was so handsome I thought I might as leave do a little courtin', spread some of my good looks around. You was still soakin' and sleepin' so I let you continue. When I come back by, your tub was empty. I figured Sundown must have took you home and tucked you in. I don't know nothing about your clothes.'

'You figured wrong,' I said.

'I often does,' he grinned. 'But I'm always eager to be set right. Where did you sleep?'

'We'll talk later. Right now they say I need a hat. Let me borrow yours.'

'My hat?' George's grin vanished. 'Now hold yer horses—'

'He has to have a hat or he's scratched, Fletcher,' one of the cowboys said. 'It's written on every registration. No exceptions.'

'Come on, George,' I begged. 'It's just for a couple of seconds.'

'A couple of filthy *calf*-rasslin' seconds.' He removed his butter-colored Stetson and studied it forlornly. He set the crease with the side of his hand and held it out to me. 'Fresh-cleaned and blocked in Boise.'

'Thank you, George. You're a real gentleman.' I nearly told him That's real white of you, but I caught myself.

I swung back up on Stoney and trotted to the arena gate. The official looked me over and waved me through. The rodeo announcer was booming out my introduction:

'Next roper up, folks, is a young cowboy from – wellnow lookee*here* – all the way from the state where they raise those *highbred walking horses* and distill that good *Jack Daniel's whiskey;* from the great state of Ten-uh-*see*' I looked up and saw this booming voice came from a short-legged man. He had to stand on tiptoe to reach the mouthpiece of a triple-barreled megaphone mounted on a pole. This had to be the wellknown prizefight announcer Foghorn Clancy.

143

'He's up and ready. Let's hear a big Oregon welcome, folks, for our Dixie visitor: Johnathan E. Lee *Spain!*'

The rope barrier dropped. A beefy yearling came bawling forth and Stonewall plunged after him. The big Oregon welcome changed into whoops of laughter when they got a look at me in the too-small coolie outfit and the too-big yellow hat. When I shoved the Stetson to the back enough to see, the sudden sun blinded me. The sky wheeled and the earth buckled but dear old Stonewall was steady as his name. All I had to do was ride and throw the loop. I couldn't tell if I had hit or missed until I felt Stoney set his heels. The calf snapped over backwards and lit on all four feet, looking back the way he'd come. I commanded Stonewall to hold as I leapt off running. A roper gets so he's got a stopwatch in his head. This was a fast catch. If I didn't mess up on the tie I was going to chalk up a real good score for my Round Up debut. I was already congratulating myself when George's hat jostled down over my eyes. I didn't even see the calf charge. The speckly devil butted me right in the breadbasket.

When things cleared up, I was back behind the chutes vomiting over a fence rail. George was rubbing my back and consoling me. I saw he had his hat on, completely unstained. On the other hand, I was a mess, I had retched the bitter residue of the night before all down the front of my blouse and trousers. George tried to get me to look at the bright side.

'Think how lucky it was you didn't have your own duds on.'

Another voice chimed behind me. 'He is going to be our light, Misteh Fretcher?'

Sue Lin stood holding my clothes. My hat sat on top of the folded bundle, neatly blocked.

144

Pendleton from the hot-air balloon *Fraternité*, 1911. The Round Up grounds are shown in the lower left-hand part of the picture, with the Indian teepees skirting the Umatilla River. Main Street runs horizontally through town, from the white hotel building past the railroad station, up the south hill to the high school.

Marchers and riders jostle into line for the first Round Up parade. 'You ride in the parade, son, or you ante up another five dollars.' Tiny tornadoes of dust dance underfoot. High school boys dressed as clowns scoop manure into wheelbarrows.

At the finish of the parade through town, participants and steeds gather in the arena: cowboys, cowgirls, Indians, stage drivers – from Tumalum to Hideaway, from the Mexican border to the Canadian line and beyond. For the parade's grand finale the entire cavalcade swings into line and charges with wild yells over the fence, skidding to a stop at the very edge of the grandstand. 'Right Between the Eyes!' they call it.

The Oompa Band. In prewar years the German Oompa Band was a big parade hit. Its members even dressed themselves in blackface.

John Spain, the southern gentleman cowboy. In one Round Up, while he was riding the outlaw Skyrocket, Spain got bucked off with his foot stuck in the stirrup. He used what they called 'the long boot trick' to twist loose and corkscrew out of his footgear. He got up, looked down at his foot, and said, 'I need new socks.'

Long Tom was the outlaw king of them all. The big, heavy-built sorrel was a hardworking plowhorse until a cowboy tried to ride him. Long Tom 'broke in two,' as they say, and it was 'Bye-bye, cowboy.'

Two legendary Iowans: Farmer Burns feels the pressure of a Frank Gotch facelock during a practice bout in the early 1900s. Burns became Gotch's tutor in 1900 and directed him to the world's championship.

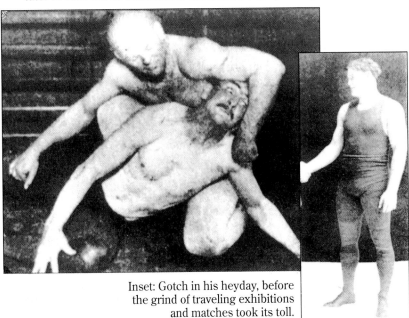

Inset: Gotch in his heyday, before the grind of traveling exhibitions and matches took its toll.

Left: William F. Cody, herder, hunter, pony express rider, stage driver, wagon master, and scout for the army: he got the name Buffalo Bill from supplying meat to railroad construction crews.

Below: A buffalo was trotted out for George Fletcher's ride and the crowd's amusement. George rode the old bull right into the ground.

Top right: Jackson Sundown with the brand new automobile he bought with his rodeo earnings.

Bottom right: John Spain in the outfit he bought with his earnings: chaps, gloves, hat, shirt, scarves, and pistol in a handtooled leather holster.

Parson Montanic. 'He could run faster, dance more gracefully, ride more skillfully, and wrestle more adeptly than any man in any tribe.' Montanic was also a renowned hell-raiser until he joined the church. He became an eloquent preacher and traveled all over the Northwest conducting meetings.

'Is he going to be our light?' George said. 'Honeypot, you see the way he managed that big roan with nothing but his kneecaps? This boy's a natural-born star, Sue honey. He might going to be *everybody's* light.'

I told George that I thought she meant to say All right. He had more important things to talk about.

'But *any* greenhorn,' he went on, wiping my chin with his neckerchief, 'is going to have to endure a certain amount of initiation.'

Another fit of retching prevented me from speaking my indignation. I'd been cowboying since the day I quit Nashville Junior, pulling down top roping money. If I was young and green, so was rodeoing, and I judged myself as familiar as the next fellow with most events of this new sport.

When I was back in my own clothes I found George and about a dozen other riders. They were trying to get their mounts lined up for what would have been a quite customary horse race – if it wasn't for the fact that all the riders were in their saddles backwards. Instead of reins they held the pack cinches, or hems of their saddle blankets, or the horses' tails.

George was happily puffing what I guessed was another of Meyerhoff's cigars. He gave me a holler. 'C'mon, Nashville. That entrance fee qualifies you for everything. Swing around bassackwards with the rest of us clowns.'

'O lord, *now* what?'

'A "Fool's Race" is what . . . and there's always room for another fool.'

He spurred his horse over to make room. As soon as I was turned backwards Stonewall commenced to stamp and fidget. My twisting around to look down the track only increased his nervous prancing. George and his big bay were the only ones at ease.

'Now listen to what I tell you,' he said confidentially. 'Lean way back for the start, keep your eyes on the tail. Twisting around to see the finish line puts you off balance. Let your horse worry about finishing. You just worry about starting; that's the hardest.'

Other riders were twisting and craning around and their horses were fretting and stamping. I forced myself to sit still. As soon as I quit fidgeting so did Stonewall. He stood calm, waiting for the other racers to be tugged up to the line. I wondered out loud why Sundown hadn't entered. George told me these clown events weren't exactly Sundown's cup of tea.

'I used to *have* to race backwards like this,' he told me. 'Just monkey business, was how they explained it. When I started winning re*gard*less, they decided to switch everybody around equal and call it a Fool's Race.' He chuckled at the memory. 'It's a curious thing: since everybody's had to ride backwards I been last as often as I been first. I'm doggoned if I can figure why that is. Alright, lean back.'

A pistol fired. The line of horses lunged forward and their riders lurched rearward. George was right about the start being the hardest part. That first lunge catches you off guard and leaves you stranded over your mount's rump with nothing to hang on to. The horse feels something scrabbling on his rear and he spooks again, then gallops in panic right out from under you. A third of the entries were spilled off by that starting lunge, and another third by that gallop. Even with George's warning I was sprawled on Stonewall's rump with nothing to hang on to. I was about to jostle off and join those other losers in the dust when I remembered

146

this was a roping horse I was riding. A good roping horse responds without need of reining.

'Stonewall, *hold!*' I shouted.

He hit the brakes just as though I had lassoed a calf. My inertia brought me back upright into the saddle.

'Now hee-up, Stoney,' I shouted. 'Eeeaw-*up!*'

Horses were pounding all around me, but most of their saddles were empty. George had to be some-where out in front. I fought down the urge to twist around and look. I slapped Stoney's rump and gave another rebel yell. We passed George right at the finish line. The crowd was on their feet, cheering.

The rodeo princess that came riding out to award me my prize was Sarah Meyerhoff. She gave it to me with a kiss for a bonus. The prize was a blue silk bandana with gold braid fringe and frilly silk letters cut out and quilted on:

FIRST PRIZE
FOOL'S RACE

The kiss was right on the mouth. It didn't need any gold braid or frilly silk in backwards writing. The message in that kiss was as explicit as the promise at the end of a matinee movie serial episode: TO BE CONTINUED!

That was my first of many Pendleton prizes, and the proudest. I tied the kerchief around my throat so it hung down my back like a cape. I found George standing in the shade beneath the stands. He was still shaking his head about the race.

'Next time I think I'll try turning the horse around. Maybe he'd run faster knowing where he's been than where he's headed. Nice hanky, Nashville. You sure you don't got it tied too tight? Your face is red as a beet.'

Before we could discuss this issue a bugle blew. It seemed too quick for another event. It blew again and the star-spangled pig came out, eyeing the arena with suspicion. His patriotic paint job glistened with grease. The horn tooted a third time and a pack of demons came screaming after the porker. The pack was all Indian children. Some wore leather clouts; some wore nothing but daubs of mud and paint. The pig squealed and scampered and the kids churned the dust in pursuit. It was no contest. This prize was a veteran, and not likely to be won.

When the novelty wore off and the kids were finally exhausted, the orange-haired woman walked out carrying a rope and a bugle. She blew recall. The pig trotted straight to her and put his head in the loop she was twirling. She led him off, waving to the stands. The unhappy kids followed, panting and downcast. George looked almost as unhappy.

'I'll be glad when we outgrow these shenanigans,' George said.

We were to endure many more. Foghorn Clancy was already announcing the next one on his three-way megaphone: 'Final call for the Squaw-Blanket Relay. Winner gets the blanket. Loser gets the squaw.' I could see why these novelty events weren't Sundown's cup of tea.

George convinced me to partner up with him for the Squaw-Blanket Relay. He said it was an easy thirty dollars if we used his big-shouldered bay.

The entries in the Squaw-Blanket Relay consisted of a team of two men and one horse. A heavy cowhide was dragged behind the horse. One man would ride the horse while his partner rode the hide. At the end of the arena they switched places for the race back. The Round Up volunteers provided the cowhides and drag ropes. I approached my hide warily, watching to see what my opponents were doing. Some were kneeling, others were sitting down with their legs stuck out. I looked up at George for advice.

'Well the *safest* way,' he said in an innocent voice, 'is belly down, like a little boy on his sled.'

I bellied safely down. The gun fired. George spurred his bay across the infield with me bouncing behind, through ruts, dirt, and filth – a damnable amount of which was kicked right in my face.

We reached the far end of the field well ahead of our competition. George wheeled the horse around and dismounted. I was a mess. My clean clothes were splattered with manure. It was under my collar, in my ears, even in my hatbrim.

'You were hitting those cow pies on purpose.'

'Only a couple,' he explained. 'For lubrication, like lard on a log skid.'

'Alright!' I sprung aboard George's horse. 'Lubrication it is.'

I spurred the gelding to a gallop, then sawed him toward the thickest pile I could find. 'Let's see how you like it, George Fletcher—' I called over my shoulder. '—getting your fancy hat lubricated!' But I saw he wasn't bellied down. Nor was he kneeling or sitting. He was *standing* up on that bounding hide, arms spread and knees bent, just like on the barrel. The filth kicked up by the bay's galloping hooves splattered nothing but his boots.

We got second place. We divied up our purse at the

watering trough while the bay drank. Fifteen bucks. I counted the silver dollars into two stacks of seven, then flipped the odd one. George snagged it from the air.

'If you hadn't detoured through that cow pie we'd be dividing thirty of these and there wouldn't be any odd one.' He dropped his dollars in a leather sack on his saddle and wheeled his horse around. 'Steer Roping's next. Let's go see what kind of mood them Texas hornytoads is in.'

I found out he meant Texas longhorns. They were in a miserable mood, stalking around in their corral, hooking at each other. Longhorns aren't fond of one another. The casual swing of a brother's head could cost them an eye. That's why the drovers from the Lone Star State had turned to other breeds; longhorns were as dangerous to themselves as to the cowboys and their ponies. I remember what one old trail boss said: 'They're like trying to herd porcupines.'

After watching these ill-tempered brutes hook and gouge I told George that perhaps I should skip the steer roping this first day.

'It's not only an event I've never tried, it's an event I've never even seen. I can study the technique.'

'There's only one technique you need to study: Mister Jackson's. He's the best there is.'

'That's a surprise, coming from George Fletcher. What makes him the best?'

'Sundown hates to get his nice suit dirty. When he brings a steer down the sucker *stays* down. It's all in the angle, he claims. Just watch.'

I watched. It's not an event you see in many rodeos anymore. Too brutal, too cruel. And back then they didn't have the stipulation that the animal had to be able to stand up afterwards to prove his neck hadn't been broken. I thought that's what Sundown did to his steer. He roped from the steer's left side, then reined to the right as fast as his fat little paint could go. The rope trailing back from the steer's horns was across his hind legs at a ninety-degree angle when Sundown reined to an abrupt stop. The animal's head was snapped one direction while his hooves were still stampeding another. He hit the ground so hard the entire stadium groaned. The steer didn't move a muscle while the Indian whipped his tie around the three legs and held up his hands. The crowd gave the steer a round of applause when it was untied and staggered to its feet.

George was right; it was all in the angle of the rope. Stonewall cut that angle across the heels of my roped longhorn like he'd been taking notes. I got third-best time, only seconds behind George. Sundown beat us all by a good half a minute.

All afternoon it was one event after another – a steady blur of animals, dust, and sun. I kept hoping I might get lucky and win myself another first place and another sweet-lipped bonus from Princess Sarah. I did share a win at one more contest: the Stagecoach Race. Sundown surprised me by asking if I would partner up with him on the driver's seat. More surprising still, he wanted me to handle the reins while he rode shotgun and threw rocks at the team. I had expected just the opposite; his experienced hands on the reins; my young arm throwing the stones. But the crafty redskin always had a trick up his sleeve. This time the trick was an Indian throwing-device called an axlotle. This is a grooved stick with holes at one end for the fingers and a notch at the other for the projectile. Indian boys use it for rabbit hunting, with a short spear positioned in the groove. The axlotle acts like an additional forearm, whipping the spear through the air with astonishing force and accuracy. Sundown said that it worked just as well with small stones.

'I'll make them run,' he said, eyeing the four rumps harnessed ahead of us. 'You keep them from running away.'

When the pistol fired the lead horse on the left must have thought the pistol bullet hit him. He nearly dragged the other three animals off their feet. Sundown reloaded his primitive catapult.

'This time the horse on the right. Be ready.'

Another stone square in the bull's-eye, as it were. We lurched past the other wagons with their feeble hand-thrown stones. By the time we reached the first turn we had the rail and the race. Nothing was going to pass us on the outside. Sundown kept up his stinging barrage nevertheless. We set a record in the Stagecoach Race that stands unequaled to this day. The use of rock-throwing devices was disallowed by the officials the following year. But our time went in the record books. You can look it up.

As luck would have it the prize was presented this time by the Round Up queen herself, Prairie Rose Henderson. The big buck-toothed girl's upper lip was swollen and blue from the steer roping, so she just shook our hands and rode away. George was sitting on a haybale in front of the dignitary seats, where Buffalo Bill's three rented cops had positioned themselves. George stood to greet us.

'Too bad she had a puffed lip. I hear Prairie Rose Henderson can give a feller a kiss and remove his tonsils at the same time.'

I was tired and hungry and not in the mood for George's jokes. The three Pinkertons didn't crack a smile, either. George fell in alongside Sundown.

'Let's go check the chalkboard, see who we drew for Saddle-bronc.'

'You two go ahead,' I told them. 'I never signed up.'

'I signed up for you,' George said, 'while you was off after them sweet tamales the Meyerhoff girls make.'

'They're called blintzes. And I keep telling you, dad-blast it – I'm a *roper*.'

'May be,' he said. 'But in about three minutes that man up there with the three-pronged megaphone is going to be calling you a broncbuster.'

My stomach growled an opinion but that very megaphone interrupted. Foghorn Clancy was informing one and all that Saddle-bronc Riding would be the day's final o-ficial event but *first!* while broncs and riders got ready, there was to be *another* added diversion, courtesy of Buffalo Bill's Wild West Extravaganza.

'Phooey,' George said. 'I thought we had that buffalo flop out of the way.'

Sundown wasn't interested but George and I angled back to the arena to have a look. A horn commenced to blow and out the gate rode the O'Grady woman. She was carrying a cavalry flag and bugling 'Charge' on her shiny brass bugle. This time the fanfare heralded Buffalo Bill himself. He made a galloping entrance on a big palomino, his six-gun blazing and his long white mane waving behind him, just like his horse's. The crowd gave him a big welcome as he made a little lope around the arena. He reared his horse to a stop beside the cowgirl's pony and gave a gauntleted gesture back toward the gate. The woman blew her bugle. Through the gate came the flatbed wagon with the prizefight ring. Only Gotch wasn't in the roped-in canvas square. It was Mister Handles and a bellering steer. The barker

153

was standing on a stool in one corner, already barking his pitch. The steer was tethered to the turnbuckle in the corner opposite.

Frank Gotch was on the ground in the wagon traces, substituting for the mules. He was wearing laced black boots and black-and-yellow-striped tights with his champ's belt buckled across his belly. A two-inch marine hawser ran back over his bare shoulder to the wagon's tongue. The giant was pulling the whole business single-handedly. He must have already heard about Montanic.

When the wagon reached the middle of the arena the crowd gave a polite round of applause. Gotch dropped the hawser and vaulted into the ring. The barker led the steer out to meet him. Gotch dried his palms on his tights and leaned over the steer. He was able to wrap those ungodly long arms all the way around the bellering bovine and lock his hands! He drew a loud breath and heaved. The animal was swung clear up onto his shoulder, its four legs kicking at the sky. Gotch held it up there, squeezing until all the beller was squeezed completely out. Satisfied, he slung the steer over the ropes. It lay without moving in the dirt, stunned senseless.

This brought everybody to their feet. They stood clapping until Mister Handles went into his pitch; then everybody sat back down. Gotch strutted around with his arms folded. When it was obvious that nobody was going to come rushing down out of the stands to take the challenge, the O'Grady woman blew 'Retreat.' The span of mules was trotted out and hastily lashed into the traces. The wagon followed Buffalo Bill's palomino back the way it had come. Gotch stood gloating as the wagon passed the silent stands. A couple of wranglers rode out and looped the horns of the steer. They dragged it off while the O'Grady woman blew a few bars of 'Taps' as a joke. The little touch of humor let the audience off the hook. George wasn't amused.

'Good thing that was a steer. If it had been a heifer I fear he mighta done more than just hug her. Let's go.'

We walked to the clerk's table with the other bronc riders. Sundown was already there, hunkered on his heels in the shade. He raised his hand.

'I got your draws.' He handed us our paper chits. 'George drew Captain Kidd. He rides first, because he's the All Round leader. I got Boneshaker. The boy got Mister Sweeney.'

'He drew *Mister Sweeney?*' George rolled his eyes. 'They must raise these Southern boys on four-leaf clovers.' He stomped away, pulling on his gloves and grumbling. 'They give him Mister Sweeney and *me* they give Captain Kidd. Suck-egg mule.'

I turned to the Indian. 'He must be some bad old outlaw, this Captain Kidd?'

'Just old,' Sundown said. 'George'll have to rake him awake.'

'Then why was George so exasperated?'

'Because you got the best draw for a big score. Mister Sweeney's a man-hater. He aint been rid but three times. George was one.'

'Who were the other two?'

'Me.' The Indian rose stiffly to his feet and we headed for the rail to watch.

Out in the arena the hostlers held a blindfolded gelding. One had a grip on the bronc's bridle; the other an end of the burlap blindfold. Foghorn Clancy's voice rolled across the arena.

'Looks like old Captain Kidd is ready to repel all boarders. And here comes his nemesis, gentlemen and ladies, the scourge of the bucking buccaneers and the pride of Pendleton, your own *George . . . Fletch-errr!*'

The crowd cheered. George came sprinting out and vaulted into the bronc's saddle. The moment his boots found the strirrups the blindfold was ripped away and the bridle freed. George rocked back and raked the shoulders and the old horse took off in a stiff-legged, teeth-rattling, erratic run, like some infernal machine coming apart.

This was what I had come to see – bad buckers and good riders. George rocked and the horse rattled, but Sundown was right. This old outlaw rattled to pieces too quick. After his initial run Captain Kidd settled down to a halfhearted bounce. George mouthed insults at the animal while spurring him from shoulder to rump. This provoked a little more action, but nothing like that first flurry.

The bell rang. George swung a leg over and landed running. He hiked dirt disdainfully after the fleeing animal, like a dog hiking. The stands loved it, but he got no great score.

After four or five other rides, it was Sundown's turn. The Indian had a style as different from George's as dark from day. Whereas George treated his bronc like it was his assistant in a burlesque routine, Sundown took the more stately approach. He walked out as if on his way to a funeral. When the snubbing ponies had the bronc steady, Sundown eased himself gently into the saddle. A curt nod and the blindfold was snatched away. There was a moment of truce between man and animal, a brief motionless peace while the ponies backed away. Then Sundown raked him and

156

Boneshaker sailed violently skyward. Yet a kind of accord prevailed, even in the violence: man and horse were partners in some ancient dance.

The animal sunfished. He skyhooked. He pawed at the clouds. Every time he landed he locked his legs so stiff the dust raised ten feet in all directions. It was clear why he was called Boneshaker. Yet, shake as the bony bronc would, the Indian's expression remained as placid as a brick. The moment the bell rang all motion stopped, as suddenly as it had begun. Boneshaker's bones were ready to stop shaking. Sundown dismounted and walked out of the arena, as dignified and unruffled as he had walked in. The roar of the crowd followed him.

After Sundown the redheaded Beeson twins each had a fair ride, followed by some more mediocres. Then it was my turn. Mister Sweeney was a hammer-headed piebald with a bobbed tail and was – as Sundown had warned – a born man-hater. He tried to bite me the moment I got near, as if he could see through the blindfold. They snatched the burlap away and he rolled his eyes back for a quick look at who it was that dared to sit on him. His eyes went red, maddened at the sight of me. He spun around the other direction and actually bit off more of his tail. This infuriated him so much he kicked himself in the jaw. Teeth flew in every direction and he took off in an insane gallop, blind with rage. He ran nose first into the snubbing post. I decided the best tactic would be to stay out of Mister Sweeney's way and let him kill himself.

I knew all along it wasn't a graceful ride to look at – a skinny kid pitching back and forth in the saddle of a hate-crazed horse. I knew as well that I wasn't going to get throwed. In one of those diamond moments of certainty I knew I had mastered the secret of wild-bronc riding. Two secrets, actually: sit loose like George Fletcher and at the same time stay composed like Sundown Jackson. Mister Sweeney knew I knew it, too, and the knowing made him furious beyond belief. He bucked and twisted and farted and snapped, but to no avail. The wilder he raved, the better I liked it. I could feel my bones and muscles learning, winnowing years of experience out of each instant. A note rang in the distance but I kept raking. I swept off my hat and slapped his bony haunch. The note grew more insistent. Then George was alongside on his tall gelding, swinging me off, behind his saddle.

'You deef, country boy? Or just plain dumb?' He was looking at me with a curious expression. 'They been banging that bell for ages.'

'I guess I didn't hear it,' I lied. I was beginning to tremble. I had managed to stay the distance on Mister Sweeney, the man-hater. It wasn't a ride to bring me much of a score but it did get me considerable advice and criticism. Sundown lit into me the moment we reached the corrals.

'Never slap a horse with your hat. It looks show-off. The judges don't give points for hat slapping.'

'Yeah, Dog, but you got to admit, he done some mighty fine spurrin'. *Too* mighty, in fact, if you hopes to last long in this bronc-riding business. You got to get you some *chaps*, Nash. See us out there? It *looked* like we was scratchin' like the devil with the hives, didn't it? That's account of these *chaps* we all wear, all unloosed and floppy. *That's* the kind of flappin' the judges give points for.'

'Another thing,' Sundown went on, 'you touched the

horn when you took off your hat. That's points subtracted.'

'The bell had already rung,' I said.

'No, he's right,' George said. 'Never let 'em see you pull leather, even after the time bell. Always keep your free hand high, see, behind your head. With your chin tucked. It makes the angle look steeper.'

This schooling might have gone on all afternoon if some of the Wild West Extravaganza troupe hadn't come by with Oliver Nordstrum to offer congratulations. Buffalo Bill stood amidst the three Pinkertons, silently appraising us through the smoke of his cheroot. Frank Gotch loomed behind, wearing a striped turtleneck and a rakish cap.

'Wellnow, gentlemen,' Nordstrum was beaming from George to Sundown. 'One day down, two to go. Which of you pulled in the top dollar, if you don't mind me asking? George? Jackson?'

The Indian didn't answer and George slid into his field-hand drawl.

'Ah calc'late Brother Sundog be about twenty dollah in de lead, 'cause he win de Saddlebronc.'

'Hunh-uh,' Sundown corrected. 'You won the Potato race and the Bulldogging.'

'You won the Steer Tripping!' George exclaimed. 'And that's a way bigger purse than any 'tater race.'

'You and the boy split second money in that Blanket Relay.'

'Chickenfeed!' George snorted. 'You and the boy split first money in the Stagecoach Race! Own up, Mistah Sundown Jackdog ... you *know* you in de lead.'

Nordstrum laughed and held up both hands. 'Let's call it neck-and-neck,' he said. 'Just the way a sporting

159

man likes it. What you say, Bill? There's still time to get down a little wager on one of our hometown stars.'

'I'm a showman, Oliver, not a sport,' Buffalo Bill reminded him.

'Mister Cody don't bet on stars,' Gotch said in that caged voice of his. 'He buys 'em. Scouts 'em out and buys them.'

'Still the Injun scout, is it, Bill?' Nordstrum's eyes gleamed with implied secrets.

'Always the scout, Oliver,' Buffalo Bill said. 'Always on the lookout for that sharpest shot, that fastest filly, that bull-of-the-woods world-beater—'

'Den listen to me, Mistah Scout.' George was dancing from foot to foot. 'Like I explain to you all on de train, if'n hits a Worl' Champeen broncrider you lookin' for for your show, den dat feller go by de name George Washington Fletcher!'

Gotch pivoted his head until his cold little eyes fell on the dancing figure. 'We already have plenty of clowns,' he said. 'All we want from you is that dancing partner you promised. If I don't get somebody pretty soon I'm gonna have to pick my own partner. *Then* you'll do some dancin'.'

Buffalo Bill and Nordstrum guffawed, and George giggled along until they hushed. The silence that followed was taut as stretched barbed wire. Sundown broke it at last.

'I got to show this boy which teepee his bedroll is in. He wasn't able to find it last night.'

He strode off toward the corrals without another word. George couldn't resist one last rib as he passed.

'Dem teepees is a lot like the folks what live in 'em, aint that right, Mars Gotch? Hard to tell 'em apart after dark.'

He shambled on without waiting for the response. But I saw it. Gotch's head rotated until the vertebrae in his neck popped, one after another, like muffled explosions in a mine shaft. I begged all present to forgive the hasty departure and hurried after my friends.

Chapter Eleven

Teepee Time

The sawtooth skyline of teepees lay ahead, edge up against the stars. The skyline was filed sharp in the blowing smoke and tempered dull red by the firelight. Drummers drummed and shadows shook. Clans chanted tribal histories around the boisterous stick games. Children and dogs scrambled in and out of the firelit teepees, yelling and yipping, just like – as Louise had put it – wild Indians. The people weren't holding back before paleface sensibilities; nor showing off for them, either. This was their stomping grounds, and it looked then pretty much the way it looks now – and probably like it had looked centuries before.

One old Indian in a worn headdress stood guard in front of the pole gate. The gate had acquired a crude sign: NO HORSE RIDING IN VILLAGE OBEY GUARD. The old Indian stepped in front of us and shook his feathered spear.

'Stand and dismount God *damn!*'

'Seems like it oughta be the other way around, Uncle Cup Too Full,' George said.

'You! George Blackfoot! Pocatello Jack! Dismount God *damn*. You got any passwords?'

'Not a one, Uncle Cup,' Sundown answered.

'I'm bare as a bone,' George added, patting his

pockets. 'Johnville, you got one of Merchant Meyerhoff's smokes left?'

'Mister Sweeney put a bad bend in it.' I held the cigar out. 'Will this do, sir?'

Cup Too Full took a sniff and nodded. 'Pass,' he said. 'Dismount on foot. Damn papooses are everywhere God *damn!*'

Sundown and I dismounted. George was staring at a noisy pack of kids running past. One dark little girl stopped in her moccasined tracks and returned his stare. She called something to her playmates and they all turned around and stared. George hollered, 'Shoo!' and the pack ran on. Uncle Cup Too Full shook his spear.

'Dismount God damn George Fletcher.'

'No, thanks, Uncle Cup; I think I'll ooze on up home. Get some oats to these cayuses and get me some shuteye.' He looked after the pack of kids. 'You noisy Injuns make a man nervous God *damn.*'

I confess I felt a little nervous myself. George leaned down for Stonewall's reins.

'No need to fret about your horse,' he assured me. 'I'll see to him like he was my firstborn. Oats and alfalfa.'

'And a little salt?' I asked him. 'I'd be much obliged. I reckon we all need a little shuteye.'

'Put your mind at ease and I'll do the same for your animal. Hey Pocatello Jack! Was I you, I'd be enjoying that lead tonight. It'll be your last opportunity.'

Sundown led his horse through the gate without a word. I told George good night and hurried to catch up.

The noise rising from the welter of teepees seemed to abate as we approached. The drumming, the stick

163

games, even the barking dogs got quieter. Sundown stopped before entering the camp.

'We maybe go first to the river,' he said. 'To water the horse and wash.'

No kids were playing in the pool. It was too near suppertime. I helped Sundown unsaddle his paint and check the hooves. He brushed out the horse's mane, then unbraided his own hair and brushed himself, using the pool for a mirror. He seemed reluctant to look toward the teepees. It was the same reluctance George had teased him about the day before. I was curious but I kept quiet. The moon rising through the dark oaks dappled the pool like a paint pony. The Indian's rigid features softened as he brushed. The shield of silence fell away, and Jackson Sundown began to talk. He talked for close to an hour, about his people, his past, his youth . . . but mainly about his long association with George Fletcher.

They had been friendly rivals since their first encounter at a baptism on this same riverbank nearly forty years before. It had been an event intended essentially to cleanse the heathen souls of the red children, but the Pendleton church had sent a black boy along, too. He was the cast-off offspring of a hotel maid. The maid had climbed out of a boxcar one Sunday, looking for work. When her apron strings would no longer tie she claimed she was married. The father was coming soon, from Denver. When the baby was born she walked out of the hospital and was never seen again. Probably left on the same boxcar, Sundown speculated. No daddy from Denver showed up, either. The hospital unloaded the baby on the city before the week was out, and the city passed it on to the church.

The boy was passed from one good samaritan to another. By the time he was school age he was wild as a mountain sheep, filthy as a pig, and unbaptized. The church fathers did not feel it fitting to allow this black sheep to join the other poor lambs in the big round pickle-barrel that served as the congregation's baptismal, but it was clear the boy needed laundering, both spiritual and physical. So they sent him along to the river with the Indian children. The Indians were a little leery of him as well. Sundown's sister, Mary Pretty Jesus, insisted that the spiritual immersion of this strange dark creature be put off until all the others were baptized.

'Mary Pretty thought he was like the Chinamen kids that made charcoal for the cooks. She said he would dirty the water. George was insulted and he hit her with a mud clod. I hit him with a free Bible. We fought all afternoon. The church fathers let us fight and started betting.'

'Who won?'

'Nobody yet,' he answered. 'It got too dark to see and the church fathers went back to town. George, he come with me, back to the reservation.'

'After fighting all afternoon?'

'It was mostly just rolling around and pinching, to make the other say uncle. But neither one of us would say it. When we got to the village Mary Pretty Jesus took George in and give him fry bread and prayed for his soul. He stayed with us many years, off and on. He liked her fry bread. George will eat anything that's free.'

The willows behind us rustled, we were no longer alone. A gang of Indian boys had slipped up to listen to their famous relative. One ragged lad stood apart from the others, examining Sundown's ornate saddle. Sundown kept talking, as if the boys weren't there.

'We tried to raise George Fletcher just like a Nez Percé. But it was no good. He couldn't hunt, he couldn't fish. He couldn't even learn how to play the stick game. When he became age-of-a-man we cut him off the fry bread. He foraged his way back to Pendleton.' Sundown dropped the currybrush into his beaded shoulder bag. 'He never would have made a good Indian. He talks too much. You! Boy!'

The lad at the saddle jumped. He had been fingering one of the saddle's silver honchos. He glared defiantly at Sundown. Sundown met his glare and dug into his bag. He flipped the boy one of his silver dollars.

'Carry that saddle to my teepee. Maybe tomorrow I will let you shine it.'

Sundown slung his bag over his shoulder and led the horse away. The boy followed, staggering under the load. Sundown ignored him, lifting his nostrils to sniff the air.

'I smell Indian tea cooking. Maybe we have some.'

The hubbub in the camp was louder than ever. Babies could be heard crying from inside Sundown's teepee, noisily but not unhappily. They just wanted to be part of the hubbub. Sundown hobbled his mare in a grassy flat behind the teepee and gave her an armful of cornstalks. He pointed to a log. The boy threw the saddle over it and hunkered alongside. In front of the tent flap a fire blazed under a steaming ten-gallon milk can. Sundown bent over and smelled the brew. Apparently satisfied with the aroma, he took a gourd ladle from a nearby basket and dipped out a taste. His face puckered like a dried apricot.

That brew had provoked the most expression I'd

ever seen Sundown display. My throat constricted just watching. One would have expected the taster to put the lid right back on, but Sundown took a tin canteen from his shoulder bag and handed it to me to hold. He began carefully ladling in the noxious-smelling liquid. I saw the tin turn a venomous green right before my eyes.

The teepee flap opened and a fat squaw waddled out, carrying a flat wicker basket with a mashed chocolate cake in it. The cake looked old as a fossil, and just as hard. She took the gourd dipper from Sundown and began ladling the liquid over the cake. When the cake was soaked to her satisfaction she return the dipper and waddled back into the teepee. In a guarded whisper, Sundown informed me that this was none other than the delicate sister George had hit with a clod, Mary Pretty Jesus.

'She gave up Jesus and fry bread for the devil's-food cake and tea.'

The babies' crying got louder. Sundown capped the canteen and returned it to his shoulder bag. He walked to the teepee and lifted the flap for a peek. The teepee was piled all around the outer edge with provisions, mainly corn and watermelons. The inner circle was piled with Indians of all ages, sitting and sipping and talking softly all at once. The talk was a crossbreed of English and Indian and some Mexican; yet it wasn't babble. It was like a treeful of jays and magpies and crows all voicing their opinions at the same time. Sundown reached in and pulled out a box of soda crackers and a strip of jerky. He let the flap fall shut.

'George Fletcher's right about noisy damn Indians. We'll have our tea on the terrace.'

* * *

The terrace was a jut of rimrock overlooking the village. Sundown had taken off his suit coat and shirt and was seated at the rim's edge, brushing his hair. He had fallen once more into that gazing silence. A long strip of jerky hung from the corner of his mouth. Between sips from the canteen he chewed steadily. I tried to follow his gaze but the only thing out there was a snowy mountain peak.

'That's some mountain out yonder.' I was trying to make some polite tea talk. 'What's it called?'

Sundown didn't cease his grooming or his chewing. 'Je'r son,' he mumbled around the jerky.

'Beg pardon?'

Sundown gnawed the jerky free and handed me the ragged stump.

'Nowadays they call it Mount Jefferson,' he said.

'What did they use to call it?'

'People used to call it Yah Kakkinan,' he answered. 'Before your president claimed it.'

'I see.' I chewed off a piece of jerky and washed it down with the tea. I was getting used to the brew; it didn't taste nearly as wicked as it smelled. 'What did that mean, Yah Kakkinan?'

'Same as it still means,' he answered. 'Damn High Mountain. Give me some more tea.'

I handed over the canteen. 'It's not half as bad as I feared. What kind is it?'

'Weed.' He took a drink, then poured some in his palm and sprinkled it on his hair. He resumed brushing.

'And this jerky?' I persisted. 'It's some of the best I ever ate? What is it, deer?'

'Not deer.'

'Elk? Antelope?'

He shook his head.

'Good Lord, it isn't *dog*—?'

Sundown let the question hang in the air a long while before he answered. 'It's turkey.'

'Turkey? Turkey jerky?' If this answer had come from anyone else I would have thought I was being kidded. The dried meat seemed much too long-muscled to be the flesh of any kind of fowl. But I couldn't imagine this somber man kidding about anything. I gnawed off another bite and we chewed and sipped a while. Sundown savored the silence. I was aching for conversation. A shout of victory from one of the games below gave me an opening.

'Say, I've been wondering, how does one win at these stick games?'

'By fooling the other tribe,' he said. 'Making them guess wrong where's the stick at.'

'Oh, it's like liar's dice,' I said. 'Only with teams.'

'Uh-huh,' he answered.

I waited for some elaboration, but Sundown began to rebraid his hair. A baby's cry arose, incensed and inconsolable.

'Is something wrong with that child?' I asked Sundown.

'No,' he answered.

'I thought Indian babies didn't cry.'

'They do when they get circumcised.'

'He sounds too old for that.'

Sundown offered no comment.

'Is he one of yours?'

'No,' he said. 'I do not have any children.'

'I thought George said you had numerous squaws—'

'George talks too much,' he said. Then he relented. 'There are many squaws in our teepee, but I have only one wife. Thirty-two years. One wife all my life. Almost one child. You ask a lot of questions.'

I told him I was sorry, and vowed to keep my questions to myself. Sundown turned his face toward the distant peak and resumed braiding his hair.

The moon climbed higher, full and stark. The camp grew quieter. The kid packs had been rounded up and corraled inside their teepees. The baby had cried itself to sleep.

Sundown put his shirt and suit coat back on against the night's chill. He took a big meerschaum pipe from his bag and loaded it from a fringed pouch. He puffed it to life with a wooden match and settled back to enjoy the smoke. He noticed me watching and passed the pipe over. I drew a little puff and smelled the bowl.

Forgetting my vow, I started to ask, 'What kind of—?' He answered before I could finish.

'Prince Albert,' he said and took the pipe back. He didn't offer it again, either.

The moon kept climbing. The stars wheeled. Down below, the private fires in front of individual teepees had died down. The council fire flamed higher as bigger branches were thrown on, then logs, planks, shipping crates. The widening circle of firelight illuminated the whole camp.

The drumming increased as more Indians converged on the firelit clearing. They hunkered on their heels, waiting, it seemed to me. Some whittled and played Mumbly-peg. Some got up and danced. One glassy-eyed man in a mangy fur robe lumbered around the fire, pretending to be a bear. Old Cup Too Full came in from his sentry post, headdress drooping more than ever. He lit the feathered end of his spear and drew

170

random shapes in the smoky sky, challenging them and demanding passwords.

I was filled with a wild urge to laugh and I didn't know how long I could hold it back. This wasn't your Currier and Ives picture of the Noble Savage; this was a comic postcard. I didn't want to appear disrespectful but, from my lofty viewpoint on the ridge, the scene below was getting sillier by the minute. Surely, even the sober-sided Sundown couldn't help but be a little amused. I glanced sideways at my companion. His eyes were closed but I knew he was awake; he was toying with that big coin. It danced in and out of his fingers as though the drums had quickened it to life. Even this struck me as funny. I turned away to keep from laughing, and saw something that froze the laughter in my throat.

Uncle Cup's glowing shapes were no longer random; the lines of sparks had joined to become a single fiery phantom, bearlike and huge in the black sky. And this trail of sparks did not disperse or dim; the shape got brighter as I stared, and stronger, until the beast leapt free of Uncle Cup's spear and reeled among the dancers with a will of its own, just like the coin. Alive! I managed to tear my eyes away and turned to Sundown.

'What kind of weed?'

Sundown stopped fingering the coin and his eyes came slowly open.

'Jimson,' he said with great patience.

'You mean *locoweed*? Isn't that a poison?'

'Enough of it.'

'You mean enough, or too much?'

'I mean too much.'

'How much is too much?'

'I heard about an Indian drunk forty-two cups once.'

'Good God!' I was frantic. 'How much too much does it take to kill you? How long? I hate to ask too many questions, but, good God Al*mighty*, man, is there an antidote—?'

He held up a hand. 'Wait. I got a question for you.' His face had changed. It was sharper, younger, and his eyes were barbed with a very disturbing glee. 'Alright?'

I swallowed hard and nodded.

'What do you think happened to that Indian who drunk forty-two cups of tea?'

'Lord, I can't imagine. Forty-two cups? What happened to the poor man?'

'He died in his teepee.'

Then, to my dismay, Jackson Sundown commenced to shake up and down. I stared at him fearfully. When he didn't elaborate on the dead tea drinker I chanced another question.

'What happens,' I asked carefully, taking pains to sound as worried as I felt, 'from drinking just a couple of cups?'

This set him shaking harder than ever. I feared he might shake himself right off the ridge, but he abruptly ceased, his palm lifted, listening. The drums and dancers had stopped. Whatever they had been waiting for around the council fire had arrived.

Two cowboys walked into the firelit circle. I saw it was the redheaded twins that had made the mules jump with their cigars. They looked drunker and feistier than ever, and were accompanied by a half-dozen cronies. They talked a while to Cup Too Full and reached some kind of agreement. The old Indian accepted a sack of tobacco and gestured toward the shadows. A pear-shaped figure emerged from the gloom, pulling a long rope. The figure was wearing what appeared to be a woman's scarlet bathrobe. Sundown turned from the sight and spit on the ground, disgusted.

'It's Nice Hawk and Flapjack. No wonder people call us sneaky.'

I ventured Nice Hawk must be the man when I saw what the rope pulled into the firelight. The animal stood, spraddle-legged, and stared stupidly into the fire. This had to be Flapjack. One of the twins pulled out a wallet and counted some bills onto a barreltop.

'Those damn fools know better than to try and ride Flapjack,' Sundown said. 'Nice Hawk will take them for everything they've got.'

Nice Hawk counted the money on the barreltop and shook his head. Not enough. The other cowboys chipped in until the wager was adequate. The pear-shaped Indian pulled a roll out of his bathrobe pocket and matched their bet. The horse stared at the fire.

'I must say he doesn't look like much,' I said. 'Compared to Mister Sweeney.'

'Mister Sweeney's been rid. Nobody's never stayed a fifteen count on Flapjack. Nor ten nor five. You watch.'

A blindfold was tied across the drowsing horse's eyes. One of the redheaded twins swung up. Nice Hawk handed the rider the reins and unsnapped the lead rope. Holding a corner of the blindfold, he looked to see if the rider was ready. The cowboy nodded. Nice Hawk snatched the blindfold away with a dramatic flourish. Nothing at all happened. The cowboy's cronies commenced counting. The horse's lolling head raised and craned around to look at the man on his back, his manner both sleepy and contemptuous. He studied the rider for a moment, then took a few little mincing steps, and leaped. Not forward or upward, like a bucking horse, but backward, like a diver springboarding up to do a backward swan – all the way over. He landed flat on his back with a sickening thump, pinning the rider beneath him.

Sundown spit again. 'A miracle somebody aint shot that man and that animal both.'

For a while it looked like the other twin might do just that, but his cronies held him back. The horse rolled back to his feet and they picked up their damaged companion. One arm was bent at the elbow the wrong way. They helped him out of the firelit circle. The horse appeared to be already asleep. Nice Hawk kissed him on the nose.

'That horse ought to be outlawed,' Sundown said. 'Nobody can ride a freak like that.'

'I can,' I said. My initial panic over the tea had subsided and I was feeling silly again.

'You can what?' Sundown asked.

'Ride him,' I said. 'I can ride him right now.'

'Didn't you see? He's a trick horse. Nice Hawk and Flapjack have been pulling that same sucker jump for years, from California to Canada!'

'Maybe we got some tricks in Tennessee Nice Hawk and Flapjack don't know about.'

'Maybe you can crack your backbone, too!'

'Wanta bet?'

Sundown nibbled at his coin, looking at me thoughtfully. Then he shrugged and stood up. We drifted downhill through the moonlight like ghosts swimming through a dream. We emerge in the middle of the fire circle. Everybody is watching. The horse is standing upright and blindfolded. Sundown and Nice Hawk hold the reins. This time the sucker on his back is me.

'One for the money?' Nice Hawk singsongs. 'Two for the show-ho?'

'Shut your mouth!' Sundown snaps. He turns to me. 'Why don't you wait, Little Brother? Till you pee some of that jimson tea off—?'

That's when I finally got it: 'Tea pee,' I laughed.

'—three to get ready—'

'Forty-two cups and died in his *tea* pee. Oh, that's rich.'

'—and four to *go*-ho!'

Nice Hawk snatches away the blindfold. Flapjack cranes his contemptuous neck around to study this new sucker. I rein his head all the way around, hard, and grab him by the halter. I lean down and sink my teeth into the tender flesh of his nose with all my intoxicated might.

The poor beast tries to start his little run but his head is twisted around too far. All he can do is hobble around in a tight circle. I hear Nice Hawk screaming and the cowboys counting.

'—three . . . four . . . five—'

It's my elongated frame that allows me to bite Flapjack's nose. No one else could reach that far forward. Round and around that horse and I went with Nice Hawk shrieking after us, waving his blindfold like a white flag. 'No fair biting no *fair*—!' The cowboys counted: '—thirteen. Fourteen. *Fifteen!* Hooray for Tennessee!'

Even the Indians were cheering. I slid off the horse and Sundown nodded and old Cup Too Full saluted. Everyone was celebrating except Nice Hawk. He dabbed at his horse's nose with the blindfold and continued to chastise me: 'If you give him in*fection* I'm going to the sheriff!'

The cowboys hooted. The drums commenced beating and the dancing resumed. The sparks spun upward.

It had been a busy day and an eventful eve. I was ready for some shuteye. I followed Sundown into his teepee. I unrolled my bed and lay there, listening. The camp got quieter. A few distant drummers drummed. No babies cried. No dogs barked. Firelight scampered up the teepee poles like red lizards. When the lizards made it to the top they turned into gray snakes and slithered away toward the stars.

I rubbed the big copper coin along my cheek. I count it the second-greatest trophy I ever won, just behind the kiss and the kerchief.

'Forty-two cups,' I chuckled.

'Go to sleep,' Sundown commanded from the dark. 'Before you get strangled.'

'Forty-two cups and strangled in his tea pee.' Then I shut up; the snakes were turning into herds of tiny horses – delicate creatures – and I didn't want to frighten them away.

No rider has ever ridden into such Round Up popularity as Jackson Sundown, a Nez Percé cowboy from Culdesac, Idaho, and nephew of Chief Joseph. He won the Championship in 1916, making a sensational ride on Angel. He was fifty years old at the time.

Top left: George Fletcher, Pendleton cowboy famous for riding the baddest outlaw as though he were in a ballroom. Merry grin, floppy yellow hat, wool chaps – 'Everything about him seemed to dance'.

Bottom left: Indians parade on the track, with the teepee village in the cottonwood grove to the rear.

Right: John Spain twirling his rope for the camera.

Below: Sundown digging his spurs into Angel's hide. The horse did his best, but to no avail. The shot rang out. 'Sundown!' came the roar from the grandstand. 'Sundown!' echoed the bleachers. 'Sundown!' re-echoed the Indians.

George Fletcher shows his classic style. The bronc rider must ride 'slick' – straight up, with a close seat, no daylight showing through – and must not shift the halter rope from one hand to the other. He may not touch any portion of his saddle (*pull leather*) or grab the horn (*choke the biscuit*). He must rake the blunted spurs, shoulder to rump.

Bonnie McCarroll takes a fall during the 1916 Round Up. Note the broken hobble, seen on the upthrown stirrup: women were encouraged to ride broncs with 'hobbled stirrups.'

Jackson Sundown handling a bad one while his friend George Fletcher looks on, at the 'Let'Er Twist!' Rodeo in Culdesac, Idaho.

Jackson Sundown in action. Outlaw buckers will try *the side wind*, *the cake walk*, *the double O*, or *the corkscrew*. They'll *sunfish*, *twist*, *weave*, *straight buck*, *circle*, *skyscrape*, *highdive*, or *sidethrow* – and may even *fallback* to kill the bronc rider.

A rare Sundown smile.

Even after he lost his hand in a roping accident, John Spain continued to rodeo and win top-dollar prize money.

Rodeo cowgirls. Prairie Rose Henderson (center) challenged cowboys and judges both. She was the first woman to compete in Saddlebronc Riding and finished only a few points behind the winner. Ruth Roach (right), known for her heart-embossed boots and satin bloomers, was the winning bronc rider at the 1917 Forth Worth Rodeo. Kitty Canutt (left) was the All-Around Champion Cowgirl at the 1916 Round Up.

Whether in beads and breechcloth or blue serge suit and starched shirt, hair wild or tied in long braids, Jackson Sundown remained the same – a champion with style, from top to bottom, beginning to end.

Chapter Twelve

Rather Ride Than Reign

The second day, then, was blame near as red-eyed as the first. But it wasn't near as rattled. The big bull calf churning across the dirt of the arena was in focus this time, and I went spurring after it with confidence. My loop was quick and true. The calf flopped down and I was on him in a flash, whipping the tie rope around the hooves. I raised my arm in a showy wave. The crowd cheered and I waved some more. I was feeling my oats. Bring on that prize; this time I would be puckered and ready.

I lingered at the ride-out gate below the judges' platform, so's I could keep an eye on my competition. Cecil Kell was the man with the stop clock. He waved at me and held up the clock. I couldn't see the numbers, but I knew it was my fastest time ever. He handed the clock to Oliver Nordstrum. Nordstrum whistled and offered it to Buffalo Bill. The old showman was seated in a special dignitary section alongside the giant wrestler. He was looking through a pair of army field glasses at the calf-roping gate.

'To-*day*, gents and ladies,' Foghorn Clancy bawled, 'a unexpected entry in our calf-ropin' contest: one of our top-dollar stars has entered this little six-bit event, right along with the young no-bodies. Here he comes, up on – well, it doesn't look like the horse has a name; but the *rider* certainly does – Sundown *Jack*son!'

Six-bit contest was right. The daily first-prize money for the calf-rope was scarcely much more than seventy-five cents back then, after second and third got their cut. Calf-roping was the ordinary task that every cowhand had already proved himself at. It was too common for top-dollar. Why was this top-dollar star taking a chance at getting busted ribs and dislocated fingers in a six-bit event?

When I saw Sundown swerve that paint stud in an effortless gallop after his veering calf, I saw why: he was a master at that ordinary task. He had probably looped and hogtied more calves than all the rest of us nobodies lumped together, and he felt obliged to show us how the task ought to be attended to. It was a study in economy: his horse followed the calf like a shadow follows a bird. His loop didn't pursue its target, it was there ahead of it, waiting. The calf popped to its back in an efficient somersault and the horse began backhauling it in like he was reeling in a big catfish. Sundown dismounted and waited until the calf had been pulled all the way to him, just as he probably waited when he was working alone, out on the range – to save a little energy – then flipped his rawhide tie around the three hooves. He would have beat my best time if he'd not elected to save that little jigger of energy.

I waited out the remainder of the roping, half expecting to see George ride out and demonstrate *his* technique with the lariat. But no other stars entered to challenge my time. I led Stoney back and forth along the rail in the shade of the cottonwoods, cooling him off, waiting to hear my name announced. I was beginning to rise in my own eyes. I might have a chance at that saddle, I ventured in a fit of sudden optimism. Hadn't I already bested the best at their own specialties? George, yesterday, in the backwards race and now Sundown Jackson in the roping? Foghorn's voice declared me the winner but no sweet Sarah came galloping out to award the prize. The event must be just too common to require a princess. Too workaday.

Nordstrum handed the purse to a Boy Scout, who carried it to me on foot. Keenly disappointed, I legged up on Stonewall and trotted away. At the home turn of the racetrack a crowd of cowboys and Indians had found a little spot of shade to watch from. Some were still in their saddles, some were perched on the top rail. Indian mamas and kids were peeking between the dangling boots.

'Find you a spot, Nashville; the peanut gallery is the best seats in the place for the big squaw race.'

It was George, sitting knees spraddled atop a pine post, like a bird. I reined Stoney around and loped over.

'Another squaw race? That would explain the tribes, but what's fired the interest of all you saddle bumpers? You must enjoy watching raven-haired maidens on paint ponies.'

'One of these maidens ain't so raven-haired,' I was informed by a redheaded peckerwood perched next to George. It was a Beeson twin, the one that had showed better sense than to get on old Flapjack. He scooted over to give me a spot. George offered me a canteen. The water had the faint taste of jimsonweed.

'Nice piece of roping,' I heard Sundown's flat voice say from the cottonwood shadows. George agreed enthusiastically.

'Certainly was! When you says you was a roper you

wasn't just whistlin' "Dixie." I've roped against Sundown afore and always come up sucking hind tit. That's how come I never bothered to enter. But, I declare, Nashville! That's a long face for a man just got the blue ribbon.'

I told him if I had a long face it was because of the way that ribbon had been presented; or the lack thereof. 'Why,' I implored, 'would the award for calf-roping be presented by a Boy Scout, whereas for folderol like yesterday's backward race we get the royal treatment? It's beyond me . . .'

'Ah-*haw!*' George raised a finger. 'It's not beyond *me*. You expected Sarah Meyerhoff to give you the royal treatment again. Goodness, Nashville; aint you heard? Princess Sarah has been – well, "disqualified" aint right. Impeached? Can you impeach a princess? Deposed? Dethroned?'

'Canned,' the Beeson said. 'They found out she's been riding in the squaw race disguised with face paint and a black wig. She won yesterday's heat going away.'

'The Squaw Race? I don't believe it.'

'Neither did Rodeo Judge Meyerhoff,' George said. 'Until some of the other squaws showed him the wig in her saddlebag. But that wasn't why they – what? – deposed her—?'

'Canned,' three or four other spectators chimed in with Beeson.

'—canned her. It wasn't because she entered and won yesterday's race under false pretenses and face paint. Pendleton folks have always let Sarah Meyerhoff get away with a lot of heel-kicking – she reminds them of her mama. No, it's because the little dickens is entered *today*, even after they caught her red-handed.'

'She's going to race?'

'In today's semi-finals. No wig or paint, neither.'

He pointed across the paddock where the racers were skittering at the starter's rope. I saw a flash of blond in the dark thicket.

'She's not an Indian!' I cried.

'She claims she is,' Sundown said. 'A lost tribe called the Levis.'

'There was a terrible fuss,' George said. 'Papa Meyerhoff pleaded with her till the world looked level. When she wouldn't back down they took back her princess crown. Whups, here they come! That's her with the willow switch between her teeth, riding the Appaloosa. Hee hee hee. The little saucebox would rather ride as a squaw than reign as a princess.'

The Squaw Race was the only race a woman could enter that first Round Up. I don't count Barrel Races, which are run one runner at a time, against a clock, and I don't count Trick Riding. Sarah Meyerhoff wasn't a clock runner or a trick rider. She was a racer, blooded to it by a blood older than any race. And she would rather ride than reign.

She was three-quarters back in the pack that first time past, sailing along on that Appaloosa mare that was as thin-bodied and economical as she was. On the next swing by she was still a good two lengths off the three other girls fighting for the lead. Just before heading into the homestretch she swung wide, close to the outside rail, where we watched. She snatched the willow switch from her teeth and raised it high, but before she gave the Appaloosa a swat she gave me another big wink, just like the night before. She cut the horse across the flank and shrieked through her teeth – 'Eee-up!' – and the Appaloosa sprang forward like an enormous jackrabbit. They crossed the finish line not two lengths ahead so much as two leaps ahead. I could tell by the pounding in my chest that the girl from the tribe of Lost Levis had won more than the Squaw Race.

I've seen high-dollar horse races and high-dollar racehorses all my life, but it's the riders that I remember. Horses come and horses go. If you want to play the racetrack forget the horses. Racehorses simply have too brief a career to draw a good bead on. Bet on the riders. They're what makes the thing go. They have a touch. Middling riders have a touch with the whip. Good riders a touch with the whip as well as the carrot. Great riders have a third touch. They have a hand for the bit and a hand for the whip and a third hand to work the heart.

When the dust settled there was as much grumbling as cheering. That blond hair didn't look very Indian. The judges' platform was buzzing with concern. Mister Meyerhoff had withdrawn from the deliberations to avoid conflict of interest and heart attack. He was sprawled back in his judge's seat red as a lobster. His two big daughters were each trying to make him take a spoonful of medicine. George clucked sympathetically at the agitated officials.

'They're in a pickle. On the one hand it don't seem right to disqualify a winner because her hide aint dark enough, whilst on the *other* if they give that towhead the Squaw Race ribbon they're liable to have an Injun uprising on their hands. What do you think they oughter do, Nashville?'

I was still too tongue-tied by that wink to have any opinion. The Beeson boy said, 'It looks to me like your friend from Tennessee has already crowned her, George – by the moon-eyed face he's making.'

Cowboys and Indians all laughed. I hadn't realized it was so obvious. An announcement from Foghorn Clancy got me off the hook.

'Ladies and gentlemen, while our judges are deliberating this predicament, I've been advised we have a special added attraction, courtesy of the Buffalo Bill Wild West Extravaganza: the world-renowned trick rider and Colleen of the Cowgirls: Miss Maggie O'Grady!'

The orange-haired woman came tearing out on her shamrock pony. She circled the track, fanning that painted rump until the fat little pony was smoking as hot as Sarah's Appaloosa. The point she was making was obvious: if they were going to open the racing up to non-squaws then shouldn't the Colleen of the Cowgirls get consideration, too? Prairie Rose Henderson galloped out and joined the O'Grady woman for the second lap, fanning just as hard and smoking just as fast. The crowd cheered approval; the deliberations on the platform became more complicated and heated. On a hunch I reined Stoney away from the rail and trotted to the watering trough.

Sarah Meyerhoff was wiping down her sweated mare with a damp bath towel. Her hair was sweated to her cheeks and forehead. She gave me a wicked grin when I rode up.

'What do you think, Colonel Spain? Can I ride?'

'You certainly can, Miss Meyerhoff. Like a bird on the wind.'

'You and your animal look a little peaked, Colonel. Are you sure you're getting proper nourishment?'

I didn't know what to answer.

'Why don't you trot over to our booth?' she said. 'I bet Papa and my sisters can come up with a nice snack.'

Like the dumbest bunny in the hutch I pointed out that neither her papa nor her sisters were at the booth; they were at the judges' stand. Her grin got wickeder.

'In that case just trot over and wait, *some*body will take care of you. You can wait in the covered wagon. It's peaceful and private. *Yah!*'

She popped Stoney with the towel. He bounded away in a startled lope. When I glanced back she was dipping the towel in the water again.

I saw what she meant about the covered wagon. It was pulled into the ash grove enough to be private yet commanded a nice view of the arena out the canvas flap at the rear. The wagon bed was loaded with sacks of flour and sugar and dried apples. A doubled quilt was arranged along one side. It looked inviting but I could not bring myself to actually crawl inside. I tied Stoney to a spoke and leaned against the wagon, waiting. Stoney nuzzled the canvas, excited by the smells. After a while I scooped out a hatful of dried apples and we chewed away, waiting. We were on our second hatful when Foghorn Clancy climbed up to his crow's nest.

'Your attention *please!* After deep delib*era*tion our panel says the Squaw Race ribbon will go to . . . Mary Elizabeth Crowhop of the Yakima Nation!' There were cheers and boos both. 'Ah, but wait! A *new* purse has been made available for a brand-new event! To-*morrow* . . . after the conclusion of the saddlebronc finals . . . a Cowgirl *Relay* will be held, the first of its kind. Three laps, three different mounts, three hundred dollars – winner take all. How do you all like *them* apples?'

There was thoughtful applause. This was a work of diplomatic genius on the judges' part; the three mounts meant it wouldn't just be the best horse that won, but the best horseman. Or horse*person*, I guess. I certainly approved. From what I had seen of Sarah's work on that bony Appaloosa I felt she could get three of *any*thing to bust a gut for her, whether they had four legs or two.

I waited until the next event was rung, then rode back to the corrals, slumped in the saddle and disappointed. Sarah nearly ran me down. She was back on the Appaloosa with two lean ponies strung out behind. She barely slowed to speak.

'My apologies, Mister Spain. I have to test out these other two nags for tomorrow. You understand. Yee-*up!*'

She tore out of sight in the maze of corrals. Of course I understood. But I was stung, nonetheless. When you got down to the rub, it looked like Little Miss Saucebox would rather ride than romance, too.

I set my jaw and spurred Stonewall back toward the jousts – a knight alone.

Chapter Thirteen

*Put the Shine Back
on the Shoes*

The derned old rodeo reeled on, one event dissolving
into the next like shadows into smoke. That Indian tea
was still working its spell. I think that's why Sundown
partnered with me that second day more than George.
Maybe it's also the reason that day's events are lit so
strange in my memories. I can still see Sundown's face
across the horns of the first steer I ever bulldogged.
The sharp dark mouth looks chiseled into the sunlight.
'Not yet,' he kept repeating as he hazed the steer closer
to Stoney's line. 'Not yet, not yet.' Then he nodded and
I dived. I got a good hammerlock on the steer's horns
but the beast was too heavy.

'Bite 'em!' Sundown yelled, reining around. 'A
cow's nose is just as tender as a horse's.'

I leaned all the way over the animal's head and sunk
my teeth into his upper lip. I bowed backwards and he
flopped over in my lap, bellering. I stuck both arms in
the air and held him with my teeth.

'Bite 'em lip!' the crowd cheered.

Sundown caught Stoney and led him over. When we
rode out there was George sitting on the haybales with
the Pinkertons again, just to make them ill-at-ease. He
had his big watch in one hand. He pursed his lips and
gave a low whistle.

'I calculate you got second money, Nashville. Right behind that Injun friend of yours there. Look like this ol' black bunnyrabbit is going to have to wake up and get to hoppin', or you two turtles is going to sneak off and leave him.'

His calculations were a shade hasty. A last-minute entry employed the same toothy trick I had used and edged me out. It was Prairie Rose Henderson. She had the better equipment, teeth-wise. George joined the three of us under the platform while the clerk was counting out our silver dollars. He doffed his hat to Prairie Rose.

'I aint surprised you knows how to bite 'em down, Miss Henderson; you been wrestling beef for old Abner Henderson since you could walk. But where do you suppose our lanky Tennessee twister learned that trick?'

The big girl grinned and shrugged. Sundown answered for her.

'You ain't the only teacher in this cow college,' he let George know. 'Some of the rest of us knows a couple of tricks.' Sundown often remarked that there really aint but two basic skills to rodeoing: there's catching holt and there's staying on – ropin' and ridin'. Everything else is just tricks.

Another memory that stands out was Saddlebull Riding. Teams of three were allowed for this event, so Sundown and George and I got to team up. A bunch of angry young bulls were herded up to the gate, along with one grumpy old buffalo the Round Up promoters had mixed in for the novelty.

'Can you bring them out for us, Bill?' Foghorn Clancy called. Buffalo Bill stood up and leveled a Sharps rifle. It blew a cloud of phony smoke. The latch flew open wide and the bulls stampeded into the arena. Cowboys took off running after them with ropes and saddles, leaving the three of us in their dust. For all my partners' skill and tricks, they were not footracers. Out of the saddle they were poky and gimpy, and rather circumspect about extending their enery too quick. Soon the only animal in sight was the sullen old bison.

'Rope the buffer,' George panted to his friend. 'I can ride him if the boy can saddle him.'

He heel-snagged a hind leg and Sundown got his rope over the massive head. When I tried to slip up on his hind side the brute spun to face me and stepped on my foot. I dropped the saddle and grabbed my boot toe. George and Sundown were being snapped to and fro like poppers on two bullwhips.

'Get a shoeshine later, Nashville!' George yelled. 'Saddle him afore he jerks our livers out.'

I threw the saddle over the buffalo's hump and grabbed a quick cinch. He didn't give me time to double it back.

'Close enough!' Sundown yelled. 'Rules say the saddle has to be secured. It's secured. Get on, George Fletcher!'

George Fletcher got on. The animal bellered with indignation. Buffalo guns he could understand. Arrows. Spears. But a saddle and rider? He erupted like a volcano blowing a plug of brown lava into the sky. But his fury made him clumsy. He got his hindlegs tangled in my heel rope. He teetered a moment, then crashed to his belly with a thunderous grunt. This allowed George to hop back into the saddle. When the bison thrashed to his feet he took off the way he'd come, straight back toward the finish line. The uncinched saddle started slipping. George let it slip and knotted his fingers in the curly mane. The saddle slipped all the way under the belly. George grabbed the cinch belt. Sundown and I chased the buffalo soldier and his wooly steed across the finish line to the enormous delight of the spectators. We were rapidly becoming the crowd's favorites.

The Barrel Races were scheduled after the Saddle-bull Ride. I checked the roster. Dozens of cowgirls were signed up but no Sarah Meyerhoff or Lost Levis Woman. She was concentrating on tomorrow's race. A lot of formalities were to follow the Barrel Races – speeching and parading and official folderol – so we had a long break before the Saddlebronc competition.

Sundown collected our little purse from the Saddle-bull Ride, and the three of us rode down to the little waterfall to divvy up and wash off. There was a shady stand of Russian olives along the pool. We unsaddled our horses and let them crop at the graygreen leaves. From his saddlebag George took his toilet kit: a bar of soap, his jar of pomade, and a straight razor rolled up in a ragged towel. He lathered up and got down on his knees to shave, using the pool for a mirror. When he was finished he passed his toiletries on to Sundown and me, not that we asked. Or even thanked him, as I recall. Things had become that familiar.

I washed off as much of the red Pendleton dirt as I could but declined the use of the razor. So did Sundown. He unbraided his hair and set to brushing it. George's lilac pomade was all the cosmetic he cared for.

It was peaceful there by the little river. There didn't seem to be anything to say, and nobody said anything. The sound of applause carried occasionally down from the rodeo stands, polite and respectful. The cliff swallows came out of their mud nests across the river and dipped and dived at the gnats.

George dried off with the towel and put his shirt back on. He settled down with his back to a boulder and his hat over his face. I decided to study the inside of my hat a while, myself. I felt clean and comfortable, listening to the swallows and the water gushing over that big boulder.

By the time Clancy's bell signaled an end to the formalities in the arena the sun was plopped on the horizon like the yolk of a big egg. Our horses were standing heads down, dozing; the swallows had flown back to their cliffs and Sundown was still brushing.

George stood up and stretched. 'You better stuff that mane in your hat, Sundog. Them broncs don't care if you're braided.'

'No hurry,' Sundown replied. 'Plenty time.'

He was right. We were loping for the gate when we recognized the sound of the O'Grady woman's bugle. Foghorn Clancy announced another added attraction. There wasn't much applause. The audience's enthusiasm for these added attractions seemed considerably diminished. When we reached the rail we saw the show wagon in the arena with its sideboards spread. Someone had accepted the challenge.

Up in the prizefight ring with Gotch and Mister Handles were two cowboys. They were in the near corner with their backs to us. They were dressed completely identical except one of them had his arm in a white sling. The Beeson twins. They looked identically drunk, too. The broken-armed one was trying to help his brother off with his boots. They kept stumbling over the three-legged stool in their corner. Sundown shook his head and gave a mournful grunt at the sight. George tried to take the brighter view.

'Grunt if you will, Mister Jackson,' he said. 'When it comes to sportin' events, you got to give them Beeson boys credit: they got spunk.'

The Indian wasn't giving anybody credit for acting the fool. 'More spunk than sense,' he said. He'd seen what happened with Flapjack; he knew this was likely to be a repeat. He turned his back and rode off toward the clerk's table before the wrestling match began.

Sundown was wise not to watch. It was as ugly as it was uneven, with nothing sporting about it whatsoever. There wasn't even a bell. When the carrot-topped cowboy reached to shake hands the giant simply scooped him up in the flying mare, spun him around, and slammed him on his back. Dust rose like smoke from the canvas mat. Gotch then rolled the groggy lad over, grabbed a foot, then sat down on the base of his opponent's spine, hard. The boy gave a wheeze that could have been a breathless attempt to say uncle, but Gotch wasn't about to let up. He twisted the cowboy's legs into a toehold with the swift skill of a pretzel maker and heaved back on the toe. The denim ripped and the freckled knee popped out through. The other brother was rushing back and forth outside the ropes, shouting, 'He gives up, you sonofabitch! He *said* uncle!'

Even after the white arm-sling was tossed over the ropes to signal surrender, Gotch still would not relent. The giant had to have one last heave. Everybody in the stadium heard the knee crack.

It was both unfair and uncalled for. I thought the crowd would surely boo, but they didn't. When Gotch clasped his hands over his head in victory the citizens gave him the same applause they would give a calfroper or a bulldogger. So some dumb animal gets stove in or knocked silly? You can't run a rodeo without busting some bones any more than you can make an omelette without cracking eggs.

George and some of the other cowboys trotted out to have a closer look at the damage, but I'd seen enough. I reined about and rode away before I upchucked all those dried apples. It wasn't just the cruel cracking of an innocent boy's kneebone, it was all the cruelty, to all the innocent bones. Riding past the judges' platform, I overheard a tirade that made it clear that at least one of those officials shared my disgust.

'I by Christ will not stand for any more of that pug-ugly crap, Oliver, I don't give a hoot in hell *how* much publicity Mister Buffalo Bill Cody might throw our way. We're the one's got this tiger by the tail – the people of Pendleton! It might whup us or we might whup it, but I'm goddamned if I'll let a bunch of bullies and bullshitters cage it up as part of their *traveling* show!'

Mister Kell had Oliver Nordstrum cornered against the rear rail of the platform and was giving him what for. Nordstrum was um-ing and ah-ing and trying to mollify the old rancher.

'Cecil, you're right. Absolutely. No more pug-ugly cruelties. But, if you recall, the esteemed Mister Cody has paid for the privilege of advertising his Wild West Extravaganza out in the arena, and paid handsomely. He was also the one that contacted Mister Clancy for us, to say nothing of his contacts in the Boise banking circles.'

'Alright, alright! But I want you to tell the esteemed Mister Cody that come tomorrow he does his advertising *after* the show. I don't want that zoo of his dirtying up our arena until our final go round is finished.'

'Why don't you tell him yourself, Cecil? He'll be at my railroad dinner party tonight.'

'I don't know as I'll be at your damn party. I got chores, you know. A wheat farm to work—'

'I know you have chores, Cecil. You've worked harder on this event than all the rest of us laid end to end, *plus* kept up with your farm chores. But every farmer knows there's a time to plant and a time to reap. Enjoy the reaping, old chum; you certainly have earned it.'

'Alright, Oliver. But there's another thing every farmer knows: that you got to scrape your boots on the porch if you want to keep shit out of the parlor.'

Foghorn Clancy began calling the Saddlebronc contestants on deck. The hawknosed old rancher let Nordstrum off the rail and they passed out of range of my eavesdropping. I had to grin. It put the shine back on the shoes, overhearing that. Just because some things out west were still untamed didn't necessarily mean they had to be unfair – not as long as people like Cecil Kell kept hold of the reins. When Foghorn Clancy called my name I trotted out with my spirits resurrected.

I had drawn a pussel-gutted old pinto called Jumping Beans. When he took off in a rapid rattle of little bucking jumps I concluded he must have got the name because he was raised on them. Jumping Beans wasn't anywhere near the bronc Mister Sweeney was, and my ride was pretty lackluster. But everybody else's was, too. The sickening crack of that knee breaking had cast a pall over the animals as well as the riders. It had been two hard hot days, and the cowboys needed a break from the dusty arena. Everybody headed to that half-built bar under the stands without waiting to hear the day's point tally.

Even this place was strangely subdued. Cowboys lounged about the walk talking soft and smoking. Dignitaries exchanged confidences, gamblers compared scores. The only loud voice was a woman's: Nadine Rose. The leather-lunged reporter was striding to and fro in front of her tent, dictating from a shorthand pad. The telegraph operator tapped out the message, wincing at the louder phrases.

'*So*, stop. One more *anxious night*, stop. Before history crowns the *First* All Round *Champion Cowboy* of the *Western World,* exclamation point. Will it be the Rough Riding *Redskin*, dash. Or the *Brown Buckeroo*, question mark. And *where* do these uncrowned *kings* pass this *auspicious eve*, question mark. *The noble Indian* we see standing in picturesque solitude on the *idyllic banks* of – What? Idyllic?'

Her voice was louder still when she had to spell a word for her telegraph man. '*I-D-Y-L-L-I-C* . . . On the *Idyllic banks* of the *Umatilla* River – What? Umatilla? *U-M-A-T-I-L-L-A!*'

The conversation on both sides of the swinging door was cowed by the woman's stentorian voice. And her purple prose made a lot of riders a little sheepish with embarrassment. I found me a place back near the wall where somebody had brought a bucket of wash water and a tray of half-drunk drinks. Rather than let warm water or the neglected whiskeys go to waste, I sat down on a barrel, took off my boot, and put my foot in the bucket. The drinks were half warm and the water half cold but it felt good on the buise that buffalo had given me.

George and Sundown came in and I waved at them

through the cigar smoke. They helped me consolidate the drinks and stack the glasses so they could share a seat on the barrel. The reporter had resumed her dictation.

'The *coal-skinned cowboy*, question mark. We see him on the bank opposite his Indian friend, spitting the seeds from one of Oregon's famous *Hermiston melons* into the *babbling brook,* stop.'

'Stuffy as a tomb in here,' George observed. 'Like as if somebody was hogging up the air.'

'These *simplehearted spirits* are a credit to their races as well as our young nation, semicolon, and I say Raise your goblet to these rough riders, America, semicolon, for these are the heroes of your *future*, exclamation point.'

'Pipes like dat,' George said, 'I don't see why she need de telegraph wire.' He stood and raised his glass. 'I pre-pose a toast to the *real* Rough Rider. President Theodore *Rose-y-velt*, exclamation point!'

Never one to be cowed sheepish, George boomed this toast in a baritone voice far louder than any woman could come close to, however leather-lunged. Everybody cheered. Someone refilled his glass. The moment Nadine Rose started to resume her dictation George raised his drink in another toast: 'To the mighty E-*Man*cipator: Honest Abraham *Lincoln!*'

Everybody cheered louder. The embarrassing dictation stopped. The roomful of cowboys grinned at each other. Nadine Rose started up again and another cowboy bawled a toast to John L. Sullivan. Another to Daniel Boone. And Jim Bridger, and Johnny Appleseed. Every time the reporter started, someone gave a toast. We tried not to laugh ungraciously at the woman's consternation, but it was difficult. No longer were we chance strangers; we were comrades, stirred together by the day's common blood, amusing ourselves at the expense of a non-combatant. George really had the knack of getting things stirred together.

The cowboys toasted until they were about toasted out. I reckoned it was about time to honor the noble South. I managed to stand and raise my Stars and Bars boot like a goblet.

'To the Great Gray *Soldier!* General Robert! E! *Jeee-sus*—'

Sue Lin had materialized out of a trapdoor to pour a bucket of steaming water over my foot. She gave me a smile and vanished back down the steamy portal. Sundown completed the toast for me:

'General Robert E. *Custer!*'

The toasting might have gone on all evening but for the appearance of Buffalo Bill and his troupe. Mister Handles was toting a round leather mapcase and Gotch had a peppermint stick stuck in one corner of his humorless grin. Nordstrum limped along behind with the O'Grady woman on his arm like a gaudy walking cane. The Pinkertons loitered at the door, eyeing the crowd. The troupe came to a halt in front of George and Sundown. Buffalo Bill squinted down at the Indian.

'You. Jackson. Spare us a minute? Mister Handles and I would like your opinion on some sketches. There's a table . . .'

Without waiting for an answer, the old showman and his barker headed for a crowded table. It cleared of customers as they approached. Sundown frowned, then rose to his feet and followed. George stood as well, hat in hand, deliberating whether to join them. Gotch stepped in front of him and pressed him back to his seat with his heavy blue gaze. Nordstrum beamed with affection and rubbed George's head.

'You monkey. Been making speeches, I hear.'

'Just perposing a few toasts, Mistah Oliver.'

'Capital idea.' He waved to the bartender. 'Pour 'em all around. Have you proposed one for the president, George?'

'Yessir, first off.'

'And the state?'

'Three or four times. Plus Washington and Montana.'

'Then let us lift one—' He surprised me with a quick smile. '—to the Volunteer State, the great state of Tennessee.'

I stood to attention as well as I could with one foot in the bucket of water. The O'Grady woman noticed my plight and bent to look.

'I *saw* that humpy divil step on you, Johnny. A monster! It's a great boon the hunters done us to rid the earth of their ugly multitudes. I trust you're all right?' Her voice was soothing and her smile sympathetic.

'Just mashed my great toe, ma'am. All I need's a little beans and shuteye and I'll be fine by tomorrow.'

'Why not have him join us, Oliver? What better place for him to recuperate? I could drive him over and you could come in the show wagon, later. I'd have time to examine his wound and see to his sustenance both at once.'

'Excellent idea, Madam O'Grady. I'm sure we could offer him better fare than beans.'

I looked at George. The only advice he offered was a raise of eyebrows. I glanced over at Buffalo Bill's table but Sundown was busy studying a large Wild West poster that Mister Handles had unrolled. The poster depicted a warpainted savage holding the reins of a pinto stallion. The face beneath the warpaint was obviously intended as the likeness of a much younger Sundown Jackson.

'I am a certified nurse as well as trick rider, Johnny,' the O'Grady woman prompted. 'Just ask Mister Nordstrum.'

'Upon my word, she is, son, and an absolute jewel with podiatric problems. Such a touch! I guarantee she'll make you comfortable.'

'That I will, honey-lad, that I will. What do you say?'

What could I say? I was utterly tongue-tied by the invitation. George raised his shoulders this time.

'Free food and a foot rub is a hard invite to turn down, Nashville. Ride with the lady. I'll lead your horse on up to the barn . . . soon's Mars Gotch and me finishes our business. He says he's gonter put me in breeches of contract if I don't make good on the match I promised. What size is them breeches, Mars Gotch?'

'Tight,' Gotch grinned. The grin spread wider and tighter until the peppermint stick shattered. Even his lips had muscles. The O'Grady woman picked up my boot and pulled me toward the swinging doors.

'Look at you staggerin' about. You're perished with exhaustion. Where did you sleep last night?'

'I slept in Mister Jackson's teepee, ma'am. Tried to, anyways. I could use a night's rest.'

'Why of course you could,' she said. She leaned me against one of the two-by-four studs where the wall never got finished. 'You wait right here and I'll get Oliver's hoopy.'

I wasn't sure what a hoopy was till I saw the gold hood-ornament come boring out of its own dust cloud to pick me up.

Chapter Fourteen

Mint Juleps and Dark Intrigue

While you was resting, Number Nine and I took a little voyage out of the hospital. 'Going to take the air,' I tell the nurse. Since my blood sugar is stabilized she thinks that's a fine idea.

'Now you'll see,' I tell Number Nine. He says Sure, right. Number Nine is a doubter.

The old path alongside the river is still there. The falls is still there. The Russian olives . . . the pool . . . but that's all.

'The rock is gone!'

'Always been gone,' Number Nine says. 'All my life.'

'Then look here! These chips and chunks!'

'Just riprap and rubble. It's everywhere in Umatilla County.'

'Not like this.' I hold one up so the moon can shine through. 'It's mahogany obsidian! Somebody dynamited it.'

Number Nine says, 'Sure, right.'

I'm not surprised by his skepticism, so I don't press the issue. *Mister Spain*, I tell myself; *learned a long time ago doubters have to be shown everything twice and told it three times* . . . I learned the lesson well, waiting for that hoopy to arrive.

The O'Grady woman tooted her way through the

loitering crowd right to the walk. 'Whatcha say, Sugar Pie? Ever been for a roll in a Rolls?'

'I never been for a roll in any machine, ma'am, unless you count steam trains. I thought you was spoofing.'

'I am not one to spoof, Johnny. Get in.'

Now both feet were getting cold. 'I kind of hate to go off and leave my friends and my horse.'

'Your friends are occupied, Sugar, and your horse could use a rest. So could you, in my professional opinion.' She reached across. 'Get in. That great toe's swole to perishin'. If it isn't drained and wrapped you won't be gettin' it back in that lovely boot for months, much less a saddle stirrup. So *whisht* amd climb aboard, you teeterin' stork – everybody's glimmin' at us . . .'

That's what in fact convinced me: the thought of everybody watching me being chauffeured through town in a Rolls-Royce with a golden hood-ornament by a woman with orange hair – especially the thought of a certain snooty cowgirl. I whisht and climbed aboard and we went dusting toward town. I sneaked a last casual look over my shoulder but the only girl I saw was Sue Lin. She was standing in the swinging doorway, a wooden bucket in one hand and a towel in the other.

Nordstrum's private railcar sat on its own little siding alongside the Round Up Special. Telegraph wires ran through a window and a telescope was mounted on the railcar's rear platform. I followed the O'Grady woman across the cinders in a one-booted hop. She unlocked the door and pulled me up the steps. The car room was even more sumptuous than I remembered – walnut gun cases; maroon carpets;

gilt-framed pictures of horses and riders. At one end, above an ornate mahogany desk, the head of an ugly mustang was mounted on the wall. At the other end the huge leanback chair waited like a plutocrat's throne.

'Ah, it's near ruined you look, Sugar. Sit there and rest in Oliver's therapeutic leanback while I get us some privacy.'

Nordstrum had built himself walls that accordioned out. The woman smiled through the crack. 'I'll nip to the train next door and fetch my kip.' The walls closed and I was alone with the chair. Therapeutic was right; I was asleep before the leather stopped creaking.

When I opened my eyes again the car's oil lamps had been turned on and my damaged foot was once more immersed – in ice water this time, in a porcelain basin.

'I hated to wake you, Sugar, but it's past time we were taking the pressure off that toe. Now open wide, there's a lad. You'll soon be grinnin' like the moon of May. Lean back and let Nurse O'Grady entertain you with the story of her wicked life.'

When I could unscrew my face after the spoonful of bitter syrup she'd forced in my mouth, I looked her over. Nurse O'Grady had attached a white cap with a red cross atop her orange hair but that was as far as her medical uniform went. She had changed out of her doeskin cowgirl outfit into a gauzy gown. You could see the lamplight right through it, among other things.

She said before she had thrown in with the Wild West gang she had been a head nurse at Bronx General Hospital, hard though it might be to believe. I believed it the moment she touched me. It was a nurse's touch, for all the calluses and rope burns. And under her rough talk the woman's voice was as smooth as Irish

201

cream. She prattled on about her family in Galway and about her training at St Brigid's in Brooklyn. She was proud that she had paid for her schooling by herself entirely, though she often had to do some things good girls from fine families would not have been proud of, surely. But she got her certificate, just like the good girls. I asked how it came about, her going from being a New York City nurse to a Wild West Show queen.

'Queen indeed,' she laughed. 'How it came about, Mister Honey, was purely a slice of chance, and I just happened to get the side with butter on it. You see, certain sportin' occasions at Madison Square Garden required a nurse on duty. I *chancet* to draw that duty for Buffalo Bill's Wild West Extravaganza the night himself chancet to have a little "riding mishap" – was what the newspapers later called it. He got a trifle too fortified from that silver canteen is what I called it – *over*-fortified – and his saddle got away from him on one of them grand gallops that's his specialty. Not a bad fall. Rather elegant, as a matter of fact. But he just *chancet* to land on the sharpshooter gal coming out with her basket of target bottles. Broke her collarbone and most of her bottles. Nicked old Buffalo up like a loser in a knife fight. I stopped the bleeding, sewed shut the nicks, and patched up his injured pride. So?' She smiled and shrugged her gauzy shoulders. 'It's ridin' and shootin' and patchin' I was doing at the very following show at Coney Island. Nurse Maggie Pageen was now also Maggie O'Grady, Colleen of the Cowgirls.'

'Certainly, you must have ridden previously.'

'Previous to that I had never been on anything with more than two legs, nor fired as much as a cork gun.'

'That is positively amazing.'

'You develop a good shootin' eye in the nursin' duty.' She pulled my foot from the ice water and felt it with her wrist. 'Cold enough for a numbness. Has the throbbin' stopped?'

I told her it almost had, and that the numbness had worked its way clear up to the tip of my nose.

'That would be the tot of J. Collis Brown's I spooned you: the British Empire's greatest contribution to the merciful science of medicine. If you could move that lamp on Oliver's desk this way?'

With the lamp shining on my foot she pulled out the long hatpin that held her nurse's cap in place. She removed the lamp's chimney and held the pin in the flame.

'Whoa!' I protested. 'That toe's been plagued a-plenty—'

'Not a dollop to plagued it *will* be if we don't relieve that congestion of blood. See how purple swole it is? Tomorrow that unhappy toe will be as big as an eggplant and throbbin' like one of those Indian drums if we don't drain it. The pin point's gone red. Lean back and trust your angels, Sweetface; Nurse O'Grady guarantees you won't feel a blessed thing but relief and gratitude.'

She set the red-hot point of the hatpin on top of the purple toenail, but she didn't stick it in. She let it burn down of its own weight. A curl of smoke rose but I felt no pain.

'Smells like a hot horseshoe on a hoof, doesn't it? Same blessed thing: no nerve endings in horse hooves or toenails. So there's no pain until you reach the — steady now – the *quick!*'

Pain shot up my leg and a gusher of black blood

spewed into the air. She held my foot in her callused palm and toweled at the spew until it stopped. The throbbing was completely gone.

'I swear, ma'am – Miss O'Grady – that's a new one on me.'

'Maggie will suit us fine.' She smiled up at me. The spew of black blood had freckled her throat and shoulders, and her gown looked ruined. She dipped the towel in the ice water and wrapped it tight around my foot. 'Now relax your skinny bones and I'll give you the Galway version of the Swedish massage.' She rose and walked to the rear of the chair and tilted it farther back. 'You can be regalin' me with *your* life story, while I rub, Mister Honey . . . by way of payin' for the service.'

Regale I did. As those callused hands worked down my collar under my neck, coaxing out the kinks and rubbing them away, I found myself running on gloomily about pretty near everything, especially about my feelings for George and Sundown and Sarah Meyerhoff and how I yearned to impress them.

'Why so down in the mouth about that? They're all three darlings worth doting over.'

'But why am I so all-fired anxious to impress them? All my life I've been among gentlemen of state and ladies of distinction. Bluebloods and highborns that I never cared a fig about impressing. Now look at me: I'm busting my dern back to measure up in the eyes of an Indian brave, a Negro man, and a Hebrew girl trying to pass herself off as a squaw! Can you explain a highborn Southern gentleman acting so silly?'

I felt something drip on my face. The woman withdrew her hands and turned away, wiping her cheeks.

'No, Sugar, I cannot explain it,' she said. 'But as a lowborn shantytown tart, I can certainly be moved by it. Whisht! Is that a surrey cloppin' across the track?' She pushed aside a curtain and peeked out. 'Blast! It's Oliver and the Buffalo Billy Goat himself. Well, Johnny-love, it looks like our time is up. I'd best be gettin' out of this silly frock and spongin' off the spots – somebody could get the wrong idea.'

She bent quick to kiss me on the cheek and was gone through the folding partitions, taking the lamp with her. I knew I should rouse myself and slip away as well, just like Goldilocks before the rightful residents came home. But I was too deep in Papa Bear's chair to move, and too numb to care. I remember the walls parting briefly and a pair of shadows peeking in. They were talking in whispers.

'It's our pretty boy, Oliver,' Buffalo Bill's voice said. 'In the arms of Mother Morpheus, if I know Nurse O'Grady.'

'Boys need their mothers,' Nordstrum said. 'Let's leave him nap. What do you say to a nip of the good stuff before our guests arrive?'

The shadows retreated and the walls closed. Sometime later I heard other voices and then a lot of other voices, engaged in the festive tinkle of party talk. I couldn't make out any words until the familiar female bray of Nadine Rose joined the conversation. Then everybody had to turn up their volume to compete.

'I've never had a *mint julep* before in my *life*,' Nadine Rose said. 'Don't stir it, you say?'

'That is correct,' Oliver Nordstrum replied. 'Don't disturb the ice or the straw and sip from the bottom of your vessel.'

'And *small* sips, too,' a voice added. It was a voice I

knew but couldn't place. 'Oliver's juleps kick like a damn mule.'

There was laughter. Nordstrum confessed the drinks were strong but the fault was not really his, it was Mister Cody's. 'I coaxed the recipe from him after his show in Louisville last fall, and merely passed it on to my help. The secret is the shaved ice.'

'The secret is *not* the shaved ice.' That voice again! 'The secret is having the hired help to *shave* it. Oliver's always been slick at hiring help.' I knew it as certain as I knew my father's voice, or my uncles' – but I was danged if I could get a handle on it.

'What ex*act*ly,' Nadine Rose interjected, '*is* your position with the Wild West Extravaganza, Mister Nordstrum?'

'With the Buffalo Bill Show? Good God forbid. I deal in grain commodities, madam. Just a simple wheat broker that enjoys a little light sport now and then.'

'I witnessed you betting a pretty weighty wad for *light sport*, Mister Nordstrum. Which one of them have you got it riding on?'

'My wad?' Nordstrum laughed. 'Why on neither of them, dear woman, as well as both. I've been covering all bets on George and Sundown, either way. The money will just about even out, give or take two bits.'

'Oliver hedges his bets,' that voice said. 'Even when he's got an ace up his sleeve he hedges his bets.'

'E*specially* when I've got an ace up my sleeve, old friend. Protect your privates first, I say. *Publicly*, Miss Rose, I'm pulling for both of our noble savages. A simple gesture of impartiality. My old schoolchum here is pulling for George Fletcher, for sentimental reasons. Just like Merchant Meyerhoff and the underground

Chinamen. Mister Cody is pulling for the Indian because he hasn't had a Red Star in his Wild West Firmament since Chief Sitting Bull died.'

'Is that so, Mister Cody?' Nadine Rose asked. 'Do I sur*mise* that you hope to feature Jackson Sundown in your traveling *show?*'

'You surmise correct, dear woman. The first World Champ cowboy and a Injun to boot. The Madison Gardens won't be big enough! Mister Handles is negotiating with him right now.'

'Ah! But what if the *black* rider is the one that wins, Mister Cody?'

'Mister Gotch is on his way to negotiate about *that* problem.'

When Nordstrum was sure the interruption was over he resumed his commentary. 'But *privately*, Miss Rose, my wad is riding on a different cowboy altogether.' I could hear his heavy-heeled boot pacing around on the other side of my cardboard wall. 'I have been an avid supporter of George Fletcher and Sundown Jackson since the first day I saw them ride, decades ago. Geniuses. Wizards! I've stood their entrance fees in penny-ante pony shows from California to Calgary, and never dunned them a *dime* interest. I've gone their bail when they needed it, and I have had them locked up when they needed that.'

The pacing stopped. His tone had become secretive, filled with conspiracy and intrigue.

'But there is more going on here than a one-time sporting event. For all that Nigger George and Indian Jack are wizards in the saddle, to be frank and off the record, Miss Rose – put away your little notepad – neither of them is the cowboy the Pendleton Round Up needs for its poster. Not for the long haul.'

'Yessir, the long haul,' that voice said. 'Oliver's right about that, too.'

'Our trademark cowboy has to be a fair-haired All-American Youth Eternal!' Nordstrum went on. 'An ageless face for the ages! Sundown and George have served in good stead to get us this far, but they are getting rather long in the tooth to be called cow*boys*. We need a trademark that is a little longer-futured and lighter-complexioned, and I think we have found him. Or he has found us, rather.'

'I surmise you mean Tall, Dark, and Handsome from Dixie?'

'Tall, Dark, Handsome, and *Young*, madam. That's who my wad is riding on.'

I tried to keep my ears perked but the rest of me was sinking fast. Truth is, I was more interested in sleep than intrigue. I couldn't remember how long it had been since I got a good night's rest. That first night I had spent clambering all over a train like a drunk hobo. The next night I traipsed all over town and ended up in a hole in the ground. Last night I had bedded down in a teepee full of flapping shadows. So I let myself sink, perfectly satisfied that I had *earned* this deep-leather therapy. The moon leaned in the window and promised to stand guard against any disturbance.

The moon is not a reliable sentry. When a hard hand shakes me the moon is gone from the train window, and it is Nurse O'Grady leaning over me. She is in her Arabian Nights outfit and carries a brass lamp smoky enough for a dozen genies. As my eyes grow accustomed to the light, I see that Louise and Reverend Linkhorn are with her. On the other side of the thin partition Nordstrum's railroad party is still scheming away.

'See if you can get your boot on, Sugar,' she whispers. 'It seems that at least two of those three darlings you dote on are in trouble. This might be your opportunity to do some impressin'.'

Chapter Fifteen

Go in de Tank?

My foot went back in the boot just fine. Nurse O'Grady
had even darned my sock. We slipped through the
accordion walls and ducked on out the car's shadowy
back door, completely unnoticed by the revelers in the
gaslit glare up forward. The whole railyard was festive
with the lamplight and laughter spilling from the
windows of Nordstrum's party car. A dozen or more
horses were parked alongside the surrey and the
automobile. The mule-drawn show wagon was there,
too, its wrestling ring folded up for town travel. Louise
kicked cinders the wagon's direction, cursing Cajun
curses. I asked her for a little more explanation about
our midnight mission.

'You know that ape-armed mistake-of-nature and his
keeper?' Louise said. 'The Reverend and me were
outside shaving ice when they pulled in on that damn
circus wagon. They was drinking and jawing and
never seen us. Mister Buffalo come out on the steps
and the Reverend and me heard them insinuating
some nasty business—'

'Beasts out of Babylon!' Reverend Linkhorn
declared. There was still some clown white around his
mouth. 'Foxes that spoil the vine!'

'Gotch and Mister Handles are curs and bullies for

certain,' the O'Grady woman agreed. 'They're also dreadful liars. So there may be nothing at all to their insinuating, as Miss Jubal calls it. Drunk bully talk. However, to be on the safe side—'

'Insinuating what business?' I was waking up fast in the midnight cool. 'What did they say?'

'They told Mister Buffalo that Mister Nigger George and Mister Injun Jack thought themselves to be pretty tough customers, until they got a bit of tenderized,' Louise said. 'Then they were more 'menable to the offers they were being offered.'

'Offers? What kind of offers?'

The O'Grady woman answered for her. 'The kind they been offering a lot of the influential citizens,' she explained. 'The kind you don't say no at.'

That's when I finally placed that familiar voice. It was Cecil Kell's! This jarring realization made my gorge rise hot in my throat, worse than the sight of the Beeson twin's knee bone. The Wild West gang must have decided to tenderize the old rancher, too, after the way he came down on Nordstrum so hard. It was a reliable technique they used. First, ply the sucker with strong drinks and smooth talk, then make him one of those offers he can't afford to turn down. I kicked some cinders at the railcar myself.

'Come on, Nashville.' Louise tugged me out of the grasp of Nurse O'Grady. 'We can worry about them Wild West weasels later. Thank you most kindly, Miss Grady. And don't think that I include you with them damn weasels. You're what my Cajun granma call a "deep-root lady."'

The woman smiled and shook Louise's hand. 'Miss Grady the Deep-Root Lady it is. Luck to you all and yer ride-to-the-rescue,' she said and headed back for the railcar, spurs jingling across the cinders. Reverend Linkhorn called after her.

'The Good Lord bless you, ma'am. If Mister Oliver need more shaved ice tell him his colored help is gone to strop the razor.'

Nurse O'Grady waved and vanished up the steps.

Our ride-to-the-rescue was accomplished in the Reverend's ancient balloon-tired baggage wagon. This venerable vehicle was pulled by a Percheron gelding, equally ancient and ballooned. He was blowing gas from his huge hind end at every ponderous step. The Percheron is a slow animal, bred for heavy loads, not rescue missions. The slow pace was making Louise antsy.

'A little faster, Reverend. See if you can't get this big-butted wind-breaker to break into a trot! That Miss Grady has me a little bit worried.' She took the buggy whip from the Reverend. 'Hum up, Big Butt, or I'll light a match to you!'

Louise's threat was enough to hum us all up, even the Percheron. Not only could he trot, he could almost run. He was blowing steam both fore and aft by the time the black mass of George's barn hove into sight. Lamplight showed through the windows and cracks.

'The damn old dickens is still up!' Louise cursed, relieved and exasperated. 'You blamed cowboys! You think your candle has got wicks at both ends with tallow enough to—'

She stopped. Something was wrong with the big barn door. One side hung crooked, half off its hinges. Reverend Linkhorn set the brake and Louise jumped down. She caught up her skirts and hurried toward the barn, calling, 'George? You, George?' I legged after her. We reached the broken door together.

George's living quarters looked like a tornado had dropped by for a visit and made itself right at home. Fluff and feathers were everywhere. The mattress was gutted in the twisted brass tangle of the bedstead. The chest of drawers was overturned and its contents scattered. All the trophies and pictures lay smashed on the floor. A single stool stood in the middle of the ruin with a kerosene lamp sitting on it, turned up as bright as it would go. Somebody wanted to make sure the ruin was thoroughly appreciated. The Reverend came through the unhinged door, his clown frown gloomier than ever. He shook his head.

'Them that plow wickedness will reap iniquity.'

Louise made a red-clawed swipe at the air. 'Not if I get to them first they won't. Even a mistake-of-nature giant is got his sensitive places. Ah!' Her threat stopped in a sob. 'Ah sweet Lamb Jesus look at that.'

I had already seen it, dangling in the dim barn space, forlorn and ruined: the barrel. It still hung from its network of plowlines, but it had been crushed, its hoops collapsed, its polished staves turned to splinters. George wouldn't go dancing with Jenny Lynne anymore. I immediately began searching the rest of the barn, fearing more grisly remains might be waiting. The horse stall was empty, its gate trampled flat by panicked hooves.

'George?' I called. Reverend Linkhorn joined me.

'Where you at, Cousin? You stove in somewhere? Sing out so we can find you—'

'George ain't here,' Louise declared. She was on her knees at a lifted floorboard. 'His jug of kill-devil is missing. He aint here and he probably aint stove in, neither!' She was talking through a clenched smile.

'He's having one of his yearly hissy-fits, is what I think; and I bet a dollar to a doughnut hole I can deduce right exactly where! Let's go hogtie the old rip before he hurts hisself.'

This time Louise took the whip and the reins. She sawed the carriage around and headed back downriver. She muttered furiously the whole way, denouncing everything male – horses, apes, and present company notwithstanding. The Reverend and I didn't say a word. We were as overpowered by her fury as we had been by her worry.

Louise whipped the puffing horse across the moon-streaked riffles at the ford. She kept on along an old riverbank road – a dim pair of ruts through the dew-bright weeds. This brought us along the back of the rodeo grounds, the way Montanic had come with his three-wheeled wagon. The foreboding sight of teepees in the mists ahead loosened the Reverend's tongue.

'I hope that aint where you deduce our poor sheep is lost. Because if it is you aint going to talk *this* shepherd into tiptoeing teepee to teepee looking for him. Certain parties in that primitive pur-loo still aint shed their bestial natures.'

'Certain parties on that modern steamtrain where we works aint, neither, as you pointed out.' Louise let the horse ease to its plodding walk. 'Now, sit still and don't talk or we'll set their damn dogs off. Then we'll have the beasts of beasts to contend with.'

Louise didn't continue on to the breach Montanic had opened into the camp, but reined the horse left, outside the rail fence.

'Yonder's the Jackson tent,' I whispered. 'I don't see Stonewall or George's gelding. I don't even see Sundown's pinto stud.'

'Of course you don't!' Louise's whisper was more of a hiss. 'They's all off together, studs, geldings, damn fools, and all!' You could tell she was still talking through her teeth, the way the words were shredded. She suddenly reined the horse to a halt and cocked her head. 'Uh-huh. Uh-huh, didn't I tell you? Have mercy just *listen* at that. You ever hear such deliriums? Sound like two swamp creatures fighting in the gumbo.'

I realized I had been hearing those deliriums for some minutes, but had chosen to dismiss the sounds as something less unnerving – disturbed night-birds; ungreased wagon wheels; the old horse's gasworks boiling up fresh gas – but certainly nothing human. Human beings *couldn't* make sounds like that, I thought, not even in the most inspired throes of delirium. 'Have mercy indeed,' I said. The Reverend crossed himself and went to Hail-Marying like the devoutest Catholic.

'Hail Mary isn't going to do one speck of good,' Louise said through her teeth. 'You think this is any affair of Mother Mary? Or Baby Jesus? No, preacher, this is the affair of menfolks, full-grown *men*folks. Giddyup!' She popped the big rump with her buggy whip; the startled horse lurched again into movement toward the glistening river. 'Let's fish 'em out before they float away.'

Our horses were tethered in the Russian olives, stamping and rearing. Stonewall and George's big bay were tied at opposite ends of the same lariat, without hackamore or halter. They were white-eyed in the moonlight, snorting at each other. Sundown's stud was so spooked he had collapsed to his hind haunches and was baying at the moon like a wild dog. The spectacle in the pool was enough to spook any animal.

215

Two men were wallowing and wrestling in the foam below the dark obsidian boulder just like the little boys had wallowed and wrestled in their King of the Mountain game. Only this game was deadly serious. Both were naked except for scraps and tatters, and both were armed and bloodied. The Indian had a big twisted tree-root clutched by one end, like a transmogrified snake, and George had his finger through the handle of what was left of a broken jug. The jagged shard of crockery gleamed like a battle-ax as George hewed the air in front of him. Sundown was deflecting and parrying the ax blows with his root. The only reason they weren't bloodied worse was because they were so drunk. Hip-deep in water, they stumbled and went under with almost every swing. Then they would surface, bellowing and babbling. This was what had given their raving the swamp-beast quality. The voices belched from the water and echoed off the big rock, water to boulder, bank to bank, until it sounded like an entire riot of gumbo monsters. The dry crack of Louise's whip finally got their attention.

'Time out, Dog Mouf . . .' George shaded his eyes our direction as though he was looking into the sun and not a cold moon. 'I think we gots company.'

He began splashing and teetering through the water toward us, still shading his eyes. When he finally teetered near enough to perceive it was Louise, he tried to wrap what was left of his patchwork underwear around his nakedness. '*Wo*man company.' His act of modesty so unbalanced him he stumbled to his allfours and stayed that way, up to his mouth in the water.

Back at the falls the Indian was trying to take advantage of the opportunity and climb the rock

uncontested. He was pawing the slick stone ineffec-
tually, his loosening braids tangled with the water-
weed; and all the while he was chanting, singsonging
away in a whiskey-thick tongue:

> 'Witchie-tie-tie gimme raw,
> Hooraw-nickle, hooraw-nickle,
> Hooraw-nickle *hey!*
> Water-spirit feelin' running round my head,
> Makes me feel glad that I'm not dead.
> Witchie-tie-tie . . .'

George had regained his feet but seemed reluctant to
take the last few steps to the bank. Louise and her pony
whip looked more dangerous than a drunk Indian with
a tree root. He raised his broken jug in a greeting to me
and the Reverend.

'And man company and boy company, too! My, my,
all deeshere social callin' . . . *Mus'* be de full moon.
Dat's howcome me and Mars Sundown elected to
wander down disaway. The bes' time for talkin' tongue
with de spirits is when ol' Mama Moon she—'

A loud crack silenced him. 'Never mind any moon!'
The whip was not quite long enough to reach its target,
but she cracked it again, anyway. 'This is no social
call. We was up to your place and seen the ruckus. We
been fretted to a frazzle, you nappy old nitwit.'

'Why dat was nice of y'awl. Awful nice, but no ways
needful. Mars Gotch and Mars Ticket Man, wiff de
mushtash and de sleeve pistol, dey pay Uncle George a
little visit, is all. We have a little d-d-*dis-scushon*.'

He was beginning to shiver and chatter in the cold.
He looked quite old and feeble, trying to pull his rags
about his trembling frame. He smiled but that made

the picture even more pathetic. His whole face was caved in; his famous flashing grin a loose-lipped mockery of itself. Louise checked a gasp with her hand.

'My Lord. What happened to your teeth? Never mind, never mind. I don't want to know. Just come on out of there. I'm not going to ruin my blue boots lifesaving the likes of you. Ah Jesus what a sight.' Try as she might, she wasn't able to hold back the sobs. 'Ah bleeding Jesus . . . if those unnatural sonsabitches hurt you—'

'You mean dem Wil' West gennelmens? Hurt Uncle George? Naw, nary a hair. All they did was have a little interview and make a little deal. Den dey give a demon*strashun* – is how they 'splain it – to con*vince* me. Mars Buffalo got my hat for c'lateral. An' my teeth is in Mars Gotch's keepin' to remind me to *stay* convinced—'

'Convince you of what?' I asked him.

The Reverend Linkhorn slumped sitting on a mossy log. 'To convince him to lose tomorrow, of course,' he said with a gloomy sigh. 'There goes the church piano.'

'To convince me n-n-*not* to win, is more like,' George said through the shivering. 'Seems de *crown heads* of Europe is all fired up to see a *champeen cowboy* from America. And it seems it's okay if this cowboy be young or old, purty or ugly, polite as a barber or spittin' terbaccy like a grasshopper – it seems it even okay he be a *Injun* – cowboys an' Injuns go together; dass what they was discussin' with Sundown at *his* interview. They wants him to shed dat blue serge suit and ride in full savage glory, just like you sees him now . . . but *no*body, they explain very carefully to me, *ever* heard of cowboys and niggers.'

Reverend Linkhorn raised a knobbly fist. '"The iniquitous have made crooked paths; who go there shall not know peace but shall fall into the pit." Isaiah.'

'Amen, Reverend,' George said. 'And I bet ol' Isaiah be *right,* too . . . by an' by in de sky.'

'"By and by" be damned!' Louise shouted. 'I'll kill the iniquitous sonsabitches this very night.'

'Uh-huh? And how you do dat, girl? In a big western shootout?' George grinned his collapsed grin. 'In the middle of mainstreet?'

'We could get the sheriff. Til Taylor won't stand for this kind of business, crowned heads or not!'

'Uh-huh? And what charge does we bring? Barndoor-breakin'? Barrel-squeezin'? No, Miz Jubal, girl – we don't get nobody, thanks all the same. We struck a deal, see, clear and simple: Uncle George, he lose the rest of de rodeo or the rest of de teeth. "Go in de tank or in de drank," was Mars Gotch's way of puttin' it. So I says okeedoke.'

'George!' I cried. 'You can't do that.'

'I can't?'

'No, you can't.'

'And why I can't? The money they offer is better than I get for winning *two* saddles. Plus I gets back my grin and I don't have to get in the ring with that skinned gorilla. Injun Jack Sundog yonder gwine get paid double for stayin' on a bronc with no clothes. What's de matter with Nigger George gettin' de same for fallin' off fully dressed?'

A mealy-mouthed tone had come into his voice. It reminded me of the calculated whine of the old colored winos that shuffled along the low end of Beale Street. I forced my eyes from George, only to be revolted anew by the sight of our noble savage.

Sundown had staggered to the shore downstream and stopped there, bent over strangely and muttering his chant at the sand. His tangled hair stuck out every which way, like one of those wild men from Borneo you used to see in carnivals. He had his breechcloth pulled to one side and was bent over examining himself in the moonlight – for fleas? wounds? or just searching for the shrunken stub so he could take a leak? I poked my hands in my pockets and watched, considerably disillusioned. When my fingers came across that big coin I took it out and flipped it away. If this was what big medicine led to I elected to pass. Sundown was oblivious to the audience his obscene fumbling had attracted.

As we watched he fell to one side and lay there in that same bent-over posture, like a carved gargoyle cracked off the cathedral wall. Louise sobbed at my side.

''Least the poor soul made it to land,' she said. 'Alright, Grampa Fletcher, your sorry carcass is next.' Louise lifted her skirts and began wading toward him, blue boots or no. When the water reached the boot tops she held out the stiff buggy whip. 'Grab on before you float away like an old cow chip. Grab on, I say! I'm sick to death of you cussed men – expiring from old age before you get around to growing up! I *told* you to stay away from this nonsense, didn't I? You two oughta heard the racket you was making. Spirit tongues my foot! I say it was ol' Poker Tail, talkin' to his joker fools . . .'

'Yes'm,' George shivered. He took the braided leather of the whip and let himself be towed through the black water to the riverbank. 'But den who else ol' Poker got to talk to?'

We hauled the two sodden wrecks home in the baggage cart, the horses tied in a line behind. I carried the unconscious Sundown to the rail fence behind his teepee and propped him there. Louise tied his horse alongside. We lobbed clods against the hide of the teepee until a woman wrapped in a blanket came out and looked at us. Without a word she fetched out another half-dozen blanket-wrapped females and they took our charge off our hands. He was still in that self-examining posture as they dragged him through the flap.

George, on the other hand, was limp as a noodle. Ribby and hollow as he looked, I wasn't able to carry him into his barn by myself. He was like a long balloon full of water. I'd get one end on my shoulders and the other end would siphon him back to the ground. It finally took the Reverend and me under each armpit and Louise at the feet; even then he siphoned out of our grasp several times before we could get him to the pallet Louise had spread for him on the hay. Louise was sure that enough of his bed could be salvaged to accommodate me but I was no more inclined to spend what was left of the ruined night in George Fletcher's barn than I was in Jackson Sundown's teepee. I began saddling Stonewall.

'I know a nice hole,' I told Louise and the old man. 'It's the only place I've had any peace in since I came to this crazy country.'

As I trotted off into the dark they were arguing with each other who got to go back to the train and who had to stay behind to make sure George didn't siphon away to permanent oblivion.

Chapter Sixteen

Fair Maids, Tarnished Knights, Castle Rats

Today's Sunday. I was outside the hospital this morning dozing in the hot sun with Number Nine and Young Miss Sweet. She's got a big radio in her lap, tuned to a church program. Young Miss Sweet is a believer much the same way Number Nine is a doubter. Who can blame him? He ate a box of stale Crackerjacks all the way to the bottom and never got a prize. Now he's searching through the crumbs dribbled all down the front of his red SURVIVAL shirt. And who wouldn't be a believer, graced with the equipment Young Miss Sweet was born with? She's untied her candystriper apron top so she can raise her T-shirt and get some tan on her tummy. It's the white shirt she won at the Let 'Er Buck. With the hem lifted all you can read is I LET IT ALL HANG OUT. Our bench is reflected in the hospital lobby windows across the fresh-mowed lawn: red, white, and me in my time – bleached denim – blue. We could be a billboard celebrating American Brotherhood. A loud female voice rattles our reverie.

'SPAIN!' I think for a silly instant it's Nadine Rose. 'SPAIN, JOHNATHAN!'

It's Young Miss Sweet's aunt. She's spotted us and comes striding across the grass in her head-nurse

222

stride. Young Miss Sweet just has time to get her apron top tied. Number Nine hides the Crackerjack box behind the bench, just in case.

'They're going to trepan him,' she tells us. 'They drill a little hole to bleed off some of the swelling, to relieve the pressure. You understand?'

I nod that I do, and my big toe gives a single throb of sympathy.

'A neurosurgeon is flying down from Deaconess General in Spokane. It's a longshot, but who knows.'

She shades her eyes and squints over our heads towards the town. Tiny shouts drift up from the midway; the carny workers are breaking down the rides.

'His EEG showed some favorable lines,' she continues, still squinting. 'And the intern thinks she detected movement while changing the IV. I doubt any of this is anything to get your hopes up over but, like I say, who knows? You can wait outside Surgery, second floor. But no more cigar smoke or vodka breath! And you, young lady. Tomorrow you wear some kind of foundation garment. You are supposed to look like a Red Cross candystripe volunteer, not some loose lollipop.'

She turns and heads back the way she'd come, her white shoes clearing a clean path through the green grass clippings for us to follow. The scent she leaves in her wake is just as clean and clear. Fresh laundry. I could track her with my eyes closed.

The sunbeams of that third and final day found me again underground, swaddled in that reassuring smell of fresh laundry. I had passed out the moment I lay down on the bench full of folded sheets, unable even to remove my boots. I awoke to find myself once more undressed completely. Sue Lin was there waiting, as still as a porcelain doll, holding a porcelain teapot and cup on a porcelain tray. She might have been standing there for years except the tea was steaming. I snatched a sheet over me and she smiled.

'Good morning, John-E. You sleep o-kay fairly much?'

I told her I slept okay but not very much. I drank the tea and she refilled my cup. I saw my clothes on one of the wooden benches, washed and dried and folded. How she had accomplished this without sun or clothesline is as much a mystery as how she was able to disrobe me in my sleep.

I finished my second cup, then a third, so I could shoo her away for more tea and get dressed.

As the hot brew rinsed last night's murk out of my head yesterday's events began to emerge. It was a joyless emerging. Not one image could I come up with that still shined. The night had tarnished them all. My frontier Camelot was turning out to be infested with rats and riddled with weakness and greed. The fair maid Meyerhoff, for whom I would have gladly ridden to glory or doom the day before, was evidently more interested in racehorses than in a shining knight from Nashville. The pair of paladins whose footprints I had aspired to follow had indeed developed feet of clay and were staggering toward a drunkard's ignominious end. I hoped I was mistaken. I certainly wished them no ill. But I didn't wish them the sort of success the Wild West gang offered, either; and I hoped and prayed the harsh light of morn had prompted my embattled heroes to forswear whatever dark deals they'd been tenderized into. These hopes and prayers were dashed the moment I trotted onto the rodeo grounds.

There at the participants' gate was Sundown looking abashed and ridiculous. He'd been costumed to fit some kind of New York publicity agent's fantasy of the American Indian. In place of his stiff serge suit and flat-brim hat, he wore a beaded breechcloth. He was tricked out in all kinds of barbaric fetishes, feathers, and bones and a couple dozen cheap bead necklaces. His face was striped with warpaint. Worst of all was his hair. It was as wild and tangled as it had been last night in the river, only with feathers tangled in it instead of riverweeds. The hair on top had been deliberately hacked off in uneven lengths, then waxed to stand up in an outlandish coxcomb. That publicity agent must have read the illustrated adaptation of *The Last of the Mohicans* at an impressionable age.

Sundown was trying to obey a photographer's demands to stand still and control a very jumpy horse at the same time. The horse was an inbred palomino, probably picked for his picturesque qualities, too. Just as well. It would have been a mortification for Sundown's stallion to pose alongside such a mockery of his master. I rode on through the gate without a word or wave. You still see that photograph, in Round Up–history paperbacks and on postcards.

I encountered my other tarnished Galahad not long after. I loped Stoney to the corrals, looking for hay, and saw George off by himself at the edge of the cottonwoods. He was slumped against a tree trunk, nursing a roll-your-own. The smoke curling from beneath his floppy old hat brim was the only sign of life. It was the first time I'd seen him puffing on anything except his ceremonial cigars.

His bay gelding was tied back in the trees, munching at a big flake of alfalfa. He recognized Stonewall and whickered an invitation. Stoney was eager to accept but I reined him on. Our horses might've been ready to have a pleasant little brunch together, but George and I certainly were not. There wasn't time for tea talk anyway. Foghorn Clancy was ringing the bell in his tower and announcing the first event.

The event was Bulldogging. I was scheduled third from last, with Sundown and George after me. There were already some prime scores to beat when my turn came. The cowboy with the leading time wasn't even a cowboy. It was the cowgirl queen herself, Prairie Rose Henderson. I reined up at the barrier rope with a grim resolution: I was *damned* if I was about to let myself get bested by a couple of clay-footed old stumblebums, or a bucktoothed belle, either. Bulldogging never has been my favorite event but I was disgusted enough to get reckless. I gave a rebel yell the moment my steer churned into sight. The barrier rope dropped and I took off after him like hell boiling over.

The Beeson twin with the broken arm hazed for me. He might not have had much sense but he had good timing. He hazed the steer perfect for my jump. I swung under the trampling hooves the moment I hooked the horns. When the dust cleared I was the one with the leading time, Prairie Rose a distant second.

Sundown came next. If he felt abashed about the caveman costume he wore, his face didn't show it. He looked as severe and capable as ever. His fashion advisers had mercifully allowed him to put on trousers, but he was still hatless and crazy-haired. His hazer's horse shied and balked at the sight of him. He looked like the Borneo wild man more than ever as he made his leap. Yet he pinwheeled that steer to the ground with such precision he made the barbaric business look almost civilized. He would have been close to my score if that hazing horse hadn't shied.

As All Round leader, George Fletcher had the final slot. When I saw him ride out I better understood his desire for solitude. George looked dreadful: his toothless face was collapsed; his polished teak complexion had turned ashen; his eyes looked like two burnt holes in a dead man's blanket. Who could have foreseen the performance that followed?

For all his down-at-the-mouth stumblebum appearance, George Fletcher was as remarkable as ever. Bulldogging was just right for his circus-acrobat ability, and he couldn't resist looking spectacular at it even while looking dreadful.

He made his dive not three lengths from the drop rope and caught both horns. He was in position to chalk up the fastest throw of the day, but he had a statement to make with that steer. He stayed on the steer's back, on his knees, guiding the animal as if it were a bicycle and the horns were handlebars. Then, with an incredible and outlandish and rebellious motion, he kicked up his heels and went into his famous handstand. He rode this way until his shabby hat dislodged and fell beneath the hooves, then (I remember thinking, 'Ah! *That's* why he didn't wear his yellow Stetson!'), with a grace no amount of old rags could conceal, he swung under the animal and brought him thundering down. Gotch and them might have rendered him toothless, but not graceless.

My time, while not the most spectacular, was still best. George and Sundown tied for runner-up. Under the judges' stand I was catching the rain of silver dollars in my hat as they rode up for their share. To avoid awkward hellos I pretended interest in the scores being chalked up by a number of disputing officials. George and Sundown waited in silence. The second- and third-place purses had to be lumped together, then divided down the middle, because of the tie. All Prairie Rose got for her troubles was a red consolation ribbon and a black eye. She gave us her happier-than-lucky grin.

'Good 'dogging, fellers. Maybe I'll finish in the money in one of the next romps. They're for woman-kind only.' She stuck the ribbon in a breast pocket and rode off singing, her voice a surprisingly dainty soprano:

'Hard luck is the fortune of all womankind.
 They're always controlled, they're always confined;
 Controlled by their daddies, until they are wives,
 Then slaves to their husbands the rest of their lives.'

The three of us sort of had to politely linger until Prairie Rose's singing exit was over. We feigned interest in the mess of chalk marks over chalk smudges on the scoreboard. It looked like George was still in the lead by one official's calculation, Sundown by another's, and me somewhere in the smudgy in-between. George was the first to break the silence.

'I give up, Dog. I simply can't decipher it. Is our young protojay catching up to us, or are we keeping up with him?'

'I should never lost him that penny,' was the Indian's response.

I didn't mention that I'd thrown it in the river. I was glad we were getting cordial again. 'I can't understand how the scoring can be all this complicated,' I said. 'Don't they usually just add up the prize money and the one with the most wins the All Round? That ought to be simple enough.'

'But this aint your usual punkin roller anymore,' George said. 'This affair has gotten too big to be simple.' He reined his bay back from the blackboard. 'Too complicated for a simple man like me to cipher out, not on a empty stomach. What do you say we lope over to the booths and see if handsome Johnny can charm any more blintzes off the Meyerhoff girls? That's something I can cipher.'

The blintz works was shut down. There was no smoke from the cookstove chimney, no steam rising off any plump daughters. I was relieved and a bit mystified. Why would the Meyerhoffs shut up shop the best day of the Round Up? They couldn't have run out of supplies, not with that supply wagon back in the ash grove. If they had run out of anything it was the public's demand for their product. Those blintzes were filling.

We had to settle for ham-and-cheese sandwiches at the Pendleton Garden Society booth. And we had to pay for these, for all of George's shucking with the four pink-cheeked proprietresses. Without his winning smile George was as feckless as Sundown without his suit and braids. The four Garden Society women were decked out in gowns tailored from the same lot of cloth – purple lilacs. Their wide chapeaus were draped with silk lilacs and lavender lace. They were all middle-aged, overweight, and given to giggling, except for one. I recognized Missus Kell's thin face beneath all the lace and lilacs. She edged away from her three colleagues.

'Sorry, boys,' she said. 'If it was my shop it would be different. I wouldn't be wearing this dadgum hat, for one thing.'

229

I told her I would much rather pay for a good ham sandwich than eat another free blintz. 'But I do miss that Meyerhoff coffee. I hope they haven't shut down permanent.'

Missus Kell told me they had not, not the Meyerhoffs. 'They went to watch the youngest ride in the barrel race. Mister Meyerhoff says he won't let her enter the Cowgirl Relay unless she wins the barrel event; then he *might* consider it. "Might" my foot! He's never kept that sassypants from doing exactly as she pleased. Still, it is a wise condition. She'll be up against some very capable young ladies on that barrel course. A good drubbing might dissuade her of itself. How about some warm root beer instead of coffee? With a scoop of vanilla ice cream?'

Sundown and I declined, but George slid down from his dilapidated saddle, eager. 'Root beer and ice cream goes good after ham and cheese.' I said I thought I would mosey back around to our spot at the far rail – I might like to see a certain sassypants get drubbed myself. Sundown reined alongside.

'George Fletcher would drink horse water if somebody served it to him free.'

A good drubbing for Sassypants? Not hardly. We reached the rail just in time to see Sarah Meyerhoff come looping around the last of the three barrels on her sorrel pony. Her thigh was right against the wooden staves, she was banked in so tight. She brought the sorrel out of the loop with a delicate jerk of the reins, then spurred him, highballing for the finish line. You didn't need to see the rides before or after Sarah's; you could tell by that last highballing finish that nobody else's time would be close. Her father presented her with the blue ribbon, weeping with pride and joy and worry and grief and who knows what else. When Sarah took her victory trot around the track she made a point of passing close by our rail.

'If it isn't Cuh'nel Spain!' she exclaimed in a mocking drawl. 'Ah expected you to award that prize, not my stuffy old daddy. Ah was considerably disahpointed.'

The cowboys laughed and she spurred her pony on, giving me no chance to come up with a comeback. My face felt as red as Sundown's.

On deck after the Barrel Race was Trick-and-Fancy Riding: 'The boots-and-bloomers portion of our show,' is the way Foghorn Clancy categorized it. The story behind that portion alone would fill a couple of books. Trick Riding was a popular change of pace in those early rodeos, often with a purse equal to the money awarded in more masculine contests. The event wasn't actually limited to Womankind Only, but a man would no more have entered a Trick-and-Fancy competition than he would have a biscuit bake-off or a quilting contest. It simply would not have been manly. Imagine how surprised everybody was by the unscheduled rider.

'Wait!' Clancy rang his bell for attention. 'Here's *another* last-minute entry, Trick-and-Fancy fans – name unknown and masked to boot. Let's hear it for – Missus *Mystery!*'

A great laugh went up as Missus Mystery galloped into view. She was wearing a flour-sack blouse and gunny-sack skirt. Baggy old patched-up long johns and socks showed beneath the burlap hem. Her outfit was crowned with the lilac-crested bonnet Missus Kell had complained about only minutes earlier.

The lavender lace veil fooled the majority of the

paying crowd, but all of us in the peanut gallery knew immediately who it was. There might be other riders in the world who sat a saddle like that – supple as taffy and just as tight – but only one who would do it in a flower hat and flour sacks. I was dumbfounded. All I could think was that somebody had paid to see one of the old clown rides, Nordstrum or Meyerhoff or somebody, for sentiment's sake.

Whatever the motive, Missus Mystery was competing in earnest. She first did a couple of sock hops off each side of the galloping horse, then stood up in the saddle and twirled a lariat. She twirled the loop larger and larger as the bay circled the track, until the rope was played out to the end. 'Spinning the Wedding Ring,' the cowgirls call it. Next she jumproped with the loop, first on one foot, then the other, and finally backwards. Without turning back forward, she cast the rope aside and bent to place her palms on the big bay's rump, then she shot her stocking feet high and stood on her hands, just like on that steer in the bulldogging, except now there weren't any handlebar horns to hang on to and it was about twice as far to the ground. I've seen other trick riders accomplish this feat a time or two since; but it's usually done by grasping the saddle on each side of the horn. I've never seen it done from a backwards stand.

The lavender bonnet finally jiggled off just like that floppy workhat had, revealing Missus Mystery's true identity to everybody. The stands cheered and applauded and whooped with delight. They were still cheering when Nordstrum cried down at us from the judges' platform.

'Jack! What's this about? What is our amusing associate up to?'

Sundown didn't answer. Gotch appeared at Nordstrum's side, his hairless countenance purple.

'Yeah, Chief. What's Uncle Funny thinking to prove?'

Sundown still didn't answer, electing, rather, to gaze down the track. I was moved to answer for him.

'I don't think he's thinking to prove anything, Mister Gotch. Trick riding is a generous purse and George Fletcher hopes to add it to his poke for the All Round. He's thinking to *win*, is what I think he's thinking.'

Gotch glowered down at me for a long withering while, his eyes going smaller and harder, like nail heads. 'That's bad thinking,' he said at last. 'For a brittle old darky with dental problems and dangerous debts, that's terrible thinking.'

George would likely have been awarded that Trick-and-Fancy purse, too, even against such accomplished trick riders as Laura Tricky and Kitty Canutt, if it hadn't been for yet one more surprise entry – the O'Grady woman. Then it was no contest. She was too much the seasoned pro, too smooth a showgirl. She could do all the hop-off-again-on-again riding stunts the other contestants could do from their galloping ponies, only do them slicker. Smoother. She finished her routine, boot soles to the sky, like George's grand finale. It's true she did a three-point headstand instead of George's far more difficult handstand, but the sight was far more appealing aesthetically. Bowlegged Missus Mystery had to settle for runner-up.

By now the whole stadium was buzzing like a beehive. Everybody sensed something had changed even if they didn't know what. Then George retrieved Missus Kell's beautiful hat and blew a big kiss toward the dignitary seats, where his own beautiful hat gleamed on the head of Buffalo Bill Cody. Cody acted like he hadn't seen the taunt, or was above it, but Frank Gotch responded by breaking a make-believe neck with two huge hands. This symbolic exchange of gestures was seen by one and all. It clarified the adversaries, if not the issues. From that moment on, everybody, spectators and riders alike, understood that a die had been cast, a gauntlet thrown. Without knowing it, everybody knew everything. Excitement hummed through the grandstands. Gamblers scampered to change their bets. Indians hurried up from the teepee camp. Cowboys crowded the peanut rail.

George and Sundown entered every event after that, and I stuck with them like a cocklebur sticks to a coyote. Sometimes we went head to head, sometimes we coupled up, to haze or snub for one another. We got another opportunity for all three of us to team together, too: in the Wild-Cow Milking.

This novelty tradition used to be even more insignificant than it is now. The purse was puny and the entries usually the same – Boy Scouts, Indian kids, rowdy drunks taking a dare, and barbers hoping to show their clients that they could be regular fellows, too. That buzzing in the stands got ten times louder when the three of us came traipsing out amidst this comical collection.

There was also one trio of women. Prairie Rose Henderson had enlisted a couple of diminutive barrel-racing beauties. She was taller than them by a head. I was taller than anybody by two, three heads. I felt like a playground bully, the way I towered over all the women and kids and barbers. I hunched down in an attempt to look shorter, hoping no one would sass me to go pick on someone my own size. Sass wasn't something I was in the mood for. So who comes promenading out in her silver-toed Spanish boots to hand us Wild-Cow Milkers our milk bottles? Sassy-pants herself.

'Why here's a strapping bunch of dairy hands. Good afternoon, Mister Jackson ... Mister Fletcher. Sakes alive, George; what happened to your pretty hat and teeth?'

'Being kept for security, is all, Miss Meyerhoff,' George told her. 'Same as Sundown's.'

'They're keeping my hat and *suit*,' Sundown wanted it understood. 'My teeth are my own.'

'I see. And how about you, Colonel Spain?'

'Me?' Before I could avert my eyes she caught me with that look – snap! 'What do you mean, what about me?'

'Did they take anything of yours, is what I mean – for security?'

I shook my head to get free but I was hooked. 'I didn't have anything worth securing, I reckon.'

'Colonel, sometimes you make me worry that maybe you're just a saddlebum after all.' She held the jangling case full of bottles out to me. 'Take your choice.'

'Hold on, now,' I protested. 'What makes you assume I'm the milker? George here's the one with experience as a dairy hand.'

'Us cowgirls can tell who's best with a cow,' she said. 'We know hands.'

'I'm not so sure. Appears to me that some of you cowgirls are a lot more interested in racehorses than cows. Or in cowboys, either.'

'Sulky,' she laughed. 'Just like a saddletramp: a

cloudy past, murky future, and a sulky nature. I think I have the very thing for your condition, if you can keep it quiet.'

She leaned near and lowered her voice just enough to pique the curiosity of everybody within fifteen steps.

'One of these crystal chalices is enchanted. If you can choose that magic bottle from among all the others you have a chance to change your fortune. Your cloudy past will clear up. Your murky future will open like a blossom, and your sulky nature will cheerfully pour forth fruit forever. Treasures untold will be yours. Choose one.'

She braced the wire case against her hip and made an offering wave of the hand. There were half-pint cream bottles in all twenty-four available spaces. I pointed at the one in the corner against her hip.

'The obvious choice!' She lifted out the bottle and proffered it into my hand, her face grave. 'Now, here's what you must do: fill it with milk from the sacred cow; bring it warm to the apple bough. You follow that, Colonel?'

I nodded like a halfwit and she jangled away to the other milkers. The bottle already was warm when I put it in my pocket. There was no doubt in my mind that I had chosen the right one. The promised spell was already working.

The half-pints were distributed, the teams ready at the barrier rope. The chute gate swung wide and a harlequin herd of wild cows came bellering in. And I mean to tell you: a wild cow in them days was *wild*, combed out of some wild and wooly country. There were tens of thousands of acres of open range back then, perfect for a headstrong heifer with a free-thinking philosophy to hide out in – meet a nice wild bull and start a nice wild family. She probably hadn't even seen a human until a week ago. That was when her torment began. The loud-talking upright-walking bastards had dragged her and her terrified offspring out of their nice home on the wide-open range and confined them behind vines with thorns of iron. Then, scant minutes ago, they had heartlessly separated her from her offspring! The predictable result of this treatment was a mistrust of anything on two legs. A dislike, a downright animosity, even. Those wild mothers of yesteryear didn't skitter away in panic like the grain-fed Bossys do today. You didn't have to go after them, they came after you. All a milking team had to do was agree on which one they wanted to milk and get in her way. Our team's experienced dairy hand picked us out a knobby-kneed Jersey runt.

'Lay for the mousy one, fellows!' George lisped. 'She's the least of the lot.'

In size only was she the least. In ferocity and frenzy and fight, she was a giant. And what a contortionist! She could hook you, kick you, and bite you all in one spine-twisting move. It was like trying to milk a three-hundred-pound shrew.

I finally got a good crank on her matted tail while George and Sundown wrestled her front end. She drug us back and forth across the arena until the grandstands were howling with laughter. At length Sundown managed to wrap the mangy fur mantle across her eyes and this gave George the chance to loop his belt around her neck. The three of us waltzed her to the rail and George got a half-hitch with the other end of his belt. I pulled the milk bottle out of my pocket and went to work. Mousy was not generous with her bounty. Her teats weren't much bigger than my little finger and about as dry. George wasn't impressed by my milking ability.

'Don't be dainty, Nashville, strip 'em hard! This aint no time to fondle around.'

George had her by his belt on one side and Sundown had her by the fur piece on the other. She was hooking for them blind, left and right, and snapping like a gator. I finally found a spigot that worked and stripped enough milk in the bottle to make it look full if you sloshed it around.

'That's enough,' Sundown panted. 'She's give me a charley horse. Look out, I'm letting go.'

The warning didn't help. The moment the belt and blindfold were off she corkscrewed around and tromped me on my sore toe like it was what she'd had in mind all along. The bottle went spinning in the dirt. Then she hooked a horn in Sundown's five-and-dime necklaces and sent beads spilling after the milk. She tried for George with her farewell kick but missed. What she did hit, though, was my enchanted chalice. It shattered in a million crystal slivers. It didn't matter anyway. When we come up for air we saw that we were the only ones still out there. All the other teams had finished. or surrendered. Prairie Rose and her team had turned in their bottle so long ago they were already at the judges' platform, collecting their first-place money. Even so, as the three of us charley-horsed and mumble-mouthed and sore-footed our way across the field of combat and back out the gate, dead last, we were given as big an ovation as if we'd paraded off first. Everybody loved us.

Well, not everybody. Gotch and his handler happened to be driving their wrestling wagon through the gate just as we were walking out, and they weren't giving us any ovation. Mister Handles was at the reins, cursing the mules. O'Grady rode behind, at a distance. She wouldn't look at me.

The wrestler was in his wrestling tights, bare from the waist up except for his head. He was protecting his naked dome with Sundown's flat-brimmed hat. A purple ribbon around his neck displayed his other trophy: a set of false teeth. This obscene pendant bumped back and forth across his naked chest as he went through his strongman flexes. When he saw us he came right to the ropes.

'Okeedoke, Fletcher. You said to get ready to lock horns. I'm ready.'

'I see that you is, Mistah Gotch. Please be patient wiff Uncle George a hair longer. I promised to give you a tussle and George Fletcher is a man of his wahd. A deal is a deal, and it aint to be broke.'

'Is that so?' Mister Handles twisted around on the wagon seat to join the conversation. 'What about all those that got broke this afternoon? Ever occur to you some people was wagering real jack on your so-called *wahd*?'

'It aint like I *tried* to win, Mistah Bowkah! Just the opposite. Can I help it that them other yayhoos wahnt capable of forpassin' my wuhst effuht?'

'There's *one* that's capable,' Gotch snarled. 'Right here. And *this* yayhoo is tired of being put off.'

'Be patient, Mars Gotch, and let me catch my breff. Do some mo' dem constipation exercises you do so good.'

Gotch was puffed up to say more but Nurse O'Grady gave her bugle a timely toot and the mules lurched forward. From his tower Foghorn Clancy began the now-familiar introduction. 'Ladies and gentlemen! for your enjoyment *another* special added attraction compliments of Mister Cody. This is the one *everybody's* been waiting for—'

'Not me,' I said. 'I've enjoyed about as much of these special added attractions as I can stand.'

'Never can tell,' Sundown said mysteriously. He was scanning the corrals like he expected somebody. 'This one might actual be special.'

'I need to lick my wounds and rest my bones and get revitalized. I know a place in those ash trees where I can catch a couple of winks. Give a holler if I'm not back for the Saddlebronc.'

George gave me a wounded look. 'You wahn' abandon a partner in his time of trouble, wuh you?'

Sundown cut him off. 'Don't listen to him, Johnny. He aint that big a fool, even drunk. Go on like you was.'

'The Dog is right, Nash,' George said with as much sincerity as his toothless mouth could muster. 'I'm not that big a fool. You go on about whahevah business you got in them twees. Thuh ain' nuffin' like a nice nap to re-*vibe*lize a fella hee hee hee.'

So once more I found myself slipping through the ash trees and climbing into the fruit-scented cool of Meyerhoff's covered wagon. Only this time it wasn't just me and a bunch of dried apples.

'I almost gave up on you, Colonel Spain!' a voice scolded. 'You're not the farmhand I took you for. That piddling little chore took you about half of forever.'

I told her to hush. I wasn't in the mood for scolding, neither.

'I'm just curious,' she kept on. 'What was it that detained you so long? Ineptitude, or enjoyment? I saw the way you pawed that poor cow.'

I hushed her myself, the best way I could think of. I wasn't in the habit of cutting someone's conversation short, but felt strongly that Miss Sassypants and I didn't have need for any more talk. Time for it, either, though I didn't know that at the moment. I found that out later, that same afternoon. I don't know that Sarah Meyerhoff ever found out. She was too much the full-tilt horse racer. Full-tilt racers don't have time to find out how much time they don't have.

It never occurred to me or anybody else back then, but, in her way, Sarah Meyerhoff was almost as talented a horseman as George Fletcher or Sundown Jackson. And who can guess how good she might have become? A girl is potentially a better horseman than any man can ever be, by the difference of her design. It's that difference between a rider and a driver. Girls love to ride horses the same way boys love to drive cars. Horses you get on; cars you get in. Boys dive under the hood and tinker with the carburetor – find out what makes a thing go and try to figure out how to make it go faster. A girl just rides. There's no diving, no tinkering. All a girl needs to do is straddle the steed and stay light in the saddle, the lighter the better. And oh me ... Sarah Meyerhoff's touch was light as a shadow, as the promise of apples, as the brush of a cool fall breeze. What steed wouldn't respond? What spirited stallion wouldn't run his heart out beneath such a touch?

Oh me, Sarah Meyerhoff ... at the Pendleton Round Up year nineteen-eleven. In the Round Ups and Go Rounds that followed I enjoyed other relationships, with more than my share of other great cowgirl riders. I found Prairie Rose Henderson to be quite the delicate little damsel once you got past the porcelain portcullis.

I got to know Laura Tricky and Kitty Canutt, too. And Fox Hastings. They were all fine riders, but they never ranked anywhere close to Sarah. Where Kitty Canutt was deep-willed and powerful, Sarah was power itself. While Fox Hastings was able to control a mount with knees and ankles alone, Sarah could do it with nothing but hints and hips. Bighearted Prairie Rose was like being rocked in the bighearted cradle of Mother Earth; Sarah was like being forked by lightning. Our covered wagon was still sweetly sparking with that lightning bolt's aftermath when we were harshly interrupted by a squall of unnamable agony from the arena.

'OW GODDAMMIT LET LOOSE UNCLE UNCLE UNCLE OW OW OW!'

Chapter Seventeen

Dreen Off Some Pizen

The squalling went on and on, unabated, and with such deep-lunged agony one began to expect it could go on till the cows came home. But it began to change. The squalls became howls and the howls became feeble curses. By the time Sarah and I got presentable and made to the arena fence for a look the curses had diminished to moans and whispers. 'Looks like we missed the best part,' Sarah said.

The wrestling wagon was parked right in front of the most expensive seats in the place. Exactly the spot I would have picked if I were a foxy fight promoter like Mister Handles. Except he had outfoxed himself this time. The wagon was close enough to the stands that the hoi polloi were clambering into the arena to join the action. Up in the ring Nurse O'Grady had her medical bag open and she was splashing something on the gory posterior of Frank Gotch; it looked like iodine and from the grin on her face she looked like she was enjoying splashing it on him. You couldn't see her eyes. They were covered with a pair of dark glasses. Those were the first colored glasses I'd ever seen on anyone except for a blind person. The rear end of Gotch's tights was ripped to bloody tatters, and his front end was buried in a corner of the prizefight ring.

He was chewing the turnbuckle to stifle his unseemly whimpers. The three Pinkertons were stationed in the other three corners, nervously trying to present some semblance of control. Two of them had their coats thrown back to display their shoulder holsters and the third carried a double-barrel riot gun. Every time Gotch emitted a loud cry this Pinky would spin around with his shotgun to make sure the wrestler wasn't attacking him in a blind rage. Sarah got a big laugh out of the spectacle.

'Looks like the big brute tried to bully the wrong dumb animal this time.' She turned to the rubber-neckers at the fence. 'What was it, a mountain lion? A bear?'

'A Indian,' they all answered.

'Yeah, a funny little *round* Indian,' one of them elaborated. 'With a jaw on him like a snapping turtle. I guess he musta thought those storeboughts Gotch had hanging around his neck meant this match was bite-as-bite-can.'

'Parson Montanic!' I said. 'That was what Sundown was hinting about. What happened?'

The story was served up piecemeal from a score of different narrators, in bits and bites spiced generously with additions and asides. It seems Mister Gotch and Mister Handles and just about everybody else took it for granted that George Fletcher was to be the op-ponent. Hadn't they all heard about the promise he made that first afternoon? Hadn't they seen George baiting the giant as he flounced past in his Missus Mystery getup? According to Mister Handles' derisive preamble from the ring George Fletcher had put up his dime-store dentures against Frank Gotch's World Champion belt.

'That makes the handicap more *serious* than twenty-to-one,' Buffalo Bill pointed out from his picturesque perch on the beautiful palomino. 'So this is going to be a serious wrestling match. No holds barred, no time limit, the first man to cry uncle loses all.'

'Hair, hide, and *all*,' Gotch had reiterated with sadistic gusto. 'I got a nice leather pouch in mind for a particular piece of Uncle George's hide. All it'll need is a drawstring.'

But instead of George Fletcher, a reluctant mudball of a man was escorted into the ring by Sundown Jackson. Sundown introduced him as Parson Montanic Killdevil, the undisputed Indian-wrestling champion of Idaho, Washington, Oregon, and some of northern California. This set off protests and complaints and cries of Foul. What if this unsavory-looking mudball had lice? A concealed tomahawk? Parson Montanic stood in a corner with Cousin Sundown while the gamblers and the rodeo officials and Mister Handles and everybody else within arguing range argued. Gotch insisted it was George Fletcher he had been promised and it was George Fletcher he wanted, not some second-string ringer too slow-witted to realize what he'd been roped into. But George was nowhere to be found (Louise had wisely coaxed him to the river, I later learned, with hints of a sweeter tussle and a nicer purse) and the spectators grew impatient. Mister Kell came down from the platform to deliberate with Mister Cody. Cody contended that the judges should refuse to proceed with the rodeo until the cowardly Fletcher was shamed out of hiding – teach him he can't get away with this kind of monkey business in a homeo-sapian society! Mister Kell said he doubted that George Fletcher could be shamed out of or into anything, and what's more he was getting pretty damned tired of all this bullroar! If nobody was going to wrestle then back this by God meat wagon out of the arena so things could get back to business; it was getting late and an ominous stormcloud was building to the northeast and they had a by God rodeo to finish! The barker saw things were about to take an unprofitable turn.

'We aint backing out!' he said. 'Champ? What say you honor the fans with a little *Indian-wrestling* exhibition? There's a good sport! Come on Parsnip Montana or whatever you're called – shake hands with Fearsome Frank Gotch.'

Sundown gave a push and Montanic walked obediently to the ring center. Grumbling, Gotch removed the flat-brim hat and the denture pendant and hung them on his corner post. He spread his arms and grabbed the ropes and did a couple of squats to warm up, then, without warning or greeting, either one, spun suddenly around and attacked Montanic at a dead run.

One narrator said it looked like a big pink locomotive running into a little brown bear that had stopped to sun itself on the tracks. But to the locomotive's and everybody else's amazement, the little bear didn't budge. It embraced its attacker in an affectionate bear hug, swung him high in the air, then returned him gently to the mat and let him loose. Everybody in the stadium was speechless. Gotch was so astounded that all his muscles seized up against each other, like a courthouse clock wound too tight. Mister Handles seemed to be familiar with the condition. He dipped a peppermint stick in spirits of ammonia then screwed it between the giant's lips. Gotch came out of his shock, roaring curses.

Two more times the huge wrestler attacked the impassive lump, two more times he was swung aloft. After returning him to the mat for the third time, Parson Montanic told Frank Gotch that Jesus loved him, then turned to leave the ring. In Indian wrestling, the match is decided by balance, not dominance. Wrestlers can tell when balance has been won and lost. After that, what's the sense in belaboring the issue and getting all bunged up? – was how the Indian wrestler saw it.

Gotch didn't see it that way. With a snarl of triumph he caught the departing Indian from behind in a flying scissorlock. They crashed to the canvas, Montanic's head imprisoned between Gotch's murderous thighs. Gotch grinned and put the squeeze on. This was more like it. Now he could crush that skull at his leisure, until he was ready to crack it like a hazelnut in a vise. He could even work the little red runt around to where he was able to crush the skull and sit on the potato face at the same time! This was the beginning of his undoing; he hadn't been there to watch that bent coin get straightened.

Thus, it was Frank Gotch's own brutality that placed his prideful flesh within the jaws of his downfall. Parson Montanic chomped down in an unbreakable bite to the finish. That was what set off those squalls of agony Sarah and I heard from our wagon rendezvous. The reason they went on so loud and so long was because nobody could unchomp that bite – not the barker, not the Pinkertons, not the whole crowd of concerned citizens who climbed into the ring – pound and pinch and pry though they tried! Nurse O'Grady finally poured a bottle of smelling salts into the whole predicament. Water began to gush from the Indian's

247

eyes and nose in such copious quantities that he was compelled to release his bite to catch his breath. Sundown Jackson dragged his cousin away from the ravaged rear. As he pushed the Parson through the ropes, Sundown grabbed his hat off the turnbuckle and retrieved George's dentures in the bargain. Montanic was still weeping when I saw him in the hayshed behind the chutes. I wondered aloud if smelling salts perhaps had a fiercer effect on Indians, like firewater. Sundown said it wasn't the smelling salts.

'Wasn't that pinching and pounding, neither. It was remorse.'

'Remorse?' George exclaimed. 'Was he remorseful about biting the big booger, or about *stop*ping biting him?'

'About having to wrestle him in the first place.'

'Let's not be signifying here, Dog. He didn't *have* to wrestle him.'

George's speech had its spunk and sparkle back, now that his teeth were in.

'I was buck-ready to go through with the match. I'd be all right. I may be old and foolish but I aint fragile. Could that ape do more harm to me than animals twicet his size been trying to do for the best part of my life? I will admit I was a mite relieved when I heard the Parson was going to pinch-hit for me. I am grateful to Mister Jackson for that. And for getting my grinders back as well; the American Legion booth is got leftover roastin' ears for free. So in front of God and everybody I want to thank you most kindly, Mister Jackson.'

God and everybody consisted of a dozen or so of us bunched up at the hayshed looking through the slats at Parson Montanic. He was on his knees in the chaff, hands clasped in prayer. His lips and chin were caked with blood. The Pinkerton with the double-barrel had been posted at the gate, presumably to keep Montanic from crashing out after another taste of ape rump.

'I thought he had vowed to wrestle no more forever,' I said.

'I had to lie to him,' Sundown confessed. 'I claimed devils in the night had tricked us into evil bargains. I said it would be George Fletcher's immortal soul he would be wrestling to save. Now he's found out it was just false teeth. You! Cousin!' Sundown rattled the gate. 'How come you didn't let go? He hollered Uncle many times, why did you keep biting his butt?'

Montanic raised his conscience-smitten face. 'Why did he keep squeezing my head?'

Everybody got such a kick out of this answer that it became quite famous over the next few years. Versions of it could be used for all kinds of responses: 'Why did you keep kicking that hog in your bare feet?' 'Why did he keep breaking my toes?' Too bad Sarah missed this snapper at the end of the tale; she was nowhere to be seen when I looked around the hayshed crowd.

That stormcloud Mister Kell referred to wasn't very big. It looked more curious than ominous, like a young mustang full of juice and on the prowl for a little excitement. It found a spot up on Cabbage Ridge just in time to catch the highlight of the whole show – Saddlebronc Riding. It plunked itself down and commenced taking flash photographs and whooping like a tourist. 'Eee-*haw*, this is the *cat's pajamas!*'

The tourists thought so as well. When the officials had all the Saddlebronc contestants take a promenade around the track the crowd whooped just like the stormcloud. Things were down to the wire and everybody could feel it. Because George and Sundown and I were one-two-three in the All Round, the officials saved us for last. The entire stands stood and cheered when they saw us come loping past at the tail of the parade, side by side.

George the Show-off was on the outside, nearest the grandstands. He was sitting loose on his single-gaited bay and had his big smile flashing. He cut quite the figure, even in his floppy old work-hat.

Sundown was on the inside, astride his paint stud. He had been washing off warpaint and shredding beads and feathers all afternoon. Now he was back in his severe serge suit and black flatbrim, and his braids were plaited neatly together beneath his chin. The gold-nugget tie clasp was his only ornament.

I was in the middle, sitting tallest of all, as full of juice as that young storm. Except for Prairie Rose Henderson I can't remember a single name of the other buckaroos parading ahead of us. All fine riders, I'm sure, and some of them likely went on to be stars and champions in their own day. But this parade was ours. We took our own sweet leisure. By the time we'd tied our mounts to the peanut-gallery rail and walked back to get our draws the shady square beneath the judges' platform was deserted of riders. Only Mister Kell was there, waiting with his hat in his hand. His aspect was still somewhat hangdog and hungover, but at least he could look you in the eye again.

'You lag-behinds must be looking for these.' Three folded pieces of paper were left in the hat. 'Who's first?'

George and Sundown raised their palms in their simultaneous gesture. Mister Kell laughed and held the hat to me. 'Pick one, Spain, Johanthan E. Lee. Those two old Junebugs might fiddle around till the snow flies.'

I took the nearest chit. Then George, then Sundown. Mister Kell wished us good luck and headed back up the wooden steps. He hesitated halfway. 'Just forget any of that other bullroar you mighta heard going around, boys . . . like which complexion would make the best poster and so forth. That was just backroom smoke. You go out there and do your stomp-down damnedest.'

He put his hat back on and continued on up the steps like a weary old judge ascending a scaffold, solemn and more than a little shaky. The name scrawled on my chit was so shaky in fact I couldn't read it. I took it back out of the shade, hoping the sun would help me. George finally had to decipher it for me.

'Captain Kidd! Hear that, Jack? Captain Kidd, hee hee hee. Our young colt got the old cob this time. I *knew* he'd eventually come to the bottom of that barrel of four-leaf clovers.'

Sundown looked at me with sympathy. 'Captain Kidd's strong but lazy, Little Brother. You need to rake him good to wake him up.'

'That's the truth. You sure should have got you some chaps to flap, like Uncle George told you. On a lazybones like Captain Kidd you need all the flapping you can get.' He held up his chit. 'I drew ol' Hot Foot. He's mighty showy. Who'd you draw, Dog?'

'Mister Wiggles.' Sundown was still looking at my skinny legs like a worried old uncle. 'Fletcher's right. We shoulda got you some chaps.'

I told them much obliged for the concern but not to anguish over me – they'd helped me plenty. 'Besides, I don't have a prayer of catching up with you hombres, not even with the best of broncs and chaps. You're the stars in this shindig, everybody knows that.'

'Catch *up* with 'em?' It was Oliver Nordstrum leaning around the judge's tallyboard up on the platform. 'You're a half-dozen points in *front* of 'em, Johnathan E. Lee, and the favorite of staying there, according to some pretty cagy odds-makers.'

'Odds-on favorite,' another voice agreed. 'Now that our Nigger and our Injun is proved uncooperative.'

It was Frank Gotch's husky purr. The show wagon had plodded into the chute lane while we were dawdling. The sides of the rig were folded up and a tent had been strung for a locker room. Buffalo Bill and Mister Handles shared the driver's seat while Gotch rode behind. There was a stool available but the wrestler looked disinclined to sit. He stood spread-legged outside the tent flap, leaning on Mister Handles' heavy hickory cane, the kind stock handlers wield in auction pens. He had on his checkered suit and striped turtleneck. His features had muscled back into the wicked grin and his face looked as impervious as bleached rawhide. His brow and dome, however, revealed that this hide might not be as impervious as it looked. It was cooked to that rosy-rare blush of Meyerhoff's corned beef. This was not lost on George the Gourmet.

'Ooo-wee, Mars Gotch! Look lak you done burn the top of your face. What 'come of that hat you was sportin' earlier? Nice black flatbrim?'

'What become of that nice one of *yours?*' Gotch shot back.

This caught George from such an unexpected angle he couldn't find a quick retort. His nice hat was in plain sight, still crowning the snowy mane of Buffalo Bill Cody up on the driver's seat. I noticed that neither the old showman nor his barker held the reins. They were dragging in the dust between the mules. The barker was trying to direct the mules with muttered threats and curses but they plodded along with heads hanging, completely deaf to Mister Handles' commands, by all appearances. Then he muttered something and they both raised their heads our direction. He spoke again and, all of a sudden, they laid their long ears back and sawed straight for us, at ramming speed. We had to move fast to keep from being penned against the chute wall. I jumped one way and my two friends the other. The mules rammed into the rail, right between us.

'Godamighty man!' Cody shouted at the barker. 'Haven't I warned you to keep a grip on those wild jackrabbits? You nearly trampled these gentlemen and — blast! I feared as much. You have thrown my inarticulated knee out of socket. Now pick up those reins while I pop it back.'

As Mister Handles scrambled down over the wagon-tongue the old showman tried to push himself standing. The kneejoint creaked to a stop before he was all the way up. He reached a beaded gauntlet toward me.

'Give an old hoss a hand, won't you, son? I think we ought to get better acquainted anyhow.'

What I ought to have done was told him to go jump in the lake, but I'd been brought up to show respect for my elders whether they deserved it or not. I reached up and steadied him while he popped the knee back into place. He kept hold of my hand and climbed over the side to the ground. Old and creaky as he was, he had a grip on him like a blacksmith.

'It's a nuisance getting old. You wake up one day to discover you're just a moth-eaten saddlebag full of memories and miseries. This knee, for instance, was first unhinged on the banks of the Yellowstone River, forty-four years ago. It was a little goodbye kiss from Chief Yellow Hand before he went to meet his maker. You wouldn't think a skinny old Injun with two barrels of buckshot in his sweetbreads would have the strength to all of a sudden sit up, would you? Let alone swing a war club.'

He released my hand but I could tell I was not yet dismissed. He pushed George's yellow hat back on his head and gave me a long look up and down. He appeared pleased with what he saw.

'You're a nice-looking lad, Johnny Spain, and that's a fact. No, please, don't hurry off; there's plenty time before your ride. Don't you think he's a nice-looking lad, Mister Handles?'

'Real nice.' The barker had retrieved the reins and was brushing the dirt off his trouser knees. 'Never seen nicer. Makes all the ladies' little hearts go pitty-pat. Just ask Miss O'Grady.'

'He also cuts a very impressive figure a-horseback, for the men's benefit,' Buffalo Bill continued. He gave my shoulder an appraising squeeze, like a housewife shopping for a roast. 'Johnny, we might have a little turkey to talk sometime. You ever consider going into show business? It's easier money than rodeo contests, and more of it.'

I told him no, never, and that I did not anticipate considering it in the future. He kept squeezing my shoulder and talking easy money, and I kept shaking my head. I shook loose just as Oliver Nordstrum came down from the platform and caught my other shoulder.

'Don't hurry off, Johnny. Remember what Ben Franklin says in his almanac: "At a great bargain,

254

linger a while."'' He gave me a sincere squeeze for emphasis.

I didn't see any great bargain and I didn't have time to linger. 'I'm gratified with all this interest, Mister Nordstrum – Mister Cody . . . and I hope you won't think me rude if I postpone this discussion until the Broncriding is over. I have yet to fetch my saddle. We were on our way to get our saddles when your mules—'

That was when it dawned on me: I had been finagled away from my friends again, just like last night in the saloon. I excused myself with a few curt words and pushed past the treacherous trio. The mules still barred my way. Rather than risk getting bit or kicked trying to get by them at the head or the heel, I climbed right up on the wagon bed. George and Sundown were nowhere to be seen, and neither was Gotch. But a puff of smoke from the tent opening caught my attention. The O'Grady woman was sitting back in the dim canvas cave on one of the fight stools. She had her legs crossed and a cigarette between her lips. Her orange-colored coiffure was gone and so were the colored glasses, revealing a head of ordinary gray hair and a spectacular black eye. She gave a nod toward the high-walled chute that led to the stock pens.

'That way it was the big bastard herded 'em,' she told me around the cigarette. 'But you best get a handgun first, love, or lots more help. You and your two old mates aint enough advantage against that abomination.'

Frank Gotch used to be a clean-cut all-American farm boy from Iowa who won the U.S. amateur championship before he was out of his teens. He was clean-cut even after he fell in with Mister Handles and won the professional crown. For a few years, anyway.

Then something happened. One winter Mister Handles took his champion on a swing down through the Mexican wrestling circuit, and young Gotch either caught something or bought something in one of those border towns that changed the all-American farm boy forever. His hair all fell out. His nose got thicker and his brow and chin wider in that typical look that sideshow giants always have, and he began to swell. It was like whatever gland it is that turns a normal kid into an outsized freak had suddenly woke up after thirty years and started pumping giant juice. He swole all over like leavened dough and kept swelling. Sportswriters that had seen him the season before wrote that the change was more than physical, that he changed deep down. Some of his loyal fans insisted that the hairless ogre stalking the wrestling ring was not Frank Gotch at all but a ringer Mister Handles insinuated in Gotch's place; that the real Frank Gotch had been rubbed out because he wouldn't take orders from the odds-makers. Others sadly said No, sorry, it's the same Frank Gotch – only with everything turned opposite. Jack London wrote in the *Police Gazette*, 'The swarthy hand of some Nameless Mexican evil has reached down the throat of a perfectly healthy young man and grabbed him by the tail and jerked him inside out – re*versed* him! – and turned him into a diseased brute.'

I think that was the invisible haze you always sensed hovering around the wrestler: the cloud of some kind of contagious disease. Far more terrifying than the thought of him catching hold of you was the possibility of you catching something from *him*. Like getting bit by a dog foaming at the mouth – the foam far more dangerous than the fangs. So I knew Nurse O'Grady's warning was accurate: the fact we had a three-to-one advantage over Gotch afforded us no consolation whatsoever. What advantage does three have against one if that one's got hydrophobia? On the other hand, I didn't have time to round me up any side arms or army. I leapt off the wagon and charged down the deserted chute, alone.

I was charging so hard around a little bend that I charged right up alongside him.

'That's far enough,' I declared brashly. 'This isn't some Bronx back alley where you can bully people and get away with it.'

Gotch was delighted by my presence, if not my declaration. 'Well well well,' he purred, 'if it isn't Gentleman John. You come to join your pals, Johnny? Well then go ahead and *join* 'em!' – and slapped me between the shoulders in what would have been a gesture of goodfellowship were it not that I was slapped flat three yards away with the breath knocked out of me. George lifted me to my feet.

'Stand up, Nashville. You shoulda run when you had the chancet.'

'Run away and leave his pals? A Dixie gentleman wouldn't do that, Uncle George—'

'I aint mean run away, Mister Champion. I mean run get help.'

'The more the merrier.' Gotch said with an amiable smile.

'Help what's got a *gun*, then! Some moon-crazed bears is said to get so ugly they need put outen their misery!'

Gotch's smile vanished and he started advancing toward us. I caught my breath enough to tell George I didn't think bear-baiting was the wisest tactic in this situation. 'Maybe we can talk things over.'

Gotch shook his head, 'Huh-*uh*,' and kept coming.

'Maybe we can rush him, then,' I suggested to Sundown. 'Surround him—?'

All three men shook their heads, 'Huh-uh,' at this suggestion. We kept backing up and the giant kept coming. He had his arms outspread now, and with the cane held out they were wide as the chute. His shirt cuffs were split and his forearms were showing through all veined and hairless. He *did* look like something turned inside out, with all the workings of muscle and sinew and gristle now on the surface, nasty and visible.

We tried to split up a time or two, duck this way and dart that, but he was as nimble as he was wide. He could spring sideways in the chute faster than we could duck and dart – and we were running out of chute. This was before rodeo builders had learned to leave gap enough between the plank rails for a boot – being more concerned that a prize bull might get a horn caught and bust his neck than worried that some hapless wrangler might need a quick getaway up the fence.

There were three gates at the end of the runway – one to the left, where they kept the bulls and steers and wild milking cows; one in the middle, where the broncs were corralled; and the gate to the right, where all the roping calves were penned. This was the least heavy of the gates, so some gaps had been left between the rails. The calves were nosed up to these gaps and bellering to their mamas in the pen across the way. It was long past lunchtime and they were good and tired of all this rodeo foolishness. This calf gate presented the only stretch of the chute that wasn't a sheer

258

wooden wall. Everybody saw at once that it was our only hope.

George was closest. He scrambles up the planks with me right beside him. Sundown chooses to try the latch. Gotch says 'Huh-uh' and springs forward, kicking the Indian's legs out from under him and hooking George with his cane. He grabs my ankle with his other hand. I remember looking down and wondering, Is his hand actually that big or is my leg that skinny? Then I was in the dirt for the second time with the wind knocked out of me. This time I had George and Sundown for company.

'Maybe you was right,' George said. 'Maybe we should have surrounded him.'

Gotch loomed down on us, dreamlike and even biblical in his enormity. He was purring something to us between his clamped teeth but I couldn't tell what; the calves were raising too big a fuss. I feared his intention was to cudgel us senseless with his hickory cane but he cast it aside. He liked to be close to his victims. He rolled us together as though he were a woodsman and we were cordwood that had to be gathered into a proper bundle so he could get his arms around the load. It was all so matter-of-fact, it seemed like the normal thing to do, even when the bundle of us was swung high and spun around and around. It was the classic old wrestling crowd-pleaser called the 'flying mare,' only this was the flying mare times three, and the crowd of calves were not pleased. Their bellering whirled past, again and again; plank walls and chute and beller; walls and chute and beller; then – crash ! – we were slammed against the calf gate wholesale. The pine boards splintered like slats in an apple crate and the calves surged away somewhere in

259

the spinning corral, scared silent: I could smell the sharp cheesey reek of their fear-loosened bowels. Gotch bent down out of the wheeling clouds overhead and bundled us together for firewood again, this time with splints and splinters of broken pine for his kindling. I found myself face to face with Sundown. I gave him a smile of Aint this something? It all had that soothing logic of a dream at work. Then, as we were swung high once more, I beheld something in the Indian's eyes that shattered the dreamy calm and set my bowels churning as bad as any calf's.

I saw a fear. I don't mean that this was the first time I had seen fear in the man; no rodeo rider ever lived that didn't have an occasional fear for his life when he was caught in a bad predicament by a bad animal. It's natural! You can get your neck broke! But what I saw in Sundown's eyes was a fear that was so far beyond the natural fear of getting killed that it was meaningless to compare the two, and it froze the blood in my veins to realize it. *That's* why my usually brave buddies had been crawfishing so! They had understood all along what had dawned on me at last: that this wrong-way-about creature was capable of doing worse than killing you. He could break you.

He slammed us down in the manure and I just lay there, paralyzed with terror like a girl. I remember thinking of the story Nurse O'Grady had told me: how a hurt from the outside can be survived even if it kills you, whereas there's some hurts that are done you from the inside that kill you even if you live – and I felt my churning bowels begin to loosen. Then, as he stooped to roll us again into a convenient armload, I saw a miraculous circle appear like a golden halo above the giant's sunburnt head. It descended gently down over his shoulders and jerked taut. He turned with a roar to see what had frustrated his fun. Another loop descended from the other direction, rusty red. It was the strawberry-roan horsehair lariat the slope-nosed kid had beat me with the first day of calf-roping. The first rope led to the Beeson with the broken leg. His cast had been whittled back so he could get his bare foot in the stirrup. He was grinning with pleasure as his horse back-walked, dragging the wrestler to the calf-snubbing post. Gotch roared again. The calves broke out of their corner and surged past the snubbing post, right over us. They shied at the splintered gate and surged back. By the time George and Sundown and I got to our feet there were two more loops around the raging Gotch. His whole head was as red as the end of a thermometer. He was beginning to look like a rabid animal now, as he heaved and raved against the lariats. The horses reared and rolled their eyes but they were roping horses, they knew how to keep the slack out of the line. The cowboys were snubbing him closer and closer as they circled the post in the corral's center. When Gotch felt his spine against the post he heaved with such violence that all his suspender buttons snapped, front and rear. His trousers fell to his knees and so did he, raving louder than ever. When the cowboys had him snubbed securely, his back against the post and his naked knees in the dirt, the other Beeson came riding through the calves and arranged the final loop over Gotch's head with his one good hand. He took care that the rope was across the man's raving mouth, then hauled it tight around the post and half-hitched it. The giant gnashed and chewed at the rope until, at last, there was foam.

We all stood – calves, cowboys, and all – in the

settling dust, panting and staring at the trussed-up spectacle. He was just as hairless below. Slope-Nose was the first to speak.

'Wal, boys, what do you suggest we oughter do with him?'

The question was clearly directed to George, the oldest boy. George had picked him out a piece of pine and was leaned against the gatepost, trying to scrape some of the filth off his sheepskin chaps. He was in no hurry to answer. Everything had become very peaceful, even the calves. They were sniffing cautiously closer and closer to the trouserless man, as impressed as the rest of us. George finally tossed his scraper aside.

'Why not let's just leave him here?' he suggested in a benevolent tone. 'These hungry little dogies ack like they might enjoy Mars Gotch's company for a spell, and Mars Gotch might enjoy theirs. And who can tell? Them sweet things might even dreen off some of the poor man's pizen.'

He flipped Gotch the silver dollar he owed him and walked off.

Chapter Eighteen

Head for the Barn

The malarkying was out of the way at last. We could get down to what we all had come for. Mister Kell spelled it out for everybody, using Foghorn Clancy as his mouth. George and Sundown and I were the only broncriders left and we were still in the lead. So our final three saddlebronc rides would decide the championship. He should have kept this to himself. It made the other riders feel a little resentful and got the crowd buzzing. Our three broncs weren't any help, either. After Gotch they seemed tame. Sundown went first on Mister Wiggles. Mister Wiggles started off a fairly ferocious squirmer and twister. The Indian rode him with such funereal dignity that Mr Wiggles ended up plodding like a hearse horse.

And George was right about Hot Foot. He was mighty showy. George had to do some fancy spurwork to outshine him.

They were both right about Captain Kidd. He should have been called Rip Van Winkle. I had to rake him to wake him, and keep on raking. By the time the bell sounded he was raked to a dangerous pitch but it was too little too late. I knew my score would be no match for the other two. I waved off the pickup man and slid down by myself. I kicked a clod after the horse the way George had the day before, and sore-footed my way to the sidelines. I was mighty disappointed.

The crowd was, too. The whole stands were grumbling over such an irresolute ending. Up on the platform Mister Kell and the other four judges were conferring in a wad at the muddled blackboard, people hollering at them from all sides. Nordstrum's voice had lost all its amiable goodfellowship; he was shrieking like a hysterical housewife: 'No *fair!* That horse is a glue candidate. He didn't buck worth a hill of beans. Get the kid a better horse or it's no contest.' From the other direction Meyerhoff was shouting through cupped hands: 'Ah? And is this a contest for the best horse, or the best rider? George had the best ride – George Fletcher!' Mister Handles was barking, 'The Injun! The Injun!' He paused for his boss to jump in but Buffalo Bill was busy peering out over the corrals for Gotch. 'It was the Injun, clear as day,' the barker went on. 'The Nigger was all show and the kid was too slow.'

The whole last act of our western melodrama looked like it was going to shake itself apart before the curtain fell. The five judges were beginning to shout and shove and the platform was pitching like a ship in a typhoon. Into the midst of this manly turmoil a delegation of the weaker sex came pouring, like rose oil on troubled waters. It was the cowgirls, reminding us that we seemed to have forgotten something in our excitement: the special Cowgirl Relay. The whole stadium breathed an audible sigh; this was just the diversion needed to give the officials time to untangle this annoysome tie. They huddled in discussion while the cowgirls and the broncriders and thirty thousand irritable fans waited. Sarah looked over the rail at me and stifled a devil-may-care yawn. Finally Mister Kell motioned Foghorn Clancy down from his crow's nest. The announcer listened, nodding and grinning, then climbed back to his megaphone.

'Today's Saddlebronc Ride! Has been *won!* By George Fletcher of Pendleton, *Oregon,* Jackson Sundown of Culdesac, Idaho, second, and John Spain of Tennessee, third. How*ever—!'* He held up a hand to thwart the protests. '–the score for the *All Round* World *Champ*ionship! . . . after a very *careful* tally . . . has been judged a *three-way draw!'*

The crowd moaned and grumbled. Clancy held up both hands.

'But in an un*precedented ruling* – after considering the me*diocre quality* of the nags in that last draw . . . three of the best of the baddest broncs in *O*-reegun . . . will be put in the hat for *another* draw . . . for a *Extra! tie*-breaking! *Last go round!'*

When the crowd finished roaring its approval the announcer continued. '*Al*so, ladies and gents . . . while this momentous event is being ar*ranged* . . . you will be entertained by these lovely ladies . . . in the world's first Cowgirl Relay Race!'

This suited everybody. The female delegation trooped back down the platform steps and the crowd settled back in their seats. And that curious cloud edged eagerly closer: this was the cat's pajamas and then some!

I didn't wait to see what three horses were picked. I headed straight for the participants' peanut gallery at the final turn. The rail was packed. All the contestants and volunteers had forgone their poker games and bottles and bull sessions to come watch. This was turning out to be some grand finale after all. I was stretching my neck at the back of the pack until I was noticed. Then the cowboys scrunched aside to make a place for me. They shook my hand and slapped my back, wished me good luck and my sweetie, too.

Sue Lin and the ancient Chinese sentry came working their way through the waiting pack, administering to the weary riders. The old man had a basket of rolled hot towels. He presented one to each of us, along with a little bow. Sue Lin followed in her voluminous black coolie outfit carrying a tray full of tea and treats. She handed me a cup and a fortune cookie.

'Your toe hurt great, John-E?'

'Great toe still hurts a mite, Sue Lin. Thank you.'

'You come to see you girl friend ride? She a good rider fairly much to you, I bet.'

The cowboys sniggered and my face went hot. So much for secret rendezvous. Sarah and I might as well have sent engagement announcements.

'Why, you're my girl, Sue Lin. You know that. Who else has been looking out for me in this distant land? Feeding me. Seeing to my hygiene and my clothes—'

This got another laugh. 'Too bad she never seen to get you some chaps, Johnny Reb,' one of the older riders teased. 'Then you might could give that pair of old cobs a run for their money.'

'I reckon so,' I said, glad to get off the subject of girl friends. 'That pair of old cobs told me the same thing themselves, more than once. I just never chanced to pass a chaps shop.'

Foghorn Clancy's voice began bellering out the rules for the cowgirl race. I handed back my towel and empty cup and returned to my place on the rail. The puzzling message in my cookie was attributed to Will Shake Spear: 'Golden lads and girls all must as

266

chimneysweeps come to dust.' I wasn't clear what ol' Will meant by it until the cowgirl race was almost over.

The rules were three laps on three different mounts, each girl having to change her saddle unassisted. I suspected the officials had tacked on this rule specifically to handicap Sarah Meyerhoff's top-dollar string of quarter horses. They calculated that in a straight-out race the light-framed Sarah would have run off and left the girls with the larger builds and the smaller assets. They calculated correctly. She exploded out of the pack on a bullet-headed mare like they had been fired from the starter's gun. She started in the outside lane but was in the lead on the rail before she was into the first turn. She blew me a reckless kiss as she flashed past. She went into the homestretch a good five lengths in the lead and still pulling away. Nurse O'Grady was riding second, on a quarter horse of her own. Big Prairie Rose was dead last, on a broomtail as homely as she was.

The next time around, on the second steed, Sarah was only two lengths ahead, with Nurse O'Grady and Prairie Rose Henderson neck and neck behind her. Whoever had come up with the saddle-changing dodge had figured it right. Sarah was a rider, as I said, not a hostler. She most likely had a stable boy on her daddy's payroll who usually readied her ride. Those other women were stronger. As she rounded the bend her face was grim and her jaw set. She didn't throw any kisses, either.

Her final saddle change must have been her slowest. I couldn't see; it was too far away, too dusty. When she came out of the dust cloud she was next to last. But this was the long-legged Appaloosa with the stretch that got longer and faster with every stride. They came blazing down that backstretch passing horse after horse. The whole crowd was on its feet screaming for her, and so was I, decorum be damned. She came into the back turn with only two riders ahead of her. Nurse O'Grady was in the lead, on that fat little show pony with the four-leaf clovers, and Prairie Rose was right on her heels The show pony wasn't so fast as he was experienced; once in front he knew how to keep you from getting around him. The shamrock-spotted rump was right in the way every time Prairie Rose tried to make a move. Frustrated, Prairie Rose swung her mount wide coming into the turn, hoping to pass on the outside. This left a gap and Sarah saw it. She touched her Appaloosa on the shoulder and the mare streaked through against the rail, right at the tightest tip of the turn. The big cowgirl was gaping after her in bucktoothed disbelief, and all the cowboys were cheering, me the loudest. Until I saw Sarah's face as she flashed past.

Her expression had gone past devil-may-care, past reckless. Her eyes were moon wide and her lips were pulled back from her teeth, just like her horse's. She and the mare both looked like they were snapped loose, broken away, cut clean from the restrictions of time and gravity. They would keep on accelerating, unfettered and completely free, lighter and lighter and faster and faster and faster until they reached the speed of light, just like they always wanted. Or thought they wanted, until they found out it didn't come completely free. It was a horse trade. Her saddling must have been short-shrifted, to save a few seconds. A bad swap. The cinch wasn't cinched enough to handle that abrupt swerve she made to get around the shamrocked rump that kept cutting her off. She made it past all right, and took a clear lead, but she was slipping. She could have reined up, eased off. She might have coasted in to easy victory. But she didn't. She was betting she'd reach that wire and light speed at the same time. A foolhardy bet, on top of a bad swap. She wasn't more than a half-dozen lengths from the finish when the cinch lost hold and the saddle slid under. Sarah pitched sideways right in front of the show pony. The O'Grady woman reined her best to avoid the falling girl, but her pony heel-clipped Sarah's Appaloosa. There was a cart-wheeling tangle of hooves and boots, of green sham-rocks and Appaloosa spots . . . and flying tresses the color of Golden Delicious apples on the branch.

Prairie Rose Henderson loped on around the tum-bling cloud to finish first.

The O'Grady woman was barely scratched, just a chipped tooth and another black eye. She was already in charge of the accident by the time I had vaulted the rail and run the distance. There were officials and cowboys and fans and even the Pinkertons crowded around, being useless and in the way. Meyerhoff was the worst of the lot. He was on his knees as close to Sarah as he could get, pounding his fat breast and blubbering like a babe. Nurse O'Grady commanded a couple of rubberneckers to drag him and his belly both some bloody where out of her hair. She was pointing fingers and giving orders like a sergeant.

'You, you, and you! Kneel down this side – one at the knee, one at the belt, one at the armpit. You three on the other side, do the same. Good. Now, one of you coppers kneel at her head and very gently – Jesus! will ya put yer bleedin' *gun* away for the love of Mary! If you want be shootin' something go shoot that wretched pony of mine.'

I pushed the rented lawman aside. 'I'll take her head,' I said. Nurse O'Grady acknowledged me with a chip-toothed smile. 'Good on you, Johnny-love. You've the gentler fingers, surely. Get situated . . .'

Sarah lay on her back as she had fallen. Her eyes were closed but her lips were still drawn back in that racing grimace. She was breathing through her teeth. Her hair lay about her like spilled honey; I had to gather it back around her face to make a spot for my knees. I spread my fingers and cradled her skull, trembling. Her eyes came open at my touch.

'What was it she called you? "Johnny-love"?' Her face was eggshell white but her eyes still shined blue and sassy. 'Who would've guessed you were such a Don Juan, Colonel Spain . . . ?'

'Whisht that!' Nurse O'Grady ordered. 'Everybody ready on the count of three. Slow and even, all I need's a few inches. One . . . two . . .'

She came up feather light. The head in my hands might have been a hollow mask were it not for the lively eyes. When Sarah was clear of the trodden dirt Nurse O'Grady whipped the prepared blanket beneath her with the same practiced ease she'd shown with her lariat. We lowered her back and Nurse O'Grady stood up, shouting at the judges' platform. 'Where the bloody hell is that flamin' doctor? Where's the ambulance car where's the stretcher? God's *balls!* this poor girl is perishing weary of layin' out here in the flies and cow flop!'

Sarah laughed through her clenched teeth, appreciative of the colorful expletives in spite of her obvious pain. I asked her what hurt most.

'My pride, what do you think? That Prairie Rose Henderson went on and won it after all, didn't she?'

'I'm afraid so,' I told her, brushing a lock of hair from her face. Her skin was damp with sweat yet very cold. 'You'll get her next time. You just take it easy and don't talk. We'll have you to the hospital in a quick shake—'

'But I *like* to talk, Johnny-love, if you haven't noticed. And what's this "we" baloney? Unless I been knocked out longer than I thought you still have a bronc to ride for the title. My long-drink-of-water All Round champion—'

'Forget that bronc and hold still! The only thing I intend to ride is that ambulance. Somebody has to keep your hair out of your eyes.'

'Forget the blazes! Your scarecrow carcass would be in the way as bad as Papa's belly. If either of you tries to come along I'll order the doctor to slam that ambulance door right in your face. Am I not correct about this, Miss Copperhead?'

Nurse O'Grady gave me a grave nod. 'She's correct, lad. You take your ride while we take ours. She's not needing to play honey-tongues just now.'

It turned out there wasn't any doctor to order or any door to slam. The ambulance and crew had left at 6.00 p.m. Oliver Nordstrum had refused to pay them overtime. There wasn't even a stretcher. Cursing, Nurse O'Grady dashed away to take care of the problem herself.

I waited on my knees. The stadium was deathly quiet. Somebody passed a canteen and I poured a few drops through Sarah's teeth. They were beginning to chatter. A couple of citizens removed their jackets and spread them over her. She apologized for the delay she was causing. 'Why don't you boys bring out some hazing gates?' she suggested. 'You could build a little corral around me and get this dismal rodeo done with. It's get-get-getting dark, time to head for the barn . . .'

Her eyes were going glassy. 'Hush,' I told her. 'Just hush and hold still.' This time she did. She didn't speak again until Nurse O'Grady returned with the Rolls. An Indian travois was sticking up from the rear seat, dangling beads and feathers from its peeled-pine frame.

'If it isn't a s-squaw sled,' Sarah chattered. 'I told you I had Indian blood.'

We blanket-lifted her onto the travois, then lashed the device on top of the right-hand seats, feet forward. Nurse O'Grady climbed in back beside her. 'Somebody who can drive and knows the way, get in and drive. Everybody else get the hell out of the way.'

The bartender that had refused to serve us at Hookners took the wheel. Papa Meyerhoff made a pathetic wobbling run to catch the car but Nurse O'Grady urged the driver on through the park gate. I took his arm and maneuvered him back toward his other daughters, at the concession booths. He'd just about run out of tears; his sobs were sounding drier and drier.

'Sarah'll be all right, sir,' I kept telling him, over and over. 'Don't worry about Sarah, Sarah'll be all right.'

He wouldn't believe me. He pulled a handful of bills from his apron pocket and waved them in the air, sobbing that he would give twice that amount to anyone who would give him a ride to the hospital. One of the Pinkertons took him up on it.

Chapter Nineteen

Last Go Round

George and Sundown had been watching from the
starter's tower with a score of other cowboys who had
sense enough, consideration enough, to stay out of the
way. They climbed down and fell in beside me.

'How's your girl friend, Johnny?' George asked. 'Can
she wiggle her toes?'

I told him she could, and her fingers as well. 'But
where did everybody get the notion Sarah Meyerhoff is
my girl friend?'

'I got the notion at the Meyerhoffs' dinner table, days
ago. The first time she gave you that look. I guess it
took a while longer for you to get it. How's Mister
Meyerhoff?'

'Beside himself, as you can imagine. He thinks the
accident was his fault. I worried at first that he would
drown himself in tears, but it looks like he's hit
bottom. He bought a ride to the hospital from one of
the Pinkertons.'

The pair nodded at this and were silent. They had
the good manners not to ask the next obvious question.
I answered it anyway.

'I didn't ride to the hospital with her because there
wasn't room,' I said. I could've squeezed in somewhere, I knew, and I was feeling more and more mean

273

that I hadn't. 'Sarah admonished me in no uncertain terms to stay here. Finish what I started, she said.'

George wanted to know how the horse wreck happened. They'd been back at the corrals, advising the officials which three broncs they personally considered the baddest. When they heard the moan from the crowd they came running. They climbed the platform just in time to see us lift her on the blanket. I gave a curt description of the pile-up and found myself fighting back tears.

'I knowed it was Sarah,' George said. 'The instant I heard that crowd, I knowed it. Sarah Meyerhoff's been getting busted up since the day she was born almost. She wiggled off the baby scale and split her chin before she was more'n a couple months old.'

'I asked her how she got that cleft,' I recalled. 'She told me a cleft on the chin means the devil's within.'

'Once, when she was about five,' George went on, 'after her mama was killed . . . Mister Meyerhoff took to bringing her to the store with the other girls so's not to hire a baby-sitter. The big sisters were already pitching in, waiting on customers. Sarah didn't like waiting on nothing. What Sarah liked was prowling, especially in places she wasn't supposed to prowl – like back in the feed-and-seed warehouse, where me and the barn cats ground grain and chased rats. There was a one-eyed calico mama with a litter hid somewhere. We could hear them but we couldn't find the nest. I finally give up. Then, one afternoon when I was dozing, Sarah trailed her to her hideout, way high behind a stack of seed corn. She went to rooting after the kittens and pulled the whole stack over on herself – eighty pounds to the sack! Broke both her arms right

274

above the wrist. That time it was me drove her to the doctor, in their old supply wagon. Mister Meyerhoff sat in back, begging her not to cry, though she never cried a drop the whole ride. Mister Meyerhoff, he bawled like a crazy man. He said he wasn't any better a father than he'd been a husband.'

'He didn't use to be crazy,' Sundown said. 'He used to play the clarinet.'

'That's so,' George said. 'And Missus Meyerhoff played the harp. They met at a Independence Day concert. The Christmas Eve night her hansom slid off the road, in fact, she was coming back from a recital up at the old high-school gym. Mister Meyerhoff didn't go, because he didn't know any Christmas carols. He blamed himself for not going and he blamed himself for letting her go – not that he could've stopped her. She was just as willful as Sarah.'

This comparison didn't make me feel any better. I said I was thinking I ought to ride after her. They hit me from both sides with reasons why that wouldn't be a good idea. George said the hospital was way the other end of town, and hard to find. Sundown said even if I found it they wouldn't let me in, filthy as I looked. 'They wouldn't let me in the time my wife lost our baby – and I had on a clean suit.' They were still arguing at me when we reached the judges' platform. Cecil Kell was waiting at the top of the steps.

'Come on up, boys. This last draw is going to be drawn in front of everybody.'

The judges' platform wasn't all that high, yet how different things looked from up there. The stock in the corrals behind us appeared diminished and tame. The grandstand across the way looked like it was full of dolls. A horse-and wagon creeping toward us across

275

the park looked like a schoolboy's toy. Foghorn Clancy broke my reverie.

'Here they *stand*, Gents and Janes . . . the best three broncbusters in the *world* . . .drawing the names of the *three baddest broncs!* Okay, boys; who goes first?'

Cecil Kell removed his hat and dropped in three folded chits. George and Sundown reached in together. I took the one that remained. We took our time unfolding our draws. Foghorn Clancy couldn't stand it.

'Don't keep us on *tenter*hooks, Chief! Put it in the basket. *I'll* read it to the folks . . .'

'I can read,' the Indian replied before he dropped his chit in the woven basket. Clancy pulled it up and unfolded it. He stretched his neck to the big megaphone like a rooster.

'Up *first!* On *Whirl*wind – a Lazy M bronc out of the McCormick stables: Mister Jackson *Sun*down, from Yakima, *Wash*ington!'

From the Indian camp a savage ovation of drums and warhoops and coyote howls rose in response to the Nez Percé's name.

George turned to his stonefaced partner. 'Ain't that properly Sundown *Jack*son? From Culdesac, *I*daho?' He dropped his slip of paper in the basket. Clancy reeled it up and read it.

'Number *two!* Riding *Long Tommm!* the Cheyenne bronc that has never allowed *any* human to sit on him more than *eleven seconds! . . . is Mister George Fletcher* from Pendleton, *O* Ree Gun!'

Now it was the grandstand's turn. The crowd let out such a roar the slow-motion horse pulling the toy cart was spooked into a slow-motion gallop. It was the luggage wagon, with Reverend Linkhorn and Louise on the seat, and all the help from the train on benches in the back. The Reverend finally sawed the lumbering Percheron to a halt directly in front of the grandstand.

'Look there, Kell!' Buffalo Bill was standing up in his dignitary box, pointing across the arena. 'Didn't I tell you? You let one monkey in, next thing you know you got a whole wagonload crashing the gates to root for him, *then* has the brass to park square in front of the most expensive seats in the show! Boys—?' he called over the rail. Only one Pinkerton remained. 'Mister Lovejoy, meander over and help those brass monkeys find their way back out.'

The man rose and brushed the hay off his trousers. He started to cross the arena but Mister Kell had other ideas. 'Leave them stay,' he ordered. 'Everybody needs rooters.' The man stopped and turned, looking from Cecil Kell to Buffalo Bill. 'Leave them stay, I tell you,' Kell said again. 'You're off duty. You been off duty for—' He took out a watch the size of a sugar cookie. '—about half a minute. Close that gate behind you.'

The detective wavered, watching his boss. The old Indian fighter removed George's hat and wiped his brow on his buckskin sleeve. He looked pretty abandoned in his box seat. Gotch was missing. The barker was off looking for Gotch. Maggie O'Grady the Colleen of the Cowgirls had become Nurse O'Grady and had apparently defected. All that was left of his army was the clubfooted Oliver Nordstrum and that wavering mercenary. Buffalo Bill had learned a thing or two from George Custer. He dismissed the Pinkerton with a wave and sat back down. Foghorn reeled my draw up and stretched to his megaphone.

'Last up . . . on a broomtail name of *Star* Going *Some!* donated, it says here, by the *Calapooya Nation!* . . . is a young Star going Some himself: Johnathan E.

Lee Spain from Ten-ah-*see!* Give our Southern boy a big hand Ladies and Gentlemen.'

'You notice, Dog?' George teased when the applause stopped. 'The folks that gave our Tennessee stud the biggest hand was mostly *lady*folks?'

I wasn't in any mood for teasing. 'This Star Going Some must be a pretty sorry bag of bones for the Indians to get shed of him.'

'That isn't why they got shed of him,' Sundown said. 'They suspect he's a *waw-noosaway*, a devil horse.'

'What gives them that suspicion? Has he got horns and a forked tail? Asides, didn't you two pick the broncs? You all was wanting to draw him, is what I think.'

Sundown ignored my accusation. 'Star Going Some has killed folks. At the Warm Springs spring powwow I saw him break a good rope so he could take after a young buck that had rode him the year before. He run the boy down in the sagebrush, rammed him over, and trampled his shinbone. Crushed it so bad the doctor in Bend had to cut it off at the knee. Let's get you another bronc, Little Brother. This one's mean and dirty.'

I told him No thanks; Star Going Some suited me just fine, the mean dirty way I was feeling. But when I saw him in the chute pen in the flesh, standing humped up and sinister among the lengthening shadows, the sight had the effect of strong lye soap: it scoured my dirty meanness off like scum off a slop jar.

He was standing a little apart from the other two broncs, but he gave the impression of being as far removed as though he were an entirely different species. He stood with blunt head lowered and pink eyes hooded, looking down into the hoof-hammered sod like he expected something to rise from the very dust and he intended to trample it the moment it emerged. A large brand marred his left flank: a four-pointed star, burned clumsy and thick, like something a child might have drawn with a charred piece of firewood. George saw me staring.

'It ain't a brand. It's a birthmark. And a four-pointed star is a sign for danger. You can see how primitive sorts like Mister Jackson's kin would assume the ugly devil was hexed.'

'Worse than hexed,' Sundown said.

I nodded without comment. Civilized sorts would as easily assume the same. The animal's sinister pink-eyed aspect alone was enough to make most riders suspect that this sorrel skin enclosed an evil spirit. That four-pointed birthmark star would have clinched it.

The other two broncs were stamping nervously along the rail, anxious to get down to business. George's draw, Long Tom, I already knew: I had watched him buck Slope-Nose – Cantrell, that was his name – halfway to Idaho the day before. Long Tom was a bony old veteran, stretched thin and black as the late-afternoon shadows. He had one white sock on his right front leg. Legend had it he bucked the other three off.

Sundown's horse was a cloudy-gray mare, spinning from corner to corner in the tight pen. She was very long-lashed and glossy-maned and rather ladylike. But when she rolled her eyes she revealed a pent-up hysteria beneath those lashes. And when she spun round at the corral's corner the long mane wafted and whirled like wind made visible.

Star Going Some. Long Tom. Whirlwind. It was easy to see how this trio of outlaws got their monickers. The peeled-pine gate opened and the bronc wranglers rode in, swinging their loops. 'Better grab your saddles and skedaddle, gentlemen,' one of them advised. 'These peaches are ripe.'

His name was John Muir, ever hear of him? The nature-loving buddy of Teddy Roosevelt? I remember him on account of he was the most unlikely-looking cowboy you ever saw – wide-browed and full-bearded and wearing bookworm spectacles. He'd come all the way from Washington, D.C., to see if Oregon had any land worth making a national park out of. He entered the rodeo as a lark. I saw him go up on Whistling Annie the first day of saddlebronc. He pulled leather at the first little jump she made and got his nose broke anyway. After that he did his larking from the saddle of a wrangling horse. It was a good thing he had that naturalist dodge to fall back on, because he wasn't any better with a lariat than he was with a bucking bronc. He did more stampeding than wrangling. His partners finally had to drive him out of the corral.

The wranglers got loops on George and Sundown's broncs first, because they were the rowdiest. Star Going Some was still staring at the dirt between his hooves. Muir rode back in as the two broncs were led out. He rode slowly up behind the humpbacked sorrel, a finger on his lips, telling everybody to hold still and keep quiet. He was aiming to simply sneak up on the dozing bronc and drop a loop over its head from behind. It was as if Star Going Some had been waiting for just such a sneak attack all along. He uncoiled from his repose sudden as a snake, and sunk his teeth in the shoulder of Muir's mount. When Muir flailed at him with the rope the sorrel turned loose the horse and went for the man. The terrified wrangling horse bolted for safety and John Muir the nature student got a chance to study some Oregon land close up. The two backup wranglers rode in to protect the thrown rider and the crazy sorrel went after *them*. They finally got the sorrel double-roped and quieted a little. Muir rose from the dirt, his specs now a match for his broken nose.

'Experience is the mother of widsom,' he declared. This was too pompous for Star Going Some. He lunged again for Muir, snapping his teeth and slicing the air with his hooves. He was still lunging and snapping as they dragged him away. *'Waw-noosaway,'* the Indian repeated gravely. George put a hand on my shoulder.

'Whatcha think, Nashville? This one gritty enough to suit you?'

I swallowed hard and told him Time will tell. We shouldered our saddles and followed the three surging broncs and their half-dozen wranglers toward the arena. A whispered hiss from the shadows stopped me.

'Fssst, John-E, here. I fix them for you.'

It was Sue Lin, peeking at me around the white-washed gatepost.

'Here. You accept it, please. I fix them for you fairly much.'

She thrust a ball of black silk at me. I wasn't sure what it was or whether I wanted to accept it, please. She peeked around the other side of the post.

'Misteh Fretcher? Misteh Jackson? Tell him to accept, please.'

George took the cloth and commenced to unroll it. I had already guessed what it was by watching Sue Lin. Slim though she was, parts of her were wider than that post. She was bare from her bottom down. George

281

held the garment up, laughing. Even Mister Jackson couldn't stifle his chuckles.

'Take it, Little Brother.'

'You better,' George said, no longer laughing. 'Sue Lin's been your Guardian Angel for days. You dasn't tempt the fates by refusing.'

I couldn't much say no. The pantlegs had already been ripped open up the seams. She peeked back around the post at me, still without raising her eyes. She asked that I return the garment as soon as I was finished please fairly much. I promised I would, honest Injun.

The old-fashioned saddle-'em-in-the-arena would never work nowadays. It would be too slow for television's impatient audience with their remote click-clickers. But audiences back then had a lot less options to click from, thus a lot more patience. They enjoyed the riga-marole. It gave folks a chance to get to know the broncs and the riders before the bucking began. The horse is drug out in full view, wild and naked. The rider follows on foot with saddle and tack and helps blindfold and saddle him before he mounts up.

Sundown's storm-gray mare is first. She leads easy between the wranglers' horses, twitchy but restrained. They stop in the center of the arena and she stands between the wranglers' horses, nervous as a bride. The snubbing rope is passed through the fork of the snubber's saddle on her right, then under her jaw, through her halter, and back over her neck where it's hitched close around the snubber's saddle horn. Then a doubled strip of red muslin is tucked in place on each side of her halter. She submits to the blindfold as though the grimy swatch of muslin were a lace veil.

Then she waits, her ears pricked for the approaching footsteps. Sundown carries his beadwork saddle across the sod and hefts it to the mounted wrangler on her left. The wrangler eases it to her back. Dropping to one knee, formal as a bridegroom, Sundown makes the cinch snug beneath her ribs. He waits until she empties her lungs, then cinches again and fastens the latigo. Satisfied, he steps back around to the outside of the hazing horse and springs up behind the wrangler. From there he's able to ease himself gently over into his saddle without stirring the mare up prematurely. The crowd watches in rapt silence as the Indian works his boots deep into the stirrups. This is classic, their silence says. This is grand. The historic union of elemental royalty. The mating dance of Sun and Wind. And as if to emphasize how classy, a delightful little coincidence occurs. At the north end of the track, where the concession booths are set up, a dust devil whirls to life and hops the rail into the arena. This dervish is spinning toward the ceremony, tossing torn tickets and peanut sacks into the air like flower girls tossing rose petals. It happens so matter-of-course nobody thought twice about it until the *Oregonian* mentioned it the next day.

The stands are as twitchy as the mare by now, straining to imagine the nuptial vows being exchanged in the blood-blessed chapel before them: 'Do you Sundown take this mare? Do you Whirlwind take this buckaroo?' Man and animal nod together. The snubbing rope is flipped free from one side as the blindfold is jerked away from the other. 'We now pronounce you cowboy and bronc. Let 'er buck!'

Sundown rocks backward and rowels the neck and shoulders. The mare makes a mighty kick at the sky.

The crowd thunders to its feet and we're in business. Sundown is leaned so far back the mare's high-kicking rump knocks his hat off. Man and mare are both impossibly perpendicular for a heart-stopping tick – the mare actually walking on her front hooves, like a circus acrobat walking on his hands; the rider standing straight up in the stirrups, hatless, his Wild West coxcomb flaring. When the mare's hind hooves come back to earth she plants them very neatly to the right of the prints left by her fore-hooves. She paws at the clouds, then jackknifes back down, twisting her fore-quarters to the left with a sling of her head. She does it again. And again. And again! Teeter-tottering up and down, round and round, more like a Brahma bull than a horse, spinning counterclockwise, faster and faster. This is more than the dust devil can resist. It waltzes right in, casting clutter before it like confetti. For a blissful moment all are joined in a single gawdy dustcloud – man and animal, earth and air, clutter and confetti . . . twisting together until nobody can make out front from rear. Then the mare plunges out of the cloud and takes off in a last-gasp run across the arena, bucking double-hard in a straight-legged, spine-jarring series of bounds that makes your kidneys ache just watching. The rider is raking just as hard. Rake and buck, spin and spur. The nuptials are obviously over and so is the honeymoon. Still, Sundown doesn't allow the contest to degenerate into a mere domestic squabble. On and on he rides, stonefaced and straight up, and curiously considerate. Every watching wife is uplifted; every husband's heart made proud.

The fifteen-second time bell wasn't mandatory back then. The judges judged you for as long as they considered your ride worth judging. That's why you run across the old records that go sixteen seconds, twenty seconds, *thirty-seven seconds!* That's how long they let Pete Wilson ride a little buzzbomb called Shelall in nineteen-seventeen. Look it up in the library if you doubt my word. More than half a minute and he never even placed. Pete was actually docked some points! Some judge thought he detected something in Pete's ride he didn't care for, and had let him ride the extra time to make sure.

But this extended ride between Sundown and Whirlwind wasn't like that. The judges weren't looking for any flaws. They were enjoying the ride, like everybody else. I don't remember any bell signaling the end, to tell the truth. The end was obvious. The mare quit bucking, simple as that. Bowed before the superior power. Remember the kid's tale about Wind arguing with Sun that she was stronger? She tries to blow the coat off a passing pilgrim to prove it. The pilgrim just wraps the coat tighter against the blast. Then the sun comes out and warms the man until he takes his coat off on his own.

The crowd roared acclaim as the Indian rode from the arena with Whirlwind beneath him, obedient but unbent. Dignified. Sundown hadn't broken her, exactly – he had instructed her. As they passed I got another look into the horse's eyes. The storm had passed and her craziness was cured. Her bucking-bronc seasons were over as well. Last I saw Whirlwind she was pulling a milk wagon for The Dalles Creamery, and letting schoolkids sit on her back . . . with dignity, still.

George's ride was the other end of the stick. He knew he was going to have to go some to top his partner's showing, and dignity was not his strong suit. He knew he looked the fool in his floppy work-hat and rundown boots and a shapeless saddle over his shoulder like a carcass too decomposed to identify – so that's how he played it. He gave the saddle a dainty polish with his shirtsleeve before he handed it up to the wrangler. The crowd laughed. Then he folded the brim of his hat up like a muleskinner and made a foolish fuss with the blindfold and cinch. When the saddle was secure to his liking he motioned both the hazer and the snubber to turn Long Tom free and get clear. Finger to his lips, George began to tiptoe backwards from the blindfolded bronc. Back . . . back, he tiptoed.

'What's he aiming to do?' Nordstrum wondered from the platform. Buffalo Bill's boozy voice answered.

'Ah, he's just jigabooing. He's gonna mount him leapfrog, from behind.' Then to everybody's discomfort, the old man went into a bleaty rendition of that bawdy schoolboy song:

'I jumped for the saddle
But the saddle wasn't there,
And I druv ten inches
Up the old gray mare!
Come and tie my pecker
to a tree to a tree—'

Nobody laughed, not even Nordstrum. The ditty dwindled to silence. The famous showman was rapidly losing his audience. But he was right about George's intentions. The blindfolded horse stood sniffing the air, baffled by the delay. George made a dash, slapped both palms on the tall horse's rump, and leapfrogged. By the time he hit the saddle Long Tom was already bucking, blindfold be damned. George grabbed the braided rope with one hand and snatched the muslin away with the other. The long-boned bronc made a couple considerate bucks to give George a chance to find the stirrups, then decided he was ready to get serious. Except George had decided different. He knew whatever chance he had to top Sundown's stately ride had to lie in the opposite way – in the buffoon, the clown, the *minstrel* way – and he went the whole nine yards that direction. As he'd been advised by his venerable daddy, 'If you're gonna eat watermelon – eat watermelon!'

I don't mean he forced his clowning; he just followed the natural path, one step after the other, dealing with problems as they popped up. First off, he had that blindfold in his hand to deal with. He tried it for a riding crop. Too limp. He pretended to twirl it like a lariat, as if the pile-driving outlaw he was riding were a trained roping horse. Too short. Finally he chomped the buck rope between his teeth and tied the strip of muslin around *his* eyes. He rode this way, feeling the air in front of him with both hands like a blind drunk. The grandstands rocked with laughter.

Long Tom wasn't accustomed to being made an object of ridicule. He took off at a full gallop in search of something to scrape the tormentor off his back. The blindfold jounced down just in time for George to see the rail coming up. He loops his railside leg over the horse's neck, out of danger, and lets Long Tom scrape his right flank full of splinters. Seated primly side-saddle, George whips the blindfold over his floppy hat and holds it at his throat, scarfwise, like a lady in a bonnet out for a ride around the plantation. This insults the proud old bronc more than ever. Back our direction he comes galloping flat out for the other rail. George feels for the right stirrup but it is gone.

George tries to saw him away again but this time Long Tom is not to be dissuaded. Right through the bunting-draped two-by-fours he smashes, straight up into the VIP seats. Dignitaries scatter screaming with their wives and children. A hellacious sight, that black horse and horseman invading their privileged world like something escaped from the pit. Clancy is ringing the gong that the ride is over but George and the bronc both know better. They are going to continue ascending right onto the top seats and over, to Ethereal Glory, if Long Tom has his way. George persuades the horse that there are yet some worldly glories they haven't exhausted and gets him reined around. Back down they come, through a different section, scattering a fresh bunch of VIP's. Long Tom misses the breach he made in the rail and has to smash a fresh one. He hits the arena dirt already going at his flat-out gallop. George makes his running dismount off one side just as his old army saddle tumbles off the other. It hits the ground and scatters completely to pieces – tree; horn; fork; gullet; cantle; shirts and fenders and leathers and brads . . . like the Deacon's Marvelous One Hoss Shay that was made so well in all its parts it lasted one hundred years, then disintegrated all at once. But it wasn't the time to be mooning after departed riding tack.

The crowd is on its feet and howling its appreciation. George doffs his hat and sweeps it low in one burlesque bow after another. When he finally straightens back up he doesn't return the ancient hat to his head. Instead, he turns back to the dignitary bleachers and sails it side-arm, up over the splintered pine into the VIP seats, like a bullfighter slinging the bull's tail to a señorita.

The hat catches a breeze and sails incredibly, up and up, then it stalls and turns, like it saw an old acquaintance, and goes sailing for the judges' platform. It comes to roost in the empty box seat alongside the venerable William Cody. Everybody's as amused as they are amazed. Buffalo Bill tries to ignore the shabby visitor and this amuses the crowd more than ever. They're still heehawing when George comes bowlegging out the gate. He's lugging the saddle parts in his horseblanket. I have to ask him if he made that throw at Buffalo Bill on purpose, or was it just a lucky accident.

'My pappy used to say, "Son, everything is a accident—"' He digs the blindfold from a hip pocket and hands it to me. 'The trick is making believe it's on purpose.'

Chapter Twenty

My Turn

My turn is mostly a blur. The biggest ride of my seventeen-year-old Cinderella life and all I can make out is the stuff in the background. Like one of those daguerreotypes taken with old film plates: everything that held still for the required exposure time is in focus, sharp as a razor – the oval track; the grandstands; the flags hanging red-white-and-blue against the golden roll of wheatland; the cast-iron sky sitting tight on top of it all, like a lid on a pressure cooker . . . that stuff I can picture clear. But me and Star Going Some are just a smear across the picture's middle. I do remember what I was thinking about before my turn: I was thinking about George and Sundown's fantastic rides. One classical, one comical, both unforgettable. Those two had pretty much stacked out their respective ends of the stick, was my thinking. The only place left for me was the middle. The best way I can think of to explain my strategy is with a story Sundown told me a few years later (exactly three years later, because I was soaking my fresh stump in this very hospital while he told it) . . . about a couple of legendary Nez Percé knife makers. They were always in an argument over which one of them could chip the sharpest edge. The best obsidian in the world comes from a hill east of

290

Bend called Glass Butte. It's mahogany obsidian, swirls of yellow and brown and amber. That Ko Shar rock that's not there anymore was a big boulder of it, either dragged there a distance of several hundred miles, or blown there by a volcano. Personally, I think it was dragged there, for its beauty and power. Mahogany obsidian was so highly prized that blades and arrowheads of it were found by the first white settlers, clear back on the East Coast. Indians came to Glass Butte from all over America to get it. You can imagine their squaws: 'Go out to Oregon and get me some of that pretty obsidian like Doe Next Door has . . . and don't come back until you do!'

Anyway, these Nez Percé knife makers decided to have a contest to see who could chip the keenest edge. They asked their old knife-maker teacher to referee it. The tribe staged up the contest in a meadow with a shallow little creek meandering through it. The first Indian steps forth and sticks his knife hilt down in the stream's sandy bottom. The blade protrudes above the water, edge into the current. Upstream he floats a big maple leaf. The leaf floats slowly down into the edge and is cut in half. The tribe yips and yells.

Then the second fellow sticks his blade in the sand and floats his leaf. It floats down and is sliced in half just like the other one – only this leaf joins back together on the other side of the blade! The tribe drums and dances. The knife makers go to arguing again: Which is sharper? The cut that stays, or the cut that closes?

They put the question to the old teacher. He doesn't say a thing. Instead he pulls his own blade out of its scabbard and sticks it in the stream, hilt down and edge upstream. He floats his own maple leaf. The leaf drifts down, slowly, slowly, then just before it touches the blade, takes a smart right turn, and goes *around* it.

That's how I planned to make my ride. I could sense that bronc's lethal edge before I even touched him. Sundown was right; Star Going Some was a man-hater. I could actually smell his hate; he was giving it off like a grizzly gives off musk – on purpose. He in*tended* for me to smell it. He wanted me to understand straightaway that he wasn't interested in just bucking me off – he wanted to trample me to death. Bucking me off was merely a way of getting my brains and briskets within reach of his hooves. Get a bronc rider thinking about that, was Star Going's scheme, and you got him hexed before the ride even starts. So I tried not to think about it. It's one of those Sunday-school mind tricks: How do you *not think* about Old Scratch's right eye? You think about His other eye, is how. So every time that vindictive devil would crane his neck around to give me his pink-eyed hex, I thought about something else – apples and tunnels; corned beef and kraut – anything to keep from being drawn into that blade that Star Going Some had waiting for me. Like the maple leaf, I took a smart turn right.

That's why I can't find myself in the old pictures my memory took of that final ride: I wasn't exactly there. My mind was elsewhere. My time? I don't remember. Score? I haven't the scantest. All I have is that blurry smear across a black-and-white background, back and forth, up and down.

Then my toe was throbbing and I knew I had dismounted. Wranglers were towing the Star-marked stud away and he was still Going Some, thrashing and gnashing his teeth in a fit of frustration. People were on

292

their feet applauding as I gimped back toward the riders' gate. It was not the full-throated roar of acclaim that had followed the other two finalists. I hadn't expected that it would be. Star Going Some's murderous grace wasn't something a crowd could see. I was content with my ride, but I knew that, to the crowd's eye, it was nowhere near as flashy as George's flamboyant performance, or as stately and splendid as the Indian's. Yet I knew my ride had been right – graceful, even – though I could not remember a single second of it. I could tell by the afterglow. Grace cannot be its own witness, but it leaves a tingling residue in its wake.

The Beeson twins stepped out from beneath the platform and shook my hand with a squeeze that told me they knew it, too. Then Prairie Rose grinned her generous grin and give me the okay sign with her thumb and forefinger. Her two cowgirl buddies bobbed their heads in agreement. I found George sitting on the ground at the edge of the cottonwoods, gazing forlornly at the pieces of his destroyed saddle spread out in front of him. He brightened when he saw me. 'That was some prime ride, cowboy.'

Sundown's flat, formal monotone concurred from the peaceful shade where their horses were resting. 'Real prime.'

Who needs the roar of the multitudes when they have tribute like that from experts like those? I was more than fulfilled, I was foundered. I had had enough of too much already. All I wanted now was a few minutes of peaceful shade of my own and a swish of water to rinse the dust out of my goozle, then wrap it up – get finished and get gone, go locate that damned hospital.

In fact, everybody was eager to get the dickens out of

Dodge, as they say: the townspeople as well as the tourists. The riders and the ropers, the dignitaries and the shit-shovelers, the corn-poppers and the ticket vendors – even that grumbling cloud up on the ridge . . . all were yearning that this punkin would soon roll to a stop.

Thus we come to the famous final scene – the wild-card ending that every Pendleton Round Up fan knows about, yet doesn't know about. I've read several so-called eyewitness accounts of it, and listened to several dozen more. Most of them were really How-I-had-it-*told*-to-me-by-eyewitness accounts. Go look at the Round Up–history books that come out every few seasons, with all their facts researched and documented. If you find any two of them alike I'll eat your hat. They all agree up to a point – that the three of us were tied after three days; that we had to ride an extra go round to settle it. But the thing that follows, *that's* where the historians and the researchers and even the eyewitnesses part company and go whirling off every which way. It's no blessed wonder. Even those of us actually there that afternoon were left a little dizzy by the spin of events.

So, as you were forewarned, this is not the truth the whole truth and nothing but the truth, certainly – this is merely my version. Take it or leave it.

The weather was turning. You hear it in hum of the wind: 'September's just about over,' it was humming, 'put the tools and toys of summer away.' I had just dipped a gourdful of water out of the barrel when Clancy's bell began to clang. I spit out the mudball I had worked up and limped wearily back toward the field of combat.

Cowboys and Indians and a hoi polloi of behind-the-scenes laborers were headed the same weary way. Women smiled at me; men nodded; and kids pointed and whispered: 'That's one of the three.' I was a star.

In the middle of the arena the wranglers have towed out a sheet-shrouded shape on wheels. It's too small to be a buggy and too big to be a vendor cart. George and Sundown are standing in front of the mysterious shape, waiting.

'Shake a leg, Nashville,' George calls. 'Before Mars Foghorn break his bell.'

Clancy sees me and stops clanging. When I have joined my two friends he holds up a big brown envelope.

'In this envelope, gents and ladies all . . . I possess the *name* of the first World Champion *cow*boy – exactly as it was passed to me by our diligent judges. Before I open it I insist we show these officials our appreci*ation!*'

He also insisted on praising each of them separately and lavishly. His voice was growing rapidly weaker but the praises went on and on. I kept craning my neck the direction the Rolls-Royce had gone, wondering why it hadn't returned. Pendleton wasn't that big. George could tell I was getting irritated. He edged over. 'Aint no good getting anxious, Johnny. Louise told me Sarah Meyerhoff is done headed for the Portland Hospital.'

'To Portland? How could she—?'

'On the train. It had already hung around way behind schedule, waiting for the passengers from the Round Up. When Mister Meyerhoff offered the conductor and the engineer a hundred dollars apiece they decided it was time to pull out. The O'Grady woman went along, Louise said, nursing Sarah and Mister

Meyerhoff both. She was trying to nurse one of them awake and the other one to sleep.'

'Which was which?'

'Mister Meyerhoff was who she was trying to put to sleep. He was about to pop a gut, Louise says. Sarah was acting a little woozy. But Louise says don't worry; your gal can still wiggle her toes.'

'How far is it to Portland?'

'Too far to ride a played-out horse,' Sundown said.

'Way too far,' George said. 'According to Louise, the engineer left all the cars here but Nordstrum's private coach and the mail car. Another engine is due tomorrow from Boise to haul the rest. You can probably get your same fresh-air accommodations, if you want.'

I was wanting to hear more about Sarah but the preamble to the awards presentation was about to be over. Foghorn was beginning to lose his voice. George and I edged back apart and listened to the announcer's croaking conclusion.

'—to these and the many other volunteers far too numerous to mention, I would like to say Well Done and Hip-hip-*hooray!* And now—' He took a folded paper from the envelope. '—without further *ado* . . . the first World! Champion! All Round Cowboy *is*—' He unfolded the paper and read it to himself several times, blinking to be sure he had it right. He swallowed hard and croaked into the megaphone. '—is Johnathan E. Lee *Spain!*'

Thirty thousand jaws drew a simultaneous gasp of shock. Every soul on the grounds was taken completely by surprise, the knowledgeable as well as the naive. The dignitaries were surprised. The cowboys and cowgirls were surprised; the vendors and the volunteers were surprised. (The gamblers were stunned!) Even some of the judges seemed bowled over by the outcome of the tallying, and they had been the tally men. There were only three people in the place who weren't surprised: Mister Kell, who had counted the tallies and placed the winner's name in the envelope; and the two men standing on each side of me.

'You did good, Johnathan E. Lee,' George said. The Indian grunted his customary agreement. 'Real good.'

The crowd wasn't so agreeable. Things were going awry fast, and that gasp of shock was turning into suspicious murmurings. I figured it out later, what must have happened . . .

There were five judges: Cecil Kell, Jacob Meyerhoff, Oliver Nordstrum, Abner Henderson, and a barber named Whiffletree, or Wigglesworth, or some such rose-watery name. Meyerhoff was off with his daughter on the truncated train, so that made four. Kell was for George and that left three. As a junior member of the William Cody Wild West Extravaganza gang, Oliver Nordstrum was supposed to vote for the picturesque Indian; but that gang seemed to have dwindled down to one fading western star with a silver canteen for his sidekick; so Oliver made a quick reappraisal. A red-skinned poster boy might be a big Wild West attraction in the Eastern environs and Europe, but out here in the real Wild West they were a dime a dozen. And since a black-skinned poster boy was out of the question in any environs, Oliver Nordstrum decided to take a longshot on me.

Abner Henderson took a longer shot still: he cast his vote for Prairie Rose. It was more than a disgruntled gesture of protest from a disappointed father. Abner felt that, with George and Sundown and me tied for first place, the cowboy with the next-highest score was technically in second place and should have had a shot at the All Round, even if that cowboy happened to be his daughter.

That left Barber Whitherhorse. He cast the deciding vote my direction. It was the following fall before I heard why, from Whitherhorse's mouth itself. I was tilted back in his barber chair at the time with my hair freshly trimmed, waiting for him to give me my full two bits' worth. I asked him outright: Why me? He acted a little disappointed that I hadn't grasped the obvious.

'Why you? Good golly, Mister Spain – what likelihood was there that wooly-headed George Fletcher or long-braided Jack Sundown would ever be sitting in that seven-hundred-dollar chair? You were a potential *customer*.'

So I was given the title by a clubfooted stockbroker and a perfumed periwinkle, neither of which knew anything about horseflesh beyond what the limited vista from the seat of a buggy afforded them. The murmur of the crowd was getting louder and angrier. The grandstands were buzzing like a paper-wasp nest in a hailstorm. We were glad to see Prairie Rose Henderson come riding out, her sunny smile still shining. The murmur quieted a little.

For the first time since the opening-day parade, our Round Up queen is resplendent in her royal regalia. A cape of purple velvet trails from her shoulder and halfway down her horse's hind legs. A rhinestone crown has been laced to the hatbrim of her hard-used hat. Christmas tinsel has transformed her leather quirt into a queenly scepter. She holds it high as she rides. This is the final duty of her reign. She was to ride a circle around us waving the scepter, then dismount and unveil the prize. The cumbersome cape makes dismounting a problem. Her horse gets skittish. She decides to make another wide circle, then grab off the shroud from the cart as she gallops past. She makes a good grab but the sheet snags and billows like a ghostly-white stallion. Her horse bolts. The cart is jerked over sideways, dumping the gleaming saddle into the filthiest spot in the whole arena.

It should have been humorous, but it wasn't. It was viewed as one more thing gone awry. Prairie Rose dismounted and hurried to the saddle, purple velvet dragging behind her a country mile. We started to give her a hand but she waves us aside with the scepter.

'Stand back, boys. This is my doings.'

The whole stadium watching impatiently as she shouldered the chariot and saddletree upright. She tossed the saddle back where it belonged and fell to cleaning the soiled leather and silver with her cape.

It was sad and awkward. It made you long for Clancy's garrulous singsong: aggravating as he often was, he was better than this strained silence. Prairie Rose rubbed and shined. The crowd watched and waited. It got so solemn that George couldn't resist poking a little fun. He flounced away toward the judges' platform, shading his eyes.

'Mars Buffalo? Mars Buffalo?' His voice was as high and clear as a girl's. ''Scuse me, sir, does I get my hat back now? I didn't win, jes' lak you tole me not to, so does I get my yeller hat back?'

The old hunter took a thoughtful sip from his canteen, then returned it to the pouch, pretending not to hear. George politely repeated his question, louder and clearer still.

'"Scuse me, Mars Buffalo! Does I get my yeller—?'

'Yes!' Cody lurched angrily to his feet and swept the hat off. He was drunk enough to be defiant even if all his allies had disappeared or defected. 'Yes blast your infernal hide, you get your damned yellow hat back. But *first*—' He drew his knife from its beaded scabbard. 'What do you say I hang on to a little souvenir *keep*sake, *Mars* Fletcher?'

George didn't know what to say. He looked sorry he had taunted the feeble old fogey.

'A little re*minder*?' Cody continued. 'To remind me the next time I chance to be passing through Pendleton to keep right on passing *through!*'

He stabbed the blade up through the hat's crown. There wasn't a sound while the old man sawed at the yellow felt. He managed to hack out a chunk about the size and shape of a fried egg. He held it up in triumph.

'You don't begrudge an old man a little keepsake, do you, Fletcher?' He tucked the chunk in his belt like it was a scalp taken in battle. 'You still got plenty hat left, and this little hole can be *your* keepsake. Here—'

He drew back to side-arm the trepanned Stetson, but a voice all the way from the stadium roof across the arena hit him like a cannonball.

'MISTER. CODY *SIR*—'

Every head turned to see what caliber muzzle could fire such a blast. The door out of the press box opened and Nadine Rose came clomping purposefully into sight. The huge pair of binoculars was having to compete for space on her heaving chest and her hands were balled in fists of wrath. She continued to address the old scout as she descended, her words ringing like a Valkyrie's sword.

'I would not *mind*, Mister Cody, having a *souvenir* of that historic hat my*self*, if you would be so kind. As a matter of *fact*, Mister Cody, I would be willing to *pay* for such a memento the *amount* of—' She thrust a fist into a khaki pocket and pulled out a banknote. '—*five dollars cash!* What do you *say*, Mister Cody? Does *five dollars* sound fair?'

Now Mister Cody was as much at a loss for words as George. Cecil Kell cupped his hands to his mouth and answered for him.

'Five dollars sounds fair to me, Miss Rose. And I reckon I'll purchase *two* – one for me and one for Missus Kell.'

Sundown and I shrugged at each other, as puzzled as the rest of the crowd. Mister Kell stepped over the bunting into the box seats. He took the knife and the ventilated Stetson from the bewildered scout and hurried away down the seats. He sawed a yellow crescent from the brim, then cut it in two. By the time he was at the breach that Long Tom had opened in the fence, he had two swatches of felt in one hand and a wad of greenbacks in the other.

'Ten dollars more, Miss Rose!' he called. 'It's a good start.'

'*Very* good, Mister Kell. Excellent! Now . . . who else?'

Nadine Rose had made it to the arena floor and turned to address the grandstands. She was puffing hard, but between puffs her voice was as powerful as ever. Foghorn Clancy and that thundercloud both must have been green with envy.

'Who else is *in*terested – in acquiring a *priceless souvenir*? It's an opportunity doubly blessed. Not only will you be contributing to an *extremely worthy cause*, you will be helping out a – *most deserving gladiator!*'

'*What* worthy cause?' a cynic from the north bleachers wanted to know. '*What* gladiator?'

Nadine Rose swept the stands with an accusing glower. 'I am disappointed in you Oregonians. *What* cause indeed! *What* gladiator indeed! Is there not one among you who will at least make a considered guess?'

The guess didn't come from the stands or the bleachers. It came from the participants' peanut-gallery rail.

'It's a saddle, aint it, mum? For George?' I recognized the voice. It was Slope-Nose Cantrell, the slim-wit from Canada. He had solved the puzzle before us Americans could. 'Am I correct, mum?'

'You are *indeed correct*, young man. A *saddle!* George Fletcher *needs* a saddle, dear people, and – in my candid opinion as a visiting journalist – I think you Pendletonians *owe* him one!'

The only response she received came once more from the peanut gallery.

'That lets me oot then, mum; I'm a To*rontonian!*'

The crowd would have been glad to have a chuckle over this and be on their way. The newspaperwoman had other ideas. She kept them pinned to their seats with her condemning glare. Cecil Kell fielded the argument from his side of the field.

'It aint only Pendleton. It's Arlington and Walla Walla; it's Lewiston and Winnemucca and far away as Chico. It's *any*body that's ever been tickled or thrilled or by God *flabbergasted* by George Fletcher!'

Kell's importuning wasn't any more effective than the reporter's. It wasn't that people weren't sympathetic to the proposition – you could see the heads nodding – but that seemed to be all they could manage.

302

They were numb with fatigue and stymied by a predicament they hadn't expected. They also were irked to find themselves still having to be a crowd when all they wanted was to get away to their separate suppers and peaceful privacies.

The woman reporter turned her back on them in disgust and resumed her purposeful tramp toward us. The crowd commenced to buzz and fidget again. In another minute they were going scatter apart worse than George's worn-out saddle. I decided to have my say first.

'Mister Kell!' I hollered. 'Let me *give* George the saddle! It's too heavy for a working roper and too ostentatious for a Dixie gentleman. Why, if it had not been for George Fletcher's guidance I—'

'No, son, absolutely not!' Mister Kell had climbed on through the breach and was striding across the arena dirt, the hat and knife in one hand, the money in the other. 'This aint charity. This is a cause, as Miss Rose stated. You will be paid what's right – four hundred dollars, as I recollect? – even if I have to purchase all the rest of this historic hat by myself.' He waved the hat above his head like a drum major. 'Any more takers? Going ... going—' Sundown's flat voice came to his rescue.

'Wait!' The Indian had his palm raised. 'I might want three pieces. One for me, and one for my wife, and one for the tree behind our cabin in Idaho.'

This gets a bleat of derision out of Buffalo Bill. 'What kind of tree, Injun Jack?' he shouts. 'A hat tree?'

Sundown squints up at the old scout a while before answering. The answer is not shouted. His voice isn't even raised. But it cuts across the distance like one of those obsidian blades from his knife-maker yarn.

'It is a burial pine, Mister Cody. A ponderosa, hollowed out by lightning. I keep the bones of our little boy in the hollow. It is very old and very scarred, but it stays alive and keeps standing. I say prayers to this tree. I give thanks for it in church. When I go away I try always to bring back a good gift. What do you think, Mister Cody? I have heard the Blackfoot elders tell of Buffalo Scout Eyes. They say you know the ways of the Indian spirits as good as the Indians. So I ask: Do you think a piece of George Fletcher's hat would be a good gift to that tree? Or is this just some more "Crazy Injun talk"?'

The old scout drew a breath and raised a gloved finger, preparing to deliver some sarcastic bombast. But something stopped him. I thought he must have suddenly remembered that crack he made about 'Injun talk' that night on the train. I later learned he and his wife had also lost a child, a six-year-old boy. Died in the flu epidemic. I learned that Sundown was aware of this, too. The old man lowered the hand and sagged.

'I think that tree will like a piece of that hat just fine, Mister Jackson. And so will the little bones.'

'Thank you, Mister Cody.' Sundown pulled the jangling purse from inside his shirt and began untying the drawstring. 'I want three pieces, then, Mister Kell.'

The air had become completely windless; the words hung like smoke. The stadium was so still you could hear the clink of silver dollars as Sundown counted. One winter I took a steamer all the way from Astoria to Frisco Bay, to hear a famous orator named William Jennings Bryan. Ten thousand seats had been set up in the San Francisco Cow Palace and a lot of us general admissions still had to stand. The occasion was the publication of Edward Curtis' photographs. Big accusing

Indian faces were displayed in a vast ring, around the audience in the middle like the accused. The title for Bryan's speech was 'Broken Promises, Broken Peoples . . . the Tragedy of the Vanishing American.' He began with Pocahontas saving John Smith's neck. He reminded us of Squanto, bringing corn and yams to the Pilgrims for our first Thanksgiving. He told of cavalry campaigns and massacres, treaties and betrayals. He detailed the disease and degradation suffered by the Cheyennes on the Trail of Tears and he made us feel the jagged lava shredding the feet of Chief Joseph and his followers as they made their desperate try for freedom. The golden-throated orator spoke without notes or intermission. He touched every heart and wrung tears from every eye. It took him about three and a half hours. Jackson Sundown touched three times that many in thirty seconds, and touched them deeper. When the Indian had clinked the fifteenth silver dollar into his hand, Prairie Rose removed her velvet-lined crown and held it out.

That did it. The silvery clash of these fifteen cartwheels was like a lock being opened. The audience was on their feet at once. '*I* want a piece!' was the cry, and here they came, the whole American crazy-quilt of them, from tailor-made business suits to hard-washed blue collars; from happy-go-lucky straw skimmers to luck-is-where-you-make-it gambler derbies; from hand-me-down high-button shoes to the latest patent-leather pumps from Paris – by the dozens, by the droves, by the hundreds, by the herds – rising up with whoops of laughter and shrieks of delight, and pouring straight down the wooden bleachers in a thundering wave, Booma looma bumpa *boom!* straight down the stairs . . . the kids all giggling and tugging to bust loose; the mothers all fluffed up and chattering and trying to hang on to the kids; the fathers exchanging cigars and slaps on the back . . . Blue Collar with his Little Woman and Small Fry shoulder to shoulder with Business Suit and his Lady of the House and his Heirs Apparent . . . booma-looma-thumping all together in happy accord, because this was what they had been waiting for all along: to get down out of those confining wooden seats and into the wide-open dirt, to see how it felt to kick those clods and raise that dust a little bit before they said goodbye and went home.

They were a crowd again. They were very nearly a mob.

Fortunately Nadine Rose was up in the saddle cart by the time the throng got there, spieling away about the historical value the piece of hat would soon have. Mister Kell manned the butcher knife and Prairie Rose ran the till. The three of them were like a crackerjack auction team. They could have sold smoke rings and doughnut holes.

A horseshoe-sized remnant of George's hat still remained when Prairie Rose declared the four-hundred-dollar saddle price had been reached. The crowd was still hollering and waving bills – *big* bills, some of them. I saw Oliver Nordstrum brandishing a whole fistful of fifties. But Kell and I were both adamant: four hundred and no more, no matter what the bids. The white-haired rancher laid the felt remnant on the wooden sideboard of the cart and commenced carefully sawing off tiny slivers and giving them to the kids. He was still slicing when Sundown and I escorted the dazed George Fletcher from the arena. It was fun seeing him flabbergasted and tongue-tied for a change. He was so overcome with this last hairpin turn of events he could barely carry his new saddle.

So the drama turned out to have a medium-happy ending, I guess, with a certain amount of sadness and a twist of irony. The Bad Guys had been routed, their last low act transformed into an uplifting solution by Nadine Rose's hat trick. Just about everybody was satisfied, one way or another. The Business Sorts were pleased to see things handled with such efficiency and dispatch. The Working Stiffs were heartened to see that a stiff even lower than they were could still get a fair shake in this Northwestern Land of Opportunity. The Bigots were appeased that it was a White Boy that had really won the Championship. The Anti-Bigots were gratified to be able to contribute toward moving the prize on to the Colored Man they felt should have won.

The Red Folk could take pride in the undeniable dignity of their cousin's performance – in the way he rode and the way he stood, and especially in the way he responded to the drunken old Indian Fighter's jibes. Besides, Sundown won the All Round Cowboy Competition fair and square four years later, anyhow. Look it up.

Even all those cloudy disputing versions that came out in the newspapers had their silver linings. The debate over who really won and what really happened stirred up such a fuss that next fall the crowds were bigger and the rewards richer.

The ones most rewarded, though, by the switch-ending of that first Round Up were the citizens of Pendleton themselves. They had been fond of George Fletcher for years – proud of the old rip, when you got them to own to it in private. Now they had been afforded the opportunity to step up and show off that pride in full public view. And that made the citizens of this primitive little backwoods sticker patch proud, themselves. Backwoods they might be, but on this one weekend in September, they had shown themselves to be more modern than many big Eastern metropolises. More civilized, too.

And me? I had the four hundred bucks raised by Nadine Rose's Worthy Cause, my rodeo earnings, plus that hundred-dollar bet I made on myself on the train – a thirteen-to-one longshot in a field of fourteen. I was suddenly rich. I could afford to put Stonewall up in the Meyerhoff livery stables and reserve a Pullman berth for the ride to Portland.

I intended to hike over to Hookners when I got Stonewall comfortable – celebrate my good fortune, stand a few all around like a flush cowpoke is supposed to. But the long room was practically deserted. The supper crowd had already left, Missus Hookner told me, and the Saturday-night crowd hadn't yet come in. She hadn't seen hide nor hair of my two friends.

'Sundown never comes in here. His wife wouldn't stand for it. I can't imagine what happened to George. I put the word out by way of Sylvester Linkhorn that he had a turkey dinner waiting, on the house. But he never showed up. George Fletcher must have found something pretty dadgum tasty to keep him away from a free meal. But I bet he shows up in about an hour and a half with the night crowd, hungry again.'

I bet he doesn't, I said to myself, but I walked back to the stables to wait. Stonewall was leaned against the stall wall with his eyes closed and his oat bag still half full. He had decided to take a little nap before finishing his supper. I decided to join him. I stretched out on the bales of alfalfa and closed my eyes. When I opened them it was burning daylight.

The stationmaster said the engine wouldn't be there until noon. I gimped back down Main. The wide street was deserted and I heard church bells ringing. Hookners was closed but I talked a dishwasher out of two turkey tails around back. The only place I could think of to eat them was down by that pool below the little falls. It gave me a chance to soak my foot and wade around for that damn coin. I was glad to hear the locomotive come whistling out of the east. The Pullman berth was a waste of money, though – too soft and crampy. I got better rest on the alfalfa.

It was long dark by the time we pulled into Portland. The porter told me how to find the hospital. He said it was just a good stretch of the legs. I'd been walking about ten minutes when it commenced to rain. I got good and soaked.

The woman at the hospital desk was busy reading *Ben-Hur*. She looked up at me over her reading glasses and told me Sarah Meyerhoff was there all right but visiting hours were over. She wouldn't of let me upstairs anyway, she said, wrinkling her nose – not in my decrepit appearance.

'Get you a two-dollar room at the Rose and get cleaned up. You look like you been starved, stomped, and *drownt*, for Pete's sake!'

It was raining harder, but the Rose Hotel was only three blocks away. The bed wasn't any longer than that Pullman berth, so I pulled the mattress off the springs and made a pallet on the floor. I slept so hard I nearly missed the evening visiting hours again. The bifocaled receptionist looked me over. Her nose still wrinkled but she cleared me through. A giddy nun escorted me up the stairs. She was happy to inform me that Mister Meyerhoff had procured the largest room in the hospital by contributing generously toward a statue they were having made for the chapel.

'A pietà! Just like that one in the Vatican. Only *prettier*,' she giggled. 'Every inch gold-plated with fourteen-karat gold leaf! That one in Rome looks like it was carved out of cold beef tallow, by the pictures I've seen of it. Here we are.'

The room was big enough to provide accommodations for the generous benefactor as well as his private nurse. Mister Meyerhoff was overcome with emotion at the sight of me, squeezing my hands and sobbing out sonnets of gratitude and guilt until I was wet to the elbows.

The O'Grady woman was slumped on a cot filing her nails. She had traded her tangerine wig and cowgirl skirt for nurse white. She loked twenty years older.

'I hope you brought a fresh shoulder for him to weep on, Johnny. Both of mine is about destroyed.'

Sarah was asleep behind a divider. They had cut off all her hair, checking for cracks. Her head looked like a peeled apple on the doughy hospital pillow. I stayed until the nun showed me back out. 'Come back in the morning,' she giggled. 'Things are brighter in the morning.' I never could figure out what she was giggling about.

From then on I sat with Sarah two hours in the morning, two hours in the evening. I read to her when I couldn't come up with any more chitchat. Church pamphlets were handy in neat stacks everywhere. When I had exhausted the pamphlets, the receptionist loaned me *Ben-Hur;* she thought an unconscious cowgirl ought to enjoy the chariot disaster.

After a week Nurse O'Grady was as weary of me as she was of Mister Meyerhoff. To give me and her both a break, she got me on the guest list to the Wild West Extravaganza at the Portland Armory.

It was a complete sellout, and featured a rematch between Fearsome Frank Gotch and Parson 'Lockjaw' Montanic. I had to stand in the rain at the ticket window for an hour before they cleared my pass, and caught the devil's own cold for it. I should have known better. 'Lockjaw' Montanic wasn't even an Indian. He was a bloat-bellied Mexican migrant they had daubed with warpaint and decorated with feathers. Gotch squeezed the bloat out of him so many times the ringside spectators had to escape up the aisles for fear of their eyes. The giant finally got his scissorlock locked, and it looked like he was settling in with intentions of squeezing the poor man slowly in half, but some wise guy in the cheap seats distracted him. 'Look out, champ!' the voice warned. 'Here come them calves!'

Gotch released the scissorhold and leapt to his feet, glaring about, his features a turmoil of tics and twitches. The wrestler's expression – if we can call it that – was a boiling stew of fear and fury, shame and suspicion, and what looked like – on my honor – anticipation.

I never saw Sarah Meyerhoff full awake again. She lapsed in and out. After nearly two weeks I caught a train to a Barnum and Bailey tent show in Seattle. World Champion Rodeo Rider George Fletcher was scheduled to make a special appearance. Again, I should have known better. It was just some bronc rider in black-face, and mediocre one at that.

I was back at the hospital the following evening. The giggling nun managed to tell me that Mister Meyerhoff and Sarah and their private nurse had caught the morning train east. To Boston, to see a famous specialist of brain injuries. I caught the midnight special.

I never found any Meyerhoffs in any of the Boston hospitals. I spent a week looking and asking questions, tramping from doctor to doctor, until I was down to my last pair of Aunt Ruth's knitted socks. My fortune was dwindling fast. I gave myself a realistic talking-to and bought a third-class ticket back west.

I stopped off in Pendleton to get Stonewall and my tack. It was snowing. The rodeo arena looked like a big ice-skating pond. The Meyerhoff mansion was boarded tight with a NO TRESPASSING sign in the yard. The neighbor told me the Meyerhoff sisters had suddenly announced they were going to live with a relative in Brooklyn and the next day they were gone. I've often wondered if that wasn't what the giggling nun meant by Boston.

The livery stables and store were being tended by the Beeson brothers and a Meyerhoff relative. Crippled up the way they were, they had lost their ranching jobs. They didn't know where the new Meyerhoff had come from; he didn't speak much English. George? He had taken a position with the school district, they told me. He was what you would nowdays call a 'mainten-ance technician.' Back then they called them janitors.

Sundown, I was told, had spent his winnings on a motorcar but couldn't figure out how to drive it. He rode in the backseat and let his wife taxi him around. He was down at Warm Springs but was due back through any day, if I wanted to wait. And George would likely drop by sometime tomorrow, it being a Saturday and the school out. I told the twins I thought I would put off any further reunions until another time, maybe next fall, when we all could go parading in blue-chip style.

I slipped back through the warehouse to the livery stables to check on my horse and gear. Stonewall looked fat and lazy and none too happy to see me.

'Don't act so worried,' I told him. 'This year's rodeoing is done.'

My saddle was still treed where I left it, under the saddle blanket. I snapped open the saddlebag in hopes of finding one more pair of Aunt Ruth's socks. Black silk bowled out instead. Some honest Injun I was turning out to be. I tucked the scented garment in my coat and took out for Main Street. Snow was piling up and the cold was coming right through my boot soles. I could have bought a new pair of socks in the Mercantile; I wasn't *that* broke. But I figured if I got frostbit I deserved it.

The sporting house was closed. So were the tunnels; not a whisper of rising steam. I went into Hookners to ask what had happened to all the Chinese and nearly tripped over Sue Lin. She was on her hands and knees beneath the bar, rubbing out the gouges and stains with a sandstone. I pulled the black wad from my coat.

'Here's your coolie bloomers back, Sue Lin. Sorry fairly much I took so long . . .'

She looked up at me. It was the first time she ever met my eyes. She stood slowly, brushing her knees. She wore a frayed brown dress and plaid shirt that had Charity Box written all over them, and her hair had been cut, boy-short. Her eyes did not leave mine even when she shook her head.

'No, John-E. I do not wear coolie bloom-ers any more now. I am a Merican citizen now. I work for Missis Hook-ner.'

Her deliberate pronunciation was as unnerving as her gaze. I asked what about the laundry? Her grandfather?

'Grandfather left. He sold the lawn-deree and left. He will go back to Bay-ging, I think.'

'And left you *nothing* at all to live on? The yellow dog! Well, I don't have much left but—'

She shook her head again. 'No. Missis Hook-ner pays me six bits a day of woman's work. She says I will soon be old enough for night work and she will pay more. She is teaching me to be a lady. I will make out good. Now excuse me.'

I was dismissed, just like that. I stood fumbling at the silk while she went back to her sandstone. I told her I'd see her later, maybe stand her to one of Missus Hookner's hot turkey suppers. She kept sanding. She wasn't in a mood to talk turkey.

I walked back to the store and bought a block of cheese and a half-dozen apples and had a very cold supper with my horse. Then I shivered all night under all the feedsacks I could round up. I could have afforded a room but it was just like with the socks.

I got Stoney and me on the first freight to Portland the following day, in a boxcar this time. I rode bundled up by the half-open door, watching the snow whirl and feeling pretty blue and uncomfortable. Had I waited a few hours I could have taken the passenger train. There was no logical reason to scoot off so quick. I just wasn't ready to see my heroes labeled as janitors or backseat drivers, either – or imagine my guardian angel as a lady of the night.

As long as we're sticking on labels, I guess I was what you would call Star Struck – marked as bad as old Star Going Some. I never was a cowboy, really, not a common workaday waddie. Even after my accident, when I had to take what ranch work I could get, I never thought of myself as a cowboy. I thought of myself, always, as a rodeo star – down on his luck a little, but on the mend, on the road back to the top. Maybe you always think of yourself as what you were in that short high noon of fame, not what you are all the rest of the long twilight and dark.

I'm closing in on nine-tenths of a century, and it was only a couple quick thrill-filled seasons out of this near ninety that I was a rodeo star. Not a very bright one at that. Still, I count myself among luminaries like Jim Shoulders and Yakima Canutt and Mark Toogood, and Mahon and Tibbs. And you. Yep, you're branded, too, like it or not, live or die, recover or don't. Because the thrill doesn't come free, we all know that. Everybody has to pay the merry-go-round man with something; and the more you relish the ride, the more you have to pay. Sarah was what I paid for taking that last go round. I was the price she was charged for racing that last race.

Let us say, just for discussion's sake, that you suddenly wake up out of that bed one morning and find yourself blessed with illumination and fated for fame and fortune. Say you invent perpetual motion and make a hundred million dollars and even become the first colored president and wear ritzy made-to-order double-breasted suits . . . you and I both know that the mark hidden beneath that ritzy double breast is the four-pointed rodeo star. That's the brand that owns you. No running iron can alter it, it's cooked clear to the bone. It's how your hide will be tallied and judged at the Great Round Up. You will be glad that this is so. Which mark would you rather be judged by? The Presidential Seal or that Bucking Star?

I hear the carny trucks out the window, loaded up and grinding out of town. Time for this old punkin to be rolling. I surely hope you can do the same before long; Number Nine says that too much time in the hospital has a way of ossifying a man's organs.

'Yep, what I say all right.'

But first, here. I'm going to put this in your hand for luck. That's good! Clench that fist around it tight. It's a little bent but aint we all? So this is so long, it looks like. Number Nine? Want to give that fist a little squeeze so long?

'You rode the piss out of that bull, kid.'

Sailor Song
Ken Kesey

'THOROUGHLY REWARDING . . . STILL RETAINING
HIS TRADEMARK VOICE OF MUTINY, KESEY MAKES
SAILOR SONG A MARVELLOUS GIFT: A SHARP AND
DARK AND FINELY TUNED SONG OF OURSELVES'
San Francisco Chronicle

After writing *One Flew Over the Cuckoo's Nest* and
Sometimes a Great Notion in the early Sixties, both now
established classics, Ken Kesey abandoned the novel.
Sailor Song is his first for 25 years and displays, once
again, his full powers as one of the truly great American
writers.

Set in the future, the story takes us to the Alaskan village
of Kuinak, a rundown fishing community of Deaps
(Descendants of Early Aboriginal Peoples) and lower-48
refugees perched on the Western Edge of history. It's a
scene rich with characters – Alice the Angry Aleut, Ike
Sallas (the Bakatcha Bandit), Billy the Squid and the Loyal
Order of Underdogs, who meet monthly for the Full Moon
Howl. Into their midst sails a ship of last hopes loaded to
the gunwales with a big-bucks Hollywood film company,
come north to film a classic children's book, *The Sea Lion*.

Sailor Song is an epic novel that revolves around the
question: does love make any sense at the end of the
world? It's about things that endure and come back at you
again – back at you, and back to you.

'A DARING BOOK, A HIGH-RISK PERFORMANCE
WHOSE VIRTUOSITY, ENERGY AND COMPLEX,
MATURE VISION MAY CHALLENGE, EVEN OUTRAGE
. . . A WHOLE LOT OF FUN'
Chicago Tribune

0 552 99567 3

BLACK SWAN

Coyote Blue
Christopher Moore

A cult novel for people too smart and too hip to be part of a cult.

Sam Hunter's life is more or less complete: he's a very successful insurance salesman, he's got a new Mercedes, a great home and a 52-inch television. But he hasn't got a girlfriend. Then he sees Calliope. She's gorgeous, exactly the kind of woman he's always wanted in his life but never had the courage to even approach.

Enter Coyote, an ancient Indian god famous for his abilities as a trickster, wise in many ways, in others a total fool. He's got just the medicine to bring these lovers together, but after that he hasn't got a clue.

In fact, Sam Hunter was actually born Samson Hunts Alone, a Crow Indian. He left the reservation aged fifteen, after a run-in with the law. Now, twenty years later, he's safely ensconced in his yuppie persona, and that earlier life is just a distant memory. Until Coyote enters the picture. From then on, nothing is the same . . .

Coyote Blue is the story of how Sam Hunter becomes a brave man, of how he finds love, redemption and release. Reminiscent of Kurt Vonnegut and Tom Robbins, with more than a suggestion of Carlos Castaneda, *Coyote Blue* is a wonderfully funny, spiritual and totally uplifting tale, by turns mysterious, terrifying, and outrageous.

0 552 99597 5

BLACK SWAN

Adam's Wish
Paul Micou

Adam Gosse, Belgian-born but England-raised, is to be best man at an aristocratic wedding in France. Envious of the groom, disappointed in his career, lonely in a flat that is at once cramped and cruelly expensive, Adam's fondest wish is that he might meet a woman, love her, and marry. Thanks to the bride and groom, a match is made between Adam and Natalie – the most celebrated person within the perimeter of Adam's social circle. Famed for what Adam considers superficial reasons – exotic parentage, great beauty, a way of making herself appear to be the centre of any gathering – Natalie is not someone he expects to take him seriously.

She does. To Adam's astonishment Natalie latches on to him as if he were the only sane man she had ever known. Drawn immediately into a marathon of European travel in Natalie's company, Adam feels alternately like her chauffeur and her fiancé. In a short space of time he tastes tabloid fame, rubs shoulders with what the world has come to think of as the New Aristocracy, becomes the envy of those who seemed to tower above him only days before.

The decision is his: he has played along in all sincerity, but how far is Adam willing to go?

0 552 99603 3

BLACK SWAN

A SELECTION OF FINE WRITING
AVAILABLE FROM BLACK SWAN

THE PRICES SHOWN BELOW WERE CORRECT AT THE TIME OF GOING TO PRESS. HOWEVER TRANSWORLD PUBLISHERS RESERVE THE RIGHT TO SHOW NEW RETAIL PRICES ON COVERS WHICH MAY DIFFER FROM THOSE PREVIOUSLY ADVERTISED IN THE TEXT OR ELSEWHERE.

☐	99550 9	THE FAME HOTEL	Terence Blacker	£5.99
☐	99531 2	AFTER THE HOLE	Guy Burt	£5.99
☐	99524 X	YANKING UP THE YO-YO	Michael Carson	£5.99
☐	99599 1	SEPARATION	Dan Franck	£5.99
☐	99616 5	SIMPLE PRAYERS	Michael Golding	£5.99
☐	99466 9	A SMOKING DOT IN THE DISTANCE	Ivor Gould	£6.99
☐	99609 2	FORREST GUMP	Winston Groom	£5.99
☐	99487 1	JIZZ	John Hart	£5.99
☐	99169 4	GOD KNOWS	Joseph Heller	£7.99
☐	99538 X	GOOD AS GOLD	Joseph Heller	£6.99
☐	99208 9	THE 158LB MARRIAGE	John Irving	£5.99
☐	99204 6	THE CIDER HOUSE RULES	John Irving	£6.99
☐	99567 3	SAILOR SONG	Ken Kesey	£6.99
☐	99542 8	SWEET THAMES	Matthew Kneale	£6.99
☐	99037 X	BEING THERE	Jerzy Kosinski	£4.99
☐	99595 9	LITTLE FOLLIES	Eric Kraft	£5.99
☐	99594 0	SWEET MISERIES	Eric Kraft	£5.99
☐	99384 0	TALES OF THE CITY	Armistead Maupin	£5.99
☐	99569 X	MAYBE THE MOON	Armistead Maupin	£5.99
☐	99502 9	THE LAST WORD	Paul Micou	£5.99
☐	99603 3	ADAM'S WISH	Paul Micou	£5.99
☐	99597 5	COYOTE BLUE	Christopher Moore	£5.99
☐	99536 3	IN THE PLACE OF FALLEN LEAVES	Tim Pears	£5.99
☐	99546 0	THE BRIDGWATER SALE	Freddie Stockdale	£5.99
☐	99547 9	CRIMINAL CONVERSATIONS	Freddie Stockdale	£5.99
☐	99500 2	THE RUINS OF TIME	Ben Woolfenden	£4.99